Pr...

"[A] l... keep you entertained for ... number of hours — the perfect read for a rainy day. . . . Shopping, St. Louis culinary treats, and mayhem abound, providing for a satisfying read."
—*Front Street Reviews*

"*High Heels Are Murder* takes Josie into the wicked world of murder, mayhem, and toe cleavage. From the sweat and toil of having to work three jobs to afford a Prada knockoff to the glamorous world of stiletto shopping, Viets spans the female psyche with panache and wit."
—*South Florida Sun-Sentinel*

Dying in Style

"Finally, a protagonist we can relate to."
—*Riverfront Times* (St. Louis, MO)

"Laugh-out-loud humor adds to the brisk action of *Dying in Style* . . . with an insightful look at the bonds between mother and daughter, the challenges of living in a multigenerational household, and the rewards of nonjudgmental friendship. Viets's fast pace is complemented by realistic dialogue and well-drawn characters in believable relationships. Viets affectionately uses her native St. Louis as the backdrop for this new series."
—*South Florida Sun-Sentinel*

Praise for the Dead-End Job Mystery Series

Murder with Reservations

"[H]umorous and socially conscious . . . rollicking fun."
—*Publishers Weekly*

continued . . .

Dying to Call You

"Viets writes a laugh-out-loud comedy with enough twists and turns to make it to the top. . . . In fact, she's been nominated for a truckload of awards this year. . . . There is a good reason why Viets is taking the mystery genre by storm these days. . . . She can keep you wondering 'Who done it?' while laughing all the way to the last page."
—Florida Today

Murder Between the Covers

"Wry sense of humor, appealing, realistic characters, and a briskly moving plot." *—South Florida Sun-Sentinel*

"A great writer . . . simply superb."
—Midwest Book Review

Shop Till You Drop

"I loved this book. With a stubborn . . . heroine, a wonderful South Florida setting, and a cast of more or less lethal bimbos, *Shop Till You Drop* provides tons of fun. Six-toed cats, expensive clothes, sexy guys on motorcycles—this book has it all." *—Charlaine Harris*

"Fresh, funny, and fiendishly constructed . . . a bright start to an exciting new series. This one is hard to beat."
—Parnell Hall, author of the Puzzle Lady crossword puzzle mysteries

Also by Elaine Viets

Josie Marcus, Mystery Shopper Series

Dead-End Job Mystery Series

ACCESSORY
TO MURDER

JOSIE MARCUS, MYSTERY SHOPPER

Elaine Viets

AN OBSIDIAN MYSTERY

OBSIDIAN
Published by New American Library, a division of
Penguin Group (USA) Inc., 375 Hudson Street,
New York, New York 10014, USA
Penguin Group (Canada), 90 Eglinton Avenue East, Suite 700, Toronto,
Ontario M4P 2Y3, Canada (a division of Pearson Penguin Canada Inc.)
Penguin Books Ltd., 80 Strand, London WC2R 0RL, England
Penguin Ireland, 25 St. Stephen's Green, Dublin 2,
Ireland (a division of Penguin Books Ltd.)
Penguin Group (Australia), 250 Camberwell Road, Camberwell, Victoria 3124,
Australia (a division of Pearson Australia Group Pty. Ltd.)
Penguin Books India Pvt. Ltd., 11 Community Centre, Panchsheel Park,
New Delhi - 110 017, India
Penguin Group (NZ), 67 Apollo Drive, Rosedale, North Shore 0632,
New Zealand (a division of Pearson New Zealand Ltd.)
Penguin Books (South Africa) (Pty.) Ltd., 24 Sturdee Avenue,
Rosebank, Johannesburg 2196, South Africa

Penguin Books Ltd., Registered Offices:
80 Strand, London WC2R 0RL, England

First published by Obsidian, an imprint of New American Library,
a division of Penguin Group (USA) Inc.

First Printing, November 2007
10 9 8 7 6 5 4 3 2 1

PUBLISHER'S NOTE
This is a work of fiction. Names, characters, places, and incidents either are
the product of the author's imagination or are used fictitiously, and any resemblance to actual persons, living or dead, business establishments, events, or
locales is entirely coincidental.
   The publisher does not have any control over and does not assume any
responsibility for author or third-party Web sites or their content.

For Christopher Jackson,
who loved St. Louis

Acknowledgments

Many people helped me with this book. I hope I didn't leave anyone out. Thanks to Christian and Jeanne Ruperto, who patiently answered my questions about scarves.

Thanks to my St. Louis experts, Jinny Gender, Karen Grace, and Janet Smith.

Librarian Anne Watts did extensive research on various subjects. Thanks also to Valerie Cannata, Colby Cox, Susan Carlson, and Kay Gordy. Kathy Sweeney helped cook up the diabolical plot at Jake's law office.

I also want to thank Emma, my expert on nine-year-olds. She used to be one last year. Emma gave me deep background on what it's like to be nine years old. I wish I could use her real name, but the world is a dangerous place these days for little girls.

As always, thanks and love to my husband, Don Crinklaw, for his extraordinary help and patience. It's not easy to live with a writer, but he manages.

My agent, David Hendin, is still the best.

Special thanks to my editor, Kara Cesare, who devoted long hours to editing and guiding this project, to the Obsidian copy editor and production staff, and to publicist Catherine Milne.

Many booksellers help keep this series alive. I wish I had room to thank them all. Thanks to Joanne Sinchuk and John Spera at South Florida's largest mystery bookstore, Murder on the Beach in Delray Beach, Florida. Thanks to Pam Marshall at the Hollywood Barnes &

Noble and to Susan Boyd in Plantation. Thanks also to Mary Alice Gorman and Richard Goldman, to Barbara Peters at Poisoned Pen, to Bonnie and Joe at Black Orchid in New York, and David and McKenna at Murder by the Book in Houston. Kim, Jamey, Jim and the gang do a terrific job at the Waldenbooks in Pompano Beach.

Special thanks to the law enforcement men and women who answered countless questions on police procedure. Some of my police and medical sources have to remain nameless, but I want to thank them all the same. Particular thanks to Detective R.C. White, Fort Lauderdale Police Department (retired). Any mistakes are mine, not theirs.

Thanks to the librarians at the Broward County Library and the St. Louis Public Library who researched my questions, no matter how strange, and always answered with a straight face.

Thanks to public relations expert Jack Klobnak, to Patti Nunn, and to my bookseller friend, Carole Wantz.

Chapter 1

"I can't believe anyone would pay a thousand dollars for a scarf," Alyce Bohannon said.

"Excuse me," Josie Marcus said, "but aren't you the woman who spent a thousand bucks for kitchen knives?"

"Those weren't kitchen knives," Alyce said. "Those were carbon-steel blades from Williams-Sonoma. They were works of art."

"And this scarf isn't?" Josie said. "Look at that color: Halley blue. It's three-dimensional. Feel it. It's Italian silk. The weight is perfect. It drapes beautifully."

Josie loved Halley blue. It was deeper than sky blue and richer than the color made famous by Maxfield Parrish. It was the blue of a bottomless lake. The color was magical with any skin tone from vanilla white to dark chocolate.

Josie held the scarf up to her face, reveling in its luxurious feel. Next to a Halley-blue scarf, her plain brown hair had glamorous red highlights and her brown eyes were deep and exotic. Her ordinary looks were her fortune, or at least her living. Josie was the ideal mystery shopper, able to melt into any mall. She couldn't wear a scarf that made her stand out.

She traced the swirling bird-and-bluebell design with a manicured finger. Like all good designs, it was simple yet sophisticated.

"Josie, quit fondling that scarf before security picks us up," Alyce said. "It's pretty. But I could buy one almost as good at Target for thirty bucks."

"I could buy a whole drawerful of knives there for the same price," Josie said.

Alyce winced. "OK, so I'm conventional. I like my art in a frame."

Josie held the blue and white scarf against Alyce's milk white skin. The fabulous scarf turned her eyes into sapphire smoke and her pale hair into platinum silk.

"When you wear something this beautiful," Josie said, "you are the frame for the art."

"Honey, I'm the whole exhibition." Alyce looked down at her generous curves. "I'm not built to be a clotheshorse, Josie. I'm too practical to spend money on something that isn't useful."

"Nothing in Pretty Things is useful," Josie said. "That's the whole point of this boutique. I wish I could afford this."

"You mean they don't give you a thousand bucks to spend here as a mystery shopper?"

"Not so loud," Josie said. "I'm supposed to be a *secret* shopper."

"We're housewives," Alyce said. "We're invisible. Those skinny sales associates are too busy being hip to notice us."

"Don't worry. I'll get them," Josie said. "I have thirty dollars to spend here, and it's not going to be easy to find something."

"How about those gold earrings?" Alyce said.

"You have excellent taste. They're two hundred dollars," Josie said. "I may be able to buy a scarf ring for the scarf I can't afford. That's twenty-eight dollars."

"You know, she lives on our street," Alyce said.

"Who?" Josie said.

"Halley. Her house is trimmed in Halley blue. That color is a little loud for shutters."

"Let me buy that scarf ring, and we can get out of here and talk," Josie said.

Only one sales associate was free. SABER, her name tag said. She had dark red hair and an air of chic exhaustion. Saber ignored Josie and stared straight ahead.

Josie recognized her type. Saber was a Captive Princess. The Captive Princess knew the universe had made a terrible mistake. She wasn't a salesclerk. She was royalty, brought low. She did customers a favor by deigning to wait on them. They should be serving her. The Captive Princess took every opportunity to let the customers know they were inferior.

A lesser shopper would have begged, "Can anyone help me?"

Josie kept silent. She counted the minutes ticking off on her watch. One. Two. Three. At three minutes and fifty-two seconds, Saber finally said, "May I help you?"

"I'll take this," Josie said.

Saber picked up the inexpensive scarf ring with two fingers, as if it were a cockroach. "Anything else?" Saber was nearly paralyzed with ennui.

"This is enough." Josie smiled sweetly. She couldn't wait to write her report.

"You from New York?" Saber said.

"No," Josie said.

"I figured you didn't buy that here," she said with a nod toward Josie's garage-sale Escada. "St. Louis is too Dutch and dumb."

"That's not fair," Alyce burst out.

Josie was surprised. Alyce rarely spoke when she was mystery-shopping with Josie. But she was a fierce defender of St. Louis. She hated to admit her city had any flaws.

Saber stared at Alyce's blue silk pantsuit. "How old is that?" She didn't bother to hide her contempt.

"I buy classic styles," Alyce said. "It's five years old. OK, six."

"Old enough to start school," Saber said. "Too old to wear. That's why Halley is moving her business to New York. St. Louisans have no style. New Yorkers understand fashion. This cow town doesn't."

Saber slouched into the back room and slammed the door.

"Thank you for shopping at Pretty Things," Josie said to the air.

Alyce stood there, openmouthed. "Did you hear what that little snip said?"

"There goes her score for personal service," Josie said.

"How can she say that about St. Louis?" Alyce said.

"Uh, I hate to agree with Saber, but nobody would call us a fashion capital."

"Some of the richest women in the world live here," Alyce said.

"And buy their clothes in New York and Paris," Josie said. "Where do your rich friends get their clothes? Chico's, Ann Taylor, and Talbots?"

"There's nothing wrong with those stores," Alyce said. "They give good value."

"Absolutely," Josie said. "But they aren't cutting-edge. Find one high-style woman in this mall."

"Right at the end of that counter." Alyce was too polite to point, but she radiated well-bred triumph. Josie followed her gaze to a classic type, the lady who lunched. The woman's ash-blond hair was lacquered into impossible swirls. Her patrician nose was so heavily powdered, Josie wondered if she was hiding the telltale veins of a tippler. Some of those lunches were very wet.

"That's a designer suit, isn't it?" Alyce said. "That lumpy pink, green, and yellow weave looks like oatmeal with sprinkles. She's wearing it with a mustard blouse. Those colors are so bizarre, she has to be rich."

"Her suit is Chanel," Josie said. "The bag is Kate Spade."

"What about the scarf?" Alyce said.

"What scarf?" Josie said.

"She had a Halley-blue scarf in her hand a minute ago. She took it off the counter."

"Alyce, there were three scarves on that counter," Josie said. "I looked at one and put it back. You say she had the other. Now there are two. I bet she took it."

"Are you sure?"

"I think she stuffed it in her purse," Josie said.

"Tell someone. You're mystery-shopping this store."

"Don't have to. Security is already on the alert."

"Where?" Alyce said.

"See that woman pawing the evening shawls by the

door? Her hair is too black to be a customer here. She does her own color. No high-style salon would let a woman over forty walk out with coal-black hair. It drains the color from her skin and makes it look yellow. Also, it's too short to be flattering for her face."

"Why not grow it longer?" Alyce asked.

"If it's short, suspects can't grab it. Besides, her shoes are lace-ups."

"So she likes comfortable shoes," Alyce said. "She's wearing a nice suit."

"It's secondhand, like mine. The hem's been let down. She's probably an ex-cop. Her shoes tie so she can chase suspects. Slip-ons would slip off when she ran."

"She's letting Ms. Chanel get away," Alyce said. "The shoplifter is heading for the exit."

"Security is playing it smart to avoid a false arrest," Josie said. "The suspect has to be out of the store or she can say she meant to pay for the scarf. See the hard-faced blonde near the cash register? She's the other security person."

"How do you know this?" Alyce asked.

"Malls are my life," Josie said. "I can't tell you how many takedowns I've seen. Watch this one."

The two security women tailed Ms. Chanel out the door. Josie followed the trio into the mall and took a seat on a marble bench near a planter. Between the leaves, she had a prime view of Ms. Chanel. Alyce sat beside her. "What—"

"Shhh," Josie said. "The show's started."

The black-haired security woman flashed her ID at Ms. Chanel. "I'm with Pretty Things Enterprises, ma'am," she said. "I'd like to ask you about the Halley scarf you have in your bag."

"I am sure you are mistaken." Ice encrusted each perfectly enunciated word.

"Please return to the store, ma'am, so we can clear this matter up."

"I do not wish to return," Ms. Chanel said. "You are forcibly detaining me. I shall call my attorney. I have the receipt here."

She pulled a receipt from her purse. Josie thought the blond security woman turned a shade paler. But the black-haired one studied the receipt, then gave a small smile. "Your receipt was issued at nine ten today at our Clayton location, ma'am. It's eleven fifteen at the Dorchester Mall. You're using an old receipt with a new scarf. Step inside, please, so we can discuss it."

"I'm sure it's a problem with your cash register," Ms. Chanel said, but she didn't resist when security steered her inside the store and escorted her to a door behind a Japanese screen. The scene was conducted so quietly, the customers didn't notice.

"An old scam," Josie said. "Ms. Chanel buys an expensive item at one store in the chain, and keeps the receipt in her purse. Then she goes to another store and shoplifts the same item. If she's caught, she tries to convince security it's a mistake. If she gets away with it, she'll return it for cash at a third store in the chain, or sell it on eBay."

"Do you think she's a pro?" Alyce asked.

"No, a professional would have spotted security closing in and dumped the scarf or paid for it. She's an amateur trying to get a thrill and a five-finger discount. I'll bet her mortified family will bail her out, and it won't be the first time they've had to deal with Mummy's hobby. She's pretty good, but security was alert."

Bass thumps from loud hip-hop vibrated down the corridor, drowning out the soft classical music on the mall's speakers.

Josie sighed. "I try to appreciate that music," she said. "It's supposed to be modern poetry."

"Yeah, a lot of words rhyme with 'bitch,'" Alyce said. "A store like the Gangsta Boyz Home is out of place at the Dorchester. Josie, you have to agree with that."

Three baggy-pantsed teens came out of the Gangsta Boyz Home and shoved their way through the mall crowd, leaving behind a trail of outraged glares.

"I'm sorry, but I don't want to shop with gangstas," Alyce said. "I don't feel safe. Jake would be furious if he knew I was at the Dorchester Mall. He made me promise I wouldn't go here anymore."

Statements like that made Josie glad she wasn't married. She didn't like making promises to a man—or sneaking around when she broke them.

"Jake's afraid you'll be attacked by the cane-and-walker crowd in Cissy's Tea Shoppe?"

"Don't be silly. Everyone knows crime is out of control at the Dorchester Mall, and it's the fault of the Gangsta Boyz Home. All the good stores are moving out. I don't know why it's here."

"Because the Dorchester invited them. The mall put in a gangsta clothes store and a video arcade. Those businesses aren't for the tea shop crowd."

"But why?" Alyce said. "Our crowd is so well behaved."

"And so tightfisted," Josie said. "The women who shop here buy one cashmere sweater at Lord and Taylor and wear it twenty years. You can't keep a mall open with that kind of spending. The mall wanted a younger crowd who spend money on clothes, sneakers, and CDs."

"Instead, they brought in the people who shoplift them."

"Alyce!" Josie said.

"Well, it's true. Lucy Anne Hardesty's mother had her purse stolen when she left the tearoom. The young thug broke her elbow. Ruined her golf game. Another friend was held up in the Dorchester parking lot."

"I haven't seen anything about a crime wave in the papers," Josie said.

"Jake says that's because the Dorchester is a major advertiser in the *St. Louis City Gazette*. Jake says they're not going to report a rise in crime and risk the mall pulling its ads."

That was the other thing Josie hated about her married friends. The women quoted their husbands as if they didn't have a thought in their heads. Yet Josie knew Alyce had put Jake through law school.

"Jake says—"

"Hey! You! Stop!"

Josie saw one of the tough teenagers racing down the marble concourse, clutching something in his huge hands. The security guard made a flying tackle and brought the kid down hard. They rolled on the floor, while another guard jumped on top of the young man. A third yelled, "Call 911."

"Those security guards are good," Alyce said.

"They're stupid," Josie said. "Subduing a suspect like that is the best way to get slapped with a lawsuit. The kid's bleeding. The guards used excessive force. What did he take, anyway?"

"A biography of Donald Rumsfeld," Alyce said. "Why would he steal a book when he could get it free at the library?"

"He isn't going to read it," Josie said. "He's going to take it to another store in the chain and try to get a refund. If he can't get cash, he'll use the store credit to buy a CD. Where are his friends?"

"I don't see them anywhere," Alyce said. "I guess they took off."

"Unless he was supposed to create a diversion for the real action," Josie said. She heard a popping sound.

"Is that a car backfiring inside the mall?" Alyce said.

"It's a gunshot," Josie said, and pushed Alyce down under the bench. Two young men with short dreads were running for the stairs.

"Help me!" A young woman with wide dark eyes, four eyebrow rings, and spiky pink hair staggered out of the athletic-shoe store three doors away. Her face was bleached with shock. She could talk only in short gasps. "Two men. With dreads. They've got a gun. They held up our store."

Six shoppers with cell phones simultaneously punched in 911.

Josie ran to the young woman's side. Her name tag said COURTNEY.

"Are you OK, Courtney?"

"I'm fine," she said—but her teeth were chattering. Josie picked a sweatshirt off a display rack and wrapped it around her. Josie saw blue smoke and smelled cordite. "What happened? Did they try to shoot you?"

"They shot the cash register. Two guys in Crips clothes came in." Courtney stopped to catch her breath. "The tall one had a Glock 9. It looked like the ones on TV. He said he'd shoot me if I didn't open the cash register. My hands were shaking so bad, I couldn't hit the keys. He pushed me aside and blasted the register. He scooped up four hundred dollars. His friend grabbed three pairs of athletic shoes. They got away with a thousand dollars altogether."

"But you're not hurt," Josie said.

"No," Courtney said. "Except my ears are ringing. Shit. I don't want to cry."

Josie gave her a handful of tissues, and she dabbed angrily at her face, smearing her dark eye makeup. "I've never had a gun pointed at me before."

Alyce poured a cup of coffee at the courtesy counter. It was black as old motor oil. Courtney took a sip and made a face, but she drank it.

"I can't believe they'd hold up a mall shop in broad daylight," Alyce said.

"It's that freaking gangsta store," Courtney said. "I don't care if the manager did give me a raise. It's not worth it. Today's my last day." She tore off her name tag and threw it on the counter.

Mall security and uniformed cops rushed through the store door. Josie and Alyce faded out the side entrance. They hadn't seen the holdup and didn't want to be questioned by the police.

"I need some coffee," Alyce said. "Let's go downstairs."

They stopped at a kiosk for double lattes, then plopped down on the wrought-iron chairs in the mall's indoor garden. A pink froth of flowers poured from terra-cotta pots. Sunlight streamed through the skylights in shimmering shafts. The fountain's soft patter soothed them.

"This is such a beautiful mall," Alyce said. "It's a shame I'll never come back."

"Why? Because you saw two thefts? That goes on at every mall in America."

"Not where I shop," Alyce said.

"Yes it does," Josie said. "One million Americans shoplift every day. They boost roughly twenty thousand dollars a minute. I know the gangsta kids looked scary, but what really happened? A white woman stole a thousand dollars and so did some black kids."

"No, you can't explain it away, Josie," Alyce said. "An old woman who shoplifts a scarf and an armed robbery are not the same. That holdup was frightening. Maybe I'm sheltered, but I like my life. I'll never come back here again, not even for you."

Josie shrugged. "OK, if that's how you feel."

"I do. My suburban neighbors can be crooks, but we don't shoot people in malls."

"You just hold them up on paper," Josie said.

"That isn't funny," Alyce said.

It wasn't. Soon, more gunshots would shatter their lives. Nothing would ever be the same for Alyce and Josie.

Chapter 2

Josie could find her way blindfolded to the food court at any mall in America, but she was lost in a kitchen.

Alyce was a culinary artist. After a stressful morning at the Dorchester Mall, she'd retreated to her kitchen. Every woman fought fear in her own way. Alyce subdued hers with a spatula. She'd cooked all weekend. Alyce was in the kitchen when Josie stopped at noon Monday to see if her friend had recovered.

Josie's kitchen looked like the "before" photo in a home-improvement magazine. Alyce's was the triumphant "after." At the palatial Estates at Wood Winds in far West County, kitchens did not have porcelain sinks and Formica counters. Alyce's kitchen was paneled in linenfold oak, like an English library. The fridge was so thoroughly disguised Josie couldn't find it. Somebody should have stuck WESTINGHOUSE on the paneling to give her a hint. Josie couldn't even figure out Alyce's toaster. It looked like something launched by NASA.

Alyce was a flurry of movement at her black granite island, chopping, whipping, and whisking with arcane kitchenware. Josie watched, fascinated. She had no idea what half those tools were. They looked like they belonged in a dungeon.

"I thought I'd fix us a little brunch before the plumber arrives," Alyce said. "Would you like an artichoke-and-leek frittata?"

"If you make it, I'll like it," Josie said. She took a seat at the granite island, on the lee side of the slicers and dicers. "Why are we waiting for the plumber? Is your toilet stopped up?"

"No, I need a pot filler," Alyce said.

"What's that?" Josie said.

"I'm having a tap installed over the stove to fill my big cooking pots. That way I won't have to haul them across the kitchen."

"You're joking," Josie said.

"I am not. Everyone has one."

"Not in Maplewood," Josie said. "We city women are made of sturdy stock. We cross vast kitchens carrying pots full of water."

"Slopping it everywhere," Alyce said.

"Of course. How else would I clean my kitchen floor? What's in this martini? It's red."

"It's a cranberry martini," Alyce said. "It's good for you. Something's worrying you, Josie. I mean, besides that awful business at the Dorchester Mall."

"That didn't bother me," Josie said. "Theft is a fact of life at the malls. But I admit, the armed robbery was a little extreme."

Josie lived in an old suburb on the edge of St. Louis. It was safe by Josie's standards, but Maplewood had its share of crime. Still, she preferred her town's eclectic jumble to the lockstep perfection of Alyce's safer subdivision.

"It's no joke, Josie. Those men pulled a gun on an innocent store clerk. Maybe you're used to that, but I'm not." Alyce was furiously cracking eggs into a bowl two at a time.

"I owe you an apology," Josie said. "I did some research. On Friday, we saw the Dorchester Mall die. That holdup was the beginning of the end. It's happened at other malls: They rent to a store that brings in the wrong clientele. Shoplifting, purse snatchings, and other crimes go up. The advertisers put pressure on the local papers to downplay the crime. That works for a while. Then something too big to cover up happens and the situation explodes."

Alyce broke another pair of eggs.

"How do you do that?" Josie said. "Not a single piece of shell. My eggs would come out extra crunchy."

"Thank you," Alyce said.

"For the eggs?" Josie asked.

"For taking me seriously about the Dorchester Mall. For not making me feel like a sheltered housewife. But you still haven't answered my question. What's worrying you?"

"My mom. She's taken up smoking."

"Why?"

"Peer pressure," Josie said.

Alyce laughed. "Your mom is what? Sixty-five?"

"Sixty-eight," Josie said. "Jane gave up smoking after my father walked out on us, because she couldn't afford cigarettes. She needed every penny to raise me. Now that she's retired, she has a little spending money. Her friends all smoke, so she started again. She says she's not worried about cancer—she's too old to care."

"She has a point, Josie," Alyce said. "It's her life."

"It's a bad example for Amelia," Josie said. "Nine is a dangerous age. Some of the kids at her school are starting to smoke. She doesn't need to see her grandmother puffing away. Her school has zero tolerance for smoking. She could lose her scholarship and be expelled. She—"

Josie stopped in midsentence and stared at Alyce. Her friend was packing curly greens into what looked like a fertilizer spreader. "What are you doing with that miniature farm equipment? The doohickey with the crank?"

"It's an herb mill," Alyce said, as if that explained it.

Josie guessed everyone had one of those, too. She wouldn't embarrass herself with more questions. "Here's the other problem with Mom smoking: She stinks."

"Josie!"

"I can't stand to be in her home. I'm there five minutes and I reek of cigarette smoke. It's in her carpets and her curtains. I have to wash my hair every time I see her. She lives upstairs, don't forget. The smoke seems to seep into everything in her flat. I've told her I hate it, but she waves away my protests like I don't count."

"What's the big deal?" Alyce was tearing the leaves off the baby artichokes and throwing them away. Alyce tossed everything but a thimble-sized hunk of the heart. Josie thought it was a lot of work when she could buy nice big artichoke hearts in a jar for two bucks.

"It's her home," Alyce said, eviscerating another tiny artichoke. "If your mom reeks of smoke, she'll gross out Amelia. You won't have to worry about your daughter picking up a bad habit."

"Mom smokes in my home, too."

"Tell her no," Alyce said. "It's your right to ban smoking there." She dropped the infant artichokes into boiling water.

"That's the problem when your mother is also your landlord and your babysitter," Josie said. "She smokes while she watches Amelia in our flat. Mom swears she doesn't, but she sneaks cigarettes. I can smell them the moment I unlock the door. She opens the windows, so the place is stinky and freezing cold, and I'm paying to heat the outdoors."

"Sounds like what you used to do at school. Didn't you sneak ciggies in the girls' bathroom and blow the smoke out the window?"

Alyce dropped the boiled artichokes into a bowl of ice water. Josie wondered if the little things were confused.

"How did you know?" Josie asked. "We didn't go to school together."

"I know you, Josie. I bet you smoked to rebel. Maybe your mom is doing the same thing. The more you make a big deal out of it, the more she'll light up. Let her go. It's a phase. Why did you quit smoking?"

Alyce patted the tortured artichokes dry with a towel, as if she'd just given them a bath.

"I discovered boys," Josie said. "I wanted more money to spend on clothes and makeup, so I quit the cigarettes. Ohmigod. What if Mom got a serious boyfriend? I mean, besides her bingo buddy, Jimmy Ryent. He's harmless."

"See, it could be a lot worse," Alyce said. "Men are a much harder habit to break than cigarettes. More expensive, too. My friend Liz's mother spent a fortune on a face-lift, and that got her a man who cleaned out her bank account. Now all Liz will inherit is a mountain of debt." Alyce plugged an odd-shaped metal device into a lemon.

"What are you doing to that innocent lemon?" Josie said.

"It's a citrus trumpet," Alyce said. "It's the most efficient way to extract juice from lemons and limes. Just plug this in and squeeze, and the juice comes down the funnel spout. No waste. No seeds."

"It looks cruel," Josie said.

The discussion on citrus abuse was interrupted by the doorbell.

"That's the plumber," Alyce said, and jumped up to open the side door.

There was quite a package on her kitchen doorstep. Josie took in the long legs, the tight jeans, and the soft blue denim shirt with the logo MIKE'S DOGTOWN PLUMB-ERS. The plumber's eyes were a clear gray-blue. The jaw was firm and square. Short brownish hair, *Miami Vice* stubble. Very nice, she thought.

"I'm Mike. I'm here for your plumbing," he said, and turned bright red. "I mean, you wanted a pot filler, ma'am?"

He looked at Josie and Alyce, not sure who to address. Josie bit her lip, trying not to giggle.

"Yes," Alyce said. Her pale complexion was pinker than usual. She patted the wall over the stove. "I want it here, if you can get to my pipes. I mean, my water pipes."

Josie snorted and tried to turn it into a cough.

Mike looked ready to bolt for the door. "Pipes. Right. I'm sure you have good lines. I'll get my stuff in the truck and be back." He disappeared again.

"He can get to my pipes," Josie whispered. "I may need a pot filler after all."

"Quiet," Alyce hissed. She was rosy with embarrassment.

Mike returned with a gray toolbox and a wary expression.

"We're having a frittata," Alyce said. "Would you like a piece?"

Josie choked. Alyce kicked her.

"No thanks," Mike said. "I had lunch already. A Big Mac." He looked around the kitchen. "I guess you don't go to McDonald's."

"I do," Josie said. "I love the special sauce. I could coat my whole body with it." Where did that come from?

Mike's eyebrows shot up.

"As a beauty aid," Josie added. "Not to eat."

Alyce had such a bad coughing fit that Josie had to pound her on the back. Mike tried to get her a glass of water, but he couldn't find the cabinet with the glasses in the acres of unmarked oak. By the time Alyce finished choking, Josie's ridiculous remark was forgotten.

"Can I get you any coffee? Soda? Bottled water?" Alyce said. She took a step toward the stove and Mike backed toward the door. What was going on here? Why would two housewives scare a plumber? And why did they sound like a bad porn movie?

"No, I'm fine," Mike said. "Really. I just want to work."

"Then we'll let you do that," Alyce said brightly. "As soon as I get my buns out of the oven."

"Good," he said. "I mean, thanks."

Alyce might be rattled, but she was still a perfect hostess. She cut the frittata in two and put each half on a plate with a generous helping of salad. Then she carried the plates into the sunny breakfast room. Josie studied her friend's odd gliding walk. Alyce seemed to float above the floor, and Josie could never figure out how she did that.

"How can I help?" Josie said.

"You can sit down and enjoy the view," Alyce said. She was too polite to say Josie would only be in her way.

Josie sat. The sunny bay window overlooked the garden, planted for early December with ornamental cabbages. The table had yellow linen napkins and matching sweetheart roses in a cut-glass vase.

Alyce put a pot of coffee on the warmer and brought in the pitcher of leftover cranberry martinis, a basket of warm rolls, and butter curls. Then she came back with the kitchen-counter TV. Alyce never watched television during meals. Josie suspected she wanted to provide cover for their conversation. Alyce turned the TV on low, and they talked in half whispers.

"What's wrong with me?" Josie said. "I've never sounded so stupid."

"We have *Desperate Housewives* syndrome," Alyce said. "Ever since that TV show, any halfway-cute handyman gets hit on. It's especially difficult for plumbers, and this one is hot. These men are running scared. They're used to initiating the sex, not having women come on to them."

"He's cute, but I can't believe I said those things," Josie said. "I'm so embarrassed."

"You couldn't help yourself. You fell into the Susan role, the klutzy single one. I expected you to trip over a chair any moment. That blasted show has ruined our handymen. It used to be a woman could have a little fling with a repairman and it was no big deal. I didn't indulge, but some of my friends did. Now these guys have become sex objects. They're like rock stars, except they're useful. Women find them irresistible."

"No wonder he's scared. Should I—"

But Alyce was staring at the TV screen. It had a red *Breaking News* banner across the bottom. She grabbed the clicker and turned the sound up. The announcer was saying, "The West County woman was shot and killed in an apparent attempted carjacking at the Dorchester Mall. Witnesses said a seventeen-year-old African-American male was the shooter. Police chased the suspect in the mall, where he was apprehended and taken into custody.

"The dead woman was identified as Halley Hardwicke, thirty, a designer—"

Alyce's fork clattered onto her plate. "That's my neighbor," she said. "Halley's dead."

"The scarf designer," Josie said, and upset her cranberry martini. Neither woman noticed the red liquid dripping on Alyce's floor.

Halley's photo flashed on the screen. She could have been Alyce's sister—her thinner, stylish sister. Halley's skin was pale as orchid petals. Her platinum hair was long and straight and set off by a scarf of infinite blue.

Halley. The woman who made silk scarves of heartbreaking beauty. She'd been shot down in a mall parking lot.

Suddenly, the world seemed much uglier.

Chapter 3

The news of Halley's murder spread through Alyce's subdivision with the speed of sound. Cell phones chirped and computer keys clicked. Husbands were called out of do-not-disturb meetings. Wives opened vibrating phones in checkout lines, saw the personal emergency codes, and took the calls at the cash register, a cardinal sin for polite suburbanites.

Josie and Alyce were still staring at the TV in stunned disbelief when the women of Wood Winds responded to the emergency. They ransacked their kitchens to whip up luscious cakes and hearty main dishes. Disasters this close to home could not be faced on empty stomachs.

Some women cooked special family meals, as if brewing a personal charm to protect their loved ones. The cooking wine came out for husbandly favorites, such as beef bourguignonne, and if the cook had a few slugs, well, she needed to steady her nerves.

Halley was dead. A member of the Wood Winds Christmas dance committee was murdered at the mall, shot during an innocent shopping trip. If golden, good-luck Halley could be killed, it could happen to any of them.

While some Wood Winds women felt the urge to protect their homes, others reached out to their neighbors. One of them ran straight to Alyce's house. Alyce was stacking the luncheon plates in her kitchen, carefully stepping around Mike the plumber. Josie was mopping

up her spilled martini and trying not to stare at Mike's
well-shaped rump wiggling under the sink.

The kitchen doorbell rang and a soft voice called,
"Alyce, are you home? It's me, Joanie."

"Who's she?" Josie whispered.

"My neighbor Joanie Protzel," Alyce said. "She has
the place with the mansard roof, right next door to Halley's house. She may know something."

Alyce opened the door and Joanie bustled into the
kitchen with two huge trays. She was so upset, she didn't
even notice Mike.

Joanie was about thirty, one of those tiny women who
could lift a sofa by one leg to vacuum underneath. She'd
hauled in half a deli, but she didn't have one brown hair
out of place.

"I just heard about Halley," Joanie said. "I couldn't
sit home alone. I had to talk to someone. I brought over
two shivah trays."

The mourning food took up the entire granite island.

"Joanie's family owns Protzel's Deli in Clayton,"
Alyce said.

"We're sending food to Halley's family, too," Joanie
said. "This is just a nosh."

Some people say it with flowers. Joanie said it with
food. She believed in comfort food—if you ate, she felt
better. Josie didn't think she could eat anything after
Alyce's frittata, but she took a small nibble of the corned
beef. Then she took a big bite. Soon she'd downed several slabs of meat.

The turkey looked like it had been sliced off a real
bird. Josie hated the processed junk that tasted like wet
Kleenex. She helped herself to a small piece. Yum. Juicy.
She tried a little more. Then a lot more.

How can I eat like this when a woman has been murdered? Josie thought.

Because death makes you hungry for life, she decided.
She piled life-giving salami on rye.

"I never thought someone from this neighborhood
could be carjacked," Alyce said. "We don't even lock
our doors in Wood Winds."

"It didn't happen here," Joanie said. "It was at the Dorchester. We've all heard the stories about that mall. My friend Kay's sister was mugged there in broad daylight. Kay won't go there, not even for the white sales."

"Jake doesn't want me shopping at the Dorchester, either," Alyce said.

Josie spread chopped chicken liver on citzel bread. The rye bread rolled in cornmeal had an incredible crust. It would be a shame to waste it.

"That's because Jake loves you," Joanie said.

Josie wondered why love meant saying no. She reached for more chicken liver and saw big holes in the deli platter. Josie hoped she wasn't responsible for them all. She was relieved to see Alyce demolishing a beef-stuffed kaiser roll as big as a hubcap.

"Have a little hand-sliced Nova," Joanie urged, heaping a poppy-seed bagel with cream cheese, capers, and half a pound of salmon. She handed it to Josie.

Josie ate the salmon. It was only polite.

"Jake says you wouldn't believe how bad the crime is at that mall," Alyce said. "He says there have been muggings, purse-snatchings, even rapes in the parking garage. They put in more security cameras because of the crime. Josie and I were mystery-shopping there Friday and we saw an armed robbery. Well, we saw the aftermath. That poor store manager was shaking like a leaf."

"You're a mystery shopper?" Joanie gave Josie a big smile. "I've always wanted to get paid for shopping."

"It's a lot more than shopping," Alyce said before Josie could answer. "It's hard work. Josie is part actress and part undercover cop. She really cares. She thinks women shoppers are laughed at."

"We don't get any respect." Joanie piled more salmon on a bagel for Alyce.

Alyce took it without hesitation. Murder killed all thoughts of dieting. Why be thin today if you were dead tomorrow? "Josie has all these disguises, so she can go into any store and look like a regular customer. Sometimes she wears tube tops and sometimes she dresses like us. Today, she looks like a trophy wife."

Josie was wearing her Fashion Victim outfit again.

"The job must pay well if you're wearing Escada," Joanie said.

"I got it at a garage sale," Josie mumbled through a mouthful of salmon.

"The shoes are torture," Alyce said. "Look at the pointy toes on those Pradas. The wigs are pretty uncomfortable, too, but that's her own hair today. You usually wear your blond wig with your Fashion Victim outfit. Where is it?"

"I washed it and it was still wet this morning," Josie said. "I didn't have time to dry it."

"At least it's not that black thing," Alyce said. "I've worn some doozies on our trips."

"You go with her?" Joanie said.

Josie could almost feel the admiration radiating from the tiny woman.

"Sometimes, if she needs a partner. But I don't get paid," Alyce added quickly. Wood Winds wives must never look like they needed money.

"Alyce is my best disguise," Josie said. "Nobody sees two housewives."

"They don't even see one," Joanie said. "You'd think I was invisible in some of those stores."

"Someone must have waited on you. That's a nice necklace," Alyce said.

"It's from Chico's," Joanie said.

"I rest my case." Josie crunched a dill pickle.

"What's that mean?" Joanie said.

"We were talking about St. Louis fashion earlier today," Josie said. "I said that Alyce's friends shopped Chico's and Ann Taylor. They don't buy Halley's scarves."

"Not for a thousand dollars," Joanie said. "No, thank you. I'd rather spend that money on my family. I've always said Halley would be happier in New York."

For a moment, Joanie's small, heart-shaped face clouded and her brown velvet eyes filled with tears. "It's so pointless," she said. "The TV said the police have the killer in custody. A young man seventeen years old.

What did he get for his murder? Nothing. And Halley is dead. Beautiful, talented Halley."

Suddenly, Josie wasn't hungry. She put the remains of her sandwich back on her plate.

"That poor family," Alyce said. "Her little girl will grow up motherless. What's Cliff going to do without Halley?"

"The way I heard it," Joanie said, "he was going to do without her, anyway. They were splitting."

"No!" Alyce leaned in closer. So did Josie. The gossip was almost as delicious as the deli.

"Cliff and Halley fought," Joanie said. "Like cats and dogs. Alan and I could hear them, and you know our house sits on a big lot. They were shouting so loud. The sound carried right through the yew hedge and the privacy fence."

"What were they fighting over?" Alyce said.

"Cliff didn't want the divorce," Joanie said. "He wanted couples counseling. Halley said no. She was sick of the suburbs. She was going to New York. I can't tell you how many nights they went round and round on that. Then they fought over their little girl. That fight was last night. They argued over who got custody."

"Halley wanted her daughter to live with her in New York?" Alyce said.

"No!" Joanie said. Her voice dropped to a whisper. She could hardly say the words. "She didn't want Brittney at all."

"What mother would give up her child?" Alyce was shocked.

Me, on the wrong day, Josie almost said. When Amelia was instant-messaging her friends and had the radio blaring, Josie felt like handing her over to the first person who asked. She stuffed a forkful of coleslaw in her mouth just in time. Mothers in Wood Winds did not joke about their children.

"Halley said Brittney could stay with her father and go to school here," Joanie said. "She said St. Louis was more of a family city than New York."

"Well, that's true," Alyce said. "But couldn't she wait

until Brittney was out of high school? She's what—five now? It's not that long."

"Cliff said that and Halley went ballistic. She said she'd wasted enough of her life in this backwater. She couldn't stand St. Louis another minute. Halley was too talented to live here. We were nothing but a bunch of hicks."

"You're kidding," Alyce said. "She sat there and smiled during the dance committee meetings, and all that time she despised us."

"She said such cruel, unforgivable things," Joanie said. "And her husband Cliff's a good guy. A little stodgy, but nice. He didn't deserve that. I just hope that little girl didn't hear her mother. It will scar her for life."

There was an awkward silence. They all knew if Joanie had heard Halley, so had her daughter.

"What did Cliff do when Halley said that?" Alyce finally said.

"Cliff went crazy. He started . . . bellowing. That's the only way I can describe it. He was like a mad bull. He called Halley terrible names. Then he threw something. Glass, or china, I couldn't tell. We heard it break. Halley screamed, but this time, it was fear, not anger. I think she was afraid he'd hit her. We were going to call the police and report domestic violence when suddenly, they were absolutely quiet.

"A little later, we heard a door slam and a car start up. Cliff's Mercedes. He must have gone for a drive to cool off. Cliff didn't come back until three in the morning. He woke us up when he opened the garage door. He left for work today at seven like always, but he slammed the door so hard the windows rattled. They didn't make up. I bet he never kissed her good-bye that morning. Her death has to be hard on him."

"I'd never guess they were breaking up," Alyce said. "They always seemed happy. Cliff was so proud of her. He bragged about her accomplishments. He was always smiling and hugging her. I never saw him angry."

"Cliff is one of those men who takes it and takes it

and then one day lets loose," Joanie said. "Last night, something broke and he let her have it."

"Can you blame him?" Alyce said.

"That carjacking was a terrible, terrible thing," Joanie said. "But it could have been worse."

"What could be worse than Halley's murder?" Josie said.

"If they'd had another fight, Cliff would have killed his wife. He was that angry. I'm not sure anyone could have stopped him," Joanie said. "Then where would that poor child be, with her mother dead and her father a killer?"

Chapter 4

"Cliff would never kill his wife," Alyce said. "That doesn't happen here. This isn't the big city."

Josie felt her temper flare. She lived in the city of St. Louis—or close enough. How come her neighbors could be criminals, but not Alyce's?

Easy, she told herself. Alyce is your best friend.

It was an unusual friendship. Josie knew that. Alyce was rich and she was poor. Alyce was married. Josie was a single mom with no sign of a husband. Alyce was a full-time homemaker. Josie was a mystery shopper. Alyce liked the calm safety of her suburb. Josie preferred the frenetic pace of the city.

They'd always enjoyed each other's differences, or so Josie thought.

It's the shock, Josie told herself. Alyce doesn't really think city people are violent, does she? A small worm of doubt burrowed into Josie's brain.

Alyce's phone rang before Josie could ask.

"It's Claire, over on Wood Winds Way," Alyce said to Josie and Joanie. "I'll just be a minute."

Joanie excused herself and went into the living room, where she made her own cell phone calls. Josie needed the time to cool down. She picked at the deli platter and tried not to eavesdrop. But above the crunch of kosher pickles and kaiser rolls, she could hear every word.

"It's dreadful, Claire," Alyce was saying. "It's too early for Cliff to have plans for a service. They can't have a funeral until there's an autopsy. Why? Because it's murder. I know she's beautiful, but they have to autopsy her. Please don't cry, Claire."

Alyce hung up. "Poor Claire," she said. "She was on the dance committee with Halley. She's taking her death very hard. A carjacking. This sort of thing doesn't happen."

Josie thought she heard the rest of that sentence: "to people like us." She made a show of checking her watch. "Look at the time. I have to pick up Amelia at school. Tell Joanie good-bye for me." She ran outside before the wrong words slipped out.

Back in her car, she fumed. Did Alyce really believe that money could protect her from crime?

As Josie backed out of the four-car garage, she could hear Alyce's phone ringing again. Probably another neighbor. The Wood Winds women were stunned by Halley's murder. Their reaction was more than the shock of sudden death. They could not believe one of their own could be carjacked. Mindless, brutish murder didn't happen to them. They'd spent a fortune to live in mansions with unlocked doors. Josie thought they'd bought false security. She didn't believe any place was safe, even with armed guards at the gates. She always locked her doors.

She drove past the châteaus, villas, and palaces of the Estates at Wood Winds, and waved good-bye to the pointless guard. It was a brilliant December day, with a heartbreaking blue sky. The lawns were still green in the mild winter. Wood Winds looked peaceful as a postcard.

Josie's mood seesawed between anger and shame. How could you even think those things about Alyce? she asked herself. When you needed help, Alyce was there, no questions asked, no lectures given. You have no business criticizing your best friend. The day you sent your daughter to the Barrington School for Boys and Girls, you planted one foot in Alyce's elegant, sheltered world.

The other remained firmly in Maplewood, land of lunch boxes and redbrick houses. Except these days, Maplewood was becoming trendy. How ironic was that? It was hard to decide which 'tude to use. Should I be blue-collar, upper-class, or hopelessly hip? Josie thought.

She pulled into the curving driveway of the Barrington School. Her little gray Honda was lost in a herd of Lincoln Navigators, Cadillac Escalades, and Hummers. She felt like a workhorse running with the thoroughbreds.

Josie wondered if she'd made the right decision to send Amelia here. She'd wanted the best for her daughter. When Amelia won a full scholarship to Barrington, Josie was thrilled, even though she still had a hard time affording the school. But did the richest mean the best?

You're giving your daughter opportunities you never had, Josie told herself. Then Amelia burst through the school doors like a dark-haired bomb, her backpack bumping behind her, and Josie's doubts vanished. Her daughter's socks were sliding into her shoes. Josie thought that might be genetic. When Amelia yanked the car door open, Josie saw her daughter's soft skin with the drizzle of freckles across her nose, like tiny drops of chocolate.

Amelia still had that sweet little-girl smell. Josie knew she'd turn into a surly teen soon. But for now, Josie could enjoy her. Amelia jumped into the car and Josie waited for the delicious perfume of—

"Cigarettes!" Josie said. "Amelia Marcus, have you been smoking?"

"No, Mom." Amelia's eyes were wide and innocent.

"You're lying."

"You're holding up traffic, Mom."

Josie looked in the rearview mirror. She had the driveway blocked. She waved sheepishly to a mother in an Escalade and got an insincere smile.

"Don't change the subject, Amelia." Josie pulled out onto the street and wondered what was the fastest way home. Traffic was heavy this afternoon.

"You left early for work this morning and Grandma fixed me breakfast," Amelia said. "She was smoking."

"That smell wouldn't last until two thirty in the afternoon."

"I swear I didn't pick up a cigarette, Mom."

Josie looked at her daughter. That statement was too carefully worded. The kid could be a lawyer. "But you were with someone who did, and she gave you a puff while she held it. You've been hanging around with Zoe, and she's smoking."

Amelia's eyes bugged and she said, "How—?" then stopped. Score one for Mom.

"I can read you like a book," Josie said. It's what I did at your age, she thought. What was the old parental curse? Someday, you'll have a daughter just like you. At least it helped Josie stay one step ahead. For now, anyway.

Zoe was the bane of Josie's existence. The kid was nine going on thirty-nine. She was the first one in Amelia's class to wear makeup and high heels. She was also the class sex instructor, dispensing wildly inaccurate information mixed with enough authentic detail to scare any parent.

"What have I told you about Zoe?" Josie said. The line of cars at the stop sign was backed up for more than a mile. They wouldn't get home until midnight.

"Oh, Mooom." Amelia rolled her eyes, one of Josie's least favorite habits.

"Amelia, we've talked about smoking. It causes cancer. It can kill you."

"Zoe says that's never been proven. She showed us that on the Web."

"Only an idiot believes that," Josie said.

"You think Grandma's an idiot?"

The conversation had veered into dangerous territory. Josie took a deep breath, counted to three, and tried to tiptoe around that land mine. "Grandma is sixty-eight. She's made a decision about her health that I disagree with, but she's an adult and aware of the consequences. You have your whole life ahead of you."

"But it's my life."

"When you have your own house, then you can live any way you want," Josie said. "But as long as you're under my roof—" Was she really saying this? She sounded like her mother.

"It's Grandma's roof," Amelia said.

"It's my home under Grandma's roof."

Traffic was hopelessly snarled. Josie craned her neck,
but couldn't see a thing. There must be an accident at
the intersection. She saw a wide driveway on the left,
then a long stretch of woods. It was now or never if she
was going to get out of this mess. Josie made an abrupt
U-turn. Her daughter did the same thing.

"What's a lesbian do?" Amelia asked.

Josie slammed on the brakes and the car behind her
hit the horn. Amelia often asked embarrassing questions
in the car, so she wouldn't have to look at her mom.

Josie stalled for time. She tried to remember the advice from the parenting magazines: Don't give your child
too much information, but don't tell her anything inaccurate or misleading. It sounded so simple when she read
it. It was different when she was trapped in a little car
with a big question. It would be just like her smart little
girl to ask an awkward question to distract Josie from
the hot topic of smoking.

"Uh, a lesbian is a person, I mean, a woman who likes
women," Josie said.

"Yeah, I know that, Mom. But what does she do? Zoe
has a lesbian lawn service. She says all dykes are into
lawn care."

"Amelia, don't use that word. That's a ridiculous statement. Lesbians can be anything—doctors, lawyers . . ."
She ran out of occupations, and looked around wildly
for inspiration. She found it outside her car window.
"Truck drivers."

So much for stereotyping.

"How do you know if you're a lesbian?" Amelia said.

Where was this going? What if she gave the wrong
answer and warped her child forever? Amelia could
wind up on some shrink's couch because Josie said the
wrong thing. Did her daughter have feelings for another girl?

Ohmigod. What if she fell for Zoe? It would be just
like that precocious little creep to experiment with lesbian sex. Should Josie give the "you can have feelings

for another woman, but not be gay" speech? Or the "I'll love you no matter who you choose to be" speech? She decided to keep her mouth shut until she knew more.

"How do you know you're a lesbian?" Josie bought time by repeating the question. Her mother used to do that, too. "Well, if you're a lesbian, you like to be with women more than men."

"Are you a lesbian?" Amelia said.

"What!" Josie's heart slammed against her ribs.

"You're with Alyce all the time."

"That's different. Alyce is my best friend. But that's all. We're just friends."

Terrific. Now I sound like an actress in some tacky tabloid, Josie thought. It was a chilly December afternoon, but a big drop of sweat plopped on her sweater. Her palms were wet. She was panicking. Take a deep breath and answer calmly. Amelia is only nine. Kids get strange ideas.

"A woman can have a female friend and not be gay," Josie said.

"You don't go out with guys anymore, Mom," Amelia said. "Not for a long time."

Had it really been so long? Josie remembered her last hot night with Josh and blushed. If her daughter knew about that, she wouldn't worry about Josie's sexual orientation. But Josh had hurt her so badly, she'd banished him from her bed. Too bad she couldn't lock him out of her bruised heart. There was still a place for Josh, alongside her failed romance with Amelia's father. It hurt so bad to think about Josh, she couldn't even drive past the coffeehouse where he worked.

"Things didn't work out with Josh," Josie said. "I decided it was better to wait awhile, so I didn't make another bad decision. But I'll go out again."

When I get over him. In twenty or thirty years. Maybe I can have bingo dates, like my mom. Maybe Mom and I can double-date.

"Grandma says Alyce's husband, Jake, is an arrogant son of a bugger," Amelia said.

"Amelia!" For once, Josie agreed with her mother,

although she couldn't say that. Jake was an arrogant
SOB. How did they jump to the subject of arrogant
men? Did this have something to do with Josie's failed
love life or was it part of the lesbian question? Josie
could not follow the twists and turns of the nine-year-
old mind. Amelia was amazingly adult one moment, and
a little girl the next.

The silence was nearly as long as the line of cars
creeping along Manchester Road. They were in the heart
of Maplewood. Josie could almost walk to their flat on
Phelan Street from here. She wanted to abandon her car
in the traffic and run home.

Normally, she enjoyed this part of the drive. Downtown Maplewood looked like a scene from a vintage
movie. She expected to see Jimmy Stewart having dinner
in a restaurant or shopping for an engagement ring for
Donna Reed in the Paramount Jewelers. Then the couple would go hand in hand to the model-train store and
the spice shop.

Of course, normally, she wasn't trapped in a car with
her daughter, answering scary questions about sex.

"Grandma said it," Amelia said. "I heard her talking
on the phone with her friend Verna."

"You shouldn't listen to your grandmother's conversation."

"I couldn't help it, Mom. She was right next to me on
the couch."

"You should have left the room to give Grandma
some privacy."

"But we were watching *Code Lyoko*."

Amelia couldn't miss an episode of the hottest kid
cartoon. She'd be a social outcast.

At last. The turnoff for their street. They were home,
thank God, and there was her neighbor Stan on the front
porch. Dear Stan, who bled her radiators every fall and
checked her air-conditioner filters on the first warm day
of spring. Stan, who could talk about why it was cheaper
to use two squares of one-ply toilet paper than one
square of two-ply. Aliens had abducted him and put an
old man's mind in his thirty-five-year-old body.

Was she going to have to date Stan to prove to her daughter she wasn't gay? Josie loved Stan like a brother, but that was the only way she liked him. His cheap knit shirt clung to his pear-shaped body and gave him bigger breasts than she had. If you dated a guy with breasts, did that count?

"Grandma's on the front porch, waving," Amelia said. "I think she wants to talk to you."

Jane came running out to the car, leaving a vapor trail of old cigarette smoke. Josie wrinkled her nose. Jane handed her the cordless phone. "It's Alyce. She's called three times. She can't reach you on that overpriced cell phone. What's the point of buying that thing if you turn it off when I'm trying to reach you? Alyce needs to talk to you right now. Are you two joined at the hip or what?"

Thanks, Mom, Josie thought. That really helps the lesbian issue.

"Alyce wouldn't call at this hour unless it was serious." Josie speed-dialed her number. Her friend picked up on the first ring.

"What's wrong?" Josie said.

"The police were here asking questions about Halley," Alyce said. Josie could hear the raw panic in her voice.

"Sure," Josie said. "You were her neighbor."

"But they have the killer in custody," Alyce said.

"They're probably tying up some loose ends."

"But why would they ask me about—" Alyce stopped suddenly. Josie could hear the rumble of a garage door in the background. "It's Jake. I can't talk now. I'll call you tomorrow." She slammed down the phone.

Alyce never called when Jake was home. At least that routine hadn't changed.

But why was Alyce so panicked? She was the most law-abiding person Josie knew. Alyce didn't even get parking tickets. What could the police ask that had her so frightened?

Josie would have to wait until tomorrow to find out. She'd never guess this one.

Chapter 5

"Was the staff polite?"

Ha. Josie knew that answer. She'd been waiting for the question. It was number four on the mystery-shopper form for the Pretty Things store. She'd waded through the routine ones:

"Was the stock properly displayed?"

"Was the store clean?"

"Were the dressing rooms clean?" Yes, yes, and yes. Now for the good part.

"Did the staff offer to assist you?"

"Were they courteous?"

"Did they thank you for shopping at Pretty Things?" No, no, and no.

Josie was itching to report Saber, the outrageously rude salesclerk. She'd made notes on the scene at the store as soon as she'd gotten back to her car. She was so stunned by Saber's behavior, she'd wanted to remember every word. Now she reread her notes. The questions didn't begin to cover this situation. How about:

Did the staff insult the customer? How many times? Verbally? Physically?

Let me count the ways, Josie thought. She'd been in this job for nine years, and had seen this kind of rudeness hundreds of times. But it always amazed her. Salespeople would insult, ignore, even verbally abuse customers—and still expect them to shop at their store.

"You from New York?" Saber had asked Josie. "I

figured you didn't buy that here. St. Louis is too Dutch and dumb."

Would Pretty Things's New York headquarters understand the depth of that insult? It was a slap at the city's supposedly styleless German population: "Dutch" was a corruption of *Deutsch*. St. Louisans were fiercely proud of their city, and felt it wasn't properly appreciated.

It wasn't just a tactless remark. Saber had piled on the insults. "St. Louisans have no style. New Yorkers understand fashion. This cow town doesn't."

In case Alyce thought she was attacking only the city, Saber had sneered at Alyce's clothes. "Old enough to start school," Saber had said. "Too old to wear."

That made the insults personal. Josie could still see the hurt in Alyce's face.

Saber was too much like her name. How many other customers had she stabbed? Josie's job was to make sure Saber never hurt another innocent shopper.

Josie had a mission: to protect the American consumer. Josie called her Mrs. Minivan. In Josie's mind, she was a tired woman with a job and a family. Mrs. Minivan had a hard life. She didn't need salesclerks like Saber slashing at her.

I can't feel your pain, Mrs. Minivan, Josie thought. But I can make sure it never happens again.

She wrote her account in straightforward sentences. There was no need to exaggerate. She signed her report with a flourish and faxed it from her home office—a grand name for a secondhand computer and a garage-sale table in a corner of her bedroom. It went to her boss at Suttin Services, Harry the Horrible. He would forward her report to New York. If Pretty Things liked her work, he would take credit for it.

Oh, well. The best part of this job was she rarely saw Harry. If she worked in an office, she'd have to face him every day.

Josie checked her watch. Five thirty. Amelia was suspiciously quiet, which meant she was probably instant-messaging her friends. It was time to get dinner going, but Josie didn't feel like cooking. She wondered if she could fix something easy, like Amelia's favorite, mac and cheese. Her mom had left an apple pie on the kitchen table. Maybe if Josie made a salad and—

"Mom, the toilet's stopped up in my bathroom," Amelia said. Her daughter stood in the doorway, balanced on one foot, dark hair swinging almost to her shoulders. "I flushed and it went all over the floor."

Just what she didn't need. Josie raced down the hall. There was an inch of dirty water on the black-and-white tile floor and a hint of cigarette smoke laced with lemon air freshener.

"Were you smoking in here, Amelia?"

"No, Mom. I just flushed and the water ran all over. I don't know what stopped it up. My shoes are gross."

Amelia seemed genuinely distressed. Well, the plumbing was old and cranky. It probably wasn't Amelia's fault.

"Throw your shoes in the washing machine," Josie said. She rummaged in the hall closet for the plunger. It was buried under a pile of boots and canvas carry bags. Josie stuck it in the commode and pumped the wooden handle. The john made sucking and slurping noises, and more water surged out on the floor. Yuck.

That sound you hear is the money being sucked out of your bank account, Josie thought as the dirty water swirled around her ankles.

"We need a plumber," she said.

"Grandma calls Mr. Ansen," Amelia said.

Mr. Ansen was sixty years old with a big belly and a smelly cigar. Josie had a better idea. "I'll call my own plumber." She opened the Yellow Pages. There it was, a nice big ad: "Mike's Dogtown Plumbers. Call us 24-7 for all your plumbing needs. Double the work at half the price."

Yes, indeed. Mike could fix her john and her daughter's worries, Josie decided. Two problems handled with one call. Was that efficient or what?

Josie spent ten minutes mopping up the water. Then

she dashed into her bedroom. She combed her hair, put on fresh lipstick, a crisp white blouse, and jeans that weren't soaked up to the knees. She studied the effect in her mirror. Nice, but not overdone. She also changed her shoes, since they were marinated in toilet water.

Mike was at her door in twenty minutes. He was even better-looking than she'd remembered. At this hour, he had a slight stubble she found manly. She checked out his hands: strong, clean, and free of wedding rings—not that that meant anything. Some married men didn't wear rings. Josie felt they should all be branded on the hand. It would save a lot of trouble.

"I remember you," Mike said. "You're friends with the pot-filler lady."

Josie blushed. "You got here fast. Do you really live in Dogtown?" It was a zingy little neighborhood near Maplewood.

"Right on Tamm Avenue," he said.

Amelia was standing in the doorway. "We learned about Dogtown in school," she said. "Stephanie gave a report. She said the name came from the 1904 World's Fair in St. Louis. The fair had a lot of ethnic groups on display, including the Igorots from the Philippines. The Igorots ate all the dogs in Dogtown. Is that gross or what?"

"I don't know," Mike said. "My neighbor Mrs. Riley has a yappy poodle that I wouldn't mind turning into a pot roast."

Amelia looked shocked.

Mike saw her face and said, "I'm sorry. I'd never eat a poodle. I don't even touch hot dogs." He grinned. Amelia giggled.

Mike squatted so he could talk to Amelia eye to eye, and Josie couldn't help notice the muscles in his thighs. "I've heard that story about Dogtown," he said seriously. "I think it's a legend. My guess is we got the name because we have so many dogs. We always have. Dogtown is proud of being Irish and we're proud of our dogs. A hundred years ago, when strangers came through our neighborhood, the dogs would bark like crazy to protect their territory. They still do. Everybody on my block has at least one dog."

"What do you have?" Amelia said.

"A lazy Labrador, although I think that's an oxymoron. Speaking of lazy, I'd better get to work. I have to keep Chudleigh in dog chow."

"Off to your room," Josie said. "Mike needs room to work." She shooed her daughter out of the cramped bathroom.

"I'll be in the kitchen," she said to Mike. She caught herself before she added, "If you want anything." I've avoided another attack of *Desperate Housewives* syndrome, she thought.

By the time she had the washer chugging away at their shoes, it was after six. Josie decided on pasta with marinara sauce for dinner, which was even easier than mac and cheese. She dumped half a jar of sauce in a pan and set the water on to boil for Scroodles.

When Amelia was little, she loved the name of the screw-shaped pasta. "Scroodles. Scroodles. Screwy noodles," she'd say over and over, until she and Josie were breathless with laughter. Calling the pasta by its proper name, "fusilli," wasn't half as much fun. But that was a million years ago, before Amelia knew words like "lesbian."

The pasta water was boiling when Mike walked into the kitchen with a handful of swollen, soggy cigarette butts. Amelia trailed after him. Josie could read that look on her face—half-defiant, half-defensive.

"I found the problem," Mike said. "It was stopped up with these."

"Amelia, you told me you weren't smoking," Josie said.

"I don't think your daughter wears red lipstick," Mike said.

Amelia gave him a grateful smile. "Grandma does," she said.

"That your mother?" Mike asked.

"Yes," Josie said. "But she's not supposed to smoke in my house."

"There you go," Mike said. "She must have dumped a full ashtray down your john. I bet you surprised her by coming home early and she flushed the evidence in a hurry. I've been through this. My mom smokes on the sly at my house when she babysits my dog."

"Let me guess," Josie said. "She says she's too old to die of cancer."

"Not quite," Mike said. "Mom claims she doesn't have the cancer gene. Her mother smoked like a chimney and died at ninety."

Here goes, Josie thought. "What's your wife say?"

"I don't have a wife," Mike said. "I'm not married."

The silence stretched for eons. Amelia looked at Josie. Josie looked at Mike. Now or never, she thought. If I mess this up, the worst that can happen is I'll have to call Mr. Ansen next time.

"Can I see you again?" Josie asked.

"You need your plumbing looked at?" Mike said. His blue eyes were guileless. Also, clueless.

Amelia stared at her mother as if she'd suddenly sprouted shiny green scales all over her skin. Don't look at me like that, Josie thought. I'm doing this for you, you ungrateful kid. Well, a little bit, maybe. Oh, who am I kidding? This is all for me.

Josie took a deep breath. "My fixtures are fine." Damn. There it was again: creeping innuendo. She stumbled through the next sentence, saying the words as quickly as possible: "Would you like to go out for coffee sometime?"

"No," Mike said.

Josie's face flamed red.

"I'd rather go out for a drink," Mike said, and grinned. His little-boy grin was nearly as nice as his big-boy build. "Are you doing anything Saturday night? My partner's on call that night."

"Just like a doctor," Josie said. "How about seven o'clock?"

Josie was staring dreamily at Mike's blue panel truck, watching him pack away his tools, when Amelia said, "Mom, I can't believe you did that."

"What?" Josie said. She liked the *24-7 Service* on Mike's blue truck. The white script letters were classy.

"You were, like, all over him," Amelia said. "It was so gross. You're worse than Zoe."

Funny how much my daughter sounds like my mother when she disapproves of me, Josie thought. "Hey, at least you don't have to worry that your mother is a lesbian."

"No, you're a slut," Amelia said.

What did she say now? Josie hadn't read anything about that in her parenting magazines. Jane would have grounded Josie for a month for a remark like that. When the phone rang, she grabbed it gratefully.

"Hey, Josie, that you?" The voice that oozed out belonged to Harry the Horrible, her boss. Josie's gratitude evaporated. Harry's calls were usually trouble.

"I want to see you in my office first thing tomorrow," Harry said. Josie heard him devouring something. *Crack. Crunch. Slurp.* It sounded like a giant breaking dead men's bones.

Harry was on the Atkins Diet, and had gained and lost the same three pounds for as long as Josie knew him. One look at Harry and most people switched to the South Beach Diet. It wasn't Dr. Atkins's fault. Harry never followed the diet, except to eat prodigious amounts of meat. Josie figured in another life he must have been Henry VIII.

Crack. Crunch. Slurp. The noise was unnerving.

"Harry, can I ask what you're eating?"

"Alaskan crab legs and butter. I got them on sale." *Crack. Crunch. Slurp.* Josie had an awful vision of legless crabs scooting around in wheeled carts. "Nine o'clock tomorrow morning OK?"

Harry was asking her if she liked the time? Something was haywire. She rarely went into the offices of Suttin Services, but when she did, it was at King Harry's command. He never cared if the time was convenient for her. "Is there a problem, Harry?"

"No, no. Not a problem. Just a little question about your report." *Crunch.*

"I can answer any questions now," Josie said. "I have time."

"No, no," Harry said. He was suspiciously jovial. Josie didn't like this. Harry was a screamer and a bully. When he sounded like Santa Claus, she'd better watch out.

Harry paused for several slurps. Was he licking crab butter off his fingers? She tried to push more pictures of Harry's self-grooming out of her mind.

"This is better discussed in person," Harry said. "I'll talk to you in the morning. And don't worry."

That did it. Now Josie knew there was trouble.

Chapter 6

"Please leave a message." Alyce's recorded voice was soft and untroubled, sounding so different from the frightened woman Josie was trying to reach.

Josie snapped her cell phone shut in frustration. Where was Alyce? This silence was unnatural. She'd already left two messages this morning. She made this third call sitting in rush hour traffic at the world's longest red light.

Josie could always reach her friend after seven thirty in the morning. Alyce had a baby. Even with a nanny, she didn't have the luxury of lying in bed. Baby Justin demanded a diaper change and breakfast by six. Jake was up and out by seven. By eight o'clock, Alyce's day was in full swing.

It was nearly nine now. Something was wrong. The more Josie thought about Alyce's hasty, interrupted conversation last night, the more it alarmed her.

"The police were here, asking a bunch of questions about Halley," Alyce had said. "But why would they ask me about—" Then the garage door had rumbled open and Alyce had slammed down the phone.

Last night, Josie thought her friend was following her unwritten rule: no yakking on the phone while her husband was home. That was family time.

Today, Josie wondered if there was another reason: Alyce didn't want Jake to hear her conversation. Was she hiding something from her husband?

Couldn't be. Alyce wasn't having an affair. She didn't

have the time. She didn't have money problems. Jake made big bucks as a corporate lawyer. She didn't drink, drug, or gamble. Her only addiction was Williams-Sonoma gadgets.

But the police had asked her questions. What could a Wood Winds homemaker know about a carjacking?

Nothing. Josie was sure about that. She'd seen her friend's face when the news of Halley's death had flashed on the TV. Alyce was stunned. You couldn't fake that kind of surprise.

Josie thought there was a reasonable explanation for the police interest: They were putting together a time line, asking the neighbors when they'd seen Halley leave for her fatal trip to the mall.

"But why would they ask me about—" Alyce's unfinished question hung in the air.

She's worrying about nothing, Josie thought. But she couldn't shrug off her friend's distress. That would be disloyal and condescending. She wouldn't treat Alyce like a silly housewife. If Alyce was worried, she had a good reason. Josie wished she knew what it was.

Unfortunately, she had her own fears to face this morning. There was Harry and his mysterious "little question." Josie wasn't fooled. There was a big problem with her report or her boss would have discussed it over the phone.

Josie pulled into the potholed parking lot at Suttin Services and checked her watch again: eight fifty-five. She had to see Harry the Horrible in five minutes. She redialed Alyce's number and left a third message. "It's me, Josie. I have a meeting with Harry. I'll have my cell off for about half an hour. I'll call you as soon as I get out. I hope everything is OK." She couldn't help adding that.

Josie pulled an old gray cassette recorder out of her purse and checked the batteries. That battered little machine was her job insurance plan. She flicked on the RECORD switch and dropped it back in her purse. She was ready for her meeting.

Suttin Services was in a dreary industrial row off Manchester Road. These businesses were struggling to survive, like the weeds growing between the aging brick buildings. Their paint was peeling and blistered. Their faded signs were streaked with rust. Torn awnings were whipped by an odd, unseasonable wind that blew hot and cold at the same time. It was too warm for December.

Tornado weather. Josie studied the sky anxiously, looking for the greenish black clouds that signaled a serious storm. So far, the scudding clouds were only a threatening gray.

Suttin Services was even more depressing inside. Dusty miniblinds blocked the light. The furniture looked like it had been swiped from the city dump. Most of the employees weren't in until nine thirty. Josie passed their paper-piled and coffee-ringed desks and wondered how they survived in there all day.

She never wondered that about Harry. He belonged in his cave, thriving in the grime and the gloom. Harry looked like Jabba the Hutt, except he had more hair. Every inch of Harry's visible hide was hairy, except his dome. Mother Nature had a perverse sense of humor.

Josie had grown used to the hairy clumps in his ears and on his knuckles. Now she saw little patches peeping out between the buttons on his too-tight white shirt.

Harry was munching microwaved sausages, piled on a grease-slick platter. He held a half-gnawed sausage in one hand, like a cigar.

"Hi, Harry." Josie sat on a chair with a crooked leg. It wobbled when she moved, but the other chair had a broken back.

"Wanna sausage?" he said.

"No, thanks," Josie said.

"You need to eat more protein," he said. "I bet you didn't have any breakfast."

"I can't face food in the morning," she said.

"How are you going to stay healthy like that?" Harry chomped the rest of the sausage, then glugged half a liter of diet soda. He wiped his lips with a paper napkin,

an oddly delicate gesture for such a gross man, and selected another sausage with a connoisseur's concentration.

"Uh, I read your Pretty Things report." Harry held
the sausage like a pointer. "Listen, Josie, I know she's a
pain in the ass, but could you go easy on that salesgirl?"

"How easy?" Josie asked.

"Could you forget what happened? Leave the incident
out of your report?"

"You want me to change my report?" Josie said, in
case the tape recorder didn't pick up his illegal request.
"Harry, she took nearly four minutes to wait on me. She
insulted a customer. I can't forget about it."

"Aw, come on. Saber's just a kid."

Saber. He knew her. "OK, Harry, who is she?"

"What do you mean?" Harry tried to look innocent
and failed.

"St. Louis is a big small town. Saber has to be a friend
or a relative."

Harry grinned, showing teeth like tombstones. "You
got me. She's my sister's kid. Just cut her some slack.
She keeps getting fired."

"She should be fired, Harry. She doesn't belong in
retail."

"But she needs the job."

"Not that job," Josie said. "I'm sure Saber is talented,
but her talents don't include dealing with the public.
She'd be happier away from customers, maybe in a job
like computer programming."

"She doesn't want to be stuck at a desk all day,"
Harry said. "She likes the discount she gets at this store.
She's just a kid, Josie. She's only twenty-five." Harry
made it sound like she was in school with Amelia.

"Her mouth is certainly all grown-up. She says cruel
things to customers," Josie said. "You read that report."

"It's not her fault," Harry said. "My sister, Jackie,
stuck her with that stupid name. Who calls a kid Saber?
It's from a romance novel or soap opera or something.
Kid's bound to turn out weird. You can't believe what

she had to listen to. In school, guys would say, 'Saber, baby, let me show you my sword.' If she'd been called Sarah, she'd be fine.

"It will take you five minutes to rewrite that report, Josie, and it would make a big difference in the kid's life."

"Harry, I'm sorry. I can't do it."

"You're not going to change your report?" Harry dropped the uneaten sausage on a stack of paper. Josie watched the grease stain slowly spread across the top page.

"No," Josie said.

"You're shittin' me. You won't do this one little thing for me?"

"I can't, Harry. It's against the rules. Once I turn in a report to this office, I can't change it."

His bald dome burned red with anger. "You want rules? I could fire you for not following orders."

She reached in her purse and held up the cassette recorder like a cross before a vampire. "No, you couldn't, Harry. I have this conversation on tape. The home office wouldn't like it."

The red RECORD button glared at him like an angry eye. Harry went pale as a boiled chicken.

"You wouldn't," he said.

"Harry, she's your niece. I understand why you'd want to protect her. You're a concerned uncle. I'm willing to forget your request, if you are."

Josie popped the tape out of her recorder and dropped it in her purse. He knew she'd hang on to her insurance policy.

"Go ahead," he said. "Destroy the kid's life. But don't ask me for any favors. We clear on that?"

"Yes," Josie said.

Harry picked up the phone and started dialing. She was dismissed. The crisis was over. It wasn't as bad as she'd thought. Harry would take his petty revenge by giving her a couple of rotten assignments, but there wasn't much else he could do. She had the goods on him, and she was his best mystery shopper. A lot of regular customers requested Josie.

Josie had to force herself not to run out of Suttin Services. Outside, a cold rain hit her in the face, and drops spattered her clothes. As she ran for the car, Josie was grateful that she was mystery-shopping Supertime Supermarts. She had on jeans and loafers. The rain would have ruined her Fashion Victim outfit and pointy-toed Pradas. Better yet, today she'd be buying groceries instead of useless scarf rings.

Josie popped in a CD and sang along to U2. When she warbled "New Year's Day," she sounded like a stepped-on cat, but in her mind Josie was onstage, bringing her own special pathos to the ballad. She loved that song. She'd even downloaded it for her cell-phone ring tone.

Josie pulled into the first Supertime Supermart lot on her list and tried to call Alyce again. No answer. Her message was short, almost rude: "It's me. Are you OK?"

Alyce wasn't, or she would have picked up the phone. If she didn't answer by noon, Josie would drive out to her house. She turned off her phone and pulled out her shopping list. She was ready to work.

St. Louis had beautiful supermarkets. The big chains competed with exotic items and displayed food like works of art. Josie even took out-of-town guests to see her local supermarket. "It looks like the food court at Harrods," a well-traveled friend once told her.

Josie passed green-lipped mussels and stone crab claws bedded on crushed ice with parsley, lemons, and decorative seashells, and sidestepped the pyramids of Asian apples and Greek figs. She was supposed to buy bulk-bin cashews with an outdated coupon. Then she had to order two double-thick, cut-to-order pork chops in the meat department. Next, she had to buy organic romaine lettuce and a case of bottled water.

Josie could use all that food. Sometimes, she had to figure out what to do with the things she couldn't use.

Last time, it was green tea, which Josie thought tasted like boiled grass, and a thirty-pound sack of dog food. Both went to her mother's church food drive. Josie knew poor people had dogs to feed, but she thought green tea only added to their misery. Jane claimed some people liked it.

Josie dreaded one duty. She had to put the bottled water underneath the cart and "forget" it. It was a checker test. If the checker missed the water, she'd lose points, maybe even her job. Josie didn't like that part. Reporting rude clerks like Saber was one thing. Going after overworked checkers was another.

Today, the checkers found the case of water at all three stores. They rang up all the items correctly, and refused to redeem the bad coupon. The stores were clean, the restrooms had paper, and the parking lots were free of runaway carts. This was a good day.

Josie was pulling out of the third Supertime lot when her cell phone rang. It was Alyce. Josie parked and opened her phone. She couldn't handle this conversation in traffic.

Alyce sounded almost as panicked as she had last night. "Something's wrong," she said. "The police had a long talk with me yesterday. I've spent all morning trying to find out if the other neighbors had visits from Dorchester homicide."

"And did they?" Josie said.

"Yes, but the cops talked with me the longest."

"Maybe you were the most informative," Josie said.

"I don't know anything," Alyce said.

"This is a high-profile murder," Josie said. "They're under a lot of pressure. They have to talk to the neighbors."

"Yes, but why would they ask me about Jake?"

"Jake, your husband?" Josie had met Alyce's husband only once or twice. He was handsome, careful, and conventional. She couldn't imagine him committing a white-collar crime, much less a murderous carjacking. The idea was so absurd, she almost laughed.

"What could Jake possibly have to do with Halley?" Josie said.

"Nothing," Alyce said, too quickly.

What was that about? "So what if the police asked you about Jake?" Josie said. "They've already caught the killer."

"Haven't you been listening to the news?" Alyce said.

"Nope, I've been having a serious karaoke session in my car."

"The police had to let the guy go," Alyce said. "They arrested the wrong man."

Chapter 7

Josie needed news about the false arrest—fast. She was meeting Alyce in ten minutes. While she raced through the traffic, she flipped through the local radio stations. She knew the search was hopeless. It was seventeen past the hour. No news for another forty-three minutes. Unless—yep, Jinny Peterson's show was on.

Josie was too young for talk radio, but she made an exception for *Livewire* with Jinny Peterson.

Jinny was a white woman host with a mostly African-American audience, and she wasn't afraid to discuss issues most St. Louisans would rather ignore. Josie had guessed right. Jinny's listeners were raging against the latest twist to Halley's carjacking.

"You're on WGNU, Charles," Jinny said. "Today, we're talking about Denzel Wattsson, the young African-American falsely arrested for the murder of scarf designer Halley Hardwicke at the Dorchester Mall. What do you have to say, Charles?"

"You ask me, Jinny, what happened to that young man is another case of RWB—Running While Black," Charles said. "It's closely related to those other well-known African-American crimes, DWB, Driving While Black, and DWW, Driving with a White Woman."

"I'm laughing," Jinny said, "but I know it isn't funny. Next caller, Jefferson from Moline Acres. Go ahead, sir."

This man had the rich tones of a TV preacher. "Denzel Wattsson is one more black man in a long line of local persecution. We've had distinguished scholars and other prominent people of color arrested and embarrassed, just because they happened to be black."

"That's true, Jefferson," Jinny said. "Denzel is a seventeen-year-old honor student at Priory School."

Uh-oh, Josie thought. The kid's parents have money.

"His seventy-three-year-old aunt had dropped him off at the Dorchester Mall moments before his arrest. The pastor of the Clayton African Methodist Church was in the car with the aunt."

Oops, Josie thought. Now the Dorchester was up against a major black church.

"Denzel was running through the mall," Jinny said, "because he was late for a lunch date with some friends. His only crime was to dress in the fashionably baggy clothes that kids his age wear. When he tried to tell the police what happened, they cuffed him and threw him down on the floor. He wasn't released until nine o'clock this morning. The police and the City of Dorchester have given him an apology."

"An apology?" Jefferson said, his voice ringing with outrage. "Are they going to give him back his day? I hope his parents sue the socks off the City of Dorchester."

"Should be easy," Jinny said. "Both parents are lawyers."

The denizens of Dorchester City Hall must be a whiter shade of pale today, Josie thought. Good. They were a snooty little city, fat and arrogant from the Dorchester Mall income and a speed trap they ran on Clayton Road. They'd have to hand out a lot of speeding tickets to pay for this debacle.

"We have Loretta from Belleville on the line," Jinny said. "Loretta, what's your take on Denzel's false arrest?"

An old woman with a cracked, creaky voice said, "I think that young man was asking for trouble dressing like a gangsta. He played right into the white folks's stereotypes. If he'd been dressed like Tiger Woods, he would have never been arrested."

"You are probably right about that, Loretta, but it's like saying a woman who wears tight clothes is asking for rape."

"She is," Loretta said, her voice gaining strength. "The Bible tells us—"

"Thank you, Loretta," Jinny said, unceremoniously cutting her off.

The on-air debate was still raging when Josie pulled into the parking lot at Minion's Café in downtown Maplewood. Minion's was a homey little place with light wood, soft blue walls, and handmade posters for church rummage sales and local musicians. Josie hoped it would have a soothing effect on her troubled friend. It was almost eleven o'clock. The restaurant was starting to fill up with the lunchtime crowd. Josie took a seat in the back where they could talk.

Alyce stumbled through the door a few minutes later. She looked like she'd been on a two-day bender. Her fine blond hair was flat and straggly. Her raincoat belt dragged on the floor. Her collar hung off on one side, and Josie realized she'd buttoned her shirt wrong. Alcohol didn't do this to her friend. Alyce was worn-out with worry.

Josie decided chicken salad couldn't fix this. This crisis called for dessert first. She flagged the waitress and ordered. "Two pumpkin muffins and two ginger teas."

"How are you, Alyce?" Josie asked. She could see a blue vein throbbing under her friend's right eye. Tiny tension lines framed her mouth. She was coming apart.

Alyce broke her muffin into two pieces, and then two more, before she answered. "The homicide detectives from the City of Dorchester talked to me yesterday. They wanted to ask some questions about Halley. I said, yes, of course. I thought they were trying to figure out where she went that day."

Alyce took a muffin quarter, and broke it into two more pieces.

"Who were the detectives?" Josie asked, hoping Alyce would feel comfortable starting out with a fairly neutral subject.

"Greg Evanovich and Cesar DeMille."

"Cesar DeMille? Is that his real name? He sounds like a dress designer."

"I couldn't exactly ask him, could I?" Alyce said. "DeMille looked as weird as his name. Real skinny, with a high black pompadour, like some fifties crooner. I swear it's a hairpiece. His hair was too thick and glossy for a beat-up guy in his forties. The other detective, Evanovich, was good-looking if you like guys with a little sleaze and a lot of gym muscle. I bet he hits on half the women he interviews."

"Did he hit on you?" Josie asked.

"I had on a blouse with baby spit-up. It isn't a perfume that drives men wild."

Alyce had reduced her muffin to a pile of crumbs without taking a bite. Josie had demolished hers, too, but her plate was empty. Dessert wasn't working. Josie ordered two cups of beef barley soup.

"Eat the soup," she said. "Then we'll talk."

The hot soup seemed to revive Alyce. The color returned to her face and the blue vein stopped throbbing. But she still looked like she might bolt at any moment. I've got to ease her into this, Josie thought. Otherwise, she'll keep describing those two cops down to their shoestrings.

"Tell me exactly what the detectives said, Alyce. Go through it question by question, from the beginning."

Alyce took a deep breath. "Cesar, the guy with the weird hair, did most of the talking. He kept the questions about Halley open-ended at first. He said, 'Tell us about her. Who did she know? What did she do? Where did she go?'

"I didn't know much. After Halley's design business took off, she flew to New York and Milan two or three times a month. Who knows who she met there? I said Halley was talented. I admired her work and I was proud that she was going places." Alyce sounded almost wistful.

"Then both detectives peppered me with more personal questions: 'Was she a player?' "

"A player?" Josie said. "What did that mean?"

"I think they were asking if Halley fooled around. They asked, 'Did she drink or gamble or spend too much money? Did she get along with her husband?' I told them I'd never seen her drink more than a glass of wine. To my knowledge, she didn't gamble. If she had a lover, I didn't know anything about it. I'd heard she was getting a divorce, but I'd never seen her fight with her husband. So far as I knew, she and Cliff got along as well as any married couple."

Which was not well at all, Josie thought. "Did you give them Joanie Protzel's name?"

"Yes. I said that Joanie had heard Cliff and Halley fighting the night before." Alyce stopped before she had to say that ugly word "killed." "I don't think Joanie will appreciate that. I should have kept quiet. Am I a police snitch?"

Josie nearly snorted her tea through her nose. Alyce looked so hurt she stopped laughing.

"This isn't high school," Josie said. "It's a murder investigation. The police need to know what's going on."

"I didn't know anything about the fights with her husband, except what Joanie told us yesterday, and I thought she should tell the police herself. I'd just be passing on gossip."

"I think it's OK to give them gossip at this stage," Josie said. "Isn't that how the police investigate a murder? One person leads them to another and then another, until they find a new side to the victim's life and a clue to her death."

"I'm beginning to think Halley had more sides than a Rubik's Cube," Alyce said. "And I didn't know any of them. Cesar asked me if she was loyal."

"Loyal? That's a weird question."

"I couldn't answer that one, either," Alyce said. "I told them Halley designed the decorations for the dance committee. I thought she did a superb job, even if some people groused that having Halley-blue decorations turned the ballroom into an ad for her scarves. I thought it looked magical. The more I talked, the more our lives sounded so trivial. Nobody gets killed for reasons like that.''

"It's not trivial," Josie said. "It's normal. It's ordinary in the best sense of the word.''

"That's not how it seemed to me," Alyce said. "Then Greg asked if anyone was mad at Halley. I said no. She was a beautiful woman who made beautiful things. Some people might be jealous, but not enough to kill her. He said, 'Are you one of those people? Do you want to live in New York?' ''

"What did you say?" Josie asked.

"I burst out laughing. I don't want a New York success. I want my soufflés to come out right. I'm a homebody.''

"I'd hardly call you a homebody," Josie said.

"Well, what would you call me? I'm happiest in my kitchen. I want to be with my son.''

"I'd call you content," Josie said. "I bet your laugh blew away the detectives's doubts.''

"I don't think so," Alyce said. "They kept asking questions. They pounded at me until my head hurt. There were so many questions, I can hardly remember them. They wanted to know if anyone would harm Halley to get even with someone else. I said, 'You mean, kill Halley to get revenge on Cliff for a business deal?'

"They said, 'Something like that.'

"That was ridiculous, and I said so. Cliff was a division head at a pharmaceutical company, not Tony Soprano. He was kind of dull. He was a workhorse.''

Even a workhorse kicked over the traces sometimes, Josie thought.

"The detectives wanted to know if Halley was a creature of habit. I said not lately. She was always running off to the airport at odd hours—early in the morning, late in the afternoon. She'd dropped all her committees. The only thing she did regularly was make the rounds of the stores that carried her scarves once a week. She always did that if she was in town. The day she was killed, that was her store day.''

"Did everyone know that?" Josie asked.

"I knew it, and I wasn't part of her inner circle." Alyce absently picked up a paper napkin and started tearing it into strips.

"The police asked a bunch more questions. They wanted to know about Halley's daughter, her friends, her business associates, her ex-lovers. I wasn't much help on that, either. I knew her best friend was Linda Dattilo, but everyone knows that."

"Why are you worried, Alyce?" Josie said. "This sounds like standard stuff."

Alyce looked stricken. "Because they asked me if Jake knew Halley."

"So?" Josie said. "They live in the same subdivision."

There was that odd hesitation again. "They asked if I knew where Jake was at the time she was killed. They didn't say that, exactly, but they wanted to know where he was yesterday."

"Do you know?" Josie said.

"Yes." Alyce was concentrating on rip-stripping the napkin. "He had a business meeting out by the airport in the morning. He was in his office the rest of the day. I called two or three times from ten thirty on and he picked up his private line to talk to me."

Alyce stacked the napkin strips into a pile, then selected one strip and tore it to bits.

"I'm sure it's routine to ask those things," Josie said. "The Dorchester cops arrested the wrong person, like you said. But the shooter was a young black male. That definitely isn't Jake."

Alyce managed half a smile. "Jake is the whitest guy I know." Two more napkin strips were in shreds.

"See?" Josie said. "Nothing to worry about."

"But why would they ask me about Jake?" Rip. Shred. Tear. The pile of napkin confetti grew bigger.

"I don't know," Josie said. "Maybe they needed to clear up some minor question. Do you think they'll come back again?"

"I don't know. If they do, I'm calling a lawyer. I've got the number programmed in right here." She held up her cell phone.

"Good," Josie said. "You're prepared. They can't catch you by surprise again. Alyce, I hate to see you so upset. Can I watch the baby while you get a massage or a facial?"

"I look that bad, huh?" Alyce tore another long strip of napkin into smaller strips, then ripped up those strips. The napkin was turning into a paper snowdrift.

"You need some pampering," Josie said.

"The nanny's with Justin now. I want to go home and hold him and rock him and feel his soft skin and admire his eyelashes. They're so long. They're going to break some little girl's heart."

"Sounds like a plan," Josie said. "Seriously, what can I do to help?"

"Tell me it's nothing," Alyce said. She took the last napkin strips and twisted them until they disintegrated under the strain.

"It's nothing," Josie said with complete confidence. "Jake's a corporate lawyer. How could he possibly be connected with a carjacking?"

"You're right." Alyce looked relieved for two seconds, but then her face clouded. "I've got a bad feeling, Josie. Something's wrong. I know it. I don't know why, but I feel it."

The waitress set the check between them.

"Did you ask Jake about the police questions?" Josie said.

"Yes. He said I was making a federal case out of nothing."

"There you go," Josie said.

Alyce reached for the check. "But he only says that when he's guilty."

Josie tried to grab back the check, but Alyce had already torn it to pieces.

Chapter 8

"Let's go," Josie said, "before you tear the place up."

Alyce seemed dazed by the wreckage in front of her: the shredded napkin, the minced muffin, the finely chopped check. "Did I do that?"

"Yes. You need something stronger than tea."

Josie guessed at the check total, then added what she hoped was a generous tip. She steered her friend out the door, around the corner, and into Josie's car.

"Where are we going?" Alyce said.

"The Schlafly Bottleworks. You can't tear the head off a beer. Their oatmeal stout is almost a health food. You can also wash your hair in it and use it as a facial mask."

Alyce didn't laugh. "I can't believe I made such a mess at the table."

"You've got something major on your mind."

Alyce didn't answer. They rode the few blocks to the brew pub in an unnatural silence. Normally, Alyce would have chattered about the people on the sidewalks, the new shops and restaurants, the places that went out of business. Today, she stared straight ahead.

Josie was worried. She hoped the industrial interior of the Bottleworks would give her friend a healthy dose of reality. They passed the gleaming tanks of beer, clean and hopeful in the noontime sun, then went into the bar. It was comfortably noisy. Alyce drifted along like a ghost and sat down at a table, folding her hands in her lap like a finishing-school student.

Josie took charge and ordered two oatmeal stouts. She

was relieved when the waiter slapped down two beer coasters instead of bar napkins. Alyce couldn't tear them up.

The stout lived up to its name. It seemed almost solid in the thick pint glasses. The barroom was dark and warm, a place for spilling secrets under the cover of other people's conversation.

"Drink," Josie commanded.

Alyce took a sip of the bitter brew, then another.

"I know you too well, Alyce," Josie said. "You wouldn't fall apart over a couple of questions by the police. You can run rings around homicide cops. I've seen you do it. Something's wrong, and it has to be your family, or you wouldn't be so upset. If you had a problem with Justin, you'd tell me. So it has to be your husband. What did Jake do?"

"I don't know," Alyce said. "I'm sure he didn't do anything."

Two tears slid down her cheeks. Then her face dissolved into a red, water-streaked mask of misery. Alyce rummaged in her purse for tissues and dabbed at her eyes.

Suddenly, Josie had a good idea what Jake did. Earlier this year, Alyce had suspected her husband had a fling with their pretty au pair. When the au pair left abruptly, Alyce had hired a nanny of mature years and serious girth. Jake took his wounded wife on a romantic cruise, and the subject was never mentioned again.

Amy the Slut, Wood Winds' most scandalous wife, said she'd slept with Jake, but she claimed to have nailed every married man in the subdivision. Even Amy didn't know if that was true. Her multimartini lunches impaired her memory, as well as her judgment. Alyce could discount Amy.

Now something had happened that Alyce couldn't ignore. Jake must be having a serious affair. This was more than a little slip with the au pair. He was in deep, possibly with a woman in their own circle. Alyce was so afraid, she couldn't even say the words. That would make her worst fear real.

I can't bring up this subject, Josie thought. Even the best friendship could not trespass into a marriage. Josie would have to wait for Alyce to talk.

Josie did, with all the patience she could muster. She sipped her stout and watched Alyce weep bitter tears. It tore her heart to see her friend so unhappy, but Josie knew it would ruin their friendship if she jumped uninvited into this marital mess.

It took half a tall glass of stout before Alyce had the courage to talk. "It sounds so trite I'm ashamed to say it. I tried to call Jake at the office a couple of nights when he said he was working late. . . ."

Josie didn't miss the careful wording—"when he said."

"I couldn't reach him," Alyce said. The despair in her voice said it was more than a missed phone call that made her feel so disconnected.

"Jake didn't answer his phone all evening. He came home at midnight. When I asked him about it, Jake said he must have been in the law library or talking to another partner. But he didn't check his messages."

"Anyone can forget to check messages," Josie said.

"Jake checks his office voice mail every sixteen seconds. He was somewhere else." Alyce took a deep breath and said the fatal words: "I think he's having an affair."

There. The words were out. The subject was safe to discuss. "Are you sure?" Josie said.

"No," Alyce said. "I'm not."

"Any lipstick on his collar? Phone numbers on cocktail napkins? Matchbooks from places you don't go? Strange earrings in the car? Traces of perfume on his clothes?"

"No. None of that."

"Hang-ups when you pick up the phone?" Josie asked.

"Yes, several. But Joanie complained of those calls, too. She thought it was the Markland kids making trouble with their new cell phones. She talked to their mother and the calls stopped."

"So the hang-ups were explained, too," Josie said.

"Yes, but—," Alyce said.

"But what?" Josie said.

"I'd better go," Alyce said. She was afraid to say more. The subject was too frightening and too big. It would have to be brought out and examined in little pieces.

Josie decided not to push. "Me, too," she said. "I still have one more supermarket to shop before Harry sticks me with another bad assignment. Want to come along? I'm buying pork chops. Thick, juicy ones. You can have half of my haul."

"No, thanks. I have a committee meeting. I'm working on the holiday party for Jake's firm. Sometimes I think I do more for his career than he does."

She stopped, and suddenly looked guilty. "I shouldn't complain. It's no hardship to sit with a few women over coffee. It's not like I'm working nine to five. I'm lucky." She said that as if trying to convince herself.

"You need to fix your blouse if you're going to a meeting," Josie said.

Alyce looked down in surprise at the mismatched buttons. "Right. I guess it wouldn't hurt to comb my hair, either. I look like a bag lady."

By the time Josie had paid for the stout, Alyce was back from the restroom. She'd washed her tear-streaked face, adjusted her blouse and her coat belt, even put on fresh lipstick.

"Much better," Josie said. "Let me drive you back to your car."

"It's only three blocks," Alyce said. "I need the fresh air. I'm fine."

Josie watched her friend walk away, her shoulders sagging and her head bowed. Alyce was carrying a heavy burden. If Jake really was having an affair, she would have to make some serious decisions. Would she turn a blind eye and become "poor Alyce," the long-suffering wife of a chronically unfaithful man? Or would she keep her self-respect and throw the bum out?

If she took the second road, Alyce would lose not only her husband and the father of her child, but the life she loved. Divorced wives could not afford mansions in Wood Winds—not when they'd been married to lawyers. Jake would call in one of his shark buddies and Alyce would be lucky to end up with custody of Justin and a two-bedroom condo, far away from Wood Winds. She might get a small stipend while she brushed up on her computer skills, but she'd have to become self-supporting. There would be no more Williams-Sonoma gadgets, no pot fillers and linenfold-paneled kitchens.

Keeping her eyes shut had its hazards, too. Alyce might not see when one of Jake's affairs turned serious, and he'd throw her out for a younger, trimmer trophy wife. Then she'd be banished, without even the comfort of her self-respect.

Too many women had had to make those choices. They tried to stay with men they didn't love until their children made it through college. But was that the right choice? Josie wondered. Kids had a sixth sense when things were wrong at home. Was it better to give them every luxury in a loveless marriage, or try to cut yourself free and survive?

If Josie was in Alyce's fix, she'd start slipping money out of the household accounts for a rainy-day fund. Lots of money. She was sure the dark clouds were about to open up on Alyce.

Once again, Josie thought about how close she'd come to living in Wood Winds and sharing Alyce's anxieties. Josie had had the ring on her finger when she threw it away for a wild romance. She left college and a steady fiancé for a man who flew her to Paris one week and Aruba the next. Her Canadian helicopter pilot never promised her security, and she never wanted it. Nate gave her something better: He made Josie feel that her life would never be dull again. She loved him the way she never loved another man. Josie still remembered the night Amelia was conceived. They'd made love by the light of a hundred burning candles.

Then Nate went down in flames with the law, and wound up in a Canadian prison for drug dealing. Josie had found out she was pregnant about the same time she learned where Nate got the money for his high living. She wasn't going to marry a drug dealer. She never saw Nate again. She'd crawled away from the wreckage of her romance with one enduring love—Amelia.

Now Josie lived in her mother's flat in Maplewood. Jane lived upstairs and made herself available for emergency babysitting and free lectures on where Josie went wrong. Josie shrugged off the lectures. She knew her mother meant well. She also knew how disappointed Jane was by what she saw as Josie's lost prospects. By her mother's standards, Josie had failed.

Josie didn't think so. She liked her life. Sure, it would be nice to have money. Sometimes she sat up nights worrying how she'd pay the bills. But at least she wasn't dependent on a man she couldn't trust. Josie had her freedom. She liked her job, and most people she knew hated their work. Harry the Horrible was an awful boss. But Josie felt she did something useful, protecting Mrs. Minivan. Mystery-shopping had another advantage. She got to spend time with her daughter.

Josie's cell phone rang. It was the downside calling: her boss, Harry.

"I got your next assignment." Harry sounded too happy for a man who'd been recently trounced.

"Good," Josie said, hoping she sounded confident. "I've finished the supermarkets. I'll turn that report in tonight."

"Excellent." He drew out the word, making her wait for her punishment. "You can start mystery-shopping Greta Burgers this afternoon."

Josie's stomach lurched. Greta Burgers were named after the owner's daughter. The unfortunate child's name was stuck on the worst burger in the Midwest. Lord knows what Greta endured during her formative years, when the slogans "Greta Is Betta" and "Greta's Cheap and Easy" haunted the radio. Josie hoped she was a rich woman now that her father was dead of hardened arteries.

Greta Burgers were god-awful gristly little gobs of grease. The only people who could eat them were cheapskates, drunks, and teenagers, or, more often, drunk teenagers. It took courage to down a Greta Burger, particularly if someone squeezed it and you saw the grease run out on the plate. Josie's stomach had flip-flopped like a beached fish after that demonstration.

Greta Burgers were so bad, mystery shoppers never had to visit more than four outlets at once. Eating more could be fatal. Some mystery shoppers quit at the prospect of eating even one Greta Burger. Others cheated, and made up their evaluations. But Josie had her code. She took at least one bite of a Greta Burger at every restaurant on her list. Harry knew that.

She asked the crucial question as her stomach churned. "How many?"

"All twenty-four restaurants in the metro area." Harry couldn't keep the glee out of his voice.

Josie couldn't keep the horror out of hers. "Twenty-four! You can't do that."

"I just did," Harry said.

"Nobody can eat twenty-four Greta Burgers," Josie said. "You're supposed to split up the restaurants."

"Can't," Harry said. "It's a rush job. All my other shoppers are busy."

"Harry, please, I'm begging you. Split up the assignment with the other shoppers."

"Are you asking for special favors?" Harry said. "I hope not. That would be wrong."

He hung up the phone, cackling like the monster he was.

Chapter 9

"Mom? Is that you in my kitchen?"

Of course it was. The kitchen was richly scented with warm butter, hot sugar—and cigarette smoke.

Those damn cigarettes. Josie didn't want Amelia coming home to a house that stank of her grandmother's stale nicotine.

She could feel the fury rising in her. Why did you take up such a smelly, stupid habit, Mom? Josie wanted to yell. What kind of example is this for your granddaughter? And if you have to smoke, why don't you do it in your own house, instead of stinking up mine?

Josie bit back the harsh words. Jane gave up cigarettes after her divorce because she couldn't afford them anymore. Instead, she spent the money on new clothes for Josie. Mom gave up her pleasure for me, Josie thought. She was entitled to smoke now. Maybe Alyce was right: If I ignore it, it will go away.

"Kitchen smells good, Mom," she said. "You making a gooey butter cake?"

Josie heard a low growl that could be either a greeting or a warning. Mom's mood was as bad as hers.

Josie bumped the kitchen door with her hip and humped a cooler full of double-cut pork chops and organic lettuce onto the sink. When she mystery-shopped food stores, Josie didn't leave perishables baking in the backseat. She brought her cooler.

She didn't need to put these chops in the freezer. Her

mother could have flash cooked them with one glare. She was mad about something.

Josie tried to defuse the situation with chitchat. "I've been mystery-shopping supermarkets," she said to her mother's back. "I've got some beautiful chops. Want one?"

Jane was wiping the kitchen table with short, angry strokes. Her back was rigid with tension. Josie could feel the anger radiating from her.

"No," Jane said. That word came down like a karate chop.

Oh, boy. Mom was seething. Yet she'd come downstairs to bake Josie and Amelia a delicious dessert. That was Mom: slapping Josie with her anger one moment, soothing her the next. Josie loved her mother, but she could never understand her.

Jane pulled the gooey butter cake out of the oven with a dish towel and slammed it on the cooling rack. The pan bounced.

Stay calm, Josie thought. Don't start anything. Wait for her to tell you what's wrong.

Josie crammed the lettuce in the fridge and shut the door. One look from her mother would wilt the tender organic leaves. She started freezer wrapping the chops.

Jane banged metal mixing bowls and spoons in the sink.

"So, Mom, what brings you to my kitchen this afternoon? Not that I object to baking and entering."

Jane wiped her hands on a dish towel. "I wanted to talk to you before your daughter came home." She stood at the sink with her hands on her hips, looking like a bulldog in a pink pantsuit and sensible shoes. A fierce gray-helmet-haired bulldog with a smudge of powdered sugar on her nose.

Here it comes, Josie thought. Mount Mom is about to explode.

"Josie Marcus, I can't believe you picked up a plumber!" Jane said. "In front of your own daughter, too. What's wrong with Mr. Ansen?"

"He's old, fat, and married," Josie said. She could feel her good resolutions going down the drain with the half-melted ice from the cooler.

"You don't have to get smart with me, young woman. You know what I mean," Jane said. "Why didn't you call Mr. Ansen? He's been our plumber for forty years."

Josie was in no mood for her mother's bullying. Not after Jane had smoked in her home—again. Not after she'd dumped her ashtray down the toilet. That had cost Josie a bundle. Mike didn't give Josie a price break on the after-hours plumbing call, date or not.

Add the plumbing bill to her worries about Alyce, her rotten boss, Harry, and the prospect of twenty-four Greta Burgers, and Josie quickly reached her flash point. "You can call him, Mom, next time you stop up *your* toilet with *your* cigarette butts. This is my home. Where I don't permit smoking because it's hazardous to your granddaughter's health."

Jane had the grace to look embarrassed. "I did that? I stopped up your toilet? I couldn't have."

"Yes, you did. The cigarettes had your lipstick on them. My date with Mike is your fault. If you hadn't stopped up my john with your cigarettes, I wouldn't have had to call a plumber. And what's wrong with dating a plumber? Do you know what he charges?"

"Josie, that's not why you're going out with him, is it—because you can't afford the plumbing bill? I'll pay it."

"Good," Josie said. "I'll send it to you."

Jane looked surprised. She'd expected Josie to be too proud to take money from her mother.

"And no, Mom, I'm not a hooker paying my bills with sex."

Jane turned red as a jar of Harvard beets. "Josie, I never meant to imply such a thing. How can you even say that?"

"How could you even say it?" Josie said. "Honestly, Mom, this is too much. Mike isn't some useless paper pusher. He actually knows how to do something. I find that attractive in a man." His long legs and good buns weren't bad, either, Josie thought, but that didn't sound nearly so noble.

"There's nothing wrong with someone else dating a plumber," Jane said. "But not my daughter. I expect better for you. Your father was a professional man, a lawyer."

"Who left us in the lurch," Josie said.

The words slipped out. As soon as she said them, Josie knew she'd gone too far. Jane looked like she'd been punched.

"I'm sorry, Mom. I shouldn't have said that. GBH." That was their family code for "Great Big Hug." Whenever anyone said "GBH," a hug was mandatory.

Jane stood there stiffly, her bulldog jaw thrust out stubbornly. She didn't move.

"You have to, Mom. It's the family law." Josie wrapped her arms around her mother, inhaling her Estee Lauder bath powder. She saw Jane's hair was thinning at the crown and carefully combed over. That bald little spot never failed to touch Josie's heart. Her indomitable mother was no longer young.

Poor Jane was meant for a genteel clubwoman's life in Ladue. But she'd been abandoned by her husband, stuck with an unruly daughter, and banished to blue-collar Maplewood. Instead of going to Junior League luncheons, Jane had spent the best years of her life at a grindingly dull job. She couldn't afford cigarettes, much less Lilly Pulitzer dresses and Pappagallo shoes. Josie's money worries were a picnic in the park compared with what her mother had faced.

"I am so sorry, Mom." Jane felt rigid as a department store mannequin. "I was out of line."

"I just want to find the right man for you," Jane said, sniffling. "I don't want you dating someone who handles sewage. You need a nice man with a manicure." She was crying now, wiping her eyes with a dish towel.

Josie hated when her mother cried. She hated Jane's clumsy attempts at matchmaking even more.

"I don't need a man," Josie said.

"Amelia needs a father," Jane said. "I saw an article that girls who have fathers living with them are less likely to get pregnant out of wedlock."

Ouch. Mom's turn for a low blow.

"Amelia won't get pregnant," Josie said. "When she turns thirteen, I'm keeping her in a stone tower with a locked door and a dragon." Josie went back to wrapping pork chops.

"Josie, be serious."

"I am serious, Mom. I'm renting the old Compton Heights water tower, the one at Grand and I-44. It's a landmark. Looks like a castle. The kid will appreciate the architecture. Good view, too."

"I've arranged a blind date for you," Jane said.

"You what?" Josie dropped a pork chop. It landed on the floor.

"Blind dates are the best way to meet eligible men. Much safer than the Internet. Granby Hicks is a lawyer, Josie. He's smart and handsome. I've seen him. He's so good-looking, he takes your breath away."

"So does emphysema," Josie said. She picked up the chop and washed it off. The floor was clean. She'd spilled pasta water on it last night.

"He works at Alyce's husband's law firm."

"Another reason to say no."

"At least go out with him once," Jane said.

"No," Josie said, wrapping the last chop and stashing it in the freezer. The blast of cold air steadied her resolve. She had to remain firm. She'd had enough of Jane's matchmaking. Her mother was a geek magnet. She'd fixed Josie up with one loser after another. At least, that's what Josie called them. Jane said they were good providers. Her mother's idea of a good provider was a CPA who clipped grocery coupons and had a penny jar on his dresser. As long as he wore a white shirt to work, Jane considered him a "professional man."

"Last time you fixed me up with that tax accountant who took me out for coffee at a hospital cafeteria. He told me it was cheaper than Starbucks. He was cheaper than Scrooge McDuck."

"Missouri Baptist is one of the finest hospitals in the country," Jane said. "It's on all the top-ten lists."

"It's on the bottom of my list for romantic dates," Josie said. "Even if I did look pretty hot in the glow of the aluminum walkers."

"Granby isn't like that. He wants to take you to dinner at Tony's, the finest restaurant in St. Louis. You can meet him at the restaurant. How safe is that? Any day. You can even go out with him tonight. Just name the time."

"No," Josie said.

"But I've already made the arrangements," Jane said.

"Then you'll have to unmake them, Mom. If it embarrasses you, too bad."

"Josie! You can't do this to me," Jane said.

"I just did." Josie realized she sounded exactly like Horrible Harry.

"I know you'll come to your senses," her mother said. "I won't call Granby and tell him that the date's off. You still have time to change your mind."

"I'll change my sex first," Josie said. "I won't go on another of your rotten blind dates, and that's that."

"Fine! Ruin your life. Again." Her mother slammed the kitchen door so hard, the glass rattled.

Josie paced her kitchen, muttering to herself. "Since when am I too good to go out with a man who works for a living? I'm supposed to date some jerky lawyer who bills five hundred an hour every time he picks up his phone? Ha. No wonder he can afford Tony's. A plumber can't. A plumber makes an honest living."

Josie thumbed through the thick stack of bills in the napkin holder on the kitchen counter, and took out Mike's plumbing bill. Then she went out on the front porch and shoved it through the mail slot in her mother's door. Take that, Mom, she thought. She shivered in the December wind. It was cold out here, even with the pale winter sun shining.

Josie suspected things were plenty warm in her mother's flat. Jane, who loved the social niceties, would suffer tortures trying to undo the blind date she'd arranged.

Too bad, she thought. Mom had to learn. Matchmaking was another bad habit Jane had developed recently. Maybe Josie couldn't make her mother quit smoking, but she could do something about those blind dates.

They were going to stop. Right now.

Chapter 10

Josie looked at her ninth Greta Burger of the day, and her stomach slid unpleasantly. She knew the burger would be awful. Greta Burgers were always awful. But they were bad in different ways. Each Greta Burger outlet (Josie wouldn't call them restaurants) found a new way to ruin the loathsome lumps.

The first one was gray and dry as fried concrete.

The second was so greasy it skidded off the bun.

The third had a lacy frill of fried gunk around the edge of the patty.

The fourth was mostly gristle. It was like chewing rubber bands.

The fifth was the worst so far. It had been fried on the same grill as a Fisherman's Find, and the cook hadn't cleaned the grill between orders. The only thing more disgusting than a Greta Burger was a Greta fish sandwich. The fishy burger had sent her stomach into full rebellion. Josie had to take a big gulp from the bottle of Maalox she kept in her glove compartment before her next stop.

The sixth Greta Burger was cold.

The seventh burned her mouth.

The eighth was almost edible, if she covered it in ketchup.

Now she was looking at the ninth. A little black thing stuck up out of the burger. Was it a human hair, a roach leg, or an odd piece of animal innards? Any choice was wretched. She knew better than to take it back to the counter and complain. The next Greta Burger would be worse, and the cook would probably spit on it, besides.

Maybe Josie could lie on her report just this one time and say she'd tasted it. No one would ever know. I'd know, she thought. I can't do it. I have my standards.

She looked at the grubby ground beef again. That awful thing was still sticking out of the middle.

Just cover it with the bun and take a bite out of the edge, she told herself. One bite. That's all. There was an ominous rumbling deep in her gut. Josie's stomach was sending an ultimatum. She'd better act quickly—or it would.

"I've got to do this," she told herself. "If I don't, Harry will win."

She nibbled a tiny piece off of one side, like a frightened mouse. The burger didn't taste half-bad, and that worried Josie. Was she starting to like Greta Burgers? Would she turn into one of the chain's strange, misshapen regulars—the shuffling old men, the odd women wearing dresses with dragging hems, the kids with spiked hair and homemade tattoos? Would she be one of the customers at the counter who mumbled to themselves, or put in their teeth before chomping a Greta delight?

Josie's gut shifted again, but she gulped the gray morsel. She'd officially sampled her ninth burger. The worst was over. She lifted the bun and the black thing *sproing*ed up again. She poked it with a plastic fork. It wasn't a hair or an insect part. It was a tubular bit of meat, possibly a vein. Josie's stomach hip-hopped. She dumped the burger in the trash, then fled to her car.

As she plopped down in the seat, she noticed pink and red spots on her T-shirt. The red was ketchup. The pink must be Maalox. Stains might actually improve this outfit. She wore her beat-up yard clothes and holey tennies for this assignment. She was still dressed better than ninety percent of the clientele.

Nine Greta Burgers down, fifteen more to go. At that thought, Josie's stomach made a seismic shift. She was swallowing a healthy swig of Maalox when her cell phone rang.

"Josie!" How could Alyce pack so much panic in one word?

"What's wrong?" Josie said.

"I called Jake's office an hour ago and his secretary, Virginia, said he was unavailable."

That sounded like Jake, Josie thought. Unavailable for his own wife. A car horn was ranting in the Greta Burger parking lot. Josie thought she heard Alyce say, "Virginia said he was talking to the police. They're in his office."

Josie rolled up her window and shut out some of the sound. Maybe she'd heard wrong. "The police are in his office?"

"The same two detectives who talked to me," Alyce said. "Virginia told me their names. I left a message for Jake to call me as soon as they finished."

"It's probably nothing, Alyce. What did Jake say?"

"He didn't. They're still talking to him. Something's wrong."

This time, Josie couldn't deny it. "Alyce, stay there. I'll drive out to your home. You shouldn't be alone."

"I'll be OK. You have to pick up Amelia at school."

"Mom can pick her up," Josie said. "She owes me big-time. Listen, Alyce, you may want to call the Wood Winds guardhouse and tell them I'm coming."

"Why? Most of the guards know you."

"I've been mystery-shopping Greta Burgers. I'm wearing my oldest clothes."

For the first time in days, Alyce laughed. The sound was a little wobbly, but the laughter was genuine. "Don't worry, Josie. The guards will think you're very rich."

"I'll be right out," Josie said. "I promise. I'm twenty minutes away."

Josie didn't keep her promise. She fought the traffic for nearly an hour. The highway department must have held a special meeting to create roadway obstacles. There was construction on one street, broken traffic lights on another, and sweeper trucks lumbering in the so-called fast lane on the interstate.

She wanted to call Alyce and see how she was, but

cars were darting in and out, speeding up and slamming on their brakes for no reason. She had to stay alert.

Josie didn't think she'd ever make it to Wood Winds. As Alyce predicted, the guard waved her through without question. Once the subdivision gate opened, the sun seemed warmer and breezes more gentle. Birds trilled. The dark clouds fled. Industrious work crews trimmed hedges and filled potholes. Heaven forbid that Wood Winds residents should feel a bump in the road.

Unfortunately, this magic circle of peace and protection didn't cover Alyce. When she opened her door, Alyce looked so woebegone, Josie immediately took her into her arms. Alyce wept on her shoulder. Josie wasn't used to seeing her formidable friend so helpless. Nothing simmered or sizzled on the stove. The oven was cold. Alyce was too upset to cook.

This was serious.

Josie let her cry for a bit, then said, "I'll make us some coffee."

"No!" Alyce said. "I mean, I'll make the coffee. You relax. I have cranberry muffins in the freezer I can warm up."

Josie realized she couldn't work Alyce's coffeemaker, anyway. The complicated German machine needed a learner's permit. She watched Alyce grind the beans in a screechy gadget Josie would throw against the wall on a hungover morning. Alyce used a special scoop to calibrate the fresh-ground coffee, carefully leveling it off. No heaping spoons for this pot. Germans demanded precision.

"Where's little Justin?" Josie said.

"Upstairs, taking his afternoon nap. I'm glad he's managed to sleep through my waterworks. You don't need both of us crying."

Alyce warmed the muffins in the microwave and lined a wicker basket with a yellow napkin. These homey tasks seemed to give her strength. For the first time, Josie thought she understood why someone might enjoy the mysterious and messy business of cooking.

By the time Alyce poured the coffee into thin china

cups and set the cream and sugar on the table, she was a different woman. She sugared her coffee and squared her shoulders, ready to face the problem.

"I'm sorry I cried like that. But I'd just gotten off the phone with Jake."

"What did he say? What happened?"

"He says it was no big deal," Alyce said. "He's lying. I can tell by his voice."

And you've heard him lie before, Josie thought, but she kept her mouth shut. Well, it wasn't totally shut. She was stuffing it with a cranberry muffin. It soothed her insulted stomach better than Maalox.

"Did his secretary give you any hints about what happened?" Josie asked.

"Virginia? She won't tell me anything. I'm the boss's wife. No one at Jake's office will tell me anything serious. And I can't ask. It's too chancy. It's bad enough I demanded to speak to Jake. I'm hoping Virginia won't spread that around the office. If I ask the wrong question or give any sign that something is off, it could stall Jake's career. His firm hates any hint of scandal. It's conservative, even for St. Louis."

Alyce had eaten almost half a muffin without reducing it to a heap of crumbs. She was definitely better.

Josie took a sip of coffee. She had to admit it was better than the Folgers she made in her Mr. Coffee. "The police visit could be nothing, Alyce. You don't know."

"I do know. I have a good sense of things, Josie. Don't tell me to deny it."

Josie didn't. Alyce had known her husband was headed for trouble long before anyone else. She had a sixth sense that the homicide detectives were interested in Jake.

But why? Corporate lawyers committed neat, clean crimes with computers. They didn't gun down women in parking lots. Besides, Jake didn't look anything like the carjacker the witnesses saw. What was going on?

Alyce needed answers, but she had no way to get them.

Josie knew what she had to do. It wouldn't be pleasant, but she'd already faced nine Greta Burgers. Nothing could be worse.

"Alyce, you helped me when I was in trouble. Now it's my turn. I can talk to someone at your husband's firm. I know one of the lawyers, Granby Hicks."

"You do?" Alyce looked surprised. "You never mentioned Granby before. How did you meet him?"

"I haven't—yet. My mother wants to fix me up on a blind date."

"I knew you'd never talked to Granby, or you wouldn't volunteer to go out with him. I can't let you do this. I got stuck next to him at too many office parties. He's a horror show."

"What's wrong? Is he a hound or a perv?" Josie asked.

"No, but you'll wish he was."

"It's only dinner," Josie said.

"It's your life. Don't waste it on Granby."

"Alyce, I just ate nine Greta Burgers. I can stomach one lawyer, especially if we go to a nice restaurant. Besides, he wants to take me to Tony's."

"Don't do it. It's not worth it."

"Dinner at Tony's will be a piece of cake," Josie said, finishing the last bite of her muffin. "But I dread what my mother's going to make me do."

"What's that?" Alyce said.

"Eat crow," Josie said.

Chapter 11

Josie ate crow, with a side order of humble pie. Jane danced around her daughter's kitchen, leaving a vapor trail of stale nicotine. The centerpiece for Josie's humiliation feast was a pathetic pile of crumpled tens, fives, and ones on her kitchen table—the money for Mike's plumbing bill. Jane made it look as if each bill had been stripped from her hide.

The only way Josie could feel worse was if she ate another Greta Burger.

Her mother was gleeful. Jane's eyes were shiny bright, like Amelia's on Christmas morning. For once, Josie was glad Amelia was holed up in her room instant-messaging her friends. She didn't want her child to see her being pushed into the marriage market. Or maybe this was the marriage consignment shop, for used goods.

"I knew you'd come around," Jane said. "Granby is the catch of the year. You'd be crazy to turn him down. You'll thank me, Josie Marcus, when you have that ring on your finger and that man in your life."

Josie ground her teeth in silent frustration. She liked her life. If she did invite a man into it, he would be Mike, not some briefcase-toting dweeb. Josie wanted to say this and more, but she remembered the purpose of her date. She was going out with Granby for her best friend, not for her mother.

"Where did you hear about this guy?" Josie said.

"Granby's mother is a friend of Mrs. Mueller."

Another strike against him. Mrs. Mueller was the interfering old bat who lived next door. She'd been the bane of Josie's existence since she was nine. Josie, that is. Mrs. Mueller had never been nine years old.

"I'll call him right now," Jane said.

"Shouldn't he call me? I don't want to look desperate."

"You can't waste any more time," her mother said. "There are younger, fresher girls out there."

"Women," Josie corrected.

"Girls," Jane said. "Young girls, still in college. Women, too. They're all younger than you."

Josie felt like an expired carton of milk. "But, Mom—"

Jane was already punching in numbers on Josie's kitchen phone. Her tone was businesslike while she talked with Granby's secretary. When she got the great man himself, she softened her voice to a turtledove coo.

Josie squirmed with mortification.

Jane put her hand over the receiver. "He can fit you in tonight," she said. "Otherwise, it will have to be next week."

"Fit me in? What am I, a dental appointment? I'll go out with him next week."

"She'll be delighted to see you tonight," Jane said into the phone.

Josie started to protest, then realized she needed to talk to Granby now. This wasn't a real date, Josie reminded herself. This was a mission for Alyce.

"Tony's will be lovely," Jane told Granby. "You can pick Josie up at home."

"Mom!" Josie said. "I'm supposed to meet him at the restaurant."

Jane put her hand over the receiver and said, "It's better this way." Then she went back to cooing at Granby. "We're right next door to Mrs. Mueller. You know where she lives? Of course you can find it, a smart young man like you. We're the two-family flat with the white porch."

Oh, barf, Josie thought. If the Greta Burgers hadn't turned her stomach, this conversation would.

Jane hung up in a flurry of smiling good-byes. "He'll be here at seven. It's five o'clock. I'll watch Amelia and fix her dinner. You have time to wash your hair. Run along."

Jane shooed Josie out of her own kitchen. Josie's stomach was still rumbling like a truck convoy, but she couldn't tell if it was predate jitters or Greta Burgers.

Why was Granby taking her to Tony's tonight? It was too expensive for a first date. She hoped he didn't expect her to fall into his bed in gratitude. Why was everything from a broken toilet to a dinner date really about sex?

What could she wear to Tony's? Josie rummaged in her closet and decided on a semidaring black Ungaro she'd bought on sale at a consignment shop. She'd gotten it cheap because the lining was patched, but Granby was never going to discover that secret. Besides, when Josie wore it out of the dressing room, it had left the shop owner's chatty husband speechless. Maybe it would make Granby talk.

Josie's mom flicked on the porch light at six thirty, while Josie was shaving her legs. Josie nicked her calf, and tried to stop the bleeding with dabs of toilet paper. She wondered if she should cut her throat instead, but that was hard to do with a safety razor. Anyway, she had a daughter to think about.

At six fifty-five, she gave herself a final examination in the bedroom-door mirror. Not bad, she thought, for a thirty-one-year-old single mom.

When Josie's doorbell rang at precisely seven p.m., Josie heard her mother rush to open it. "Granby," Jane gushed. "How nice to see you. You're right on time, too. I'll get Josie."

Time for Mr. Awful, Josie thought. She wondered if Granby would be a nerd or a pin-striped stiff. She took a deep breath and headed down the hall.

The guy filling her living room was ridiculously handsome. He had a jutting jaw, a cleft chin, and wavy blond hair, like an old-fashioned matinee idol. His chest was broad, his waist was narrow, and his legs were long. The old theme song for *George of the Jungle* flashed through her dazzled brain. This was a hunk-a-rama. She'd definitely suffer him for Alyce. What were friends for?

Granby wore a well-cut gray suit with a light purple shirt and tie. She'd read somewhere that purple was the new blue for menswear. That was pretty over-the-top for a lawyer. Maybe Granby was a wild one after all.

"It's a pleasure to meet you, Mrs. Marcus," he said to Josie's mother.

Jane practically pushed Josie and Granby out the door so they could begin their date.

A sporty gray car, polished like old silver, was parked in front of her flat.

"Nice," Josie said.

"It's an RSX Type-S," he said. "Two hundred ten horsepower, i-VTEC engine, seventeen-inch alloy wheels. It will do until I get my Porsche. I think the Boxster is too girlie and the 911 is too expensive, at least until I make partner. I'm considering the Cayman S. Now, that's a sweet car. Two hundred ninety-five horses and a flat-six engine. It's kicking the Boxster's ass, and it's only sixty thou."

Only sixty thousand, Josie thought. Only about three times what I make in a year.

"That's my new camera in the glove box. Tell me what you think."

Josie pulled out a slim silver camera. "Nice," she said. She seemed stuck on that word, but Granby didn't notice.

"Finally went digital," he said. "I got the Sony DSC-17. Has one hundred eighty photos and five-point-one megapixels. It was about three hundred dollars more than the Polaroid izone 300, but that one doesn't have the optical zoom. The Olympus D-630 was . . ."

Josie's eyes crossed. They weren't even at the restaurant yet and she didn't think she could listen to one more model number. She wanted to scream. She wanted to leap out of the moving car. She was the prisoner of a Sharper Image catalog.

"I still think the best pen is a Mark Cross," Granby was saying. Somehow, he'd switched from cameras to pens. "What do you think?"

"Nice," Josie said. She felt like a parrot.

"I use a Cross Townsend titanium-and-lacquer fountain pen for major contracts. The partners use Montblancs. Those are twice the price. I think the Cross is just as good. But if you really want to impress someone—"

Josie was desperate. She was never going to steer this conversation in the direction she wanted. It was like a runaway train. Her only hope was to derail it. "I know one of your firm's partners," she blurted. "Jake Bohannon."

There was a long silence. "Is he a friend of yours?" Granby's tone was carefully neutral.

"Not really," Josie said. "I heard the cops were talking to him today."

"How do you know that?" Granby asked, still cautious.

"How could I not?" Josie said. "The police questioned him for more than an hour. Two homicide detectives. It was the talk of the office."

That last part was a safe guess.

"Well, since you already know, I'm not telling tales out of school." Now Granby was eager to tattle. "They were asking about that designer who was carjacked."

"Halley? That was a gang killing, wasn't it?" Josie said.

"That's how I heard it. Of course, I'm not one to listen at doors."

"But a secretary did," Josie said. "I bet she reported every word."

"Correctomundo," Granby said. "She said our boy Jake had been very bad. He had an affair with Halley."

Josie's heart sank. Poor Alyce. "I thought he was married."

"He is. I've talked with wifey a few times at company functions. Nice dull little blonde. Girls like that are meant to be martyrs."

Josie was glad they were in a darkened car. She

clenched her fists to keep from punching the lout. Just hang on, she told herself. We're almost at the restaurant. We're in downtown St. Louis.

The Arch loomed above them, an impossible arc of stainless steel. Tonight, the moonlight made it molten silver. Once upon a time, Amelia's father had flown Josie along the Mississippi on a night like this, showing her the city's startling beauty. But that was another lifetime.

"Look at the Arch," she said. "People come from around the world to see it. We live here and forget how incredible it is."

"Reminds me of the stainless-steel finish on the PX-5—"

Josie cut him off before he could tell her what that was. "You were talking about Jake's affair with Halley."

Granby was eager to resume knifing a partner. He'd cheerfully eviscerate Jake to get his partnership. "It's a little more than that. But we're at the restaurant. Let's order dinner and then I'll tell you the rest."

Josie thought Tony's decor was old-fashioned modern: soaring space, dark wood, well-placed pools of light. Waiters in tuxes hovered unobtrusively, removing plates, bringing butter, pouring water, without the diners noticing.

She sank into her chair and patted the fine linen. She deserved this after her day. Despite nine Greta Burgers—or maybe because of them—Josie was hungry, but her stomach lurched at the thought of meat. A Tony's steak and a Greta Burger probably didn't come from the same species, but it would be a while before she could stomach red meat.

"I'll have the spinach, avocado, and Roquefort salad and the Dover sole," Josie said.

"Good choices," Granby said. "I'll have a steak."

The spinach and the fish were flown in fresh from England. Josie hoped both plane tickets were on Granby's bill.

"Would you care for wine?" Granby said.

"A glass," Josie said. A gallon, she thought. A barrel. She'd need plenty of painkillers to sit through this dinner.

"See that table over there?" Granby nodded toward three silver-haired men. "Those are the senior partners at Davis-Willingham. On your left is Ardmore Sommers, of Sommers, Caruthers and Strawn. And don't turn around, but behind you is Harrison Barnel with his new wife. I don't have to tell you how important he is." He didn't even bother with the blond wife's name. She didn't count.

More brand names, Josie thought. This was a gathering of legal eagles. Now she understood why he wanted to go to dinner here on their first date. It wasn't about her. It was about him. He wanted these bigwig lawyers to see Granby Hicks dining in the best restaurant in town. He was one of the big men. She was arm candy.

I'm not going to sit here like a Stepford wife, Josie thought. He's going to tell me what I want to know. After the salads were mixed at their table, Josie said, "We were having an absolutely fascinating conversation about Jake and Halley. Do you really think they were having an affair?"

Granby was ready to dish. Having all those hotshot lawyers around must have made him feel part of the inner circle. "I didn't actually catch Halley and Jake in bed together," he said. "But he was at the Bradcliffe Hotel with her."

"The pretty little hotel with the fountain, out by Westport Plaza?" Josie said.

"That's the one," Granby said. "The firm maintains a suite there, because it's close to the airport and has teleconferencing facilities. The suite is supposed to be for business meetings, but all the partners bang their secretaries at the Bradcliffe, except Jake. Virginia, his girl, is about a hundred years old."

Too old to be a girl, Josie thought. "Are you sure Jake took Halley there?"

"Saw them with my own eyes. They were in the lobby.

Jake looked nervous when he ran into me. He was eager to get away, which I took as a sign of guilt."

Josie was eager to get away from Granby, too, and she wasn't guilty of anything.

"Jake didn't introduce me to her, but I recognized the famous Halley. He said he was there for a conference. Yeah, right. I checked with the concierge after they got in the elevator. There was no conference."

"That's not good," Josie said. The spinach was impossibly tender. The Roquefort was creamy-sharp. The avocado was perfectly ripe. But she was losing her appetite.

"I'll tell you what's bad," Granby said. "He lied to the cops about it."

"That was dumb," Josie said. Her remark seemed to encourage Granby.

"You're telling me." Granby leaned in. "First, Jake said he hardly knew Halley. The cops pressed him on it, but he kept denying it. He said she was a neighbor and he barely recognized her. Then the cops moved in for the kill. They said Halley's cell phone records showed the woman called him several times a day."

"What did Jake say then?"

"There was this long silence. I thought he'd turned to stone." Granby forgot he didn't listen at doors. He'd switched to a first-person account. "Jake tried to weasel out of it. He said, 'You must have the wrong number. Halley must have called my wife, Alyce. They were on some committee together.' "

Josie was furious. That rat was trying to drag his wife into his mess.

"The police said Halley made only two calls to his home number and none to his wife's cell phone. They had him by the short and curlies." Granby actually giggled.

Josie longed to run her fish fork through him. Lawyers were supposed to be careful, but Granby didn't mind backstabbing a colleague. Was he that self-absorbed? Well, yes. He was also a world-class braggart. Worst of all, his opinion of women was so low, he didn't think he had to worry about Josie. She was not important enough.

Josie had to reel in her resentment. This isn't about me, she thought. I'm supposed to get information for Alyce. Boy, am I getting information.

"Jake was still denying like crazy when the cops dropped the big bomb. They said he was on the hotel security tape with Halley the day she died. Nine in the morning. He kissed her in the lobby."

"What kind of kiss? A friendly kiss on the cheek or a passionate one?" Josie asked.

"The cops didn't say. But a room service waiter saw Jake and her in the corporate suite."

"Were they dressed?"

Granby was annoyed. He didn't like being questioned. "I don't know. I couldn't hear that part. But Jake was definitely in a hotel suite with Halley, and she's not a corporate client."

"Amazing," Josie said.

Granby smiled smugly, as if she meant him.

"I bet the office rumor mill is going crazy," Josie prompted.

"There's supposed to be a big partners' meeting to-morrow, only Jake's not invited. Think he'll be forced to resign? There could be a Porsche in my future sooner than I thought."

The naked greed in Granby's eyes sickened her. She wanted to get away from him.

"Dessert?" he said.

"No, thanks," Josie said. "I've had enough."

Chapter 12

Jane was waiting up for Josie when she came home from her date. Josie felt sixteen again. It wasn't a good feeling.

"Well?" her mother said. "How was it?"

Josie saw the terrible hope in her mother's eyes. "Fine," she lied. Awful, she thought. I'd rather have my wisdom teeth pulled. At least I'd get anesthetic.

Josie was grateful that Granby didn't kiss her good night. Of course, clutching her gut in the car home probably didn't give the man romantic thoughts. She wondered if Granby even had romantic thoughts. He didn't seem to have the slightest interest in her. To be fair, she didn't have any interest in him, either. She was using him. They were even.

"Are you going out with him again?" Jane asked. Her voice trembled slightly. It meant so much to her mother when Josie dated a "nice" man. It happened so rarely.

"Yes. We have a date."

"When?"

"Next week sometime. He'll call me."

Heaven only knew why Granby asked her out again. Maybe it was the hot dress and the killer heels. Maybe because she knew what a fish fork was.

Josie knew why she said yes. She might need more information for Alyce. It was at least seven days till her next date with Granby. A lot could happen in a week. The police could find Halley's killer and lose interest in Jake. Josie prayed that would happen. Otherwise, she was facing another endless evening with Granby. How could a fully dressed man expose so much naked ambition?

Jane sighed with happiness at the news. "I'm going up to bed," she said.

"Good night, Mom," Josie said. She forgot to thank her for watching Amelia, but Jane didn't notice. She floated upstairs, wrapped in new dreams and old cigarette smoke.

Josie threw open the kitchen window to air the place out, and realized she was hobbling. Those were killer heels, all right. She kicked off her shoes. Her toes were sore, red, and crunched. She had a blister on her little toe.

She wondered if her mind looked the same way after that date: blistered and festering with angry thoughts. She longed to tell Granby what a smug, self-satisfied bore he was. He had no loyalty. He was a weasel in a suit, except she was being unfair to weasels. They ate vermin. Granby was vermin.

Oh, heck. Granby wasn't the real issue, and she knew it. How was Josie going to tell Alyce that her husband was unfaithful? His affair was so cheap and dreary: meeting Halley in the firm's hotel suite, becoming the butt of snickers and giggles at the office.

Josie made a pot of coffee, poured herself a cup, and stared into it. She didn't want to tell Alyce. But she didn't want her friend wandering in the dark, either. Alyce had to protect herself and plan for her future. She had her child to consider.

Alyce couldn't even leave Jake and go home to her mother. Her parents were dead. She was alone, except for Jake and Josie. Her husband had betrayed her, Josie thought. As her best friend, what can I offer? A preview of a frightening future, where Alyce would be always short of cash and time, worried about getting to work, and wondering who would care for her child. Josie was used to living on a shoestring. Alyce had a long way to fall.

Josie glanced at the kitchen Kit-Cat clock with the

rolling eyes and moving tail. It was two thirty in the morning. Maybe she'd have some answers after a few hours' sleep. She poured her coffee down the sink, cold and untouched, then shut the window.

On her way to bed, she stopped by Amelia's room. Her daughter had kicked off her blanket and lay sprawled across the bed, sleeping with abandoned innocence. Josie covered Amelia, tucked her in, and smoothed her silky dark hair. It was the same color as her father's, a richer shade than Josie's ordinary brown. Amelia had her father's long nose, too. She hated it, but Josie thought her daughter would soon be a dramatic beauty. She kissed Amelia on her smooth forehead. She never stirred.

Then Josie went to bed, where she tossed and turned for the next four hours, wondering how she would break the news to Alyce.

She woke up shivering at six thirty. She'd kicked off the covers during the night, but no one had tucked Josie in. She stumbled into her bathroom, hoping a hot shower would warm her. Josie dressed in her oldest clothes again for another day of Greta Burgers, but put on her good raincoat. She didn't want to embarrass Amelia at her school by wearing one of her down-at-heels mystery-shopping outfits.

By the time Josie had dropped her daughter off at Barrington, it was a golden morning, sunny and unusually warm for December. The weather was the only good thing about the day. Josie faced the prospect of eating Greta Burgers and delivering bad news.

Josie dreaded the call to Alyce so much, she ate six Greta Burgers before she got up the nerve to call her. Finally, at one o'clock, she speed-dialed Alyce's number, praying she wasn't home. Her friend answered on the first ring.

"I can't talk on the phone," Alyce said. "You want to meet me somewhere?"

"I'm at the South County Greta Burger."

"No, thanks," Alyce said. "Just walking into that grease pit turns my stomach."

"Mine, too," Josie said. "And I get paid to eat them."

"I've lost my appetite for the first time in my life," Alyce said. "Maybe that's good. I could wind up a size two like all the other Wood Winds wives. Jake did me a favor."

Josie didn't dare answer. Alyce didn't seem to expect one.

"If you're in South County," Alyce said, "why don't we meet at the Laumeier Sculpture Park? I'll be there in twenty minutes. I can use the walk. Meet you by the big red steel sculpture, *The Way*."

That was Josie's favorite. Most of the sculptures at Laumeier weren't pretty. Many looked downright industrial—vast hunks of metal sixty or more feet tall, a hundred or so feet wide. Some were sharply angled. Others were round as silos. Josie found the sculptures oddly peaceful. Maybe it was the hopeful way they enclosed space. They made Josie feel her troubles were finite.

Alyce looked small and lost beside the giant red metal sculpture. They walked along the paths in a silence that grew darker and heavier. Finally, Alyce burst out with, "I married a fool."

Josie had never heard her friend talk that way about Jake, not even the first time Alyce suspected he was unfaithful. She kept silent while Alyce vented her fury.

"What's the first thing they teach you in law school? Get a lawyer if the cops talk to you. It's basic. Never, ever represent yourself. Especially in a murder. I heard that in class after class."

Alyce wasn't a lawyer, but she'd helped put Jake through law school. She sat in on his early-morning classes and even took the tests, if it was a big class and nobody noticed her. Sometimes, Josie thought Alyce had more legal knowledge than the man with the law degree.

"I heard it, but it went right past Jake," Alyce said. "My husband, the big-shot corporate lawyer, thought he could outwit two homicide detectives. After all, how much do they bill an hour? Jake also thought because they didn't read him his Miranda rights he wasn't the focus of the investigation. I told him again and again that Miranda was custodial. So did his professors. But he didn't listen to that, either. The cops weren't required to advise Jake of his Miranda rights if he wasn't in custody. So what did Jake do? Something even stupider than representing himself: He lied to the cops."

"How did you find out?" Josie said.

"He finally confessed everything to me last night."

"Everything?" Josie said.

"He told me about Halley."

Josie was weak with relief. She wouldn't have to break the bad news to her friend.

"He swore they didn't have an affair," Alyce said.

Liar, Josie thought. "Do you believe him?" she asked.

"Of course," Alyce said.

It wouldn't be "of course" if he were my husband, Josie thought. He'd be taking a polygraph test.

Alyce must have seen the doubt in her eyes. "He swore to me on our son's life."

"Then what was he doing with Halley in a hotel suite?" Josie asked.

"He said it was business," Alyce said.

Monkey business, Josie thought. "Law firm business?" Josie said.

"Not quite," Alyce said.

Well, he was telling the truth about that. Granby had said Halley wasn't a firm client.

Josie knew Alyce was upset. She hadn't asked about the date with Granby last night.

But Josie was equally lost. They'd passed Josie's second-favorite sculpture, a fat Botero bronze called *Roman Soldier*, and she hadn't stopped to study its menacing curves. They might as well be strolling in a parking garage. Acres of groomed lawns, gigantic sculptures, and bare-branched trees stretched before them, but they saw nothing.

"Jake said he couldn't tell me right now," Alyce said, "but he would when the time was right. He promised to hire a criminal attorney. That's where he is now, talking to one. He should have called the man yesterday. He's going to be arrested anytime now, Josie. I know it. The police interviewed our nanny, Mrs. Palm. She was so upset at the questions, I was afraid she'd give her notice on the spot."

"Were they bad?" Josie said.

"The worst. The police wanted to know if Jake had a girlfriend. Mrs. Palm said he didn't have any girlfriends that she knew about. Then they asked if he had a gun."

"A gun?" Josie shouted in surprise. A woman walking a golden retriever stared at Josie.

Alyce lowered her voice. "He carries one in his car for protection. He works late and he has meetings in bad neighborhoods. It's a Glock 9, registered in his name. He hides it under the front seat."

"Where's the gun now?" Josie asked.

"Jake doesn't know. As soon as I told him about the nanny, he went out to his car to check. The gun's gone."

"Did he report it stolen?" Josie asked.

"He made a report, but there's no sign his car was broken into. He doesn't know if it was taken last night or last week."

"Doesn't he lock his car?"

"Not when he's in Wood Winds. It's a gated community. We don't lock our doors."

That again.

"So any of your neighbors—or any of the staff they employ—could have taken the gun out of your unlocked garage," Josie said.

"Yes."

Worse and worse. "Why were the police so interested in Jake's gun? Did they find the murder weapon?"

"I don't know," Alyce said. "But I'm scared, Josie. You've got to help me save my husband."

"Me? Jake can afford the best lawyers and private investigators. I'll just be in the way. I don't have any legal authority. I'm not a trained investigator. I don't even have a PI license."

"You can talk to people," Alyce said. "They like you. Jake will hire people like himself. They'll say the wrong things and no one will help him. I love my husband. I know how you feel about him—"

Josie started to protest, but Alyce said, "We've known each other too long for polite lies. Jake is a good man, Josie, and he's a good father, but I know he comes off as arrogant sometimes if you don't know him well. He's not. He's just shy. It makes him seem stiff and stand-offish.

"Jake already has three strikes against him: He's a rich, white lawyer. Cops love to put men like him in prison. Juries love to convict him. You've got to help me, Josie. Please."

Alyce was begging.

"But I can't do anything," Josie said. "I don't know anybody. I don't know anything."

"Just talk to some of Halley's friends for me. Help me get some background on her. The police need to find other suspects besides my husband."

"Aren't the police already doing that?" Josie said.

"No. Jake was dumb enough to lie. The police won't look for anyone else."

"But how can they suspect Jake if the shooter was a young black male?"

"I don't know," Alyce said miserably. "It doesn't make sense. But I think someone is trying to frame Jake for Halley's murder. I need to know who hates him enough to do this."

"Alyce, can I play devil's advocate? Are you sure Jake isn't guilty of something?"

"Besides lying to the police about Halley?" Alyce said.

"How well did he know her?" Josie asked. She wanted to say, "In the biblical sense?"

"He told me he was *not* having an affair with Halley. I believe him."

What had the sneery Granby called Alyce? The "little wifey" meant to be a martyr? Alyce must be the only person who believed Jake was innocent.

Josie knew the man was guilty of something: maybe murder, possibly adultery, certainly stupidity. What if Josie found out what really happened? Alyce wouldn't want to hear it.

The situation was hopeless. This was a lost cause.

She looked at her friend's worried, pale face, and knew it was time for a serious reality check.

"Of course, I'll help you," Josie said.

Chapter 13

A cold wind crawled up Josie's back. She shivered and turned up the collar on her raincoat. The sky had turned dark and threatening. The golden day had slipped away.

"Brrr," she said. "It's getting cold. We still have to decide who we should talk to. Want to go somewhere for coffee?"

"I want to go home," Alyce said. "I know I'm being ridiculous, but I have a bad feeling. Would you mind going back to my place? I'll make us coffee. I have cookies, too."

"Sure," Josie said.

Icy rain pinged on the windshield as Josie drove to Wood Winds. But once Josie pulled into the subdivision entrance, the dark clouds vanished, though the wind stayed sharp.

Josie was always amazed by the perfection of Alyce's home. The sun came through the breakfast room window like a designer spotlight, highlighting the vase of gerbera daisies on the table. The room smelled of coffee and warm sugar.

Alyce brought out a plate of wild-animal cookies: hot pink elephants, acid green rhinos, and yellow monkeys. "I made these for Justin. Try some."

"Are you sure I can eat them?" Josie said. "They're too beautiful. How did you get those gorgeous colors?"

"Easy," Alyce said. "All you do is whip up some royal icing and use a pastry bag with a plain tip."

"That's all *you* do," Josie said. "I couldn't tell a pastry bag from an evening bag."

"The pastry bag is the one without the sequins," Alyce said.

Josie bit the head off a pink elephant. "Let's start with Halley's life. Do you know anyone who would want to kill her?"

Alyce thoughtfully nibbled the tail off a yellow monkey. "Her husband, Cliff, according to my neighbor Joanie. She told us the couple fought the night before Halley died."

"Right," Josie said. "If Halley wasn't carjacked, Cliff would be the number one suspect. Does he have an alibi?"

"I don't know," Alyce said. "Maybe that's something we should find out."

"The shooter was wearing gangsta clothes," Josie said. "That doesn't sound like Cliff's crowd."

"Or Jake's," Alyce said.

"They make their killings in the stock market," Josie said. "Does Cliff subscribe to *Soldier of Fortune* magazine?"

"Be serious, Josie," Alyce said.

"OK, but we need to check out the husband. Any other suspects?"

"Halley lived on my street," Alyce said, "but I don't know much about her."

"You said Linda Dattilo is her best friend," Josie said. "Who's she?"

"Linda lives in Wood Winds by the lake. She runs a decorating business out of her home. You've probably seen her. She's very thin, very cute. Her little girl is best friends with Halley's daughter."

Josie checked her watch. "I have time before I pick up Amelia. Can we see Linda now?"

Alyce stood on tiptoe and looked out her breakfast room window. "That's Linda's house over there. Her SUV is in the drive. She's home."

Linda lived in an overgrown Cape Cod with three stories, three dormers, and about sixty-four windows. It was a house for aspiring presidential candidates, cabinet members, and CEOs: solid, traditional, and rich without being ostentatious.

Linda met them at the door. Her hair was a rare red gold. Her eyes were a brilliant green. The hall was done in a soft seafoam shade that set off Linda's unusual coloring.

Linda's house was a showcase for her decorating business. No ice white living room for her. The colors and arrangements were striking, but comfortable. Josie could imagine herself living here if she ever won the lottery. Too bad she never bought a ticket.

Josie studied an artful collection of photos on one wall. "How do you do that, Linda? When I put a lot of photos on a wall, they look like I threw them there. That's you in those theater pictures, right?"

Josie pointed to a photo of a younger Linda as a boyish Peter Pan. In another, she was an ethereal Laura Wingfield in *The Glass Menagerie*.

"I was in a few college productions," Linda said, and shrugged. "Unlike Laura, I married my gentleman caller. That's my husband, Tom, there."

"Very romantic," Alyce said.

"It seemed so at the time," Linda said. "Can I get you some tea?"

"No, thank you," Alyce said. "We had a few questions about Halley for the memorial service. We hope you can help us."

Josie looked at her friend's smooth face and marveled at how she lied so easily. She decided to let Alyce do the talking. This was her world.

"They asked me to write something, but I was too upset," Linda said. "I start crying every time I think about—" She dabbed at her eyes with a pale green tissue.

Alyce patted her hand. "I should think so. She was your best friend."

"My only friend," Linda said. "We married about the same time, moved into similar houses, even had our daughters within a week of each other."

"How did you feel when you heard that she was going to New York?" Alyce said.

"Like I'd lost my best friend." Linda gave a self-conscious laugh. "I didn't know how I would get along without her. She was such a big part of my life. Halley said, 'Don't worry, Linda. New York is only two hours away by plane, and you can call me anytime.' But a phone call isn't the same, is it? Now I don't even have that."

Josie wondered how she'd feel if Alyce moved away. Lost, she decided. Linda was right. A phone call wasn't the same.

"It must have been hard for you," Alyce said.

"It was," Linda said, "although it got easier as the months wore on. Halley was changing, becoming a different person. In some ways, I wasn't losing my Halley, you know?"

"I do," Alyce said. "What started the changes? Was it because she became so successful, so fast?"

"It happened before that. Her husband was pressuring her to have a second child. Halley panicked. With another baby, she'd be trapped for good. She started canceling committee meetings and going places she never went before. She went into the city."

Linda said "the city" as if it was someplace shocking and dangerous.

"Halley began hanging around with the artsy crowd in the Central West End. She took me with her at first, but I don't like hanging around bars. That's where she met Ramsey, the great American novelist."

"I've never heard of him," Alyce said. "But I don't read much since Justin came along. I still haven't finished *The Kite Runner*."

"Nobody's heard of Ramsey," Linda said. "He was supposed to be the next John Updike. He wrote this opening chapter that people say is the finest modern literature they've ever read. Ramsey spent a lot of time in the West End cultivating people, gaining their confidence, then showing them that chapter. It was powerful enough to get him six months' free rent in a carriage house.

"Instead of finishing the novel, he had a mad affair with the family's teenaged daughter. Her parents were outraged. After they threw him out, he spent a summer at a twelve-bedroom cottage in Maine, where he drank himself into an artistic stupor. Next, it was four months in a luxury condo at the Lake of the Ozarks, where he dried out. People gave him drinks and meals on the strength of that chapter. Women threw themselves at him. All because he had great potential."

"But he never wrote more than one chapter?" Alyce said.

"Not that I heard," Linda said. "I still think he's a great talent. Ramsey was the most accomplished sponger I ever met. He got free meals, drinks, luxury houses, and all the women he wanted for writing two thousand words. How many authors can say that?"

Why is she telling us this? Josie wondered. Alyce sure couldn't use it at a memorial service. Perhaps Linda needed to talk about what had happened to her best friend. She'd lost Halley long before she died.

"Did Ramsey take advantage of Halley?" Alyce asked.

Josie wanted to applaud. Alyce always knew the delicate way to ask difficult questions. Josie would have said flat out, "Did Halley have an affair with this Ramsey?"

"Maybe. Halley was an easy target. She was angry at her husband and stuck in a life she didn't want. Ramsey had a sixth sense for which women to pick. But if so, it wasn't for long. Halley was too smart to support him and Ramsey wouldn't waste time on a woman who wouldn't give him money. He did her one favor. Ramsey introduced her to a drunken artist named Evelyn. Her affair with Evelyn changed her life."

"Halley was gay?" Alyce said.

Linda laughed. "No, Evelyn is a man's name, too. Like Evelyn Waugh."

"What's Evelyn's last name?" Alyce asked.

"I don't know. He has one name, like Cher. I don't know where he lives, but his work is shown at a gallery in the West End. That's how Halley met him. Evelyn looks effeminate, but he's quite the ladies' man."

"Did Cliff know about him?" Alyce said.

"God, no. A man like Cliff has too much pride to tolerate a wandering wife. Evelyn was a safe choice for a lover. Cliff thought all artists were faggots—his word, not mine."

"He sounds enlightened," Alyce said.

"There aren't a lot of liberals in the upper ranks of corporate America," Linda said. "To be fair, Evelyn is an awful phony. He's got this British accent that's BBC one minute and Brooklyn the next. No wonder Cliff couldn't take him seriously."

"Did Cliff and Halley fight about Evelyn?" Alyce said.

"I don't think so," Linda said. "But they fought about everything else. It got bad about three months ago. At least, that's when Halley started talking to me about it. No matter what they fought about, it was really only one argument. Halley hated her life in the suburbs, and she wanted to escape. She was desperate."

"Do you think Cliff was angry enough to kill her?" Alyce asked.

"Cliff?" Linda laughed. "He wasn't violent. He might bore her to death, but he'd never hurt her. He just didn't want their life to change. It was Evelyn who got Halley out of Wood Winds. He sponsored her for a national contest, the Year's Best Design. Amateurs had to be sponsored by a professional artist.

"Evelyn hasn't much talent himself, but he recognized Halley's. She won the contest. Her design was published in the *New York Times*. The next thing you know, she was starting her own scarf-design business and headed for New York. One week she was going to the supermarket for bread, the next week she was going to Milan for silk."

"Her scarves are fabulous," Josie said. "She deserved

to be a New York success. I never understood how it happened so fast."

"She was ready for it," Linda said. "She had the training. She went to Parsons School of Design in New York. But she met her husband at the wrong time in her life and wound up in St. Louis. Cliff wasn't a bad guy. He just wasn't a good choice for her. He wanted two kids, a gas grill, and a house in the suburbs. He never pretended otherwise."

"How did they meet?" Alyce asked.

Josie was fascinated, watching how she teased information out of Linda, gently probing, avoiding the painful subjects.

"You can probably use this in your memorial," Linda said. "It's a safe subject. Besides, most people didn't know their marriage was on the rocks."

Except the neighbor who heard the fights, Josie thought.

"Cliff was working at his company's New York headquarters then," Linda said. "He met Halley and they started going out.

"I guess you'll have to soft-pedal this next part. Halley wanted a major New York design career, but poverty wore her down. When she met Cliff, she was twenty-three, tired of working as a waitress and trotting her portfolio around for rejections. Her back ached from sleeping on a futon and her feet hurt from hauling trays of food across hard tile floors. She could barely afford her dingy apartment, even with roommates. Cliff took her to expensive, glamorous places. The rich life made her restless. She was artistic, and the dump she lived in would have depressed someone far less sensitive.

"Halley told me that one night Cliff proposed after dinner at the Four Seasons. He was going to be head of the St. Louis division, making major money. He offered her a six-bedroom cottage with a picket fence and granite countertops. She said she wanted to think about it. She wouldn't let him take her home. She spent the ride home on the subway thinking about the best way to tell

Cliff no. She didn't want to hurt his feelings, but she wasn't cut out to be a corporate wife.

"She was probably so distracted composing her rejection that she didn't notice someone lifted her wallet. Halley didn't realize it was gone until she got home. That upset her. Then she opened her kitchen cabinet to make a soothing pot of green tea and found a rat sitting on the shelf. A big, fat rat. It didn't run when she screamed. It sat there like it owned the place.

"Rats and pickpockets are something you live with in a big city. But these two incidents hit her at the wrong time. She accepted Cliff's proposal. For nearly six years, she was Mrs. June Cleaver. Then she went off the rails."

"What happened?" Alyce asked.

"She was turning thirty," Linda said. "That's a milestone in a woman's life."

"Tombstone is more like it," Josie said. "Women get their midlife crises ten years before men."

Josie hoped she didn't blow it with her outburst, but Linda nodded in agreement.

"That is so true," Linda said. "I thought turning thirty wouldn't bother me. I was fine until the morning of my birthday. I woke up so depressed I couldn't move."

"Me, too," Josie said. "I could not get out of bed. I was paralyzed. Finally, my mother knocked on my bedroom door and said, 'It's seven thirty and your daughter has to go to school. Why aren't you up?'

" 'I'm going to die,' I said.

"My mother said, 'Not right away. Get your rear out of bed, Josie. You have a daughter to support.' It worked. I got up."

Oops. Alyce was looking stricken. Should she have avoided the word "rear" or the mention of working for a living? This crowd could be stuffy sometimes. Josie sent the conversation safely back to Alyce. "How did you spend your thirtieth, Alyce?"

"I had morning sickness. I celebrated my birthday with 7UP and soda crackers."

"I'm sorry," Linda said.

"Don't be," Alyce said. "I wanted that baby. But it

would have been hell if I didn't. Do you think Halley snapped when Cliff pressured her for another child?"

"Absolutely," Linda said. "That's when she started going to the West End. Most of the Wood Winds crowd never goes into the city. But Halley was a transplanted Manhattan girl. She felt at home there. She met Ramsey, and then Evelyn. The rest was history."

A short history, Josie thought. Halley was dead.

"I'd like more details about her artistic growth for the service," Alyce said. "I'll be careful not to say anything that would upset her family. Can I find Evelyn through his gallery?"

"Yes," Linda said. "It's on Maryland, near Euclid."

"What about Ramsey? He might give me some details about her artistic life," Alyce said. "I'd never use his name."

"Wouldn't make any difference if you did," Linda said rather meanly.

"Where's he living now?" Josie said.

"I don't know," Linda said. "Ramsey could be in his old haunts, or he may be hiding out from some irate husband or parent. He may have worn out his welcome and taken off for a while. He developed an unpleasant streak of self-pity after he'd had a few drinks. Wait. I think I have his cell phone number somewhere."

Linda brought out a stack of paper with doodles and numbers scribbled every which way. "Here. That's it. He changes his cell phone provider more often than he changes his socks, so I can't promise that will work. You can also try his favorite bar, Llywelyn's."

"Will he talk to someone like me?" Alyce said.

"If you buy him a drink," Linda said. "He's never met a drink he didn't like."

Chapter 14

"That was amazing," Josie said when they were back in Alyce's SUV. "I can't believe the information you pried out of Linda."

"She wanted to talk," Alyce said. "She needed to tell someone what happened. She's so lonely. Poor Linda. Their friendship was over the day Halley won that contest."

"It was over the day Halley's husband wanted another baby," Josie said. "She sounded frantic to escape."

"Can you blame her?" Alyce said. "There's nothing worse than being trapped in a life you hate. Staying home with my Justin makes me happy, but it might drive another woman crazy."

Alyce drove at a stately pace past the lake at Wood Winds. Sunshine silvered the water. A woman in a blue coat walked a golden Lab along the edge. The scene looked idyllic, but Josie knew she would go slowly crazy in Wood Winds.

"What would send you over the edge?" she asked.

"Having to work for a living," Alyce said.

Like I do, Josie thought.

There was an awkward silence. Alyce was facing that unhappy possibility, thanks to her husband. Josie wondered if Alyce was thinking the same thing. They'd asked Linda every question except the most important one: Was Halley having an affair with Jake?

The silence seemed to smother them. Josie searched frantically for a safe subject. "I still have time before I pick up Amelia. We can talk to more neighbors or eat more Greta Burgers."

Josie's stomach growled ominously. Alyce's eyebrows shot up at the sound.

"I think that was a vote for more talk," Josie said.

Alyce's cell phone rang. "I'd better take this." She pulled the SUV over to the curb and opened her phone. "You can watch the lake," she said.

Instead, Josie watched the color drain from her friend's face. "Where are you?" Alyce's voice was a death sentence. "I'll meet you there."

Alyce snapped her phone shut and said, "The police want Jake to come in for questioning."

"Has he been arrested?" Josie asked.

"Not yet. But he will be. At least this time he's taking his lawyer, Andy Cole, with him. Jake is on his way to Andy's office. I'll meet him there."

"I'll go with you," Josie said.

"No," Alyce said. "This could take hours. There's nothing you can do. The nanny will stay with Justin. I'll call you when I can."

Alyce pulled into her driveway next to Josie's car. Josie hugged her friend. "Good luck," she said. The words sounded stupid. Luck was what you wished someone who had a chance of winning.

Alyce didn't answer. Maybe she didn't hear. She hardened her pale face into an expressionless mask and squared her shoulders. Alyce was steeling herself to face the worst.

Josie waved forlornly from Alyce's driveway. Then she drove like a madwoman through the traffic and hit all the remaining Greta Burger outlets. She scarfed down the wretched burgers, but had no idea how they tasted. She could have been eating fried cardboard. She wished she had. It was probably more sanitary than a Greta Burger.

By the time Josie reached the Barrington School, her stomach was rumbling like a summer thunderstorm. She chugged some Maalox to soothe it.

Josie pulled up at the Barrington School just as the

bell rang, then waited impatiently in line for her daughter. She rolled down the car window to get rid of the stench of cheap meat and old onions.

"Eeew, Mom, what stinks?" Amelia wrinkled her nose as she plopped onto the seat.

"I've been eating Greta Burgers so you can have a decent meal," Josie said. "Don't give me any lip."

Amelia sulked all the way home. Josie belched and swigged Maalox. I took this mystery-shopping job to spend more quality time with my daughter, she thought. Maybe I should have had a son. A nine-year-old boy would love a belching contest with his mother.

Josie's worries slid over to Alyce, who was facing more than an upset stomach. Alyce's marriage was crumbling, her husband's career was on the skids, and he was a murder suspect for no reason Josie could understand. If Jake was arrested, her friend would be scalded in the white heat of publicity.

Alyce was such a private person. She would suffer in terrible silence. How would this horror affect little Justin? Josie glanced over at her own daughter, staring out the window, her small compact body bristling with hurt. We don't need two nine-year-olds in our family, Josie decided. It was time to act like an adult.

"I'm sorry I snapped at you," Josie said. "I ate too many Greta Burgers. I don't feel so good."

"I can hear, Mom," Amelia said. "You sounded just like Abel at school, except he does it on purpose."

"I'll make us something good for dinner," Josie said. "That will calm my stomach."

"Mac and cheese?" Amelia said.

"Yep." Josie had read an article in a parenting magazine about how to make quick meals more wholesome.

"Sweet!" Amelia said.

At home, she ran to her room and started her homework without being asked. She forgot to set the table, but Josie did it for her. She'd cut the kid some slack. Alyce's troubles were a reminder how quickly happy lives could disintegrate.

Josie piled the macaroni on her daughter's plate and admired her work. She thought the colorful veggies brightened a dull dish.

Amelia didn't. "What's in my mac and cheese?"

"Vegetables," Josie said. "This is a healthy meal if I add some broccoli, carrots, and peas. I threw in a few leftover green beans, too."

Amelia forked a green bean to the side of her plate. "I didn't want a healthy meal. I wanted dinner."

Amelia carefully ate around the vegetables, even the ones she normally liked. Josie didn't nag her. She hoped some of the broccoli-and-bean vitamins rubbed off on the macaroni. She was relieved when the phone rang, and grabbed it before Amelia could get it.

"Hey, it's Mike," the hunky plumber said in a luscious telephone voice. It sent pleasant tingles through Josie. Mike and his low-fat buns were her reward for an awful day.

Josie saw her daughter staring at her and blushed. Could the kid read her thoughts? Probably not. But Amelia could see her mother's burning face. Josie turned her back and took the phone to the other end of the kitchen.

"I'm calling to apologize," Mike said. "We got your check today for that job at your house. I wouldn't have charged you, but my partner and I have this agreement—no breaks for family and friends who call through the service. Otherwise, we'd be working free most of the time. Once the call is logged, it's official. Let me give you my cell phone number, and your next plumbing emergency is on me."

Josie eyed her uncertain kitchen sink and the pot of congealing vegetable macaroni. Naw, that would be too obvious. Also, too disgusting. What would it say about her cooking if it stopped up the sink?

"We still on for our date?" Mike said.

"Absolutely," Josie said. She was tongue-tied as a teenager. She managed another four words. "Looking forward to it."

"Me, too," Mike said. "I wanted to take you to dinner at a little place in Maplewood. Nothing fancy, but I think you'll like it. Oops, there's my beeper. Gotta go."

After her dreary date with Granby Hicks, talking to Mike was exhilarating. He was actually interested in her. He didn't drone on about his high-tech toys. He didn't make her feel like another accessory to impress the right people.

When Josie hung up, she heard water running. Amelia was loading the dishwasher.

"Thank you," Josie said, and hugged her daughter. She knew it wasn't only virtue that prompted Amelia to do the dishes. The veggies on her plate had been scraped into the garbage and carefully covered with boxes. Josie hid her smile just as carefully. So much for veggie mac.

She and Amelia finished cleaning the kitchen. Then both went off to write their reports: Amelia on the Great Wall of China and Josie on the not-so-great Greta Burgers. She faxed the report to Suttin Services, then started to call Alyce. No, Alyce had told her to wait, and she would. A call now might be an interruption.

More than once that evening, Josie lifted the receiver to call her friend, then decided against it. If Alyce needed her, she'd call. Josie watched the ten o'clock news. There was nothing about an arrest in the Halley Hardwicke murder. That was a relief. Maybe Jake would be questioned and released. Maybe Alyce's uneasy feeling was wrong. Josie fell asleep clinging to that hope.

It was dashed at seven the next morning when the phone rang. Josie could tell Alyce had bad news. Her friend sounded flat and emotionless, almost as if she were reading a report.

"I'm sorry to call so early," Alyce said. "But I wanted you to hear it from me first. Jake's been arrested. He's charged with conspiracy to commit murder in the first degree. He's in the county jail."

"Ohmigod," Josie said. "Can your lawyer get him out on bail?"

"Andy thinks so. The preliminary hearing is tomorrow."

"How is Jake?"

"He looks so scared, Josie, not like my confident man." Finally, Alyce's feelings broke through. Josie could hear her friend's fear. Alyce loved Jake, whatever his faults.

"How are you?" Josie asked.

"Furious!" Alyce said. "The police searched my kitchen, Josie. They've wrecked my house. They took our financial records. They took Jake's computer. They searched his office, too, but at least they couldn't touch his client files. His lawyer says there's nothing we can do about the house."

"I'm so sorry," Josie said.

"His law firm wants Jake to take a leave of absence until it's sorted out."

"Can they do that?" Josie asked.

"They have to. They have to reduce their exposure for liability."

"What happened to 'not guilty until proven'?" Josie asked.

"It makes no difference whether he's convicted or acquitted," Alyce said. "A client could claim Jake was too distracted by his own problems and missed something important. If Jake made a mistake, the client could sue the firm. Besides, who wants a potential felon representing them?"

"I'm so sorry," Josie repeated. Sorry for what? she wondered. Sorry this happened to Alyce? Sorry her friend married Jake? Sorry he got caught? The words were meaningless.

"The story is all over the radio and TV," Alyce said. "It didn't make the newspaper yet, but it will."

"I'll be at your place right after I take Amelia to school," Josie said.

"What about your job?" Alyce asked.

"I finished the Greta Burgers yesterday," Josie said. "It will take Harry a day or so to think of something worse."

Amelia was a model child that morning, dressed, breakfasted, and ready to leave on time. On the drive to school, she kept the radio tuned to 105.7, The Point. The popular kids' station wasn't interested in news about Jake. Josie let her daughter listen. She'd hear about Jake soon enough.

As soon as she let her daughter out of the car, Josie switched stations. She found Jake's story in thirty seconds.

"A prominent West County attorney was arrested today for the murder of designer Halley Hardwicke. Milton 'Jake' Bohannon was charged with conspiracy to commit murder in the first degree, a police spokesperson said."

Milton? Josie thought. Jake's real name was Milton?

"Designer Halley Hardwicke died in what appeared to be a carjacking at the Dorchester Mall," the announcer said. "Police sources say Bohannon arranged the murder for hire of his estranged lover."

Estranged lover? Poor Alyce.

Josie switched off the radio. She'd heard enough. The drive to Alyce's was a four-lane battle with the morning traffic. Then she had to fight her way into the subdivision. Reporters and TV trucks were camped at the gates to Wood Winds. Some boldly stopped the residents' cars as they left the subdivision gates.

The neighbors will love that, Josie thought.

Alyce met her at the kitchen door. She was so angry, her pale skin had a permanent flush.

"Look at this," she said. Chair cushions were flung on the floor, drawers hung open, and jars and cans were scattered on the counter. Alyce's beloved kitchen gadgets were thrown in a prickly pile on the granite island. Copper pots were dumped on the floor.

Josie caught a glimpse of the other rooms. Crooked pictures and an overturned chair said they'd been ransacked, too.

"The police did this?" Josie said.

"The bastards," Alyce said. That was shocking language for her.

"Nothing looks broken," Josie said. "I'll help you put things away."

She began gathering chair cushions, while Alyce sorted through the herb mills and other exotic devices.

"You're lucky the cops didn't arrest you for that stuff in your kitchen," Josie said. "It looks positively lethal."

Alyce didn't laugh. Josie worked beside her, straightening drawers and making chitchat. She knew Alyce would spill when she felt like it. They watched Milton "Jake" Bohannon do the perp walk several times on TV, then turned it off when they couldn't bear it anymore.

Alyce was right. Her husband looked scared and somehow smaller. Jake also looked guilty. He stumbled once on the humiliating walk to the jail. Alyce stared frozen-faced at the TV. Josie wished she'd cry. Her fearsome silence was worse than weeping.

The news stories featured the same photo of Halley, smiling, shining, successful. She looked like she would live forever. Once again, Josie was struck by the dead woman's resemblance to Alyce—a more stylish, thinner Alyce.

"She looks like me, doesn't she?" Alyce said when they saw Halley's photo again.

"There's a resemblance," Josie said.

"No wonder the cops think Jake had an affair with her," Alyce said. "Everyone at his office thinks he was her lover. But Jake swears he wasn't, and I believe him."

You have to, Josie thought. She wondered how long Alyce's faith would last. Why wouldn't Jake tell her about his business with Halley? Why didn't Alyce make him? Was she afraid of his answer? Did she need to hang on to her last illusions? Josie had had to face the truth about the men she'd loved. It had scalded her soul.

"Are you OK?" Josie asked. "I mean, for money and stuff? I have a little in the bank."

"Thanks, Josie," Alyce said. "The firm is paying Jake for now. We'll be fine financially. His parents are on a cruise around the world for their anniversary, and I'm not contacting them unless this goes to trial. They're better off not knowing. There's nothing they can do. I'm glad my parents are dead. My mother would die of shame. Justin is too young to know what's going on. All I can do is try to live a normal life."

But Josie didn't think that was possible. Already, Alyce's house was smothered in silence. Usually her phone rang almost nonstop with calls from her committee friends and neighbors.

Today, no one called or came by, except for little brown-haired Joanie Protzel.

She bustled in, hauling a huge tray. "I just stopped by to bring you a little something to keep your strength up." She looked at her watch. "Oops, I have to go." Joanie ran out of Alyce's house as if her misfortune were contagious.

Josie lifted the cover on the tray. There was an artful display of corned beef, roasted turkey, and kosher salami, decorated with onion blooms and carrot roses, and piled with Jewish rye, bagels, and knot rolls.

Joanie never said what the tray was, but Alyce knew: Mourning food.

Chapter 15

Was there an escape clause in the wedding vows? Did "in sickness and in health" also mean in jail and without a job? Jake Bohannon had dragged Alyce into a murder, and Josie was powerless to help her.

Alyce had shared Jake's success, but she deserved to. She'd devoted her life to his career. She gave dinners for the firm's partners and major clients, served on committees, ran his household, and cared for their son. Now she would share his shame.

What did Josie know about the man who could destroy her friend's life?

Nothing. I didn't even know his real name, she thought. Josie'd had no idea Jake had been baptized Milton. She wondered if that was a family name. She knew Jake came from old St. Louis money. He'd gone to the right schools. He lunched at the Missouri Athletic Club and golfed at the St. Louis Country Club. He was on the board of two or three charities.

But Josie could get that information from his résumé.

She knew nothing about Jake the man. What did he want? What would he do to get it? Would he sacrifice his wife and son? Josie had no idea.

When she'd talked to Jake on the phone, he was always polite. But people of his class wore good manners like good tailoring. Josie never knew what faults they hid. She'd met Jake a few times, but couldn't picture him clearly. She remembered a long patrician face, dark hair, broad, slightly hunched shoulders, and white manicured hands.

In person Jake had been courteous but distant, as if he couldn't quite place her. "Josie, right?" he'd said the second time he'd met her. When he went through the same routine the next time they met, Josie felt she was not important enough for Jake to remember.

About a year ago, Josie finally admitted to herself that she didn't like Jake. She struggled to keep this secret from Alyce. Josie felt she had no business criticizing any woman's mate. She'd made her own mistakes. At least Jake never sold drugs, like the men she loved.

Now she sat in Alyce's kitchen, staring at Joanie Protzel's artfully arranged deli platter and wondering what she was going to say. Josie picked up an onion bloom and absently twirled it, then pulled the leaves off a carrot rose.

If Amelia did that, I'd tell her to stop playing with her food, Josie thought. How can I help Alyce? What can I say that won't sound like I'm criticizing her husband? Josie prayed for tact, something she had in short supply. She felt no sudden infusion of wisdom. She couldn't sit there torturing innocent vegetables. Might as well start.

"If Jake's innocent—," Josie said.

"He is," Alyce said. The two words cut off any doubt.

"Why are the police so eager to go after an innocent man?" Josie asked.

"They're desperate," Alyce said. "They falsely arrested a young African-American. It was an outrageous mistake. They're facing major lawsuits, plus a boycott of the Dorchester Mall. So they turned around and arrested a rich white man. Now they're not guilty of racism."

"It's even more dangerous to arrest an attorney," Josie said. "Talk about lawsuits. Jake is a blameless corporate lawyer. He was miles away when Halley was killed. He could wind up owning the Dorchester Mall." There. That was tactful as all get-out. Josie was proud of herself. "Er, what exactly do the police have on Jake?"

Alyce poked at a piece of turkey. "I admit it looks bad," she said. "But there's a good explanation."

Uh-oh, Josie thought, and sacrificed another carrot to the cause.

"There hasn't been discovery yet," Alyce said, "so we don't know everything the prosecution has, but Jake's lawyer, Andy, has a pretty good idea. He found a leak in the prosecutor's office."

"What kind of leak?" Josie had a sudden, delightful vision of Mike the plumber and his toolbox.

"A waitress where the lawyers meet for breakfast told Andy some things," Alyce said. "The prosecutors talk too much and don't tip."

"And Jake's lawyer tips?"

"Big-time," Alyce said.

Josie wondered if "tip" meant "bribe." She'd spent enough time in restaurants to know that customers often talked freely, especially regulars with their own table.

"I don't understand how the cops can tie your husband to a carjacking," Josie said.

"The gun that killed Halley was registered to Jake," Alyce said.

"Ohmigod. But it was stolen out of his car, right?"

"Yes. But Jake didn't notice it was missing until after the police questioned him. He reported it stolen, but now they don't believe him. He doesn't lock his car all the time, especially in Wood Winds, and there was no sign of a break-in.

"There's more," Alyce said. "The police have been through his home computer's hard drive."

"Already?" Josie asked.

"I told you. They really want him for this," Alyce said. "They're bending every little fact into proof of his guilt. They found an e-mail that Jake forwarded to the women in our subdivision warning them about carjacking."

"What's wrong with that?" Josie asked.

"The police say Jake was setting up a scenario to make Halley's carjacking more believable. The carjacking e-mail is an urban legend. It's been debunked on Snopes.com, the urban legend Web site."

"So what?" Josie said. "Half the e-mails I get have been debunked by Snopes."

"There's also a videotape," Alyce said. She stuck a fork in a thick slice of roast beef and rolled it like a rug. "They have a security video of Jake in the parking garage at the Dorchester Mall. When the crime rate skyrocketed, the mall put in extra cameras.

"The video is grainy and hard to see because the tape has been used so much. But it's definitely Jake standing by his Lexus. It looks like he's handing money to some young men in gangsta clothes. One is big and burly. The other is small and thin. You can't see the faces clearly, but the person who shot Halley is usually described as a small, thin African-American male."

"There's more than one thin man in St. Louis," Josie said. "Jake knows the kids, right? They all dress that way. They're probably some client's sons guilting Jake into buying something for a school fund-raiser. Do you know how much I shell out for school pizzas, wrapping paper, and candy bars for the neighborhood kids?"

"Jake doesn't know who they are," Alyce said. "He says two young men approached him in the Dorchester garage and wanted twenty dollars to 'protect' his car. Jake paid them because he thought it was easier than going through the insurance hassle if they keyed the paint or slashed his tires."

"Can he describe them?" Josie asked. "Did he get their names?"

"If you're extorting money, you don't usually give your name. He said they looked like two young toughs."

"Did he report the incident to mall security?" Josie asked.

"No. Jake was in a rush. He was late for a meeting."

"Why was he at the mall in the first place?" Josie said.

"His watchband broke. He got a new one at the mall repair shop. He has a credit card receipt."

"What's the problem?" Josie could see Jake being too busy to bother about a mere twenty dollars. People like him threw twenties around like beads at a Mardi Gras parade.

"It happened two days before Halley died."

"Oh," Josie said.

"Jake's attorney has a private investigator looking for the young men. So far he hasn't found them."

He wasn't likely to, Josie thought. After the shooting, there wouldn't be any gangsta wannabes within ten miles of that mall. The place would be crawling with police. Nervous shoppers and jittery store owners would report a dark-skinned kid in baggy clothes doing anything suspicious—like breathing.

"Well, in that case, they definitely weren't some client's kids," Josie said. "His story makes sense to me. How would Jake know a couple of street toughs, anyway?"

Alyce kept prodding the roast beef with a fork, until Josie wanted to grab it away. Finally, she spoke. "Jake is on the board of Fresh New Start, the scholarship program for young men who've been in trouble with the law. The board meetings are in an iffy neighborhood downtown. That's why Jake got the gun. The police say Jake hired a hit man through someone he met at Fresh New Start."

"That's ridiculous," Josie said loyally. But she wondered if it was. "Besides, Jake wouldn't be stupid enough to give the hired killers his own gun."

But he was stupid enough to talk to the cops without a lawyer. He was stupid enough to believe he wasn't a serious suspect if he wasn't Mirandized.

There was more silence while Alyce toyed with a pickled tomato.

"There's more, isn't there?" Josie said.

"Yes," Alyce said. "A witness saw Jake with Halley in the corporate suite at the Bradcliffe Hotel. Plus, a room service waiter delivered coffee to the room. Jake signed the check. He says they were there for a business meeting."

"But not law firm business," Josie said.

That photo of Halley flashed in Josie's mind again. Halley was slender, confident, and beautiful. The perfect match for a man like Jake. A glamorous married mistress was safer than a skittish au pair.

"No," Alyce said. "Jake wasn't there for the firm. But

it was definitely business. He told me that. But no one believes him.''

Including me, Josie thought. But you don't like him, she reminded herself. Be fair. "Just because two businesspeople meet at a hotel doesn't mean they're having sex," Josie said. "That's so twentieth century.''

"Right." Alyce brightened. Her smile faded quickly. "But the witness heard them arguing. Halley supposedly said, 'Your wife will find out anyway.'

"Jake said, 'Not if you don't—' The witness didn't hear the rest because Jake unlocked the door and pushed Halley inside the suite.''

"Pushed how?" Josie asked. "Roughly, gently, playfully?''

"I don't know," Alyce said.

"Who is this witness?''

"They didn't mention a name. We'll find out soon enough.''

"What does Jake say?" Josie asked.

"He says the conversation never took place.''

He's lying, Josie thought. A false witness would come up with a more complete story. Alyce looked stricken. She started stacking the bagels. She knew her husband was lying, too.

"Well, it's Jake's word against the witness's," Josie said. "And you don't know how credible that person is.''

Alyce took a deep breath and said, "They also found Halley's scarves tied to the bedposts.''

"For decoration," Josie said.

"And their DNA was in the hotel suite: Halley's and Jake's.''

"Didn't the hotel maid clean the room?" Josie said.

"She didn't have time. Jake and Halley were there the morning of the day she was—" Alyce stopped. The word "murdered" fairly shrieked at them, but neither one said it.

"What kind of DNA?" Josie asked.

"They didn't say," Alyce said.

"Do you think it was DNA on a soda straw?''

"Jake doesn't use straws. He never drinks soda. They ordered coffee, remember?"

"Maybe the DNA was from the coffee cups."

"Room service took the tray back downstairs," Alyce said. "Everything was washed before the police got there."

"They leave the room service trays in the halls for days when I stay at a hotel," Josie said.

Alyce didn't even attempt a smile. She was building a wall with the sliced rye bread.

"Maybe they got the DNA off a cigarette butt," Josie said. "Does Jake smoke?"

"No."

"Did he cut himself accidentally? Have a nosebleed?"

"No."

"Leave any hair?" Josie asked.

"Not that we know," Alyce said.

There was a miserable silence, while they surveyed the wreckage of Joanie's deli tray. It looked like raccoons had attacked it.

Josie could think of only one other source of DNA. From the look on Alyce's face, she had the same thought. Jake might have left his DNA in a condom once before—in the wastebasket in the au pair's room.

"Is that all the police have?" Josie said.

"All?" Alyce started laughing as bitter tears ran down her cheeks. "All?" Then she was crying, and Josie could not comfort her.

Chapter 16

"I'm sorry." Alyce wiped her tear-glazed eyes on a deli napkin.

This was a major breach of Alyce etiquette. Also, a useless one. Alyce succeeded only in smearing her eyeliner. Tears streaked her cheeks and splotched her blouse. Alyce had had a serious crying storm.

"I hope you're not apologizing for crying," Josie said. "I'd be screaming and tearing out my hair. I'm just sorry you have to go through this. How can I help? What do you want to do?"

"Scream and tear out my hair." Alyce's attempt at a smile tore Josie's heart.

"Sounds like a plan," Josie said. "Then you can crawl into bed and pull the covers over your head, or drink margaritas until you pass out."

"Can I do both?" Alyce asked. "Look at Joanie's deli platter. I've destroyed it."

"No way," Josie said. "You mangled two slices of beef. I crippled the carrots. Everything else is fine. I'll help you wrap it up."

"Joanie was so nice to bring it over," Alyce said. "I have marvelous neighbors. I couldn't imagine living here if I didn't get along with everyone. Well, almost everyone. Amy the Slut doesn't count."

"Your neighbors should like you," Josie said. "You help everyone. You work hard for this subdivision."

"It's my way of paying forward," Alyce said. "I know Jake's situation looks bad right now, but my neighbors understand. They know Jake couldn't possibly hurt anyone. I haven't had one nosy phone call. People here respect our privacy. We take care of one another in Wood Winds. I wish the rest of the world was as thoughtful."

"Yeah. There's a zillion reporters at the subdivision gates," Josie said. "Do you want to get away from here? You can wear one of my mystery-shopper wigs as a disguise."

"No, thanks," Alyce said. "I can't face that dog pack even in a wig. Wood Winds' security called me. They're trying to chase away the reporters, but it's hopeless. When they get rid of one, ten more return."

They're hot for this story, Josie thought, and it will only get worse. Halley's murder was *Cinderella* gone wrong: An ordinary housewife became a brilliant success and then a pathetic victim. Jake was the handsome prince who destroyed her, while poor Alyce sat at home like a drudge.

"I'll make my famous margaritas and we can relax," Josie said.

"I shouldn't stagger hungover into Jake's hearing tomorrow," Alyce said. "I'd feel better doing something. We can start our investigation by talking to my neighbors. That way we won't have to leave the subdivision."

Investigation, Josie thought. A grand name for a glorified kaffeeklatsch. Still, visiting a few neighbors wouldn't do any harm. Alyce was better off surrounded by friends instead of the hostile media horde at the gates.

"What are we trying to find out?" Josie said.

"More about Halley," Alyce said. "I lived down the street from the woman, but I know so little about her. According to her best friend, Linda, Halley changed about fifteen months ago. That's when she did the ballroom in Halley blue for the annual dance. It was the talk of Wood Winds."

"I bet they raved over it," Josie said.

"No," Alyce said "Her design was overpowering. The dramatic decorations made people nervous. Remember, this crowd is happy with freesias on the table and covers

on the chairs. They complained that Halley turned our
dance into an ad for herself. I thought it looked
fabulous."

"How did Halley feel?" Josie said. "Was she upset by
Wood Winds' rejection?"

"I have no idea. But there's someone who does know:
the dance-committee chair, Renata Upton Livermore.
She can tell you everything about everyone in Wood
Winds."

"Have I met Renata?" Josie asked.

"You'd remember if you did," Alyce said. "We call
her Renata Liverspot. She's our very own grande dame.
Renata is a wealthy widow in her seventies. She believes
she rules Wood Winds society, and we humor her. Renata has wonderful white hair she wears in a Grace Kelly
French roll. She's the only woman I know who can carry
off a tiara and a lorgnette.

"If she had her way, she'd be reincarnated as Mrs.
Vanderbilt and restart the Four Hundred. We had a
hard time convincing her that every resident of Wood
Winds had to be invited to the annual dance. She only
wanted the 'right people.' "

"She sounds like an awful old battle-ax," Josie said.

"I adore her," Alyce said. "She's from another time,
but she really is grand. She gave a lovely tea for my
birthday. She served blueberry scones with clotted cream
and tea in porcelain cups. Renata is a hoot. You'll get
a kick out of her."

Josie wasn't sure about that, but she kept quiet.

"After we see Renata, we'll visit her cochair, Betty.
She's another charmer. It will be fun, Josie. I need a
good chat with my friends."

"Then let's start," Josie said. "Call and set up the
appointments."

"Oh, we don't need to call," Alyce said. "I'm in and
out of their houses all day long, thanks to the committee.
Last week, I spent four days addressing invitations in
Renata's dining room. She wouldn't allow computer labels for our big event. They had to be hand addressed
in blue-black ink."

"Should we walk to her house?" Josie said.

"Proper suburban women never walk anywhere unless they have a dog with them," Alyce said. "They run only if there's a fire or they're wearing exercise clothes. Otherwise, we are required to drive. A lady goes calling in her carriage."

They drove past the mélange of architecture that made up Wood Winds—Tudor palaces, Italian villas, French châteaus. The queen of Wood Winds society lived in a re-created Victorian mansion on the subdivision's highest hill.

"Renata likes to look down on people," Josie said as she trudged up the steep stone steps.

Alyce managed her floaty walk even on those stairs. "Josie, be nice. You of all people should appreciate her eccentricity."

"You're right. It isn't everyone who builds a brand-new haunted house," Josie said. "What is this architecture: early Addams family?"

"Gothic Revival," Alyce said. "Did you see the gingerbread scrollwork? She brought in wood-carvers from Germany. The inside is amazing: dark wood, stained glass, wrought-iron chandeliers. There's a fountain in the foyer, a gazebo in the garden, and two wine cellars."

The massive front door could have guarded a mausoleum. A red stained-glass window stared out of it like a bloody eye. A leathery-winged stone gargoyle leered over the door.

The whole place creeped Josie out. It was cheerful as a four-day funeral.

"Are the bats and cobwebs specially imported?" Josie said.

"Stop," Alyce said. "Don't you dare make me giggle." She put on her serious grown-up face and rang the doorbell.

Josie expected the front door to creak open and reveal an ancient butler in a morning coat. Instead, they saw a smiling Hispanic maid in a white polyester uniform. Her smile seemed to slip when she saw Alyce, but the porch was so dark, Josie wasn't sure.

"Hi, Carmelita," Alyce said. "May I speak to Mrs. Livermore?" She started to step into the foyer, but the maid deftly blocked her entrance.

"I'll ask Mrs. Livermore if she's in." The maid had morphed into a pit bull in polyester. Definitely no smile, Josie thought.

"It's me, Carmelita." Alyce looked puzzled.

"Please wait," Carmelita said, and shut the door on them.

"I don't know what's got into Carmelita," Alyce said. "She should have invited us inside to wait. Of course Mrs. Livermore is at home. That's her car in the driveway. Liz's SUV is parked behind it and Jessica's Mercedes is across the street. They must be having a meeting, but then I should be invited, too. I guess they didn't want to bother me."

Josie felt cold, and it wasn't from the sharp wind. She shivered and stared at the carved-wood flounces and filigree until the maid cracked open the front door. Josie saw a slice of frightened face.

"Mrs. Livermore is not at home." Carmelita said the words in a rush and started to shut the door.

Alyce still didn't get it. "Of course, she's home," she said.

"No. Not home." The maid's accent grew stronger, along with her fear.

Josie tried to shield Alyce from the blow she knew was coming. "We should go," she said, tugging at Alyce's coat sleeve.

Alyce was oblivious. "Is something wrong, Carmelita?"

Suddenly, the heavy door was flung back by a woman with wrinkled, papery skin and spun-cotton hair. She was small and thin, but there was nothing frail about her. Her back was straight and her mouth was hard. Renata Upton Livermore was a hanging judge in a beige twinset.

"I thought you could take a discreet hint, but now I will have to be direct, Mrs. Bohannon." She made Alyce's name sound like a curse. "I don't wish to see you here again. I will expect you to have the grace to resign from my committee."

Alyce went rigid with shock. "Why?"

"I don't wish to associate with the wife of a murderer," Renata said.

Josie was afraid Alyce would faint, but she stood her ground. "Jake isn't guilty," she said.

Josie could see the effort those three words cost Alyce. She was proud of her friend.

"Of course he is," Mrs. Livermore said. "The police said so. Your husband paid Halley's killer. He gave him the murder weapon. He brought reporters to our gates."

In Renata Livermore's eyes, these three sins were equal. "We have a killer living in Wood Winds." Her eyes snapped sparks. "It's a disgrace. What will it do to property values? I can't believe you would show your face in public, Alyce Bohannon. I am not at home to you. Ever."

Mrs. Livermore shut the door firmly, and Josie heard the final insult, the *snick* of the lock. Alyce stood on the porch, too stunned to move. Josie dragged her down the stairs.

"Come on," Josie said. "How can you stand that old bat?"

"I'm sure it's a misunderstanding," Alyce said.

She still doesn't get it, Josie thought. Alyce was an outcast now.

"Let's go see Betty," Alyce said. "Mrs. Livermore belongs to another generation, but Betty is our age. We've spent too many afternoons together at the club pool. I cared for her baby when she was in the hospital. She'll understand."

"Is it a good idea to see her right now?" Josie didn't think Alyce could take more rejection today. She'd need time to understand she'd been banished from Wood Winds society.

"Betty is my friend," Alyce said as they pulled into the circular drive of a pinkish semi-Spanish palace. It looked positively cheerful after the Livermore house of horrors. Josie peeked in the front window and caught a glimpse of marble tile, crystal chandeliers, and a sweeping staircase.

Alyce rang Betty's doorbell, but no one answered. A shiny blue SUV was parked in the drive.

"Is that Betty's?" Josie asked.

"Yes," Alyce said.

"Does she have another car?"

"Just her husband's Lexus. But Jerry should be at work."

Josie thought she saw the curtains shift slightly in an upstairs window. "Let's go home," she said.

But Alyce kept ringing the doorbell, while the fierce wind burned her delicate skin a raw red and twisted her corn-silk hair into hopeless tangles. Her desperation was painful to watch. The doorbell echoed madly across the marble floors. Josie was sure she heard soft footsteps on the staircase. But no one answered the door.

Finally, Josie took Alyce by the arm and steered her to the SUV. Alyce didn't resist.

"Let's go back to your house," Josie said. "We need to rethink our investigation. Why don't you let me drive? You look a little shook."

"I'm fine," Alyce said, but her pale face said she was devastated. "I don't understand, Josie. Betty and Renata are my friends."

"No, they're not," Josie said. "Your friends stand by you when you're in trouble."

"Well, they're my neighbors. They know me. They know Jake. Betty had too many eggnogs and gave him a sloppy kiss at the Christmas party. Now he's a killer and she won't come to the door to talk to me. I was good enough to watch her baby for a whole week."

"They're just two jerks in a big subdivision," Josie said. "I'm sure your other neighbors don't feel that way. We'll have some fresh coffee and play with the baby and—"

Alyce slammed on the brakes and stopped dead in the street outside her house. She gave a single scream. It was a terrible sound, as if someone had plunged a knife into her heart.

"What is it? Are you hurt? What happened?"

Alyce pointed to her Tudor mansion with the mullioned windows and the half-timber garage. She was so upset, she couldn't talk.

"My God," Josie said.

The garage was covered in blood. Dripping gore was splashed across the front and ran down the pink pavers.

"What happened? Is someone dead?"

Then Josie realized the red was too bright, the color too uniform. It wasn't blood. It was red paint.

Someone had spray-painted KILLER on the garage doors.

Chapter 17

"Red paint is a bitch to clean off mullioned windows." Josie scratched at the thick, lumpy glass with her fingernail. She peeled off a long strip of red paint, and it landed on her shoe.

Alyce giggled. She was so tipsy, anything—or nothing—was funny. Giggly drunks were a scandal in Wood Winds. Two days ago, Alyce would have been shocked if one of her neighbors had been spiflicated in her driveway at noon. For Alyce herself to be in that condition was unthinkable.

Now it didn't make any difference. She was a killer's wife. She could do as she pleased. Alyce was beyond scandal.

Alyce and Josie defiantly scrubbed away the KILLER splashed across the garage doors. Red paint had bled onto the mullioned windows and dripped on the pinkish pavers.

It had taken Josie nearly an hour and a bottle of wine to get Alyce back out to the garage. After they'd recovered from the first shock of that red word sprayed across the garage, Josie had helped Alyce into the house. Her friend had moved like a sick old woman. Josie half carried her into the kitchen, and sat her down at the granite island.

"Thank God Justin has a playdate at Hannah's house," Alyce said. "He and Mrs. Palm, the nanny, won't be home for another three hours."

"Alyce, I'm glad the baby is safe. But this is vandalism," Josie said. "We have to call the police."

"No," Alyce said. "The reporters will find out and we'll have more bad publicity. Besides, the police will never figure out who did it."

"Where the heck is your refrigerator?" Josie said, looking around the oak-paneled kitchen. No door handles or knobs gave away the location.

"Next to the sink," Alyce said. "Third panel."

Josie never understood why anyone would hide a refrigerator in a kitchen. It belonged in there. But then she couldn't figure out the herb mill, either. She rummaged through the fridge and found a bottle of pinot grigio.

"Where did you hide the wine opener?" she said.

"Wait," Alyce said. "That wine is for Jake's dinner party next week. It's fifty dollars a bottle."

"You need it more than he does," Josie said. "Cheap wine gives you a bad hangover."

"There isn't going to be any dinner party, is there?" Alyce said. She sounded dazed. "The opener is in the drawer on the left with the wine coasters and bottle stoppers."

"Don't worry, we won't need a stopper. There won't be any leftover wine." Josie filled a water glass with the pale gold wine and set it in front of Alyce. "Drink."

Alyce drank, while Josie abused her friend's faithless neighbors. Alyce made excuses for them between sips.

"Renata comes from another time," Alyce said. "She looks at life differently than we do."

"Humph," Josie said, and realized she sounded like Renata. "What's Betty's excuse? She's young and gutless. Hey, maybe we could make that into a soap opera—*The Young and the Gutless*."

Alyce didn't laugh. Josie felt like a court jester trying to please a bored queen. "Keep drinking," she said to Alyce.

Alyce took another sip. Josie downed a healthy swig. Expensive wine went down easier than cheap stuff.

Alyce was staring off into space.

"Drink," Josie said.

Alyce was halfway through the tall glass of wine when Josie said, "I know why Renata Upton Livermore has that gargoyle over her door. It's her portrait."

Alyce started giggling. Then she laughed out loud. "To hell with the whole bunch," she said. "I don't need them. Let's clean that paint off right now."

"Do you really want to go out there?" Josie said. "Maybe you should hire someone to do it."

"No," Alyce said. "I haven't done anything wrong. I want the whole neighborhood to see me. Come on, Josie. We'll put on some old clothes and go to work."

They piled on layers of ragged T-shirts, old flannel work shirts, thick wool socks, and butt-sprung coveralls to keep warm. Josie rooted in her car for a pair of old tennis shoes. Alyce dug some disreputable sneakers out of her closet.

"We look like bums," Josie said. "We are definitely lowering property values."

"Good," Alyce said. The giggly wine drunk was wearing off. Now she was angry and mildly hungover.

They found two scrub brushes in the hall closet, along with cleaning supplies and a big plastic bucket, and marched outside to confront the awful red word.

Vigorous scrubbing was a good way to work out their anger. Hot fury protected them from the cold wind. Soon they'd worked up a sweat. The spray paint came off the pinkish pavers with scrub brushes, cleanser, and elbow grease. Windex, soft scrubbers, and fingernails removed it from the glass.

"Oh, Josie, look at your nails," Alyce said. "They look like you've manicured them with pinking shears."

"They'll grow back," Josie said.

The hardest task was getting the gore off the white garage doors. After nearly an hour of scrubbing, Josie said, "It's mostly gone, but I can still see the faint outline."

"Maybe we can paint over it," Alyce said. "We have matching paint in the basement."

They spread out a drop cloth on the freshly cleaned pavers and set out their paint cans, trays, and brushes. Josie liked the strong, clean scent of the paint.

"Thanks for helping me," Alyce said. "I didn't want Jake to see this when he comes home. He has enough to deal with."

Josie thought Jake should see what he'd done to Alyce. If he'd been her husband, she'd paint the garage with a big scarlet *A*.

"Is he coming home?" she asked. "Does your lawyer think he'll get bail? This case has had a lot of publicity."

"Andy has high hopes and we have an ace in the hole. The judge is a golfing buddy of the senior partner at Jake's law firm."

"Won't the judge have to recuse himself?"

"In St. Louis? Those good old boys stick together. At worst, Jake may have to wear a thingie around his ankle, like Martha Stewart. But Andy is pretty sure Jake will be released on bail."

"When's the arraignment?"

"Tomorrow morning. Please don't come, Josie. I'll be fine. I need to be there and play supportive spouse."

"You *are* a supportive spouse." And a better wife than Jake deserves, Josie thought.

After that, the only sound was the whistling wind and the soft shush of their brushes as they painted the garage doors.

Wood Winds was unnaturally quiet. No SUVs cruised by. The Mercedes station wagons, Jaguar sedans, and Lexuses stayed in their driveways. No one walked a dog or ran behind a sports stroller. Josie thought she saw curtains twitch and miniblinds quiver, but she was never sure.

Eeriest of all was the streetwide response to the mail. In any neighborhood, rich or poor, people came out to get their mail. At twelve twenty, a letter carrier drove down the street, stopping and stuffing each ornamental mailbox with envelopes and catalogs. The letter carrier waved and smiled at Alyce and Josie, then turned the corner. No neighbors came out for their mail. Five minutes. Ten minutes. Fifteen. Their doors stayed shut.

"I feel like we're the survivors of some weird disaster," Josie said. "You subdivision is never this quiet."

"They don't want to come out and have to see me. Let's stay out here all day," Alyce said. "They'll go stir crazy."

They painted the garage doors three times, until Josie was nearly snow-blinded by the white paint. After the third coat, Josie stood back and took an appraising look.

"I can't see any red paint, Alyce," she said.

Alyce followed her down the drive, then pointed at the door. "There," she said. "I can still make out the letters. See the *K*, the *I,* and the two *L*s?"

The letters were gone, buried under a blizzard of white paint. But Josie knew Alyce would always see the hated red word. The accusation was burned into her brain.

"Let's paint the doors one more time," Josie said. "Then we'll go inside. I'm cold. I need to warm up with some coffee. The wind has shifted and I have more paint on me than the doors."

They finished the last coat in silence. The subdivision's unnatural quiet was getting to both of them. Nothing moved. No doors opened. No one dared to come outside, pick up the mail, and wave to Alyce.

My friend is a pariah, Josie thought. This is so unfair. Alyce is so kind and generous. How dare these twerps turn on her?

"You know the worst part?" Alyce said, as if she'd heard Josie's thoughts. "This attack had to be done by one of my neighbors."

"Kids do stupid things," Josie said.

"The kids are at school," Alyce said. "An adult did this."

Chapter 18

All morning long, Josie had paced and fretted and made a zillion calls to Alyce's cell phone. In between, she cleaned house, hoping to burn off her frustration.

Alyce had her phone turned off. That meant she was either in court or with Jake's attorney. Josie kept speed-dialing every fifteen minutes. She had to know how the arraignment turned out.

She found out at noon, when she turned on the news. The TV cameras showed Jake entering the courtroom. Josie thought he looked arrogant, emotionless, and guilty. Alyce looked like she was going to her own execution. She was pale and determined, her head at a proud angle. She wore a dowdy, high-collared black dress.

Josie wondered if the dress was deliberate. Alyce had to look like a good wife and mother, not a voluptuous woman. She also wondered if Jake's lawyer was sending a sly message: "See why her husband stepped out, folks? He didn't kill anybody, but can you blame him for his affair?"

How could Alyce endure the intrusive publicity? How could Jake expose her to such public shame? Josie called and called, hoping her friend would say she was surviving. No, that she was mad as hell.

At least the news cheered Josie. Jake was free on bond.

Alyce was in her own personal prison, suffering the subtle tortures only suburbia could inflict.

Alyce finally turned her phone back on at two o'clock. She answered with a small, mouselike, "Hello."

"How are you?" Josie asked.

"OK." Alyce sounded like she'd been beaten.

"What's the matter?" Josie asked, then wondered if there was an award for Dumbest Question of the Year.

"I feel like a Mafia wife," Alyce said. "I was on TV at the arraignment."

"Only for twenty seconds," Josie said.

"The whole city saw it," Alyce said. "Now everyone stares at me, but no one says anything. After I took Jake home, I went to the supermarket. My neighbors cut me dead. I've known them for years. I've been in their houses. I've watched their children. I've gone to their parents' funerals. Today, they ignored me.

"I was in bulk foods when Anne came by, pushing her cart. She looked through me like I was a window. Betty turned her back on me in produce. Jessica locked her car doors when I passed her in the parking lot."

"That bitch," Josie said.

"That's not the worst," Alyce said. "Hannah's mother canceled her playdates with Justin. My baby is an outcast. I don't care what they do to me, but how can they hurt my innocent child?"

"You don't want your son associating with people like that," Josie said.

"He's too young to understand why he can't play with Hannah anymore. How could I live in Wood Winds as long as I did and not know these people?"

"Has everyone turned on you?" Josie asked.

"No, Joanie's been by twice, bringing deli trays," Alyce said. "She left enough food to feed a high school football team, but she didn't stay. She doesn't seem to know what to say. Or maybe it's me. Maybe I don't know what to say to her."

"Food is Joanie's way of showing she cares," Josie said.

"It's a big help," Alyce said. "The more she brings, the less I have to brave the supermarket."

"See?" Josie said. "Joanie doesn't talk much, but she knows what to say."

"Linda was here, too. Linda Dattilo. She was Halley's best friend—but Linda came by to say hello. The conversation was awkward, but at least she tried to talk to me."

"Did she mention the garage doors?" Josie asked.

"No. Neither did Joanie. They both acted as if the incident never happened."

"Maybe they don't know," Josie said.

"Everyone in Wood Winds knows," Alyce said. "Besides, Linda would have heard about it at the meeting."

"What meeting?" Josie said.

"Linda told me there was a secret meeting of the homeowners' association. They want to buy our house," Alyce said. Her voice trembled with shame and shock.

"Under the Wood Winds association rules, they can do that if we are criminals and unfit to live here. Mrs. Livermore wanted to throw us out now, but the lawyers for the association said the homeowners would have to wait until Jake was convicted. Then they can press for a buyout."

"Those bastards." Josie grew more foulmouthed as Alyce's troubles worsened. "I'd sell your house to a drug dealer right now."

"We can't sell," Alyce said. "We put up our house when we made bail. I don't think Jake will lose this case, but our lawyer warned us that juries are unpredictable."

Andy Cole was preparing them, Josie thought.

"What's Jake say?" Josie asked.

"I haven't bothered him with it. I didn't tell him what happened at the supermarket, either. He has enough to worry about. Josie, if Jake is convicted, we'll be homeless."

Josie started to say, "You could live with me," but she looked around her kitchen. The old white fridge and the chipped porcelain sink would depress Alyce. Josie didn't even own a decent set of steak knives.

"Alyce, you shouldn't be alone now."

"I'm not alone. I have Jake."

Fat lot of good he is, Josie thought. "I'm sure he's exhausted," Josie said. "I'm on my way over."

"Who'll pick up Amelia at school?" Alyce asked.

"Mom," Josie said. "After I went out with her dream date, Granby, I can do no wrong. What can I bring?"

"Just some milk. I thought I had enough for Justin, but Jake's drinking it, too."

"Better than booze," Josie said. It was the only good thing she could say about Alyce's husband right now.

The evergreens at Wood Winds were precisely barbered. The lawns were raked and ready for winter. The mulch around the spindly trees was mounded to perfection. The homes gleamed with fresh paint. Especially the new paint on Alyce's garage doors.

Josie hauled several grocery bags into Alyce's kitchen. "Milk, wine, and chocolate," she said. "Emergency supplies."

"No wine for me," Alyce said. "I had enough yesterday. I'll make us coffee. But I'm definitely ready for chocolate. What do we have here?"

She pulled the gold-foil box out of the bag. "Ohmigod. Bissinger's. The dark-chocolate assortment. Did you ever have their chocolate-covered blackberries? Good thing they're only available for a few weeks around Labor Day, or I'd weigh four hundred pounds."

"I ate myself into a stupor once on the chocolate-covered raspberries," Josie said. "I'm not kidding. I had a whole pound and practically passed out in ecstasy."

Amelia's father, Nate, bought them for me, she thought. *My life was filled with little luxuries then. Chocolate-covered raspberries, champagne, scented candles, silk sheets. And a man who loved me.*

"St. Louis chocolate is the best," Alyce said. "Too bad Bissinger's isn't well-known outside the city."

"That's good," Josie said. "Leaves more for us."

She studied the rows of chocolate in the box. Josie hated crème centers. If she had a darning needle, she'd try a discreet probe on the underside, but she only did that at home when Amelia wasn't around. She was pretty sure the square one was caramel.

"How's Jake?" Josie bit into the square chocolate. Yum. She'd guessed right.

"Taking a nap. He didn't sleep well in jail. Justin's curled up next to his daddy. He missed him."

Alyce picked her chocolate with equal care. "A crème center. I love those."

Did you miss Jake? Josie wanted to ask. But she didn't have the nerve. Instead, she sipped Alyce's hot coffee and studied her friend. The dark shadows under her eyes looked like bruises. Her hair was more flyaway than floaty. She had a big red pimple on her nose.

Alyce and Josie both politely picked through the chocolate box, searching for the right one. They both got what they wanted: another crème for Alyce and a caramel for Josie. If only we were as good at picking men, Josie thought.

"We need to get our investigation going again," Alyce said, between neat bites.

Josie didn't think it had ever started. But maybe it would distract Alyce. It couldn't hurt to talk to people.

"We won't get anywhere in this subdivision," Josie said. "But there are a couple of ways we can go. We can look for Ramsey, the great American novelist." She found a truffle in the box.

"Why should we talk to him?" Alyce ate the bear claw.

"He knew Halley when she was restless, before she got famous. Maybe she did something desperate then that led to her murder."

"You mean like hook up with Evelyn the artist?" Alyce said.

"Exactly. We should talk to him, too. Then there's Halley's husband, Cliff. I still think he could have killed her."

"Shouldn't the police be doing this?" Alyce said.

"They should, but they aren't," Josie said. "Jake is their chosen bad guy. They can't say, 'Oops, we screwed up again. It's really the husband.' They're going to do everything they can to prove Jake was the killer.

"There's one more potential suspect: Granby Hicks."

"The lawyer? Are you kidding?" Alyce said.

"Do you know how gleeful he was when the homicide detectives talked to Jake? He practically did a happy dance in Tony's. He thinks he'll be the next partner if Jake is out. Granby wants that partnership so bad he'd sell his soul on eBay." Josie found another square chocolate. It had to be more caramel.

"Let me get this straight," Alyce said. "You think Granby murdered Halley to ruin Jake's career."

"Yes," Josie said. "The carjacking was designed to frame Jake. Granby used his inside knowledge about Jake's"—Josie put on the brakes before she said "affair"—"dealings with Halley."

Alyce carefully chose an almond toffee. "Josie, I've never had a good word to say about Granby, but that's crazy."

"You didn't see Granby's face when he talked about Jake's downfall," Josie said. "He's eaten with ambition and envy. Does Granby know where you live?"

"Of course," Alyce said. "He's been here on business often."

"When was the last time?"

"Three days before Halley died. He had to talk to Jake about a client. I think he brought some papers, too. What's that got to do with anything?"

"He had access to Jake's unlocked car. He could have taken the gun when he was here."

"I don't think so, Josie. Even if it's true, how are you going to prove it?"

"I'm going to do some computer snooping," Josie said.

"We don't have a computer," Alyce said. "The cops took it, remember?"

"I can do a search at home," Josie said. "I've already made another date with Granby."

Alyce shuddered. "I'd take the veil before I went out with him. If you really think he's a killer, you don't want to be alone with him. Josie, don't do that for me."

"I'm doing it for me," Josie said. "I want our old life back. You're too notorious to go mystery-shopping with until this cools off."

Suddenly, Alyce looked infinitely weary. "Do you think I'll ever have a normal life again?" she said.

"You will. I promise. I'll do everything I can to make it happen." Josie looked at the gold box, piled with empty frilled cups. So far all she'd done was help Alyce eat chocolates.

"We can't hang around here any longer," she said. "Let's go into the Central West End. They're more tolerant in that part of town."

"Not to the wife of an alleged murderer," Alyce said. "That's what they called my husband on TV, an alleged murderer."

"Don't worry. They'll call him innocent soon." Josie reached into her purse and pulled out a wig. "Here. Wear this. You'll make a killer redhead."

"Alleged redhead," Alyce said.

Chapter 19

You can do this, Josie told herself. You should have done it years ago. Her heart was pounding as she eased her gray Honda onto Kingshighway.

Josie was going back to the Central West End for the first time in nearly a decade.

Kingshighway lived up to its grand name. Hanging baskets of greenery in ornate holders paraded down the center. The boulevard hadn't looked this good the last time she'd been in the West End.

That was almost ten years ago, when she and Nate were wildly in love. They'd had champagne brunches at Café Balaban and late-night drinks at Llywelyn's Pub. They'd dined at the fashionable restaurants, shopped for antiques, stopped at Big Sleep Books for the latest mysteries.

The West End belonged to St. Louis's old money. The inhabitants lived in massive mansions on private streets guarded by iron gates. She'd met some of these privileged people at Nate's parties. Josie felt sorry for them. They were prisoners of their great wealth and family expectations. They had everything but their freedom.

Nate had had loads of new money and limitless freedom. Now he was behind bars, too, and Josie would never see him again. She thought about him almost every day. How could she avoid it? Amelia looked so much like her father.

Josie had faced the loss of her lover, single motherhood, and her angry, disappointed parent. But she couldn't summon the courage to return to the scene of her extravagant happiness. Josie couldn't bear to go back to the neighborhood where she and Nate had been in love.

Mercifully, mystery-shopping kept her mostly in the county malls.

Now she was returning with Alyce. This is no time to whine about my past, Josie told herself. My friend has real problems, right now.

Alyce was fighting off her fears with chatter. "I haven't been in the city in ages," she said. "I love these fabulous old robber-baron castles. Look at the carved fleur-de-lis on that doorway."

"They're amazing," Josie said.

I was at a cocktail party at that house years ago, she thought. The furniture belonged in a museum. The host had served jug wine, deviled eggs, and yellow cheese on Ritz crackers. Nate had laughed about the cheap hors d'oeuvres and taken her out for caviar afterward.

"I wonder what people will make of Wood Winds in a hundred years?" Alyce said. "Will they laugh at our turrets and towers and make fun of my half-timber garage?"

They already do, Josie wanted to say, but that would be cruel. "Your citrus trumpet will be the highlight of the house tour. That red wig is growing on me."

"I hope it's not growing on me," Alyce said. "I feel like a hooker."

"You're not far from work. The Stroll's only a few blocks away," Josie said. "Weird, isn't it? The city's richest people live within spitting distance of the poor."

"Stop! There's a parking space, and it doesn't have a meter," Alyce said. "Grab it."

"Spoken like a true suburban woman," Josie said. "You'll spend a hundred dollars on gas, but not a nickel on parking."

"We have principles," Alyce said as Josie eased her gray car into the spot. "We're starting with the novelist Ramsey, right? Which bar do you want to try first? Drinks are on me, as well as bribes and tips."

"I could learn to like this investigating," Josie said.

Three hours later, she wasn't so sure. "If I have another club soda, I'll explode," Josie said. They were in the dark, wood-paneled depths of Llywelyn's, munching warm, salty potato chips.

"These chips are terrific," Alyce said. "I can't stop eating them."

"Crispy grease is my favorite food," Josie said.

"Do you ever eat anything healthy?" Alyce said.

"If broccoli was so great, Bissinger's would cover it in chocolate. Just don't tell my daughter."

"I think she knows," Alyce said. "I've been passing out twenties like yard-sale flyers, but there's no sign of Ramsey."

Josie pulled out a small notebook. "This is bar number six. You've dropped two hundred dollars so far, but no one has seen the successful failed novelist. I don't think they're covering for him. You're offering a cash reward and he has too many unpaid bar tabs."

"You've been calling Ramsey every fifteen minutes from a different pay phone," Alyce said. "He's not answering his phone."

"It's my patented Josie Marcus speed-dial assault."

"Have you left any messages?" Alyce said.

"Are you kidding?" Josie crunched a chip. "What could I say that wouldn't drive him deeper into hiding?"

"Let's give it up and track down Evelyn." Alyce ate the last chip.

"That should be easier." Josie checked her notebook again. "His Gallerie Evelyn is around the corner."

Josie didn't know much about modern art, but she liked most of what she saw at Gallerie Evelyn. The man had an eye for color and form. She spotted only six duds: a group of muddy oils near the entrance.

A skinny man barely larger than a boy met them at the gallery door. Josie couldn't believe anyone would wear a black turtleneck and a beret. He even had a cigarette holder in one hand. In the other was a wineglass that never seemed empty.

"May I help you, ladies?" the man said, with a blast of wine fumes. He was wasted.

"Are you Evelyn?" Josie said.

"EVE-a-lyn," he said. "EV-alyn sounds like a waitress. Can no one in this benighted city pronounce my name right?" His accent wavered between BBC and Brooklyn.

"We certainly admire your lovely art," Josie said.

"Lovely is for calendars," he said. "My work is powerful. Thought-provoking. It's supposed to make you feel uncomfortable."

"I'm definitely uncomfortable," Josie said.

Alyce shot her a look. "We understand you have some early works by a St. Louis artist," Alyce said. "Halley Hardwicke."

"They're gone," he said. "So is Halley. She's dead." Evelyn gave a dramatic sigh and took a long drink. "She was dead to me long before that."

"You knew her before she was famous?" Alyce said.

"I discovered her," Evelyn said. "I awakened her from her bourgeois existence. Before she met me, she thought a painting had to match the living room couch."

"I thought you carried her early works," Josie said.

"Sold them all." Evelyn took another gulp. "There was quite a run on them after her death. Even her minor sketches. I sold all twenty-one pieces."

The artist could be as bourgeois as any stockbroker, Josie thought. She didn't like the portrait of this man at all. He was a cliché, and greedy, besides.

"But I have works that are related to her." He pointed the cigarette holder at the group of muddy paintings on the wall. "If you want works of great personal meaning, may I suggest these? I call them *Halley, One Through Six*. They show the six stages of love, from the springtime budding"—he flicked the cigarette holder at a bilious green canvas—"to its inevitable death." The flat gray canvas looked like a basement wall.

Josie peeked at the price tag on the gray one. Eight thousand dollars. No matter what color he used, Evelyn liked green.

He skittered across the floor and made a sweeping gesture that took in all six canvases. He didn't spill a drop of wine. "This is the story of our love. Alas, there was no happy ending."

Alas? Josie thought. Did he really say "alas"?

"I brought her up from nowhere," Evelyn said. "I believed in her. I made her a New York success. Then, suddenly, she didn't know me. Still, it's better to love, even if I was betrayed. I've put my suffering on canvas. I've painted out my pain. It's made me a better artist."

Josie couldn't imagine how Evelyn could be worse. The six paintings looked stale and derivative, even to her untrained eye.

The artist waved his cigarette holder at a white canvas with a rusty red slash down the middle.

"That is my love, engulfed by my loneliness," he said. "White is the color of mourning. Red is for our passion."

Josie thought it had the passion of a paint sample at Home Depot.

"I can see your feelings," Alyce said.

"Of course you can," Evelyn said, throwing his arms wide. "But are you capable of feeling them?"

"I think you're still angry at her," Josie said.

"I am, dear girl." Evelyn smiled at her as if she were a prize pupil. "Halley threw her talent away on silk scarves. Trifles for the rich. I would have never let her enter that contest if I thought she'd abandon her art for commercial success."

Especially when she didn't cut you in, Josie thought.

"We'd like to find someone who knew her in the early days," Alyce said. "Before you, I mean. We're willing to pay."

Josie was startled by Alyce's blunt statement.

"How much?" Evelyn said.

Alyce understood the man. Josie had underestimated his crassness.

"Two hundred dollars," Alyce said. "We're trying to locate the novelist Ramsey."

"Forget it," Evelyn said. "He's in deep hiding. An unhappy papa is chasing Ramsey with a shotgun."

"Is the daughter pregnant?" Josie asked.

"Worse," Evelyn said. "Crazy. Ramsey romanced her, promised to marry her, then skipped. Poor girl tried to slash her wrists. She'll miss at least a semester at Smith. Very sad. Her parents are positively homicidal. Ramsey took off after the father shot out his car windows—while he was sitting inside. He didn't tell a soul where he's hiding. Ramsey dare not show his face until she's out of the loony bin. He won't be back for months."

Evelyn sounded gleeful. He took another gulp of wine. "I'd like to take your money, dear lady, but I have no information to give you. Are you sure you won't consider my Halley series?"

"Sorry," Josie said. "But here's my card if you spot Ramsey."

"And there's another hundred dollars if you can find him in a week," Alyce said.

Evelyn stared at her. "I know who you are," he said. "That wig may fool some, but I have an artist's eye. You're the wife of Halley's killer."

"He's innocent," Alyce said.

"Your secret is safe with me, dear lady. I admire your faith. I'll do my best to find Ramsey," Evelyn said. "You will remember that bonus, won't you?"

"How could I forget?" Alyce said.

On the walk back to the car, Josie said, "Did you see what Evelyn was charging for his awful paintings? Eight thou apiece."

"Charging is one thing," Alyce said. "Getting it is another."

Josie stumbled over an uneven sidewalk. "Do you really think he'll call us for three hundred dollars?"

"He'd sell his grandmother for fifty cents," Alyce said. "If he finds out where Ramsey is, he'll call. We've got to find Ramsey. He spends so much time on the city's seamy side, he's bound to know something useful."

"I have a plan," Josie said, unlocking the car doors. "Watch this."

She waited until Alyce was in the car, then pulled out her cell phone. Josie speed-dialed Ramsey's number.

"Congratulations, sir," she said. "This is Marcus Marketing Services. We are inviting qualified adults to mystery-shop hotels and cruise lines. Your name was given to us by Mrs. Renata Livermore."

Alyce's eyebrows shot up, but she stayed quiet.

"If you are willing to take a free twenty-one-day Caribbean cruise on the Rolland-Canada Line to rate the food and service, we will provide you with airfare from St. Louis to Fort Lauderdale. All your expenses will be paid, but you must fill out our thirty-page evaluation form. If you do not fill out the form, you will be responsible for payment in full for the seven-thousand-dollar cruise.

"If you are interested, we must hear from you within forty-eight hours." Josie gave her cell phone number, then snapped her phone shut with a satisfied smile.

"Think he'll call back?" Alyce said.

"I'm betting this guy is broke and desperate to get out of town. I give him fifteen minutes. Let's head home."

Ramsey called back half an hour later. Josie pulled off the road to take the call.

"Marcus Marketing Services," she said.

"Did you call and offer me a free cruise?" Ramsey said.

"It's not free, sir," Josie said, "unless you are willing to do the thirty-page evaluation. And there is an eleven-dollar port tax."

"Yes, yes, I understand that. When can I leave?" Ramsey said.

"We have cruises open in six weeks," Josie said. "Also, four weeks, two weeks, and if you are able to leave in two days—"

"I'll take that one."

"Fine," Josie said. "We'll send a courier to your home with the paperwork and tickets. What's your address?"

"I'm in St. Ann, just off St. Charles Rock Road," Ramsey said.

"Good," Josie said. "Our courier will be there in about forty minutes. Look for a woman with black hair." She hung up.

"Who has black hair?" Alyce asked.

"Me," Josie said, reaching into her bag and plopping on a straight black wig. "What do you think?"

"Cher should be so lucky," Alyce said.

"The great American novelist is hiding out by the airport," Josie said.

It was four o'clock. The afternoon traffic was starting to thicken into a rush hour stew, but Josie pulled in front of a worn green bungalow in forty-two minutes. The screen door was ripped and the front stoop was cracked.

"This doesn't look like a carriage house in the West End," Alyce said.

"It wouldn't be a toolshed there," Josie said. "Ramsey screwed up big-time. No wonder he's desperate to leave town."

She knocked on the door, and chips of paint flicked to the broken concrete.

Ramsey had used every art to preserve his fading beauty. His deep tan was fake, and so were his white teeth. His blond hair was brassy and needed a color treatment.

"Are you from the cruise line?" He smiled, and the tan cracked into a hundred lines.

"I have your papers right here." Josie held up a fat manila envelope stuffed with blank mystery-shopper reports. "This is my associate."

Alyce nodded.

"Come in, come in," he said. "Let's start signing."

The living room was bare except for a plaid couch with a nasty brown stain, a battered TV, and a set of barbells on the dusty floor.

"Well," he said, rubbing his hands together. "What do you need from me?"

"Everything you know about Halley Hardwicke," Josie said.

Ramsey turned green under his tan. "What? What is this? You're supposed to give me the papers for my cruise."

"Sorry. Your cruise is canceled," Josie said. "But I'm

offering you the deal of a lifetime. You talk to me about
Halley, or I'll tell that poor girl's parents where you're
staying."

"You can't do that," Ramsey said. "They'll kill me."

"And that would be a great loss how?" Josie said.

She pulled out her cell phone. "What's it going to be,
Ramsey? Lots of people are gunning for you right now.
I could make them very happy. I don't think that front
door would ward off a shotgun blast."

"I'll talk, but I don't know much about Halley."

"We'll take what we can get," Josie said. "Spill."

Ramsey flopped down on the stained couch. Josie and
Alyce stayed standing. "I met Halley about a year and
a half ago, when she was at loose ends. She didn't like
living in the suburbs. She wanted to go back to New
York, where she belonged. We had a few gins and grins
and then I introduced her to an artist named Evelyn."

"There were no hard feelings when you broke it off?"

"No," Ramsey said. "As soon as she figured out that
Evelyn could sponsor her for that contest, she latched
on to him like he was Brad Pitt. She flattered the little
faggot outrageously. I figured she had to blow him to
get the sponsorship. Once she won the contest, she
couldn't dump him fast enough. I don't know how she
stood him as long as she did."

Josie didn't know how Ramsey could look in the mirror without flinching, but that wasn't her business.

"Evelyn said that Halley was the love of his life,"
Josie said.

Ramsey burst out laughing, a big, ugly sound that
bounced around the nearly empty room. "Halley wasn't
his great love. She was his great meal ticket. Evelyn
expected her to introduce him to all her country-club
friends and provide him with an endless supply of rich
patrons. He was prepared to sell out and do representa-
tional art, even dog and cat portraits. Evelyn knew he
had no talent. He thought he could ride her coattails
and make major money.

"Halley wasn't going to have Evelyn prancing around
her snooty friends. He was an embarrassment. She gave

him the boot. Humiliated him, actually. I was there. She called him a closet queen and said if he ever came near her again, she'd have him arrested for stalking.

"Evelyn was heartbroken, all right, but it wasn't about lost love. It was about lost money. He was furious at Halley. If she'd been shot by a skinny white guy, instead of a skinny black one, I'd swear the killer was Evelyn. That's all I know. I can't believe someone like you tricked me."

"It's another sign you're getting old," Josie said.

Ramsey winced.

"Aren't you tired of dodging murderous daddies?" Josie said. "It's time to find a sweet old widow with lots of money and settle down, Ramsey."

She and Alyce were out the broken door before he could answer.

"Well, that was interesting," Alyce said, back in the car. "But I'm not sure what we got."

"A motive," Josie said. "Evelyn had a good reason to kill Halley."

Chapter 20

"Do you know Jake Bohannon?" screamed a bushy-haired man in a rumpled suit.

"What do you think of an alleged murderer living in your neighborhood?" yelled a skinny woman in a plaid blazer.

The unruly mob of reporters shouted questions as Josie's gray Honda slowly rolled through the gates of Wood Winds. One even shoved a microphone against the window. Josie ignored it and kept on driving.

Alyce was unmoving as a mannequin and pale as a mourner in a funeral procession. All the color was washed from her face. Her red wig looked like a brush fire.

Josie patted her friend's hand. "We're nearly home," she said. "It's almost over."

"It will never be over," Alyce said in a dead voice. "It was worse this morning with Jake. The reporters asked awful questions. One woman said, 'What's it like to live with a murderer?' "

"Ohmigod," Josie said. "I can't believe she asked that. Keep the wig. At least you can get in and out of here without being recognized."

"Whose SUV is parked in my driveway?" Alyce said. "Did a reporter get through the guards?"

A woman popped out of the driver's side with a football-sized foil-wrapped package, and Alyce gave a shaky laugh. "It's little Joanie Protzel, bringing me more food."

Joanie waited for them to park. "I've got a nice roast chicken and some grilled vegetables," she said. "I thought you'd be tired of cold cuts."

"That's so sweet," Alyce said. "Come inside."

The energetic Joanie followed Alyce into the kitchen. She plunked the foil football on the granite island and unveiled a roast bird the size of a small turkey. "That should be enough for dinner and some nice sandwiches."

"Thank you so much, Joanie," Alyce said. "I didn't want to think about cooking tonight."

She didn't? Josie had never thought she'd hear her friend say those words. Alyce adored cooking. Her life really was derailed.

"Want some coffee or a glass of wine, Joanie?" Alyce said.

"You can stay for one drink," Josie said. It was an order. Alyce needed company after surviving the media gauntlet at the gate. She had to believe all her neighbors didn't hate her.

"I—" Joanie hesitated. "A little coffee, but I can't stay long. Did you change your hair color, Alyce? It's very striking."

"You're too polite, Joanie," Alyce said. "It's a wig and it looks awful, but it's a good disguise." She pulled it off and shook out her blond hair. The floaty strands stuck straight out, thanks to static electricity. Alyce smoothed them back in place.

"Now you look like the Alyce we know," Joanie said.

The kitchen doorbell rang. Linda Dattilo was at the door. Once again, Josie was startled by Linda's vivid red gold hair and green eyes. The unearthly combination belonged on a movie star, not a soccer mom.

"I have good news," Linda said. "Mrs. Livermore has pulled some big strings. By tomorrow noon, we'll have No Parking signs installed along the road to Wood Winds. No more press vans and TV trucks. The reporters won't be able to get closer than two miles."

"Thank God," Alyce said. She gave Linda coffee *and* white wine.

"Here's the best part," Linda said. "Old Mrs. Liverspot insisted a cop should be posted on the road for the next few days to hand out tickets. She's getting one, too."

"A ticket?" Josie said.

"A pet cop," Linda said.

"Let me heat up some cranberry scones," Alyce said.

"Show them your citrus trumpet," Josie said.

"What's that?" Linda said.

Suddenly, Alyce's kitchen was filled with laughter and lively chatter. Coffee was perking. The oven was preheating. A timer dinged. Alyce was rummaging in the refrigerator and everyone was talking at once.

Alyce had a smile on her face and color in her cheeks. Josie hadn't seen her look so relaxed since Jake's arrest.

The stairs creaked, and Josie looked up. There he was, the man who'd caused Alyce so much misery. In his pressed khakis and polo shirt, Jake looked like he was ready to play eighteen holes. The arrest hadn't taken a toll on his looks.

Jake was handsome, if you liked that kind of man, Josie thought. His thick dark hair was meticulously cut. His eyes were heavy lidded and his nose was slightly too long. Josie couldn't decide if he looked aristocratic or arrogant. Maybe the two were the same.

"Hi, ladies," Jake said. "Am I interrupting a party? Thought I'd come down for a little coffee."

Silence. Josie wondered if the other women were stunned by the presence of a real, live alleged murderer.

Alyce filled the awkward silence with quick introductions: "This is Joanie Protzel. She brought us those delicious deli platters. Tonight, she fixed us a whole roast chicken."

"Roast chicken?" Jake said, and smiled. "My favorite. You're the lovely lady who's been giving us such wonderful meals. This is real comfort food, Joanie. Just what we need. I can't thank you enough."

Joanie blushed. Jake's charm was definitely working on her.

Alyce continued the introductions. "This is Linda Dattilo. She lives in our subdivision. She and Joanie both do, actually."

"Linda." Jake gave her a royal nod.

"I think we've met before," Linda said.

"Oh," Jake said. "Of course."

More silence. Then something seemed to click on in Jake's brain. "You're the decorator. Didn't you do the Hendersons' new house on Willow Way?"

"That's me," Linda said.

"Clever work with that dining room," Jake said. "That room always looked so dark until you transformed it."

"I didn't think you'd notice," Linda said.

"The Hendersons told everyone what a super job you did," Jake said, sidestepping the issue.

Linda seems as wary of him as I am, Josie thought. But Joanie was definitely impressed. Now Josie could see why Alyce fell for Jake. He could be irresistible when he worked at it.

"And you know who this is," Alyce said, taking Josie by the arm.

There was a slight pause, and Alyce prompted, "I don't have to introduce my best friend."

"Josie, right?" he said.

"Right," Josie said. Jake still doesn't quite remember me, she thought. Why am I wasting my time helping him?

"Alyce tells me you've been a huge help to her—and me, too. I hope when things are . . . resolved, I'll be able to thank you properly."

OK, Josie decided, that speech was nearly as handsome as Jake. If he forgot my name, well, he does have a few things on his mind right now. He gets a pass this time.

Alyce was beaming, pleased her husband had made a good impression on her friends. She handed him a cup of black coffee and a buttered scone on a blue plate.

Josie's cell phone played her favorite U2 tune. "Excuse me," she said. "This could be my mom or my daughter. I have to take this." She moved toward the breakfast room and opened her phone.

It wasn't her family. It was Evelyn. The artist's voice was shrill with rage. "I heard what that awful Ramsey said—that I only wanted Halley because of her rich friends."

"What?" Josie said. Why was Evelyn screaming at her? "Evelyn, what's wrong?"

"Ramsey called me, the slime. He said you'd been to visit him. He wouldn't tell me where he was or I'd tell you. If I knew how to reach that girl's parents, I'd tell them, too. He deserves to be shot."

"Evelyn, I know where Ramsey is," Josie said. "I found his hiding place. I tricked him and he's not happy. I don't know what he told you, but I'm sure he's just lashing out."

"Ramsey said it was time to set the record straight about my so-called great love. He said he'd make sure everyone knew what Halley said to me when we broke up. I'll never sell my *Halley, One Through Six* if he does that. She didn't mean it. It's what lovers say when they're angry."

"I'm sure," Josie said. She wasn't sure at all. Halley had hurled some hurtful invective.

"I loved her," Evelyn said. "My art is proof of my love. Everyone can see that. But I know someone who didn't love Halley. I'll tell you who killed her."

"Tell the police, Evelyn."

"The police won't listen to me. I'll tell you, but only in person."

Josie sighed. The silly little man was such a drama queen. No wonder Halley had wanted rid of him. Josie was tired of Evelyn after one encounter.

"You have to come here. Right now." Evelyn's voice climbed to a birdlike screech. His words were slurred. Josie definitely didn't want to meet a drunk.

"Evelyn, I can't come there. I have a family. I have to go home."

"Come here right now!" he shrieked. "Maybe you're not interested, but your friend Alyce will be. How much does a murder defense cost these days? At least two hundred fifty thousand dollars, and that's if it doesn't go to trial. Once that happens, the price goes up."

His voice turned soft and wheedling. "I can save

Alyce big money, and my information will only cost her fifty thousand dollars."

"Fifty thousand!" Josie realized she was screeching, too. She moved deeper into the breakfast room and lowered her voice. "Alyce doesn't have that kind of money."

"She'll have to have it for the trial. She can give it to me instead of some crooked lawyer. Her husband's innocent, and I can prove it. But you have to see me tonight."

"Evelyn, we can't come tonight. But we'll be there tomorrow. Say, ten o'clock?"

"All right. I don't like waiting, but I'll possess myself in patience. Bring your friend Alyce—and her checkbook."

Josie hung up the phone and saw everyone staring at her: Jake, Linda, Joanie, and most of all Alyce.

"What was that about?" Alyce said.

"Nothing," Josie said. "Just someone being overly dramatic."

"I'd better go," Joanie said. "My husband is due home any minute."

"Mine, too," Linda said.

A wail from upstairs announced that Justin was awake and demanding attention.

"My turn to check on the boy," Jake said, and ran upstairs. Josie gave him points for dealing with a cranky kid.

The kitchen party was over. A few good-byes, and Josie was alone in Alyce's kitchen, surrounded by empty cups and crumb-dotted plates.

Her cell phone rang again. If it was Evelyn, she wasn't answering. But Josie recognized the number. It was Harry the Horrible, with two more awful assignments: Down & Dirty Discount stores and Chunk-A-Chicken.

Chunk-A-Chicken lived up to its name. It served chicken elbows and knees in greasy gravy. Josie loved most fast food, but she couldn't stomach gravy-coated gristle. Harry was still making her suffer for Saber.

"How many Chunk-A-Chickens do I have to shop?" she said.

"All fifteen locations," Harry said.

Josie's stomach dropped like a broken elevator.

"Oh, Josie," Harry said. "They want you to sample the fries and gravy, too."

"You're doing this on purpose," Josie said.

"There's no connection between these assignments and the fact that poor little Saber got fired," Harry said.

"She did?" Josie couldn't keep the smile out of her voice. She'd accomplished something after all.

"Bite me," Harry said.

"It can't be worse than a Chunk-A-Chicken," Josie said, but her boss had already hung up.

Alyce came downstairs, carrying a chubby-cheeked Justin. They had a brief session of baby kissing and cooing. When Justin was installed in his high chair with some Cheerios, Alyce said, "What was going on with Evelyn?"

"Is it that obvious?" Josie said.

"That you were hiding something? It was to me."

"Evelyn says he knows who killed Halley," Josie said.

"Josie! Why didn't you say so sooner?" Alyce said.

Josie shrugged. "Because I don't believe him. Evelyn would have told the police if he really knew who the killer was. He wouldn't miss the free publicity. Evelyn would love to prance around on the six o'clock news, saying he caught the killer."

"What's this about fifty thousand dollars?"

"He says if you can come up with that much money, he'll give you proof that Jake is innocent."

"Josie! This is the break we've been looking for."

"No, it's not," Josie said. "Evelyn is a sponger. He knew you were willing to pay for information, and he's trying to take you for your last dime."

"Then why did you agree to see him?"

"Because I want to talk to him about his farewell scene with Halley. Calling a man a closet queen is one strong motive for murder. Dashing his hopes for major money is another. Look at that guy. He's skinny as a boy. With the right makeup and a stocking cap, he could pass as a young African-American male. He could be our shooter."

"So you're going to see him alone?" Alyce said. "Brilliant plan, Josie. Then he can shoot you, too."

"I'm not afraid of him. I outweigh him."

"Not when he has a gun," Alyce said.

"If he killed Halley, he caught her by surprise. He can't surprise me."

"You're not going there alone," Alyce said.

"Yes, I am."

"No, you're not. I'm going with you. Tell me what time, Josie, or I'll tell your mother."

"That's ridiculous."

"Not as ridiculous as seeing a killer alone," Alyce said.

"OK, ten o'clock. I'll pick you up at nine. I'm mystery-shopping Chunk-A-Chickens tomorrow, and I know you don't want to go with me."

"Yuck," Alyce said.

"My feeling exactly."

Josie's cell phone rang for the third time in ten minutes. "How did I get so popular all of a sudden?" She looked at the number and winced. It was her mother.

"Where are you, Josie?" Jane said. "It's after five. You have to come home. We have trouble."

"What kind of trouble, Mom?"

"The city inspector was here all afternoon. He says we have lead paint on the garage and it has to be repainted. It will cost a fortune. Someone complained about it."

Older houses were vulnerable to visits from the city inspector. "Do you think Mrs. Mueller turned you in?" Josie said.

"Absolutely not. She's my friend. Besides, he gave her a citation for the lead paint on her garage, too."

"I thought he cited us because of a complaint."

"He did. But Mrs. Mueller said something because his car was parked in front of her house, and he wrote up her garage."

Josie smothered a laugh. Her mother's next words wiped the smile off her face completely.

"The inspector also said the porch railings have to be replaced."

"I'm sorry, Mom. That's expensive."

"Someone named Skip wants to talk to you about a job at the Booby Trap."

"The strip joint?" What was going on? Josie felt her life spinning out of control.

"I have no idea what a place like that does," Jane said. "He sounded rough, Josie. You didn't really apply to work there, did you?"

"Of course not, Mom. It must be some kind of joke," Josie said.

"What about the magazines?" her mother said.

"What magazines?" Josie said.

"The mailman delivered a huge stack of them. I've counted forty-two so far."

"I'd better come home," Josie said.

Chapter 21

Forbes. Field & Stream. Redbook. Real Simple. Magazines were piled waist-high in Josie's front hall.

There were magazines she'd never heard of, like *All About Beer.* Magazines she'd never need, like *European Cigar Cult Journal.* Magazines she'd never read, like *Black Men's Swimsuit Extra.* And magazines she couldn't read if she wanted, like *Cosmopolitan en Español.*

What joker sent her *Gourmet?* Or any of the other forty-odd magazines littering her floor? Just looking at the heaps of glossy paper made her back ache. Her mail carrier must have a hernia.

"What's going on, Josie?" her mother said.

"I don't know, Mom," Josie said. "It has to be a mistake."

"What are you going to do?"

"Start canceling subscriptions," Josie said.

"Can I have this?" Amelia waved a copy of *InStyle.*

Josie handed her daughter a copy of *Inc.* "Here," she said. "Read this business magazine first. Then you'll be able to buy yourself the clothes in the fashion magazines."

"Really, Josie," her mother said. "You ought to be glad Amelia is interested in good grooming."

"I don't want my daughter to be a Barbie doll," Josie said.

"Barbies are so twentieth century, Mom," Amelia said.

Josie hugged her daughter. "Did I forget to tell you how smart you are?"

"No problemo," Amelia said. It was her favorite phrase.

Sometime after the phone call to cancel *Gourmet,* but long before *Allure,* Josie heard her doorbell ring.

"I'm stuck on the phone," she told her mother.

"I'll get it," Jane called.

A minute later, Jane was back. "Excuse me, Josie. Did you order a lot of things from L.L. Bean?"

"No," Josie said.

"UPS has twenty packages for you."

"Twenty! Ohmigod. Could you refuse them, Mom? All of them. It's a mistake. I'd do it myself, but I'm on hold to the subscription department."

"Is this another joke?" Jane said.

"No, this isn't funny," Josie said.

After more than a dozen phone calls, Josie learned that someone had used her MasterCard, Visa, and Discover numbers to make purchases online and by telephone. The thief even had her security numbers and expiration dates.

"But I have my cards in my purse," Josie said. "I didn't lose them."

"Happens all the time," a credit-card-company representative told her. "You'll have to cancel them."

Josie was on hold again when Jane returned, her forehead creased with worry. "You have fifteen boxes from the Pottery Barn."

"Refuse them, please. What?" Josie said into the phone. "What's my expiration date? Lady, I expired a long time ago. No, I'm sorry. I didn't mean that. It's February 2010."

"Josie!" her mother said. "Will you pay attention? What about The Territory Ahead? They've sent you seventeen packages."

"I didn't order anything from them, either," Josie said. "I didn't order anything from anyone."

"How about Tiffany's?" Jane said. "You have ten Tiffany's boxes."

"Do I look like someone who would order from Tiffany's?"

"You don't have to get snippy with me, Josie Marcus. I'm just trying to help." Jane stomped out of the room.

The credit-card representative came back on the phone, asking for more information. "What's my mother's maiden name?" Josie said. "It's Snead. Like Sam Snead, the golfer. You never heard of him? He was before Tiger Woods. Woods. Yes. No, my mother's maiden name is *not* Woods."

Jane came hurrying back, wringing her hands. "Josie, there is a UPS man with fourteen boxes from Victoria's Secret."

Josie was tempted to keep the sexy lingerie. After all, she had a date with Mike. But she didn't know if it was her size. What if it was something sleazy, like crotchless panties? Or were they from Frederick's of Hollywood? Josie thought she got a delivery from that catalog, too.

"Please, Mom, just say no to everything. I'm on the phone canceling the subscription to *Fitness* magazine."

"Maybe you should keep that magazine," Jane said.

"Over my dead body," Josie said, then realized that was probably the wrong answer. "I don't need *Fitness* magazine. I'll get enough exercise lifting these magazines. Hello?" she said into the phone. "What are the first six digits on the address label? Eight, two—"

The packages kept coming. Jane turned away cashmere sweaters, a flat-screen monitor, and a new computer system. Josie nearly wept when she thought of that computer going back on the delivery truck. She worked on a slow, cranky machine bought at a garage sale.

Jane refused an iPod and broke Amelia's heart. She turned away luxurious bonbons and fruit baskets from Harry & David. She said no to stylish UGG boots and skimpy bikinis.

The deliveries came by FedEx, UPS, and companies Josie never heard of.

Meanwhile, Josie's right ear grew red while she hung on the phone, canceling magazines and straightening out her credit cards.

Josie knew it was only the start of her misery. It would be months before she had all the charges removed.

When there was a lull in the deliveries, Jane came back, looking guilty. "Josie," she said. "You know I'm still seeing a psychologist for my little shopping problem."

Actually, it was a big problem. Jane was addicted to the Home Shopping Network.

"But I didn't order these things," Jane said.

"I know, Mom."

"Then who did?" Jane said.

Before Josie could answer, there was another knock at the door, and a man appeared with twenty pepperoni pizzas. Jane sent them all back.

"Couldn't we keep one?" Amelia said.

"No," Josie said, more sharply than she intended.

Amelia's face clouded.

"GBH," Josie said, and gave her daughter a hug. "I'm sorry. I'm upset about the packages and magazines being dumped on us, but that's no excuse to bark at you."

"Who did this, Josie?" Jane repeated.

"I don't know, Mom."

But Josie had her suspicions: little Saber, the seriously rude salesclerk, or her evil uncle Harry. Saber had a lot of free time now that she was unemployed.

"Mom, it's seven thirty," Amelia said. "This is our Girls' Book Night. We have a date."

Once a month, Josie and Amelia went to the bookstore. Amelia could buy one book for ten dollars or less. She was addicted to Lisi Harrison's nearly endless $9.99 Clique series. Amelia had gone through *Best Friends for Never, Revenge of the Wannabes,* and *Invasion of the Boy Snatchers.* Tonight, Amelia had her sights set on *Dial L for Loser.*

"I really—" Josie started to say she didn't want to go to a bookstore tonight. She was exhausted. But how many kids begged to read books these days?

She changed her mind in midsentence. "—don't want to make one more phone call. I need to get away. Mom, can you hold the fort while Amelia and I run to the bookstore?"

"Good. You need to relax," Jane said. "You can get a latte and read a magazine while Amelia looks for her books."

Josie stared at her mother and the heaps of magazines. "I hope that was a joke," she said.

"I forgot," Jane said. "What do you want me to do while you're gone?"

"Just say no," Josie said. "No matter what it is, send it back. I didn't order it."

It was a relief to get out of the house, away from the endless mountains of magazines. The night air was clear and crisp. Amelia chattered about her best friend, Emma, and her plans to redecorate her bathroom. Josie had given Amelia permission to repaint after the water disaster.

"I'm thinking purple, Mom. What do you think?"

"If that's what you want."

"That's my fave color. Emma's, too. Emma wants to do her whole bedroom in purple, but her mother said it's a very tiring color. She won't allow it."

"Her mother's right," Josie said.

"Then why are you allowing me?"

"It's your bathroom," Josie said. "It's going to stay purple for a long time."

She thought her daughter should learn to live with her mistakes, at least the small, easily fixable ones. It was good training. Mistakes only got bigger when you got older. There was no way Alyce could paint Jake out of her life.

"Cool," Amelia said. "Is that a cop on your tail?"

"I'm going two miles below the speed limit," Josie said.

The car was filled with strobing red and blue light.

"Sugar," Josie said.

"It's OK, Mom. You can say the real word," Amelia said. "You're entitled."

The cop who swaggered over to the car was boyishly

cute. He had a cowlick, short brown hair, and a dimple on his chin. Josie thought the long arm of the law looked good.

"May I see your license and registration, ma'am?" Officer Cutie said.

Ma'am? Josie's heart sank. She'd been hearing that too often lately. Store clerks used to call her "miss." Now she was "ma'am." Her fantasies about Officer Cutie went out the window as she handed him her driver's license.

"Do you realize that you don't have any brake lights or rear license plate?" he asked.

"You're kidding," Josie said. "I mean, of course you're not kidding, Officer. But this is the perfect end to a rotten day. Somebody sent truckloads of items I didn't order to my house, along with forty or fifty magazines, and—"

"Twenty pizzas," Amelia said. "Somebody sent us twenty pizzas and Mom wouldn't let me keep even one pepperoni."

"My credit-card numbers were stolen and I'm being harassed," Josie said.

"Whoa," the cop said. "Back up there. And go a little slower."

Josie recited her tale of woe once again, ending with, "Now you tell me my license plate and brake lights are gone."

"I'm sorry, ma'am, but it's true."

"Are you going to give me a ticket?" Josie said.

"I think your day has been punishment enough," the cop said. "But you'd better get that fixed first thing tomorrow morning, miss."

Miss. She's been upgraded to "miss."

"You're going to have to make a report on that missing license plate," he said.

"Could you do it for me here, right now, please? I don't have time to make any more calls tonight. It's all I've done for hours."

"She's really stressed-out," Amelia added. "She yelled at me for nothing."

The cop took the report. "Remember what I told you. If I see you driving around without those brake lights tomorrow, I will give you a ticket. Now, go straight home. You can't be on the streets at night without brake lights."

Josie went home. Her neighbor Stan the Man Next Door was waiting in front of her house with a flashlight and a toolbox.

"Josie, do you know that your brake lights are out?" he said.

"The police just stopped me," she said. "I'll get them fixed in the morning."

"I'll look at them now," he said.

Stan wore a shapeless hooded jacket pulled tight around his face, making him look like the Unabomber.

Josie sighed. Stan had such a good heart. If only he were as handsome outside as he was inside. She'd tried to give him a makeover, but he refused. Stan was too stubborn to change and she was too shallow to accept him as he was.

"Josie, open the trunk so I can get to work," Stan said.

Josie started to refuse. It would be cruel to take advantage of Stan's crush on her. But her credit cards were canceled, and the new ones wouldn't arrive until after ten thirty tomorrow. She'd have trouble paying a mechanic. Besides, Stan liked to tinker as much as Alyce liked to cook. It was recreation. She couldn't deny the man a little fun.

"Sure, Stan," she said. "Thanks." She popped the trunk.

"Hold the flashlight," he said. Stan poked and prodded inside the trunk and underneath the car.

"Someone did this deliberately," he said. "The wires have been disconnected. I've hooked them back together."

"Thank you, Stan," Josie said.

"I didn't do anything."

"You were there when I needed you," Josie said.

Stan blushed to the tips of his large ears.

"Mom, can we go in now?" Amelia said.

"You could have gone in anytime," Josie said. Stan's hopeless romance was a live soap opera. Her nosy daughter would rather freeze than miss a single episode.

"Thank you again, Stan," Josie said.

She left him on her sidewalk, staring at her front door. Josie felt sad. She should have invited him in, but that would only make Stan's unrequited love worse. She stepped over the mounds of magazines on the hall floor. They seemed to have grown.

"Mom?" Josie said. She heard the TV blaring in the living room. A big cardboard box squatted near the coffee table. Josie caught the faint odor of cigarette smoke. Jane had been hitting the cigs again. Josie decided to say nothing. She'd caused her mother enough worry today. If a cigarette made Jane feel better, let her have one.

Her mother was snoring openmouthed on the couch. Jane looked old and vulnerable, sprawled across the cushions. She woke when Josie turned down the TV.

"I didn't mean to fall asleep at eight o'clock," Jane said. "Suddenly, I was so tired."

"This has worn you out. Any more disasters?"

"You had two more deliveries," Jane said. "I refused the first one, but the second box was left on the front porch while I was on the phone with the handyman. He says he'll have to repaint the old garage. He has to give me an estimate on that. The new porch railings are going to cost me more than a thousand dollars."

Josie groaned. "I'm sorry, Mom."

"It's not your fault," Jane said.

But Josie thought it was. Saber's revenge was costing her mother far more than Josie.

"Look, Mom, I'll pay for the railings and the garage. It will take me a little time to come up with the money, but—"

"You'll do no such thing, Josie. This house is my responsibility. You take care of my granddaughter. That's your job. I should have had those things fixed years ago. I've been on borrowed time."

Jane somehow managed to look defiant, sitting sleepily on the couch. Her mother was always prepared to fight, and she usually won.

"I'm afraid to ask," Josie said. "But what was the other delivery?"

"It's right there by the door," Jane said. "A case of California wine."

"I'll keep it."

"Josie! It's ninety dollars a case, plus the shipping."

"Cheap at twice the price," Josie said. "Where's the corkscrew?"

Chapter 22

A pile driver pounded Josie's skull into her spine. Her stomach lurched and staggered like a seasick sailor. She managed to sit upright in the booth at the Majestic Café. For that feat, Josie thought she deserved a Congressional Medal of Honor.

Alyce sat across from her. Even her friend's diet breakfast of black coffee, dry toast, and a poached egg made Josie queasy.

The Majestic was a Central West End fixture, a dark warren of rooms and booths where the servers knew everybody and everything. Alyce wore the red wig Josie had given her. The vibrant color hurt Josie's eyes this morning.

"Here," Josie said, "have a bottle of wine." Strange how that dignified bottle had caused such roiling havoc in her gut.

Alyce read the label. " 'Topolos Vineyards. Sonoma County. Alicante Bouschet.' I'm impressed. This is first-class wine."

"It gave me a first-class hangover," Josie said. The room seemed to be swaying. A private earthquake rumbled in her head. Lined up in front of her was breakfast: a cup of black coffee, a glass of water, three aspirin, and a bottle of Maalox.

"How much did you drink?"

"The whole bottle," Josie said. "Mom didn't want any."

"Oh, Josie," Alyce said. "Don't you want some breakfast?"

Josie's stomach and all the nearby precincts rebelled. "No, I'll have more coffee and another aspirin."

"Are you sure you want to mystery-shop Chunk-A-Chickens after we see Evelyn?" Alyce said. "I don't think you should go there when you feel so bad."

Josie fought back a bilious belch. "Why waste a good day on Chunk-A-Chicken?"

"Maybe you should go home and rest." Alyce opened her poached egg with a fork, and the runny yellow inside spread across the toast. Josie's stomach shivered. She tried not to look.

"I need the money," Josie said. "Besides, if I went home, I wouldn't rest. I'd be dealing with more fallout from the festival of orders."

"Has everything been returned, except the wine?" Alyce said.

"Yep, we did that last night. Mom was a big help. I couldn't have done it without her. It was pure torture sending some of those things back, especially the cashmere sweaters and UGG boots. My winter boots are so old, the black polish doesn't cover the salt stains anymore.

"I hated returning that new flat-screen computer, too. And Amelia really wanted the iPod. Whoever did this knew how to torment me twice: first, with all the cancellation calls, then with all the things I can't have."

"Somebody really wanted to get you," Alyce said.

"It has to be Saber or her uncle Harry."

"Harry already got you," Alyce said. "He's giving you every wretched assignment he can dream up. I don't think Saber would do this. It's too much work. She's lazy. You saw how she draped herself along that counter. She hates to move. She'd have to log major time on the phone to pull this off."

"Who else could it be?" Josie said. "I haven't given any other stores bad reports lately."

"I think it has to do with our investigation," Alyce said. "Someone is trying to stop you."

"Couldn't they just slash my tires?" Josie said. "This mess will take weeks to straighten out, even if I don't get any more deliveries."

"That's what they want. To keep you tied up so you can't help me."

"What help?" Josie said. "The only thing I've found out so far is I can't drink a whole bottle of wine."

"You're making people nervous, or they wouldn't do this."

"How did they get my credit-card numbers?" Josie said.

"There's all sorts of ways to steal credit-card information, Josie."

"All three cards?"

"They can hack into your computer. They can pull your statements out of your trash."

"I tear them up," Josie said.

"In how many pieces?"

"Two. Or four."

"Too easy to piece together," Alyce said. "Look, Josie, I don't know how it was done, but someone got your credit cards. Someone wants to stop you."

"Well, they're not going to," Josie said. "This makes me angry." She swallowed the last aspirin, took another swig of Maalox, and gulped her coffee. Her head was throbbing and her gut was lurching.

"It's quarter to ten," Alyce said. "We might as well walk to Evelyn's. It's just around the corner."

"Better check the meter first," Josie said. "They ticket like crazy around here."

Alyce stashed her wine in the back of Josie's car. Josie dutifully fed the meter, and they started walking toward Evelyn's apartment. Soggy dead leaves blew across the sidewalk, and a sharp wind rattled the tree branches. Josie felt better in the cold air.

Evelyn lived on the edge of the West End, where it slid from beautiful to blighted. His Beaux Arts building must have been fashionable once. Now the bricks were covered with a century of grime and the trim needed paint. The art-glass door was missing a pane. The hole was covered with taped cardboard.

"Nice repair job," Alyce said.

"The brown cardboard doesn't clash with the red and yellow glass," Josie said.

The dingy lobby was littered with newspapers and junk mail. The marble tile was gray with dirt.

"Evelyn is on the second floor," Josie said.

"I don't trust that elevator," Alyce said. "Let's take the steps."

Climbing the stairs helped clear Josie's head. A hand-lettered sign tacked over the bell by Evelyn's door said, "Please knock."

Josie did. Evelyn didn't answer. She pounded on the door until her head hurt. Still no answer.

"Are you sure you had the right time?" Alyce said.

"Positive," Josie said. "I wouldn't forget that."

Alyce tried the ornate brass handle. "It's open. He must want us to come in."

"Maybe we'd better call the police," Josie said, pulling out her cell phone. "I don't like this."

"Why? We never lock our doors at Wood Winds," Alyce said.

"And look where it got you," Josie said. She instantly regretted her outburst. Alyce looked like she'd been slapped.

"I'm sorry, Alyce. But most people do lock their doors, especially in this neighborhood." Josie pulled her gloves off and wiped down the doorknob with them. "At least, wear your gloves if we go inside." She put her gloves back on.

"You're being ridiculous," Alyce said. "Hangovers make you paranoid."

"Shh," Josie said. "Evelyn will hear us." She dropped her voice to a whisper. "You're the one who said I shouldn't see a murderer alone."

"You don't really believe Evelyn is a killer, do you?" Alyce said.

"I think he has good reasons to murder Halley," Josie

said. "But he won't hurt us. He wants your money. From the look of this place, he needs it."

Alyce quit arguing and put on her gloves.

"Evelyn," Josie called as she opened the door.

No answer.

"Maybe he went to get coffee," Alyce said. "I'm glad you made me wear gloves. This place is so dirty, I don't want to touch anything."

The dark, narrow hall was nearly blocked by a spindly table littered with bills. Josie parted the pile with a gloved finger. The rent, electric and phone bills were past due.

Black socks were drying on a tilted lampshade. Alyce wrinkled her nose at the yellowing underwear piled in a corner, and delicately stepped over the thin, rucked-up rug.

"Has this apartment been ransacked?" Alyce said.

"I can't tell," Josie said. "He could just be a sloppy housekeeper."

Evelyn used his living room for a studio. Near the majestic bow window was a clutter of brushes and paint tubes. Impatient, discarded sketches littered the floor. A half-finished oil sat on an easel. More canvases were stacked against the wall. Josie thought the paintings were the work of a depressed man. Dark gray, charcoal black, and dirt brown were applied in angry, slashing strokes.

Alyce opened another door. "Ick," she said. "Have you seen the mold on his shower curtain?"

Josie surveyed the dark speckles and black streaks. "Looks like one of his paintings," she said. "Maybe it's his inspiration." She started giggling. So did Alyce.

"We've saved his bedroom for last," Alyce said. "I'm sure it's the highlight of the tour."

"If he's in there, we're going to be really embarrassed," Josie said.

She stood outside the closed bedroom door and called, "Evelyn!"

"Maybe we should just leave," Alyce said. "He's not here."

"No, I have to see where Halley conducted her torrid affair," Josie said.

"How could she stand it?" Alyce asked. "How could she stand him? This is so grubby."

"People will put up with worse than this for the kind of success Halley had," Josie said. "Besides, the bedroom door might be closed for a good reason. The living room is his work space. The bedroom could be the fantasy he created for his lovers. What do you bet? Black satin sheets? Fake-fur bedspread? Mirror on the ceiling?"

"Please," Alyce said. "You're painting pictures I'd rather not see."

"They can't be any worse than Evelyn's," Josie said.

"Oh, yes, they can," Alyce said. She seemed suddenly anxious and uneasy.

Josie was enjoying herself. Her hangover had vanished in the burst of adrenaline. She got a tingle from walking through Evelyn's apartment when he wasn't there. She had to see more.

"Josie, let's go," Alyce said. "Evelyn isn't here. He's not going to help Jake. You were right. He's a con artist."

"In that case, he'd try to talk you out of that fifty thousand dollars. He was drunk last night. I bet he's passed out on his bed with a bad case of wine flu. Either that or he went out for some hair of the dog. He probably left a note somewhere in this chaos, maybe on his refrigerator. We haven't seen the kitchen, either."

"OK," Alyce said. "A quick look around the bedroom and the kitchen and we're out of here. Promise?"

"Promise," Josie said. She knocked on the bedroom door and called again, "Evelyn!"

No answer.

"Here goes," Josie said, and opened the door. A torn shade blocked most of the light. It took a moment to adjust to the dim room.

"I can't imagine Halley here," Alyce whispered. "This is beyond sordid."

"It's not that bad," Josie said. "It looks like a college crash pad."

Now Josie could see a fat ginger-jar lamp squatting

on a chipped brown table. On the floor was a mattress and box spring piled with limp sheets and dirty laundry. Blooming in the center, like a flower on a trash heap, was a Halley-blue scarf.

"This place stinks," Alyce said. "He could at least air it out. Why does it smell like old diapers? Isn't he a bachelor?"

"He was," Josie said. She approached the bed cautiously. The pleasant tingle had escalated into sharp stabs of fear.

"He got married?" Alyce stayed in the doorway. She would not enter the bedroom.

"He got dead," Josie said. "That's not a pile of old clothes. That's Evelyn."

Chapter 23

Alyce stayed frozen, five feet from the rumpled bed. She refused to move closer, as if Evelyn could drag her into death's embrace.

Josie crept to the edge of the bed. It took all her nerve, but she had to make sure he was dead. As she got closer, there was no doubt. Evelyn looked like he was wearing a fright mask. His swollen face was a study in purple and red. His tongue stuck out like a gruesome slug.

Josie resisted the urge to close his popped eyes. The Halley-blue scarf around his neck was obscenely beautiful.

"He really did love her," Alyce said in a small voice. "He couldn't live without her."

"Evelyn didn't commit suicide," Josie said. "He was murdered. Someone strangled him."

"Ohmigod," Alyce said. She stayed rooted to her spot.

"We'd better get out of here," Josie said. "I hope no one saw us."

"Why? A few minutes ago, you wanted to call the police."

"That was before I knew Evelyn was murdered," Josie said. "What are we going to tell the police?"

"The truth," Alyce said. "We had an appointment."

"To buy information he wouldn't give the police," Josie said. "For more money than the average cop makes in a year."

"We don't have to tell them that," Alyce said. "It's not like I have the cash in a brown paper bag."

"Oh, right," Josie said. "No problem. We can just say nobody answered the door, so we opened it."

"It was open," Alyce corrected.

"And we walked into a near stranger's apartment and snooped around. Then we opened another closed door and found him murdered."

"But we didn't kill him," Alyce said. "He looks all stiff, like he's been dead for hours. That's rigor mortis, right?"

Josie thought Evelyn looked like a dead spider in his black turtleneck and black jeans. His beret was a black hole on the pillow. "I'm no medical examiner," Josie said, "but for what it's worth, I'd guess he was killed last night."

"Then we're safe," Alyce said. "I was home with Jake last night."

"You mean Jake, the alleged killer of Halley?"

"Jake couldn't have killed him. He was with me all evening," Alyce said.

"Wives don't make good alibis," Josie said. "Any witnesses to confirm that you two were home? Any neighbors stop by? Did the nanny spend the night?"

"No," Alyce said.

"I didn't think so. By the way, that's Halley's scarf squeezing the dead man's neck."

"Oh," Alyce said.

"Yeah," Josie said.

"Maybe I could get some coffee until you finished talking to the police," Alyce said.

"The interview with the police will take hours," Josie said. "But it will take the cops ten minutes to figure out the connection between us. Then they'll throw Jake back in jail. And maybe you, too."

Alyce turned even paler, if that was possible. She was a haunting figure in the dim light. "Let's get out of this horrible place," she said.

Alyce managed to float down the stairs, even in her shocked state. Josie tried not to run. She kept reminding herself that housewives were invisible. But she was afraid they were an oddity in this neighborhood. If they'd looked like drug dealers, musicians, or a couple in drag, they'd have a better chance of blending in.

Neither woman said a word until they were on the sidewalk, walking to Josie's car.

"Jake would have to be pretty stupid to kill Evelyn," Alyce said.

But it wouldn't be the first stupid thing he's done, Josie thought. She didn't say it. She didn't have to.

They walked another block in deafening silence. If Jake killed Evelyn, he sure wouldn't tell Alyce, Josie thought. He didn't tell her a lot of things. She didn't tell him everything, either.

"Did Jake know you were talking to Evelyn this morning?" Josie said.

"No, I didn't want to raise his hopes," Alyce said.

"Do you think Evelyn tried to call Jake last night?" Josie said.

"I don't know," Alyce said. "I don't think the phone rang, but I was exhausted. I put Justin to bed and fell asleep about seven o'clock."

Jake had heard Josie's conversation with Evelyn, the same as Alyce. He'd been drinking coffee in the kitchen. If he knew Halley, then he knew who Evelyn was. He could put the conversation fragments together, and realize Evelyn might have information that could save him. Jake could have called Evelyn while Alyce slept.

What if Jake went to see him? Would Jake try to strangle the information out of Evelyn? Jake had to be hard up for cash, facing a big murder trial. After he killed Evelyn, he could have ransacked the apartment, searching for the evidence, then left.

Josie felt sick, but a gallon of Maalox couldn't cure this problem. She had two impossible choices: If she didn't go to the police, she was withholding information in an investigation. If she did, she'd get her best friend's husband in deeper trouble.

Alyce and Josie made it to the car without anyone noticing them. At least, Josie didn't think so, and she'd been trained to notice signs of snooping. She'd lived next door to the one-woman neighborhood watch program, Mrs. Mueller. No curtains fluttered in these windows. No blinds were lifted by a finger. No one came out to check the mail. Josie didn't even see a postal worker on the sidewalk.

There was still time on her meter, so no parking ticket would give her away. For once, Josie was glad she drove an anonymous gray Honda. The staff of the Majestic Café might remember them, but Alyce wore a red wig and Josie looked like a lot of women.

That was her talent. Josie might have left some hairs or fibers at the crime scene, but the police couldn't trace them to her if they didn't know she was in the apartment.

"We can't leave Evelyn alone in there," Alyce said. "Can't we give the police an anonymous tip?"

"I'll find a pay phone," Josie said.

"Where?" Alyce said. "I don't see one nearby."

They were back on Kingshighway, driving past hospital row, the massive medical complexes overlooking Forest Park.

"I know a place," Josie said.

She pulled into the hospital garage, parked the car, and ran inside. Alyce followed, looking slightly dazed. Nobody noticed them. A running woman and a dazed one were ordinary sights in a hospital. A guard asked Josie and Alyce who they were seeing.

"Smith," she said. "Maternity."

Alyce blinked. The guard checked the computer, wrote out two passes, and said, "Take the elevator to the fifth floor."

"What were you thinking?" Alyce said.

"There's always a Smith in a big hospital," Josie said.

She found a bank of pay phones in an alcove near the soda machines. There was no one around. She covered the phone receiver with a Kleenex, which didn't look unusual in a germ-ridden hospital, and dialed 911. She hoped it would disguise her voice.

Josie recited Evelyn's address, then said, "There's a dead man on the second floor."

She hung up.

"What are we going to do now?" Alyce said when they were back in Josie's car.

"You're going home," Josie said. "Your car has been in your driveway all morning for the whole neighborhood to see. If the police ask where you were, give them a slice of your best chocolate cheesecake and play Mrs. Domestic.

"I'm going mystery-shopping. And you're right. There's no point in torturing my gut with Chunk-A-Chicken today. I'll shop Down & Dirty Discount stores instead."

"Eeww," Alyce said.

"They're depressing," Josie said. "But at least I don't have to eat there."

"I suppose," Alyce said. "But what a day."

"It will get better. My daughter is spending Saturday at her friend Emma's house. I'll swing by, pick her up, then take her to the zoo for an hour and buy a pretzel."

"This is some day when the best thing you have to look forward to is a zoo pretzel," Alyce said.

"Oh, there's more," Josie said. "After the zoo, I'll drop Amelia off at my mother's flat and go on my date with Mike the plumber."

"That's tonight? I want a full report," Alyce said.

"I never kiss and tell." Josie pulled into Alyce's driveway. "We're here."

"Come in and have a cup of coffee," Alyce said.

"What about Jake?" Josie said.

"He's with his attorney this morning. Justin is with the nanny."

Once inside, Alyce pulled off the red wig and stashed it in the closet, then patted her blond hair into place. Now that she was safely away from Evelyn's apartment, Josie's knees felt weak. Evelyn had played a dangerous game, and now he was dead. She kept seeing his purple face and the Halley-blue scarf. What had that sad, silly

little man done? Evelyn didn't deserve his horrible
death. Josie realized her hands were shaking.

"Can you try some food now?" Alyce said. "Maybe
a quick cheese omelet?"

"I'd better," Josie said. "I'm a little wobbly and I
don't think it's the wine."

While Alyce whipped up the omelet and warmed
some muffins, Josie called her mother. "Three more deliveries this morning," Jane said. "Six packages from the
Pottery Barn, three from Williams-Sonoma, and more
cashmere sweaters from Neiman Marcus. Oh, another
Harry & David fruit basket. I sent them all back."

"Thanks, Mom. Sounds like the deliveries are slack-
ing off."

"I certainly hope so," Jane said. "We'll know more
by this afternoon."

Josie snapped her phone shut as Alyce's doorbell
rang. Alyce peeked out the side window.

"Ohmigod, it's Amy the Slut," she said in a whisper.
"I can't face her today."

"Yes, you can," Josie said. "You want a witness that
you were home, in case the police ask where you were
this morning."

"How can Amy be a witness?" Alyce asked. "She's
never sober."

"She's better than nothing."

Amy the Slut breezed in with a gust of alcohol fumes
and a gift bag. Wood Winds' most notorious wife wore
a black catsuit and a wide red leather belt. A dark fur
coat was thrown over her shoulders. Her black boots
had four-inch heels. All Amy needed was a whip to complete the ensemble.

Amy plopped down at the granite island and helped
herself to a warm muffin.

"Raisin bran," she said. "How like you, Alyce. So
wholesome." Amy's skin was miraculously free of broken veins and puffiness. Her vices hadn't caught up to
her yet. "I want to thank you for taking the pressure off
me. You've made a bigger scandal than I ever could."

Alyce stood frozen at the stove, her spatula in midair.

"Your omelet is burning," Josie said.

"Yes," Alyce said, and let it smoke in the hot pan.

"I'm so grateful," Amy said. "It's such a hoot listening to all the good women in our neighborhood trashing you. Oh, now, don't look so stricken. As soon as little Jakey is declared innocent, they'll all come back and kiss your ass again."

"You think Jake is innocent?" Alyce clung to that pathetic hope in the midst of Amy's insults.

Josie got up and turned off the stove, then dumped the scorched omelet on a plate. It wouldn't be too bad if she picked off the burned parts.

"Of course," Amy said. She waved the muffin in the air. "That boy just doesn't have what it takes, no offense. He's no stone killer. I've known one or two of them. They have, shall we say, a hardness that Jake lacks."

Alyce started to say something, but Josie kicked her shin. She stayed by the stove, as if she could shield Alyce from Amy's acid.

"What about Cliff?" Josie said. If anyone knew the men of Wood Winds, it was Amy.

"What about him?" Amy said. Hatred flashed in her eyes. She didn't like to be distracted from tormenting Alyce, but she enjoyed flaunting her illicit knowledge.

"Do you think he killed his wife?" Josie said.

"Ah, Cliffee," Amy said. "The strong silent type who takes it and takes it and then one day doesn't. He could have. Cliffee likes to play rough. I'd be happy to show the cops the bruises Cliffee gave me. Especially that cute homicide detective, Evanovich.

"Oh, don't look so shocked, Alyce. Cliffee wasn't getting any at home with Halley running off to New York, so he outsourced his lovin'—and his anger. I was just kinky enough to like it, for a while. Then he bored me. But did he actually do the deed and kill Halley? We'll never know as long as the police keep focusing on the wrong man, will we?

"Well, enough about me. I brought you a little something. This is the real comfort food."

Amy opened the gift bag and pulled out a fifth of

Bombay Sapphire gin, vermouth, a lemon, and a jar of stuffed olives. "One can only eat so much corned beef in a crisis. We've watched Joanie load you down with those deli trays. Really. It's so . . . ethnic. I thought you were ready for some WASP soul food."

Amy reached in the bag again and set a silver shaker on the granite counter. "Cheers," she said. "I have to go now. But remember Aunt Amy's advice: Your neighbors will crawl back once Jake is declared innocent. Oh, one more thing. Not all your friends are really your friends. Ta-ta."

She was gone in a flurry of gin fumes. Alyce picked up the lemon and hurled it at the closed door.

"I hate her," Alyce said. "I hate her. I hate her. Thank you for keeping me from killing her. It was touch and go there for a moment."

"The kitchen cutlery was only a heartbeat away," Josie said.

"What did Amy mean by saying not all my friends are my friends?"

"Who knows?" Josie said. "She's a drunk. Don't believe that *in vino veritas* stuff. Boozers are liars."

"But was she lying about Cliff being violent? Did he knock her around when they had sex?"

"I don't know," Josie said. "But she's the second woman who said Cliff has a violent streak. Little Joanie thought he did, too, and she's truthful."

But was she? Josie wondered. Or was Joanie the friend who wasn't the friend?

"Does Amy always lie? Or is there a sliver of truth in her drunken malice?" Josie said. "If so, how do we find it?"

"It's not worth the search," Alyce said, and swept the gin, the vermouth, and the silver cocktail shaker into the trash.

Chapter 24

"So this bookstore calls and says they have an emergency," Mike the plumber said. "Their women's john is stopped up, and they want me to fix it fast."

He's so cute, Josie thought. She felt like a high school girl with a crush. But Mike was better than good-looking. He was sort of pettable. No, she didn't want to pet him. She wanted to . . . Down, girl, she told herself. The night is young and you're old enough to know better.

"I got there and the commode was blocked, all right," Mike said. "Like somebody poured concrete down it. I used my trusty snake, but I couldn't make any headway."

"Headway. Was that a pun?" Josie said.

"Not on purpose," Mike said.

Josie laughed. She'd been laughing a lot since she'd polished off half of her Maplewoodie. The potent combination of rum and tequila made Long Island iced tea look like Earl Grey. The Maplewoodie was the house drink at the Maya Café. Josie thought it would be unpatriotic, as a citizen of Maplewood, to refuse one.

She'd had plenty of guacamole, salsa, chips, and crab cakes, so she wasn't really drunk. She felt good for the first time today. Her headache had disappeared. The warm, colorful restaurant and Mike's comforting presence banished the horrible pictures of Evelyn.

Josie thought her first date with Mike was going well. He actually seemed interested in her as a woman, rather than some cutie who could impress his important friends. He looked even better out of uniform, in a soft beige shirt and well-fitted jeans. And he was staring at her.

"So you weren't making any headway with the head," Josie prompted.

"Right," Mike said. "Anyone ever tell you how cute you are?"

"I was thinking the same thing about you." Oops. Time to lay off the Maplewoodie. "You were talking about your work."

"Yeah, the case of the concrete commode. I took the whole thing apart. You'll never guess what was stopping it up. It was jammed in there, like someone had forced it."

"Anything you can mention at dinner?" Josie said.

"Sure. I found a Brussels sprout, a gold chain, and a lace garter."

"A Brussels sprout. Like a vegetable?" Josie said.

"A green uncooked sprout. It was so weird, I took a photo."

Mike pulled out a Polaroid. It was a close-up of a bright green Brussels sprout, a white lace garter, and a fine gold chain on a dark tile floor.

"Bizarre," Josie said. "It could be part of the decor at the Maya."

The Maya Café, designed by Bill Christman of the City Museum, was deliciously funky. On the wall was a cross made up of old *Time* magazine covers, with icons like John Kennedy, Martin Luther King, and the notorious "Is God Dead?" cover. A sign said SISTERS OF MERCY. Another sign was for the Dimwit Bros. painters.

"That's enough about me," Mike said. "How was your day?"

Did he really want to know? The man didn't seem like the same species as the ultra-ambitious Granby. She wished she could tell Mike about her day, but she didn't know him well enough. She couldn't burden him with her story of finding the strangled artist. The horrible vision of Evelyn's bloated face flashed in her mind, and Josie felt suddenly sick.

"What's the matter?" Mike said. "You look pale."

I can't tell him the truth. Not yet. I don't know him well enough to say I skipped out on a murder scene. But I can talk about Jake. Maybe he can help me. Men look at life from a different perspective.

"I'm worried about my friend Alyce Bohannon."

"She's the pot-filler lady, right?"

Josie blushed when she thought about the afternoon she'd met Mike. She'd spent most of it with her foot in her mouth. "That's her. Alyce's husband, Jake, was arrested for the carjacking murder of Halley Hardwicke."

"I'd been following the story on the news," Mike said. "I didn't realize that was your friend."

The waitress was standing over them. "Did you save room for dessert?" she asked.

"You have to try the sopaipilla," Mike said.

"I guess I do," Josie said.

"Another drink?" Mike asked.

"Coffee," Josie said firmly.

While they waited for dessert, Josie told him about Jake's legal troubles.

"She's a real lady, your friend Alyce," Mike said. "That word's gone out of style, but I mean it. We do a lot of work in that subdivision. Some of those Wood Winds women are aggressive. They practically tackle me when I walk in with my toolbox."

Josie, who'd had a few thoughts of her own about tackling Mike, steered the conversation to a safer topic. "The women turned meek as mice when Mrs. Livermore decreed Alyce persona non grata. They followed old-lady Liverspot's lead like little yellow ducklings. They should be ashamed. Alyce helped every one of those cowards, and they deserted her at the first sign of trouble."

"I'm not surprised," Mike said. "Money can't buy character."

Josie told him what she'd learned so far: the fight Joanie had overheard between Halley and her husband the night before she was murdered. Linda's information that Halley was desperate to get out of the suburbs. Amy the Slut's cryptic comment about false friends. And the dreadful scene with Renata Livermore.

"I know her," Mike said. "The decorator ordered a bidet for the bathroom. Mrs. Livermore wouldn't have one. Said it was unchristian."

Josie giggled. She'd never look at Mrs. Livermore the same way.

Josie told him about her talk with the rabidly ambitious Granby, although she didn't mention this was a blind date arranged by her mother. She explained how she tracked down Ramsey, the successful failed novelist.

"That's clever," Mike said. "Where'd you get the idea?"

"From a police sting on *Cops,*" she said.

"You watch Court TV?" he said.

"I'm crazy about it," Josie said.

"I think I'm in love," he said.

Was he joking or serious? Josie couldn't tell. Instead, she told him about Evelyn, the bad artist with the Brooklyn-BBC accent. She didn't mention Evelyn's murder. She hadn't heard it on the news yet.

"Evelyn sounds like a fourteen-carat fake," Mike said.

"Except he was smart enough to recognize real talent in Halley," Josie said.

"And she repaid him by dumping him. No wonder she's dead. She has another talent. She knew how to piss people off. Are you sure the artist didn't kill her?"

"I'm positive," Josie said. She packed a lot of conviction in those words. His death was proof of his innocence. "I haven't gotten to the best part." Josie told Mike about the avalanche of packages and magazines on her doorstep.

"You've been through all this in the last few days?" Mike said. "Look at you, so bright-eyed and pretty. You should be dead tired. You're amazing, you know that?"

Josie was grateful the waitress showed up with their sopaipillas and coffee. It saved her from answering. There was a respectful silence while the luscious dessert was set in front of them. Josie's was fragrant with cinnamon and rich with honey and ice cream. Her much-abused gut gave a contented gurgle. She hoped Mike didn't hear it.

They were savoring the last bites before Mike said, "You've found out a lot, but how does it help Alyce's husband?"

"That's the problem. It doesn't," Josie said. "I've talked to everyone, but learned nothing."

"Yes, you have. You don't know what you know," Mike said. "That's why all those packages and magazines were dumped on you—to keep you from stirring up the hornet's nest. This was more than a prank. Someone wants you to spend days on the phone, straightening this out. They want your time."

Mike sipped his coffee. Josie liked watching him. She could imagine Mike sitting at her kitchen table. She couldn't see herself fixing him dinner, but dessert and coffee were a definite possibility.

"You need a fresh perspective," Mike said. "That's me. Here's my take on things, and remember, I know most of the players in Wood Winds. Everyone thinks Halley's murder is about love, or at least sex. The cops say she had an affair with Jake and he killed her, right?"

"Right," Josie said.

"I think it's really about money. Evelyn, the artist, talked about love. But that novelist guy Ramsey thought Evelyn wanted money. Not cash, but an introduction to Halley's rich friends, which amounts to the same thing. Evelyn wanted to sell his art to the big-money crowd."

"Ramsey might have been jealous," Josie said.

"I don't think so," Mike said. "Evelyn and Ramsey were two of a kind: failed artists and successful spongers. Follow the money and you'll solve this."

"What money?" Josie said.

"I'll get to that. I see another hole in your investigation."

Josie liked that he used the *i* word. It made her aimless poking and prodding sound organized and official.

"Are you sure Jake had an affair with Halley?" Mike said.

"Alyce says he didn't, but she's his wife. What else was Jake doing in that hotel room?" Josie said.

"Talking business with the woman, like he said."

"Oh, come on, Mike. You've seen the photos of Halley. She was gorgeous. Do you really believe nothing was going on?"

"Yeah, I do. A man can be alone with a beautiful woman and not jump her bones. We're not all animals. Everybody thinks that's all I do all day. I'd never get any work done if I screwed all the lonely housewives people think I have.

"The way I see it, Jake slipped up maybe once with the babysitter, or au pair, or whatever you call her. But there's no proof he strayed after that."

"Except for Amy the Slut," Josie said.

"I know Amy," Mike said. "She comes on to every man who gets near her, but she's not as successful as she'd like you women to think. A lot of guys are turned off by Amy. Jake might have been one of them. Maybe he told her no, like I did, and she said she hooked up with him, anyway. That would get him in trouble with his wife. Amy gets more kicks out of causing trouble than she does out of sex. Who'd believe Jake was innocent?

"Let's give the man the benefit of the doubt. What if he really did have business with Halley—personal business?"

"What do you mean?" Josie said.

"Did you ask yourself how Halley was financing her operation in New York? She wasn't working for another designer or a corporation. She was starting her own company. Do you know how expensive that is? I have some idea, just from running a business here in St. Louis. She'd need hundreds of thousands of dollars, maybe millions. Where would she get that kind of money? Was she independently wealthy?"

"No," Josie said. "Halley was broke when she married Cliff, as least as I understand it. Cliff makes a big corporate salary, but it's not enough to finance a start-up in New York. Anyway, she was divorcing him."

"There you go," Mike said. "Halley needed money to escape St. Louis. Lots of money. Jake didn't sleep with her. He was an investor, or he was putting together a group of investors."

"But the police found Halley's scarves tied to the bed-posts in the hotel suite," Josie said.

"So? Anyone could have tied them there. Maybe someone at the firm was trying to make Jake look bad."

Granby, Josie thought. Would Granby slip over to the corporate suite and redecorate it before the police arrived? You bet. He'd move faster than his favorite Porsche for the chance to ruin Jake.

"You need to find out if Jake had any money to invest," Mike said.

"You're a genius," Josie said.

"Nope. Just good at unblocking things."

"I could kiss you," Josie said.

"Yes, you could," Mike said.

And so she did.

Chapter 25

"Then what happened?" Alyce said. "I mean, after you kissed him?"

"I'll never tell," Josie said.

"But I'm your best friend."

"Exactly," Josie said. "That's why I'm in your kitchen at nine in the morning. Mike has an absolutely brilliant idea. I think it could help. We need to talk. Where's Jake?"

"Upstairs," Alyce said. "He's still asleep. It's the nanny's day off, as you can see. I get to play with Justin."

"Daddy sleep!" Justin shrieked, and exuberantly squashed a chunk of banana on his high chair.

"Not if you keep yelling like that, big boy," Alyce said.

"Get book!" he said. "Get Bob!"

"Right. Get your book," Alyce said, helping him down.

Justin toddled off to find a board book of *Bob the Builder*. He dropped it in a plastic dump truck. "Vrrooom. Vroom." Justin made truck noises as he drove it back to the kitchen.

"Testosterone takes over long before age two," Alyce said. "I told myself I wasn't getting him gender-specific toys. I'd let him choose. No matter what I gave him, he made it into a truck. When I found him crashing his Teddy bear into his giraffe, I gave in and got him trucks. Bob the Builder is his idol."

"There are worse ones," Josie said. "At least Bob does something useful."

Justin plopped down and began gnawing on his Bob the Builder board book.

"That's a good book," Alyce said.

"Meaty plot," Josie said.

Justin drooled happily.

"He's teething, poor little guy," Alyce said. "With any luck, he'll gnaw on Bob for a while. He can take it. So what's Mike's brilliant idea? Do you care for any coffee or cheesecake?"

"I'm never eating again," Josie said. "But I would like some coffee."

She was sorry as soon as she said the words. Josie waited impatiently while Alyce fussed with her fancy German coffeemaker. She was eager to explain Mike's theory, but she needed Alyce's full attention.

Finally, Josie had a steaming cup in front of her. Justin was still testing the strength and endurance of Bob the Builder. Alyce settled into a chair at the granite island. In the harsh morning light, Josie could see how worn her friend looked. The dark shadows under her eyes were becoming permanent. All the concealer in West County couldn't help her. Alyce needed hope, and lots of it. Josie thought she could give her a good dose.

"This has to be good," Alyce said. "You're squirming worse than Justin. Tell me what Mike said."

"Let's suppose that Jake is telling the truth and he didn't have an affair with Halley," Josie said.

"Of course, he's telling the truth," Alyce said.

Oops. Josie had wandered into quicksand already. "That's what I mean. I was speaking from the police viewpoint. They think he had the affair with Halley. Jake said he wasn't at the hotel for law firm business, but it was business. That confused me, until I talked with Mike. Does Jake have any money to invest?"

"Well, there's his 401(k) and some stocks, but that's about it. How much are you talking about?"

"At least a hundred thousand, more like half a million."

"Out of our league," Alyce said. "We have a mortgage, two cars, country-club dues, the nanny—the usual expenses. And that was before Jake had to get a lawyer."

"Any savings accounts?" Josie asked.

"A small money market," Alyce said. "Nothing with that kind of money."

"I know the police took your financial records, but do you have copies of them?"

"Don't need copies," Alyce said. "We bank online and we bought a new laptop. We can check them anytime."

"Have the police asked any further questions about your accounts? Is any money missing?"

"No," Alyce said.

"Are all the accounts in both your names?"

"Where is this going, Josie?" Alyce looked wary. Her coffee sat untouched on the counter. Justin gnawed quietly on his book.

Suddenly, Josie knew Mike's bright idea was a disaster. She wanted to run out the door. She wanted to take her words back. If only you could hit rewind in real life. Now it was too late.

"Josie?" Alyce said. "What's wrong?"

"Uh, I think I misunderstood something Mike said. I'd better go."

"Josie Marcus, you're going to stay right here and tell me." Alyce's gray-blue eyes were cold and hard as slate. "I need to know. Even if it's bad, it's better to know."

There was nothing to do but go forward. Alyce had the right to know, Josie thought. No matter how painful that knowledge was, ignorance would hurt even more.

"Did you get some money when your parents died?" Josie said.

"More than eight hundred thousand dollars," Alyce said. "We spent some on the house and a trip, then put the rest in a special account for Justin's education. It was about seven hundred fifty thousand. But I don't consider it our money. It's Justin's. We never touch it. That's why I didn't mention it."

They'd need every penny of that fund to educate the

little guy gnawing on Bob. Justin's primary school would cost ten thousand or more a year, long before he got to college.

"Is the money still there?" Josie said.

"What do you mean, is it still there?" Alyce said.

"Halley needed investors' money for her New York enterprise. Hundreds of thousands of dollars."

"So?" Alyce said.

"What if Jake was putting together a group of investors for Halley, and he was one of them?"

"You think my husband gambled with our son's future?"

"I'm probably wrong." I hope I'm wrong, Josie thought. Please, let me be wrong.

Alyce looked panic-stricken. "I haven't looked at that account in months. We left it in my mother's old bank in Pittsburgh. I keep the passbook in my kitchen desk."

She pulled out *Joy of Cooking*. "It's still here. The police didn't find it. See, with interest, it's seven hundred fifty seven thousand dollars."

"Who has access to the account?" Josie asked.

"Jake and I. Either one of us can put money in."

Or take it out, Josie thought.

Alyce must have had the same thought. She ran to the laptop at her kitchen desk and logged on. It wouldn't connect to the Internet fast enough for her.

"Come on," Alyce wailed, and walloped the computer until she was online. Her fingers pounded the keys, and she was in the bank's Web site. She typed in her password wrong, yelled "Shit!" and typed it again.

The screen blinked, then unscrolled a long list of figures.

"That son of a bitch!" Alyce screamed. "It's gone. It's all gone except for fifty-seven thousand dollars. Jake stole our son's future."

"You don't know that," Josie said.

But Alyce was a wild woman, her pale hair flying as she raced up the stairs. She beat on the master bedroom door and shrieked, "Jake, open up."

Josie caught a glimpse of Jake's face, drawn and unshaven. She heard Alyce cry, "Tell me it isn't true. Tell me you didn't give our child's money to that woman."

"Shh," Jake said. "She'll hear you." He took her hand and drew her into the bedroom. The door slammed.

Josie wanted to leave. She could hear Alyce's screams coming from upstairs and cries of, "You bastard!"

Justin looked at Josie with big, trusting eyes. A little fluff of dark hair stuck straight up. He slobbered happily over Bob the Builder. Josie wanted to burst into wails, but she couldn't. She tried a crooked smile.

Justin smiled back, and showed two new sharp teeth.

"Hey, handsome, you've got what it takes to get the girls," Josie said.

Justin laughed. Josie wished she could laugh with him. "Want me to read that?"

"Bob the Builder!" Justin said.

She took that as a yes.

Josie was halfway through *We Can Do It!* when Alyce came downstairs, her eyes red and swollen with tears. One look at her friend's tortured face, and Josie knew there were worse betrayals than adultery.

"Let's go, before I'm the one arrested for murder," Alyce said.

She threw on a coat and bundled Justin for a cold day. In the garage, she transferred his car seat to Josie's Honda. "I don't trust myself to drive," Alyce said.

"Where do you want to go?" Josie said.

"Nowhere. Anywhere. Away. Just drive. I want to go home and I can't. I wish my mother was alive. I'd take Justin, grab the first plane, and go see her. I miss her every single day.

"Justin's money was special, Josie. Mom knew Jake would make enough to support us. But this was her way to look after her grandson. And now Jake's stupid, cowardly, idiotic—" She slapped the dashboard with every word.

Josie's small car didn't seem big enough to hold Alyce's rage. Josie was afraid it would melt the windows and burn the seats. She looked in the rearview mirror.

Justin had stopped gnawing on Bob. His face got that cloudy look little kids have before they burst into tears. Josie tried to head off the oncoming wails.

"Alyce, that won't help. Justin shouldn't hear it."

Alyce took a deep breath. "You're right. I'm just so angry at Jake. I wish he had screwed her."

"Daddy!" Justin crowed. He pointed out the window at a farm. "Cow! Cow goes mooooooooo."

"That's right," Alyce said. "And there's a horsie. What does a horse say?"

Helping Justin with his animal sounds seemed to calm her. Josie drove on the lonely country roads around Alyce's house, past bare woods and dead winter fields.

"This is so peaceful," Alyce said.

Personally, the woods gave Josie the creeps. She thought they were good places to bury bodies. If Jake was her husband, she'd be digging a deep hole in that stand of maples.

Justin went back to gnawing contentedly on Bob.

"Jake forged my signature," Alyce said. "It takes both our signatures to take money out."

"The bank didn't notice it wasn't your signature? Is he that good a forger?" Josie asked.

"Married people forge each other's signatures all the time," Alyce said. "I can probably sign Jake's name better than he can. But I always tell him. Usually it's something like our income taxes needed to go out right away and Jake's on a trip. I signed his name and sent it off.

"Jake said he got a 'sure tip' from a client and he put two hundred thousand from Justin's college fund in the stock market. He didn't consult me because he knew it would make us a fortune. He wanted to surprise me. Well, surprise. He lost it. Every last cent. But did that teach him anything? No."

Alyce leaned back on the headrest and closed her eyes. "Halley convinced him she was the next hot thing. The greeting-card queen Mary Engelbreit is a St. Louisan. Halley told Jake she'd have the same fabulous success. Jake was desperate enough to believe her. He had to get the money back. The more he investigated Halley's prospects, the more he was convinced she would make it big.

"Jake took the rest of our son's money—five hundred thousand dollars. He was one of five investors behind Halley. But Jake wasn't taking any chances. He made the investors buy a keyman policy for five million dollars on Halley."

"I think I know what that is," Josie said. "If anything happened to Halley, the investors would get paid a ton of money to cover their loss."

"Right. The keyman policy was Jake's idea. Now he's telling me not to worry. He says the college fund won't lose any money—in fact it will make money. He was just waiting for the policy payoff to replace it before he told me.

"He's an idiot. He's given the police the perfect motive for murdering Halley. It would take years for Halley's company to make a profit. But if she died now, they'd get rich quick."

"Do the police know about the keyman policy?" Josie said.

"If they don't, they will," Alyce said. "The insurance company is going to be looking for reasons not to pay the investors."

"You didn't know anything about this policy?" Josie said.

"No." The word came down like a hammer.

"So that conversation the witness heard in the hotel hall was real?" Josie said.

"You mean the one where Halley said, 'Your wife will find out anyway.' And my stupid husband said, 'Not if you don't—' and then pushed her inside the suite?"

"Yes, that one. Why was he with her at the hotel that day?"

"She wanted the last fifty thousand out of Justin's account for start-up costs. He wouldn't give it to her, and they had a fight."

"Terrific," Josie said. "Another motive for murder."

"He might as well take out a billboard on Highway Forty that says, 'I killed Halley.' "

"Except he didn't," Josie said.

"I know he didn't," Alyce said. "But he's so arrogant, he's going to hang himself. Nothing bad has ever happened to Jake. He can't understand why his luck has turned. He's always had everything he wanted. He thought he could make the stock market roll over like a pet dog. Instead, it bit him."

"So Jake turned to Halley, as the next-best way to recoup the lost money," Josie said.

"He did," Alyce said. "And he ruined our lives. His business with Halley wasn't law firm business, just like he said. He wasn't having an affair with her. He couldn't—no, he wouldn't—tell me. You know why? Because he was afraid. He knew I wouldn't let him touch Justin's money.

"Jake's a gambler, Josie. A plunger. He lost big in the market, so he bet again—on Halley. Like any gambler, he was sure he'd get it back when Halley's business took off. Then she died. But he'd hedged his bet with that keyman policy. He was waiting for it to double his investment. Then he'd tell me and be the big hero."

"Oh, Alyce."

"There's more. Something I haven't had a chance to tell you yet."

Something you didn't want to tell even your best friend, Josie thought.

"There's a problem at the law firm," Alyce said. "No, it's a mess. A big, big mess. Even if Jake is cleared of Halley's murder, he could lose his partnership. We're looking at years of lawsuits, maybe bankruptcy."

"Good God, Alyce, what happened?"

"Jake was working on a huge takeover of a company. The firm's biggest client. It was all very secret. Somehow, a message was sent from Jake's PC in his office to the CEO of the takeover target, alerting him that someone was trying to take over his company."

"And that's bad because?" Josie asked.

"The whole deal blew up."

"Oh," Josie said.

"Jake's not only in trouble with his firm, but the client

can turn him in to the ethics board for violating confidentiality. The lawsuits could cost the firm millions. Jake's a partner, a member of the firm, so that makes them all liable. The firm would then turn around and sue Jake. And when lawyers start suing each other—"

"They never stop," Josie said. "When did the firm uncover this?"

"They had their suspicions before Halley was killed. That's another reason they were so anxious to hustle him out of his office—so they could go through his files and computer records."

"Why would Jake do that?" Josie said.

"For money," Alyce said. "The firm claims the tipped-off CEO was going to give him major money for the information."

"Do they have any proof?" Josie said. "Do they have anything besides that one e-mail?"

"No," Alyce said. "But since the firm found out about the e-mail, they can say he didn't get any money because the CEO didn't want to be caught paying off an informant."

"Great," Josie said. "So having no money is no proof of Jake's innocence."

"Right," Alice said. "The police will say Jake murdered Halley because he heard the rumors that the firm was on to him. Jake was doubly desperate for money: He'd cleaned out our son's account and his takeover tip-off fell through."

"What a mess," Josie said, then wished she'd kept her mouth shut.

"He didn't do it, Josie. The only thing he's guilty of is stupidity. But it's enough to ruin us all."

"What are you going to do?" Josie said.

"What can I do? I'll stay with him until after Halley's trial. We have to get through that first. Then I don't know."

She started crying. Justin began wailing along with her in the backseat, and Alyce could not reach out to comfort him.

"Take me home," Alyce said. "I'm calmer now."

By the time they reached Alyce's house, Justin's face was red with angry weeping. Josie helped carry his car seat into the garage. In the confusion, Alyce didn't say good-bye. She hugged her child to her, and hurried in the house.

Josie drove around aimlessly, sick at the heartache she'd caused. Her clumsy questions had killed a man. Now she'd ruined Alyce's marriage.

She'd driven her own mother into debt, thanks to anonymous complaints to the city inspector. Days of her own time were wasted replacing the stolen license plate and canceling the mountain of packages and magazines she didn't order.

What had she learned that could help Alyce and Jake? Not a damned thing.

Josie hadn't a clue who killed Halley.

She was useless. She was worse than useless. All she'd found were more reasons for Jake to murder Halley.

Chapter 26

Josie felt like she was shopping in the seventh circle of hell.

The Down & Dirty Discount store was in a gray metal building as big as an airplane hangar. Bare lightbulbs were strung overhead, but the huge space absorbed the light. The store was dim as a cave.

Bump. Thump. Bump.

Josie's crippled cart lurched along the concrete floor, then came to a complete stop in some sticky substance. Was that glue on the floor? She struggled to free her cart. The poor metal beast was trapped like a mastodon in the La Brea tar pits.

Finally, she cleared the cart wheels, then turned into an aisle lined with shower doors. They seemed to come complete with soap scum.

Bump. Thump. Bump.

The stock was piled on unpainted wood shelves that reached to the ceiling—and threatened to topple onto the shoppers. Tired men and worn women wrestled cut-rate bathroom vanities and cheap ceiling fans into their carts. Josie rolled past them, looking for the garden-furniture section.

Bump. Thump. Bump.

She was assaulted by awful odors. The rolled rugs smelled musty. The car parts were repulsively oily. The plants in the garden center reeked of manure. But the frozen fish fingers in the food section were strong

enough to overpower everything. They smelled like
cod corpses.

Josie thought she couldn't feel any worse after she
left Alyce's house yesterday. She was wrong. Mystery-
shopping Down & Dirty stores made her even more miserable. Sunday revealed her total failure as a friend.
Shopping these stores showed her professional futility.
Monday in a D&D was a low point in her career.

Year after year, Josie mystery-shopped the Down &
Dirty stores. She always turned in negative reports.
"Poor" was the highest grade she'd ever given a D&D
store. That was one grade up from the bottom rung of
"unacceptable." Yet the corporation kept asking Suttin
Services to mystery-shop the D&D stores, and they always requested Josie.

Did the managers ever read her reports? she wondered. Or were they filed in some warehouse?

She looked at the questions on her sheet: Was the
parking lot clean and pleasant? Never. Plastic bags and
old napkins always roosted in the dying bushes in front
of the store. The lots glittered with broken glass. Today,
Josie finally learned how some of that glass wound up
on the potholed blacktop. Two winos were fighting over
a bottle of muscatel from D&D. During the tussle, the
disputed bottle went flying and smashed to the ground.
She left the winos in each other's arms, weeping over
their loss.

Josie wanted to cry with them. It would be only more
depressing inside. Now, as she bumped along the gray
aisles with her cart, she knew that was the only thing
she'd been right about today.

Most people who shopped at Down & Dirty couldn't
afford to buy anywhere else. A few were bargain hunters
who deluded themselves into believing that the cheapest
was the best. D&D boasted it carried "the best brand
names at the lowest prices."

It didn't mention that those brand names weren't the
same quality as the ones in higher-priced department
stores. The venerable brands sold out their customers

and made "special" (i.e., lower-quality) lines just for D&D.

D&D was where you bought bicycles with instructions in Chinese, pressed-sawdust furniture that wobbled when you assembled it, and pop-up tents guaranteed to collapse in the first heavy rain.

Worse was the knowledge that this cheap junk was made by slaves in third-world countries. D&D shoppers never saw those people. But they had to notice the browbeaten employees scurrying through the store like frightened rabbits.

Josie dreaded asking the staff the obligatory questions on her mystery-shopping sheet. Many barely spoke English. She was sure if she yelled "green card," she could clear out the store.

Oh, well. The sooner she went to work, the sooner she was out of here. Her assignment was to ask a clerk to assist her in the garden-furniture section.

Josie stopped a stick-thin woman with french-fried hair. She was wearing a yellow D&D smock. "Excuse me," Josie said. "Where is the garden furniture?"

"Two aisles over, in G. Middle of the row," the clerk said. The name tag around her neck was turned inward. A wise decision. Aisle G was light fixtures. Josie picked up the night-lights she was supposed to buy while she was there. She found another clerk in the "home additions" section. He was adding on a substantial beer gut and a wide back porch.

"Garden furniture? Aisle S, little lady," he said cheerfully. "On the left." A D&D EMPLOYEE OF THE MONTH sticker hid his name.

Josie trundled down to Aisle S, which seemed halfway to Iowa. It was packed with paint supplies.

She found another clerk in Aisle Q, stocking paper towels. She was a young dark-skinned woman with cropped hair. Her name tag said DANITA.

"Where's the garden furniture, please?" Josie said.

"Aisle R," Danita said cheerfully, and went back to piling packages.

"Don't leave me," Josie said. "Please. I've been misdi-rected all over the store."

"That bad, huh? I'll take you there," Danita said.

She escorted Josie to the proper section. Josie felt like she'd been wandering in the D&D wilderness for days.

"Thank you. Thank you so much," Josie said to her rescuer.

"No problemo," Danita said, sounding remarkably like Amelia. How did she stay so cheerful in this hellish place? Thank goodness for Danita. Now Josie could give someone at D&D a positive report. She felt a little better.

She picked up four bile green lawn-chair pads, as in-structed, and headed for the checkout line. Only two clerks were at the cash registers, and the lines were backed up around the store. Josie's cell phone played her favorite U2 tune. Normally, Josie didn't answer phones in checkout lines, but normal rules didn't apply at D&D.

She looked at the number. It was Harry, her horrible boss. Of course. If you were in hell, the devil would find you.

"Josie," he said. "Where are you?"

"Shopping at a D&D," she said.

"Good," Harry said. He'd know she was miserable. "Can you mystery-shop at Plaza Venetia tomorrow?"

Plaza Venetia would seem celestial after a day in the dark underbelly of discount stores. Josie tried not to sound too eager. Harry might take away the assignment.

"I guess so," she said. "What's the store?"

"Another Pretty Things boutique," Harry said. "God knows why, but the company personally requested you."

Because I'm good, she wanted to scream. Because I'm honest. Because I help weed out the bad staff, like your niece. But she didn't say it. Harry knew that already.

"Does that mean I still have to do the Chunk-A-Chickens?"

"You bet," Harry said. "Just be glad you've got work."

Josie hung up, then heard her phone again. It was her mother.

"Josie?" Jane said. "Did you order twenty-four CDs?"

"No, Mom."

"How about six reams of computer paper from Office Depot?"

"No, Mom."

"A new down comforter?"

"Are we still getting more deliveries, Mom?" Josie couldn't keep the despair out of her voice.

"Bunches of them, Josie. All new companies. Didn't you cancel those credit cards?"

"Yes, Mom. These must have been ordered before the cancellations."

"I refused everything, but I couldn't do anything about the twenty-five magazines."

"Twenty-five!" Josie yelped, and the people trapped in line with her stared. "I'm sorry," Josie said to them.

"You don't have to apologize," Jane said. "I know it wasn't your fault. Josie, can I ask you a personal question? You didn't order *American Baby* on purpose, did you?"

"Ohmigod, no," Josie said. "Mom, I don't have time to read the magazine, much less take care of a baby. I'll be home as soon as I can. Keep saying no until I get there."

Half an hour later, Josie stepped out of the dank, cavelike Down & Dirty store into a warm, sunshiny day. It had to be at least fifty degrees, a gift in cold December. Josie was determined not to waste it, no matter how bad things were.

Josie found Jane on the front porch, saying no to a shipment of Omaha Steaks. Her mother looked small and determined. Her jaw jutted stubbornly, and her arms were crossed in front of her.

"OK, lady," the deliveryman said, "but this is your address, right?"

"We didn't order them," Josie said, hurrying up to the porch. "My credit card was hijacked."

"Oh, sorry," the deliveryman said, and began loading the boxes back on the handcart.

Josie eyed the rejected boxes suspiciously. She'd seen enough Omaha Steaks on Harry's desk. Was this proof her boss was behind the package pileup? What could she do about it?

"Oh, Josie, I'm so glad you're home," Jane said.

Josie picked up her mother's cigarette, which was burning a scorch mark into the porch rail, and handed it to her. Jane took a puff, blew out a stream of smoke, and said, "I had to turn away more. Lots more, including a two-pound box of chocolates and a home exercise machine."

She was wringing her hands, a sign she was frantic with worry.

"Thanks, Mom," Josie said. "I'm so sorry you had to put up with this. GBH."

She gave her mother a hug, and felt the tense muscles in her neck. "Mom, this has you tied in knots," Josie said, rubbing her mother's neck.

"No, Josie, that's not it. I can deal with delivery drivers. It feels good to return orders when they're not mine. The handyman called. It's going to cost another thousand dollars to paint the garage. Where am I going to get that kind of money?"

"Raise my rent," Josie said. "I'm due for an increase."

"I will not," Jane said. "I'm not taking money away from my own granddaughter. It will come from somewhere. I'll have to think about it. Do you want lunch?"

"Not hungry," Josie said. "I want to start canceling magazines before I have to pick up Amelia at school."

Josie canceled fifteen magazines, including *XXL,* "the voice of the Hip-Hop Generation," *Sports Illustrated,* and *Cook's Illustrated,* before she had to stop. She pulled her old brown sweater out of the back of her closet. She loved that sweater. She used to wear it when she dated Amelia's father. Feeling its soft warmth brought back good memories. She wondered if Amelia would notice it.

"Eew, Mom," her daughter said as she dropped onto the car seat. "Do you have to wear that old thing? It's gross. What if one of my friends sees it?"

"What?" Josie said.

"That sweater. It's all stretched out. And it's old."

Amelia wrinkled her freckled nose. At her age, "old" was the ultimate insult.

"It's not old," Josie said. "It's comfortable."

"How old is it?"

"Ten years old," Josie said.

"I'm nine. It's older than me."

So much for memories, Josie thought. It's time to make some new ones.

"It's a nice day. Let's go to the Turtle Playground." Josie held her breath. Did Amelia consider herself too grown-up for the playground?

"Cool," Amelia said.

Josie tried not to show her relief. The Turtle Playground was a wonderfully loony collection of concrete sculptures on the south side of Forest Park. There were three giant turtles and four small ones, plus a curling snake that seemed to be biting the Highway 40 overpass. The biggest turtles were forty feet long. The smallest were seven feet long. There were also seven eggs.

Josie reached in her trunk for the two bottles of water and the chocolate chip cookies she'd packed. She swapped the brown sweater for the navy Windbreaker she kept in her mystery-shopper disguise kit to change her appearance.

"That's better," Amelia said. Her sigh of relief was audible. She was saved from social embarrassment.

Josie and Amelia munched cookies and watched three little girls slide down the biggest turtle's back.

"The big turtles are named Richard, Sally, and Tom," Josie said. "Those are the children of Sunny Glassberg, the woman who donated the playground. The little turtles are named for her grandchildren, Antonio, David, Adam, and Emily."

"No 'Amelia,'" her daughter said. "I wish I had a turtle named after me."

"Which one?" Josie said.

"A big one," Amelia said.

Josie splashed her water on the turtle's huge front paw.

"I hereby rechristen you Amelia," Josie said to the turtle. "Henceforth, you shall be known by that name."

"You're nutso-crazy," Amelia said. But she looked pleased.

A wedding party ran through the playground, laughing and posing on the smaller turtles.

The bride, in a full-skirted white dress and long veil, sat down on a turtle back. The groom kissed her. Four bridesmaids in frothy pink velvet dresses applauded.

Amelia watched, spellbound. Josie hoped her daughter wasn't going to ask about her wedding pictures. She held her breath.

"Do you remember when I was a little girl in kindergarten," Amelia said, "and you let me dress up in your high heels and a pink bridesmaid dress to play princess?"

Josie managed a nod.

"That was my favorite thing," Amelia said.

"It was?" Josie said, surprised. She had an album full of photos of Amelia playing, but no memory of the pink princess. Funny how memory works, Josie thought. Something that means nothing to us can be so important to someone else.

Later, after too much grief and pain, Josie would realize Amelia had given her the key to the mystery in the Turtle Playground.

Josie's one regret about that afternoon was she didn't take it.

Chapter 27

"You're driving me to Arsenal Street," an exasperated Jane used to tell Josie.

Generations of St. Louis mothers said that to their unruly children, instead of, "You're driving me crazy." Arsenal Street was the site of the old state hospital for the insane.

When Josie heard Jane say those words, she knew she was heading for trouble.

Once, Josie got caught holding a shrieking and stall-door-slamming contest in the school bathroom. Josie loved the room's echoey acoustics, and tried to get her classmates to appreciate them. The teachers were not amused.

Jane actually drove ten-year-old Josie to Arsenal Street. It was twilight when Jane showed her the creepy brick building behind the grim stone fence. "That's where you'll put me if you don't start behaving," Jane had told her.

Josie took one look at her mother's clenched jaw and wild hair, and knew Jane was at her wit's end. Josie was so scared, she was nearly perfect for a whole week.

But Josie was a different kind of mother. Amelia didn't drive her crazy. She thought her daughter kept her sane. Josie knew if she didn't spend the afternoon at the Turtle Playground with Amelia, she would be sick with guilt over Alyce. She'd spent a good part of Sunday mentally beating herself up.

An hour with Amelia giggling, eating chocolate chip cookies, and baptizing the big turtle kept Josie sane.

Josie also felt a bittersweet pang. She knew Amelia would be a teenager soon, and then she really would drive Josie crazy. Amelia would no longer want to be seen with her mother, even if Josie did change her sweater. Josie's very existence would embarrass her daughter. The saggy-sweater incident was a foretaste of the future.

Amelia was tugging on the sleeve of Josie's acceptable Windbreaker. "Mom, we gotta go," she said. "It's going to rain."

Josie shook herself free of her dark thoughts. The sky was roiling with jagged black clouds, and the light had the yellow-green edge that signaled tornado weather. The temperature was dropping like an express elevator. Amelia's teeth were chattering from the cold. Josie took off her Windbreaker and wrapped it around her daughter.

"All good things come to an end," Josie said. "And bad ones, too, for that matter."

A gust of wind blew the bride's veil over her face and ripped the bouquet out of a bridesmaid's hand. The frivolous pink bouquet rolled across the ground toward Josie. She caught the runaway flowers and handed them back to the bridesmaid.

"You're next to get married," the bridesmaid said, laughing.

"Only works for bridal bouquets," Josie said. "I'm safe."

Fat drops of rain plopped all around them. Josie and Amelia ran for the car and hurled themselves into the seats, laughing, wet, and windblown.

"My turtle is really baptized now," Amelia said.

Another gust shook the car, and it took all Josie's concentration to steer the little Honda through the flash-flooded streets.

Only after a dinner of broccoli and burgers (onions and ketchup, no pickles for Amelia), only after Amelia finished her homework, only after she IM'ed her friend Emma and was tucked into bed, did the guilt get to Josie again. The cold rain lashed the house and rattled the old windows. Equally cold accusations beat on Josie's conscience.

She had ruined Alyce's marriage with her amateurish meddling. She had interfered in Evelyn's life and now the artist was dead. Not just dead, horribly murdered. She had—

Her bleak thoughts were interrupted by the phone ringing at nine thirty that night.

"Josie, I didn't interrupt anything, did I?"

Josie nearly dropped the phone. Alyce was breaking her ironclad rule about calling during family hours.

"What's wrong?" Josie said.

"I went to bed early, but I couldn't sleep, so I called you."

"Won't you wake up Jake?"

"I'm sleeping in the guest room," Alyce said.

"Oh, Alyce." Josie wanted to weep at the damage she'd done. Alyce was totally isolated now—no husband, no parents, no friends except Josie. Some friend she was.

"This is all my fault," Josie said.

"No, it's all Jake's fault. He embezzled our son's money."

"But if I hadn't said anything—"

"I would have found out at the trial, and everyone in the courtroom would have seen my shock and shame. I couldn't bear that, Josie. I couldn't. I can't stand to be a public fool. It's bad enough the rest of his office thinks I'm the duped wife because he met Halley in a hotel suite.

"What I have to say couldn't wait until morning. I called to tell you how much I appreciate all you've done."

"Yeah, I'm a regular Sherlock Holmes," Josie said.

"No, you've been a big help. You've found out more than those overpriced private eyes Jake's lawyer hired. Please don't give up. I need you to keep investigating."

"Thanks, Alyce. I've been sitting here listening to the

house blowing down, and beating myself up about how I've ruined your life."

"Well, stop it. Right now. Let's spend our time on something productive. Where do we go next? Who should we check out?"

"My prime candidate for the killer is Halley's husband," Josie said. "Cliff had that big fight with her the night before she died. She said terrible things about Cliff and their little girl. Halley wanted the divorce, and he didn't want to let her go. A lot of men kill their wives and lovers rather than let them go."

"Cliff is my choice, too," Alyce said. "But he's not at work this week. He's home. His parents are staying with him, and he has visitors coming and going all day long. I can't go to Halley's house. They think my husband killed her. They hate me."

"I'm sure that's not true," Josie said.

"Well, I can hardly make a condolence call," Alyce said.

"Maybe we can't intrude on the family," Josie said. "But we can ask questions at Cliff's office. Let's go there tomorrow. I'll drive."

"It's a date," Alyce said. "How early can you pick me up?"

"I have to mystery-shop first thing tomorrow. Want to put on your red wig and go with me?"

"I won't go to the Dorchester Mall," Alyce said. "I can't stand the sight of that place. It's ruined my life."

"Relax, we're going to Plaza Venetia," Josie said. "I'll pick you up at nine."

"Anything to get out of here," Alyce said. "Mrs. Palm comes at eight, and she'll watch Justin all day. See you tomorrow."

Alyce hadn't said one bad word about Jake, but Josie could feel her friend's seething rage.

I don't care what Alyce says, Josie thought. It is my fault. I wish she'd never found out about Jake borrowing money from Justin's college fund. Maybe he would have restored the money before Alyce noticed it was gone.

Right. And maybe I'll get an invitation to sing with the Dixie Chicks.

OK, it wasn't her fault. But Josie still felt bad.

As punishment for her useless meddling, she set up another dinner with the awful Granby. They'd talked about it, but they hadn't agreed on a date yet. Josie thought Granby had lethal levels of ambition. He wouldn't let anything stand in the way of his headlong rush to success—including Jake.

Josie didn't tell Alyce that Granby was number two on her Halley Hit Parade and that she'd set up another date. Alyce would feel guilty, and Josie would feel guilty that Alyce felt guilty, and they would be buried in an avalanche of guilt. It wasn't worth it.

Josie decided she would just do it. If she learned anything, she'd tell Alyce. Besides, a date with Granby would make Jane happy. Josie felt no compunction about feeding her mother's false hopes. Jane should know her daughter and the greedhead lawyer were a spectacular mismatch.

Josie dialed Granby's number. He answered, his voice ridiculously rich and manly. She could see those broad shoulders and that mighty dimpled jaw. The *George of the Jungle* theme screamed in her head. Too bad the guy wasn't an oil painting. He was perfect until he started talking.

"Josie," he said. "I'm glad you called. I'm thinking of getting a new HDTV. Samsung has a model that's only fifteen and a half inches deep. That's thirty percent thinner than the old CRTs. What do you think?"

That you're a complete twit, she thought.

"That we should discuss it over dinner," she said, her voice soft and flirty. "I know we talked about going out again, but we didn't set a date. So are we going out again, or were you leading me on, handsome?"

Oh, barf. She was channeling Jayne Mansfield.

"How about Wednesday night?" he said. "I'll pick you up at seven thirty. Can you stand Tony's again?"

He hadn't found anyone better for the power brokers' floor show. "I'll try," Josie said.

"You're quite the little joker," he said. "I like a woman with a sense of humor."

Josie almost told him it was model XC3 from Sony, but she was afraid he'd pull the plug on their date.

"We may be ordering champagne," he said. "My partnership is getting closer every day."

"Oh?" Josie let her voice linger, breathy and interested.

"Turns out murder is the least of Jake's problems," he said. "He's done something big and bad at the firm that's going to get his ass kicked out no matter what. I can almost feel that Porsche under me."

Josie couldn't take any more. "Well, I can't wait to hear about it Wednesday," she said, and hung up.

In the old days, I could have worn a hair shirt and scourged myself as punishment for my sins, she thought. Instead, I have to suffer a near-eternal evening with Granby, atoning for what I did to Alyce.

No point in being a complete martyr. Josie picked up the phone again and dialed another number.

"Hello, Mike," she said. She could see him, too, and it was a much better picture than she got with Granby. She saw that quirky curve in Mike's right eyebrow. The curl that always settled on his forehead. And the soft and very kissable hollow at the base of his neck.

"You must be psychic," he said. "I was just about to call you. I really enjoyed our evening. Want to go out tomorrow night?"

Josie went to bed smiling. Alone, but smiling.

Chapter 28

A guard in a sharply pressed uniform waved Josie through the gates with military precision.

Wood Winds looked rich and secure this morning. The winter sun gilded the mansions and turned the bare trees into ebony and silver works of art.

Was this enchanted place really a hotbed of murder, adultery, and greed? It seemed as substantial as the sheltering limestone hills. No wonder Alyce didn't lock her doors. It was hard to believe anything bad could happen here.

But Josie saw her answer on Alyce's street. Black-clad mourners were gathering at the home with the Halley-blue trim, moving in clouds of expensive perfume and speaking in soft whispers. A caterer's truck was unloading the funeral feast. A little girl in a blue velvet dress stood lost in the middle of the lawn. Her mother should have told her to put on her coat.

But her mother was not there. Today was Halley Hardwicke's funeral.

Alyce rabbited out her side door with her head down, as if she were running from an angry mob. Her red wig seemed too colorful for the subdivision's somber mood. She'd covered it with a black scarf.

"Halley's funeral must be today," Josie said.

"It's at noon," Alyce said. "It's a memorial service. Linda says she's being cremated."

"Are you going?" Josie asked.

"As what—the wife of the murderer?" Alyce said. "What do I say to Cliff? 'I'm so sorry for your loss, but my husband didn't do it'? Or should I say, 'I'm sorry you think my husband boffed your wife, but he's innocent on that count, too'?

"How about, 'We've both suffered losses: Your wife took all my son's money'? Which one would the etiquette books advise for this occasion?"

Sarcasm did not become Alyce. Josie could see her friend had spent a long night alone in the guest room. She heard her hurt and loss. Alyce believed in Jake's innocence, but he'd shattered her world. She'd been ostracized by her neighbors. She was separated from her husband, though they were shut in the same house. Alyce's bedroom door was closed to her husband for the first time.

"We need to go," Josie said. "It's important. Funerals put a strain on people. Relatives fight. Friends say the unspeakable. Murderers show up to gloat over their victim. You won't be noticed if you sit in the back, especially if you wear that wig."

"A wig disguises my hair," Alyce said. "My shape remains the same."

"Then we need to make you invisible," Josie said. "We'll dress you as a nanny. Mrs. Palm will let you borrow a uniform."

"You're joking," Alyce said.

"Do I look like I'm laughing? If we want to help Jake, we need to be at Halley's memorial service."

"Right now, I don't care if Jake is locked up for fifty years."

"Yes, you do," Josie said. "What kind of future does your son have if his father is in prison?"

"What kind of future does he have with no education money?"

"If we clear Jake's name, he'll collect on that keyman policy and your boy will go to Harvard," Josie said. "Where's the funeral?"

"The Episcopal chapel on Manchester."

"We'd better get moving. We need to be back here at eleven to get you dressed," Josie said. "We have to go mystery-shopping, then stop by Cliff's office."

As Josie threaded through the last of the rush hour traffic to Plaza Venetia, Alyce said, "I don't feel the same about shopping anymore. I'm a lot more cautious, even at the safe malls, like this one."

"Good," Josie said.

"I don't want to live my life on guard," Alyce said. "I want to know there are safe places."

"There are no safe places," Josie said. "Just a false sense of security."

"I don't want to live in your world," Alyce said.

"You already do," Josie said. "Your world never existed."

Alyce clamped her mouth shut, biting back her protests. How could she argue with Josie? She knew it was true.

Josie pulled her Honda into the treelined entrance of Plaza Venetia. The shopping center looked more like a country club than a mall. The white columns could have graced a plantation house. The mall's sweeping white staircase was fit for the grandest entrance. Fountains splashed and planters created little oases where weary shoppers could rest.

"Can you really tell me this is a dangerous place?" Alyce said.

"I know it is," Josie said. "I've read the police reports. This mall has seen everything from carjackings to child abductions. This is modern life, Alyce. You can't close your eyes and wish it away."

"I wish I could make the last two weeks go away," Alyce said.

Josie felt ashamed for lecturing her friend. Alyce had been given a far bigger dose of reality than Josie ever wanted to swallow. "You look tired," she said. "Want to stop for coffee?"

"Nope, I want to nip into the restroom," Alyce said.

They opened the door, heard water running, and found a blond sprite about four years old splashing in the sinks. She wore miniature jeans, tiny pink tennies, and a T-shirt with TARA in sparkly letters.

"Hi, Tara," Josie said.

"Hi," Tara said shyly, and planted her wet palm on the mirror.

"That's a pretty shirt," Josie said.

"Mommy bought it," Tara said.

"She's not here with you?" Josie said.

"She's shopping. Mommy said I could go to the bathroom by myself. I'm a big girl."

Alyce and Josie exchanged looks.

"Yes, you are. Where's Mommy now, Tara?" Alyce said. "We'll take you back to her."

"Shopping," Tara repeated.

"Is she buying you more clothes?"

Tara shook her head.

"Is she buying your daddy clothes?"

"Daddy doesn't live with us," Tara said. "He has a bitch in Clayton."

Alyce choked. Josie figured Tara's mother was in need of serious retail therapy.

"Is Mommy shopping for shoes?" Josie said.

"Yes," Tara said.

"Then let's go see her," Josie said. She handed Tara a paper towel to dry her wet little paws. Tara took Alyce's and Josie's hands. They walked her to the shoe store halfway down the mall concourse. Tara was heartbreakingly small. Her little pink tennis shoes slapped the marble floor and her belly stuck out under her sparkly shirt.

I could pick her up under one arm and run for the exit, Josie thought. If she screamed, everyone would think I was a good mother removing a noisy child. From the grim set of Alyce's mouth, Josie suspected she was having similar thoughts.

There was only one woman in the shoe store, a trim blonde with a bitter, dissatisfied look. Watching her gave Josie a weird feeling, as if she'd seen little Tara suddenly age.

The blonde sat on a pink chair, drumming her fingers

on the arm. She was surrounded by stacks of shoe boxes. Josie figured the salesclerk was in the back, digging out more stock.

"Mommy!" Tara shouted, and ran to her.

Josie reached in her purse and pulled out her Suttin Services ID card. She flashed it at Tara's mom. "We're Plaza Venetia security, Ma'am," Josie lied. "Do you know it's against the rules to leave a child under twelve unattended in this mall?"

"I just sent her to the ladies' room," Tara's mother said. She sounded put-upon. Her shoe-therapy session was interrupted.

"Prime place for child abductions, ma'am," Josie said. "You've made it easier by putting your child's name on her shirt. She thinks anyone who knows her name must be a friend."

"You have a sweet, trusting child," Alyce said. "She came straight to us without asking questions. Doesn't she know better than to talk to strangers? We could be halfway down the highway by now."

The blonde turned a shade paler, and held Tara's hand tightly.

"If we ever find Tara wandering alone again," Josie said, "we'll have you arrested for child endangerment."

"I didn't mean to—," the blonde said.

"No parent means to have her child abducted," Josie said. "Don't let her wander again."

She saw a woman coming out of the stockroom door, loaded with shoe boxes. "We have to go. We know you're a good mother and it won't happen again."

Alyce and Josie tried not to run out of the store. They didn't talk until they were on the escalator.

"Guess we did our good deed for the day," Josie said.

"OK," Alyce said. "I'm converted. There are no safe places. I'm just another version of that trusting mother. That little girl came right up to us and took our hands. We could have kidnapped her and no one would have noticed."

They were distracted by playful shrieks and cries of, "Give me my cell phone." Four teens were hanging out by the cookie store, laughing and chasing one another around the tables.

"Is that tall one a boy or a girl?" Alyce said, then looked horrified. "Ohmigod. I can't believe it. I sound like my mother, God rest her soul."

"You?" Josie said. "I nearly said, 'You can't tell these days.' Are mom phrases programmed into our brains?"

"I think all four of those kids are girls," Alyce said. "But they have baggy clothes and short hair, so it's hard to tell. Maybe they should wear sparkly shirts like Tara's that say 'BOY' and 'GIRL.' And why aren't they in school?"

"I'm guessing they're playing hooky," Josie said, "something I'm sure you never did."

"I didn't," Alyce said. "But I wish I had. I wish I'd done a lot of things it's too late to do now."

"Really?" Josie said. "Mostly, I wish I could undo things."

Alyce laughed for the first time that day. She took off the black scarf, shook out her fake red hair, and smiled. Suddenly, they were two homemakers on a shopping spree.

Mystery-shopping the Plaza Venetia Pretty Things was easy. The store was neat and clean. The stock was handsomely displayed. The salesclerk, Trisha, was as chic and slender as all the Pretty Things clerks. Unlike the surly Saber, she seemed to enjoy waiting on customers. She chatted with Josie while she rang up the same scarf ring that Saber had despised.

"I have one of these," Trisha said. "I get a lot of use out of it."

"Do you also have a Halley scarf?" Josie said. There was a brilliant blue display on the counter by the register.

"I wish," Trisha said. "That's way out of my budget, even with my employee discount. We debated taking down the Halley display after she died, out of respect. But her signature scarves are selling better than ever. It sounds terrible, but dying was good publicity. Now everyone wants to own her."

"Death as a good career move," Josie said once she and Alyce were out in the corridor.

"Please," Alyce said. "That isn't funny."

"Sorry," Josie said. "Maybe I should have bought a muzzle instead of a scarf ring. Let's swing by Cliff's office in Clayton. It's only ten fifteen."

Cliff's office was in one of the tall mirrored glass towers that infested downtown St. Louis and nearby Clayton. In the nineteenth and early twentieth centuries, businesses built impressive offices. Now they put up mirrored monoliths that reflected the city's past glories.

The vast black marble lobby was empty except for a dark reception desk and a monster two-story gray and white painting.

"What is that?" Josie said. "It looks like a burly aspirin."

"That pays the rent," Alyce said. "It's the ScratchLess allergy pill, the big seller at Cliff's company. ScratchLess produces the scratch."

"No wonder they made a shrine for it," Josie said. "I'd recognize those shades of gray anywhere. Guess who painted that masterpiece? No, you won't have to guess. The signature is two feet high."

"Evelyn," Alyce said.

"The portrait of the artist as a total sellout," Josie said. "I thought Cliff didn't know his wife had an affair with Evelyn. What's he doing with art by his wife's lover in his office lobby?"

"Good question," Alyce said. "Maybe Cliff wasn't blind to Halley's affair after all."

"You certainly can't miss this," Josie said. "Guess Halley was fooling herself when she thought her husband hadn't tumbled to her affair."

"Either that or she didn't tell her good friend Linda everything," Alyce said.

"Can I help you, ma'am?" the guard at the dark desk asked. He was a thin man with a hawk nose and a country accent.

"Yes," Josie said. "We stopped by to see Mr. Cliff Hardwicke."

"Mr. Hardwicke is off this week," the guard said. "There's been a death in his family."

"I'm sorry," Josie said.

"We're all sorry," the hawk-nosed guard said. "He's a nice man. Does a lot for the community." He indicated a display of photos on the far wall. "You can see some of his good works over there. They're for real, too. He's a fine person. Is there any message you'd like to leave for him?"

"No, thanks," Josie said. "Our business can wait."

She and Alyce strolled over to the photos. They saw Cliff hugging bald children in a hospital ward. Cliff holding a squirming puppy at an animal shelter. Cliff presenting a check to the American Red Cross. And Cliff shaking the hand of a huge, tattooed man under a banner that said, CON READ—SOLID, EDUCATIONAL READING FOR PRISONS AND PENITENTIARIES. The big man's T-shirt said, KNOWLEDGE IS THE ULTIMATE DEADLY FORCE.

"My, my," Josie said. "You really can help yourself when you help others."

"What do you mean?" Alyce said.

"I know where Cliff could find a hit man to kill his wandering wife."

Chapter 29

The large woman lumbered out of Alyce's guest bedroom and smiled at Josie. "I can't thank you enough," she said.

Josie blinked. That was Alyce's voice. She could hardly believe the old woman in the nanny's uniform was her friend.

The baggy brown uniform added twenty pounds and twenty years. The lumpy polyester thickened her waist and flattened her breasts. The heavy rubber-soled shoes made her feet seem large and graceless. Her floaty walk was now a down-to-earth stomp.

Too bad the tired lines and shadows on her face were real. Combined with the short, frizzy gray wig, they made Alyce look like her own grandmother.

"It's important to go to Halley's memorial service," Josie said. "I'm glad we found you a good disguise."

"No, I want to thank you for making me wear this uniform," Alyce said.

"You do?"

"It's been ages since anything was too big on me," Alyce said. "This outfit hangs like an old sack."

Josie helped Alyce pin the skirt at the waist so it didn't slide off.

"I've never looked worse," Alyce said with undisguised satisfaction.

"Your own mother wouldn't recognize you," Josie said.

"Of course not. I look worse than she does, and she's dead."

"Alyce!" Josie said.

They dissolved into a fit of giggles that lasted all the way to the church. That was the last laughter they would hear for a long time. The day suddenly grew dark and cold. The gilded sun disappeared behind glowering clouds. The rain started as they ran for the church, but this wasn't a romantic funeral mist. The cold shower soaked their clothes.

Josie and Alyce arrived half an hour early, expecting a crowd. Already, the Episcopal chapel was half-full. On a sunny day, the church must seem simple and beautiful. Today, its stark white walls had the warmth of a refrigerator. The blue stained-glass windows looked like shards of ice.

Alyce and Josie slid into the second-last pew, where they were least likely to be noticed. They pulled out prayer books and breathed in the scent of damp wool, candle wax, and hothouse flowers.

The altar was a cloud of white lilies tied with Halley-blue ribbons. An easel held a photomontage of Halley: golden, glowing, and lucky—until the last moment of her life.

"It seems so empty up there without a coffin," Josie said. "Why was she cremated?"

"It was Cliff's idea," Alyce said. "He told Linda that Halley didn't want to be buried."

How convenient, Josie thought. There would be no body to exhume if the police asked awkward questions later. Josie would give a lot to know if Halley's last wishes were in writing.

"That's her in the blue jar?" Josie asked.

Alyce nodded. "Horrible, isn't it? It looks like a candy jar."

Halley's ashes were in a blue glass urn surrounded by white candles. A ring of fire, Josie thought. The woman was trapped for all eternity in that tiny jar. Cliff had won. He'd kept Halley in St. Louis.

Josie shivered, but not because her clothes were soaked in cold water. The blue glass urn seemed to pulse in the dancing candlelight. Josie wondered if Halley were inside, beating against the hard glass, like a genie trapped in a bottle. No magic could free her. No friend could save her.

Friend. Something nagged at Josie. She'd seen something today at the mall, or maybe at Cliff's office. Something about a friend. The thought niggled and nagged, darting around her mind like an irritating fly. Cliff's friend? Halley's friend? Alyce's friend?

She tried to concentrate on the service. She and Alyce were here to observe the principal players in this drama.

Alyce kept her face shielded by her prayer book. Josie studied the Wood Winds neighbors parading down the aisle. Amy the Slut flounced in first, wearing a black dress as tight as a pressure bandage. Her boobs bulged like forbidden fruit. The mourners looked deliciously scandalized. Amy always gave people what they wanted.

Joanie bustled in next, a small brown bundle of energy. She looked incomplete without a deli tray. Amy gave her a wicked grin. Joanie managed a tentative smile, hesitated, then scurried into the pew behind Amy.

Good for her, Josie thought. Brave little Joanie would not be bullied into sitting next to someone she despised.

Renata Upton Livermore sailed in with her coterie of Alyce cutters. The old woman made a dramatic sight in lavender trimmed with black jet. Betty and Liz trailed behind her, perfectly turned out but somehow diminished in Mrs. Livermore's magnificent wake. Old Lady Liverspot selected a pew two rows from the front, and glared at a black-clad couple until they scooted to the other end. Then she sat down with her attendants.

Last came Linda Dattilo in somber navy. Once again, Josie was startled by the striking combination of green eyes and red-gold hair. How did this rare beauty wind up driving a minivan in Wood Winds?

Linda spotted Joanie, lightly touched her shoulder, and slipped in beside her. As the dead woman's best friend, Linda was entitled to sit closer to the front, but she didn't presume on the family's grief. Josie liked that.

The church was nearly full now. A late arrival pushed into the pew and Josie slid over. Now she had a better view of Cliff Hardwicke in the front row. Halley's husband was tall, bland, and blond. Josie had seen men like him in a hundred annual stockholders' reports.

How could the wildly creative Halley have lived so long with Cliff? At last, Josie thought she understood Halley's affair with skinny little Evelyn. The artist was ridiculous, but at least he was alive. Cliff looked like a robot.

I'm being unfair, she thought. Halley's husband is probably paralyzed by grief. She tried to take the charitable view in church, but Josie disliked Cliff on sight. Besides, she suspected he'd murdered his wife.

Brittney, Cliff and Halley's daughter, sat between her father and a white-haired couple. Judging by their long, bland faces, Josie guessed they were Cliff's parents. There was no sign of Halley's parents. Were they dead? Or too infirm to attend their daughter's funeral?

Five-year-old Brittney was a perfect miniature of her mother, with the same pale blond hair and dark blue eyes, set off by her blue velvet dress. This child was Halley's real masterpiece.

Josie wondered if Brittney's mother had chosen the dress for a special occasion—something besides her own funeral.

"Where's Mommy?" the little girl asked, bunching her blue velvet skirt in her hands.

"Shhh," her grandfather said, and patted her shoulder. Her grandmother smoothed the child's crumpled skirt.

How could Halley abandon her daughter in St. Louis? Josie prayed the little girl never heard her mother's plans to go to New York alone.

"In the midst of life we are in death," the minister intoned.

"I want my mommy," Brittney said. "Where's Mommy?"

Her grandmother tried to comfort the girl, but she shook off the old woman. "I want my mommy." Now her voice was louder and her face redder.

Her father frowned.

"I want my mommy!" the child shrieked. The anguished cry seemed to rattle the windows. *"What did you do with her?"*

She's in a jar, poor child, Josie thought, and felt a tear slip down her cheek.

Brittney's grandfather gathered the struggling child into his arms and carried her out of the cold church. The little girl kicked and screamed, "Mommy! Mommy, where are you?"

The child's cries wrung Josie's heart. Alyce was weeping softly, and so were many of the men and women nearby.

Dear God, let this miserable service be over, Josie thought. She didn't know if that counted as a prayer, but it was answered. Eventually. Josie couldn't remember a word of the eulogies. But the child's cries were burned in her mind.

The mourners filed out of the ice-blue church, shocked and silent. Alyce and Josie ran through the pounding rain to Josie's car.

"That was a horror show," Alyce said. "Don't even think about going to the reception at Halley's house."

Josie started the car. The Honda's steamed-over windows provided Alyce some privacy. She pulled off the wet gray wig and ran her fingers through her own hair. It was flat and oily.

"Of course not," Josie said. "In close quarters, someone might recognize you."

"Even if they didn't, I couldn't take it," Alyce said. "That poor child cried for her mother, and Cliff didn't try to comfort her. He wouldn't hold her. He didn't even take her out of the church. Her grandfather had to do that. Could you imagine living with a man that cold?"

"No," Josie said.

She wondered if Andy, the man she'd been engaged to when she met Amelia's father, would have been like

Cliff if she'd married him. Andy was all business. He even said her engagement ring was an "investment diamond." Once again, she was glad she'd ruined her life with Nate. There were worse fates than a wild fling and an out-of-wedlock child.

"All Halley's talent was reduced to a handful of crushed bone in that dreadful urn," Alyce said.

"Do you think Cliff will keep it on the mantel?" Josie asked.

"It won't matter where he keeps it," Alyce said. "Halley will never get away from him. My Jake is just as trapped. Cliff constructed the perfect frame and put my husband in it. And Jake helped him. Josie, how are we going to get out of this?"

"I don't know," Josie said.

"Poor Halley," Alyce said. "Cliff crushed her. He burned her body. He had her ground into powder."

All that was true.

"But did he kill her?" Josie said. "That's the real question."

Chapter 30

Who killed Halley?

Was it her husband, her lover, or her investor?

They all had good reasons. Halley had used and humiliated all three men in her desperate bid for success.

Cliff had fought with his unfaithful wife the night before she died. He knew thugs who could kill her. He had her body cremated. Those were three good reasons to suspect him.

Then there was the late Evelyn, seething with rage over his lost love—or his lost income. Did he shoot her in a blind rage? Did a witness think Evelyn looked dark-skinned in the shadows of the parking lot? Witnesses were notoriously unreliable. Was his murder proof of Evelyn's innocence? Josie wasn't sure anymore.

Finally, there was Jake. The police had powerful forensic reasons for their choice: DNA and fingerprints. Plus the parking-garage video that showed him handing money to two men, one young and skinny like the killer. The murder weapon was tied to him, too.

The police also had sex and money. Josie agreed with them on that. Alyce wanted to believe her husband was faithful. Mike wanted to give Jake the benefit of the doubt. Maybe Mike was right, but Josie didn't have much faith in the faithfulness of a man with a roving eye.

She thought Jake had had an affair with Halley. If the ambitious designer was willing to slip between Evelyn's unsanitary sheets to advance her career, Halley wouldn't hesitate to seal the deal with Jake with more than a handshake.

Sex and money were a volatile and unstable combination. Halley had lured Jake into stealing his baby son's money. When Halley had tried to nail Jake's last dollar, they'd argued. Did Jake opt for a quick profit with the help of a contract killer? With that keyman policy, Jake had a million-dollar motive for murder.

Josie felt disloyal, but she still wondered if the police had arrested the right man.

You're biased, she told herself. You don't like Jake.

Jake's patrician good looks had no fascination for her. Josie saw the softness of someone who'd never had to struggle. She could never love a man like Jake. But Alyce saw him through different eyes. And Jake was charming—Josie would admit that. She'd seen him work his magic. She could understand his attraction. She just couldn't feel it.

Jake was a man's man, which in Josie's experience meant a man without much regard for women. Josie thought Alyce was the real brains of the marriage. She should be working as a corporate lawyer, preparing the kinds of torts that have nothing to do with kitchens.

But nobody asked you, did they, Josie Marcus? Plenty of people have weighed in on how you should use your talents, and they never include mystery-shopping on their list. But that's what you like to do.

Alyce loves her boy, her Williams-Sonoma kitchen, and the snooty son of a bitch she married. So shut up and help your friend.

Friend. Once again, the word triggered something in Josie's mind. What? Why did she feel so uneasy? What was the connection?

Josie had dropped Alyce off at her home at one o'clock, then drove in the cold rain, trying to sort things out, trying to believe that Jake was innocent and someone else killed Halley. Who? No matter how hard she tried, she couldn't make all the pieces fit for anyone.

Josie decided mystery-shopping would concentrate her

mind. She still had Harry's nasty little gift, the Chunk-A-Chickens.

She stopped to fill her car with gas and rummaged in the trunk for her bag of disguises. She couldn't go in that place wearing her best black pantsuit. By the end of the day, it would reek of old grease and dead chickens. In the gas station restroom, she slipped into jeans and a sweater. Better, but she was still overdressed for a Chunk-A-Chicken.

Her first stop was the Chunk-A-Chicken on Clarkson Road. The bright yellow building with the bold orange trim should have seemed cheery. But the floors were dark with dirt and the windows were yellow with air-borne grease. Grease coated the hair and face of the sad young employee who took her order.

Why didn't you study harder? Josie wanted to say to the kid. You could have had a real job.

She cleared the trash off a table, and used some of her bottled water to wipe off the sticky soda and spilled gravy. She knew what grade she was giving this place for cleanliness.

Josie sat down in the booth, and immediately cursed her boss and whoever left the wet umbrella puddle on her seat. Now her jeans were wet.

Come on, she told herself. Quit whining and get to work.

She poked around in the foam container of chicken chunks, fries, and gravy. She couldn't find any pieces she could positively identify as wings, legs, breasts, or thighs. But she didn't see any feet, heads, or necks, either. She popped a chunk in her mouth. It tasted like chicken-fried fat. The fries were soggy and slick with grease. The brown gravy was like warm glue. She salted a fry, dragged it through the gravy, and ate it. She could practically feel it clogging her arteries.

At the second Chunk-A-Chicken, Josie decided that Cliff was the most likely suspect after Jake. Halley had wanted a divorce, but Cliff didn't. He was bitter and angry. He'd given her the life he'd promised. Halley had lied to him, humiliated him with an affair, then rejected him and their child, all for a career in New York. How about that for a motive?

Two women said he was violent. Joanie heard him throw things. Amy said he'd left her bruised in bed.

Cliff knew people who could kill Halley, thanks to his charity work. Cliff had access to Jake's unlocked car. Cliff knew the artist Evelyn, and had the best reason to kill him.

But if Cliff killed his wife, why didn't he make it seem like an anonymous carjacking? Why set up Jake for the murder? Did Cliff want to make himself look innocent— or was there some long-standing animosity between the two men?

The police usually suspected the husband first. So why did they arrest Jake instead of Cliff? What did they know that cleared Halley's husband?

Josie was so distracted, she ate almost the whole order of chicken, fries, and gravy without thinking. She had to be more careful. Tonight was her date with Mike. She didn't want to be sick.

By the third Chunk-A-Chicken, she wondered if Ramsey, the failed novelist, could have killed Halley.

Not likely, she decided. Ramsey was lazy. This murder took a lot of work. Ramsey preferred to live off the work of others. Besides, how would Halley's death benefit him?

Ramsey wasn't rich enough to invest in Halley's business, and he had no great emotional investment in her.

Josie lifted the lid and looked down at her chicken-fried autopsy. These Chunk-A-Chicken bits were decidedly odd-looking. Did chickens really have that many angles? Josie ladled extra gravy over her order to hide it.

The fourth Chunk-A-Chicken slid down while she considered Granby, the greedy lawyer at Jake's firm. Was "greedy lawyer" an oxymoron?

Granby had plenty of reasons to set up Jake. The man was eaten with ambition. But why would he kill Halley? Was there a personal reason? Did Granby know Evelyn?

Josie had a lot of questions for Granby on their next date. If she could get some answers, maybe she'd be

closer to solving Halley's murder. She'd love to tag
Granby for the killer. The man was a pin-striped socio-
path, lusting for his new Porsche in the wreckage of
Jake's career.

The fifth Chunk-A-Chicken left her queasy. Maybe
that's because she took another hard look at Jake. She
knew why Jake would kill Halley. But why murder
Evelyn?

Because Jake knew about the artist's demand for
money. Evelyn claimed to know the killer, and wanted
money for it.

No, that didn't work. Evelyn said his information
would exonerate Jake. Jake had no reason to kill the
little artist. This murder investigation had more odd
pieces than a carton of Chunk-A-Chicken.

Josie nearly gagged on chicken-fried gristle. That did
it. She couldn't face another Chunk-A-Chicken. She
didn't have the stomach to look at her so-called investigation anymore, either. It was hopeless. She had no forensic facts. The police knew things they weren't telling
outsiders.

The restaurant's yellow walls made her feel bilious.
Josie had to get out of there. The cool, rainy air helped.
She belched, unlocked her car, and reached for the bottle of Maalox she kept in her glove compartment. Josie
chugged a good dose, probably more than she should
have, but desperate meals called for desperate measures.

Josie had questions that needed to be answered, and
she couldn't ask Alyce. She had to talk to Alyce's friends
Linda and Joanie. Friends. Why did that word bother
her? Why did she feel so uneasy?

Because you've eaten enough chicken grease to slide
to Arkansas, she thought.

She turned the car around and headed for the only
people in Wood Winds who would tell her anything.
That's when she remembered Amy's strange warning:
"Not all your friends are really your friends."

Now she knew why the word "friend" nagged at her.
Only one person heard Cliff and Halley argue vio-

lently. Only one person heard Halley say unforgivable things.

Little Joanie.

No one else heard the shouts, listened to the china shatter, or saw an enraged Cliff drive off in the middle of the night. Most people thought Cliff adored Halley. They were surprised to hear the couple was divorcing. Of course, people divorced all the time. But what if their split was a peaceful separation?

What if those arguments never took place?

Linda said Cliff was deadly dull, not violent.

Amy said he liked rough sex, but that didn't make him a killer. If indeed she'd really been to bed with Halley's husband. Amy embraced everything but the truth.

Only Joanie heard him fling crockery and run out of the house. Only Joanie heard those hard words.

Maybe Joanie made it all up. Did she have some reason to hate Halley? Had Halley given her some deadly insult? Or did she covet Halley's husband? Joanie wouldn't be the first woman to move in on a grieving widower—although it would be a neat twist to court him with roast chickens and deli trays made by her current husband.

No, Josie thought. Actions speak louder than words. Joanie was one of the few women in Wood Winds who didn't abandon Alyce.

Maybe she wasn't Alyce's friend. Maybe she came to the house because she wanted to know what was happening with Josie's investigation. Maybe I've finally found out something useful.

It was time to talk with sweet little Joanie, dispenser of deli trays, and find out if she really was Alyce's friend.

Chapter 31

"Would you like a little nosh?" Joanie said.

"No, thanks," Josie said. "I've been mystery-shopping Chunk-A-Chickens."

"You need real food," Joanie said. "Some nice turkey to settle your stomach."

Josie fought back a belch. She was sure it would be the first one in Joanie's perfect kitchen.

"Well, maybe just a taste," Josie said.

"And chicken soup," Joanie said. "I can heat some up. Lots of dill and nice, light matzo balls."

Josie detected an ominous, impolite rumbling deep in her gut. "No chicken," she said quickly.

"Of course not," Joanie said. "What was I thinking? You poor thing."

Joanie's kitchen was sleek with black granite, cherrywood cabinets, and stainless-steel appliances. Josie counted two ovens, two refrigerators, and a stove the size of a minivan. It was another Wood Winds showcase for the culinary arts.

Little Joanie didn't seem intimidated by her cutting-edge kitchen. She was at the granite counter, slicing a turkey breast like it was butter. How did she get a knife that sharp?

"Here," Joanie said. "Try a little of this."

She plunked down a platter piled with turkey, a basket of bread, and a dish of real mayo.

"I can feel my stomach settle down just looking at this," Josie said.

"Don't look. Eat. I like to watch a real eater," Joanie said. "Too many women around here are on diets. They won't touch real butter, fresh eggs, or good, whole cream. They're missing the best part of life. That low-fat junk will kill them. It's bad for their bones."

"Wish it was this easy to make everyone happy," Josie said, tucking into the sandwich. "If I didn't live in Maplewood, you could watch me eat three times a day."

She was surprisingly hungry. How could she scarf down a thick sandwich after five Chunk-A-Chicken stops?

Fried franchise grease wasn't food, she decided. Besides, funerals made her hungry. Memorial services, which didn't have a body, left her feeling even more empty.

"Did you go to Halley's service?" Josie said.

"It was so sad," Joanie said. "A young woman's death is a terrible thing. I'll never forget that little girl crying for her mother. It was pitiful. Afterward, we went to Halley's house. Cliff stood there like a zombie. I think he must be on medication. His parents looked so tired and frail. And there wasn't enough to eat. You don't give people little puff pastries stuffed with cheese nothings after a memorial service. They need substantial food. They need to celebrate life."

I've been celebrating all afternoon, Josie thought. I'll either live or die trying.

"I have some nice cheesecake," Joanie said.

"No, thank you," Josie said.

"With fresh strawberries." Joanie gave a beguiling smile.

That was different, Josie decided. She could get her daily ration of calcium and fresh fruit.

"Just a little piece," Joanie said. She cut a generous slice with a lethal-looking knife, then shook brown powder all over Josie's piece.

"What are you doing to my cheesecake?" Josie said.

"Relax," Joanie said. "I'm just adding fresh-ground cinnamon. They never put enough on these cheese-cakes."

The cheesecake was luscious. While she ate her dessert, Josie peppered Joanie with more questions. "Did the police know about the fights Halley had with her husband?"

"I told them," Joanie said. "But they didn't seem interested. They kept asking me about Halley and Jake."

"What sent them in that direction?" Josie said.

"It certainly was *not* me." Joanie was no longer relaxing in her chair. She shot straight up and sounded defensive.

"Of course not," Josie said. "You've been a faithful friend, which is more than I can say for the rest of this subdivision."

"It isn't Alyce's fault, no matter what her husband did—or didn't do," Joanie said.

"Did Halley and Cliff ever argue about Jake?"

"No," Joanie said. "I never heard his name mentioned once. I told the police that, too." Joanie seemed anxious to make it clear she had nothing to do with Jake's arrest.

"Did Cliff have any reason to dislike Jake? Did they have a dispute about business or any subdivision problems?"

"No," Joanie said. "I go to all the homeowners' association meetings. Jake and Cliff hardly ever attend. They both work late. There was no trouble between them that I know about. Halley and Cliff never fought about Jake. I never heard anything on that subject, and believe me, I heard way more than I wanted."

"It's funny no one else heard those fights," Josie said.

"It's not funny at all," Joanie said. "We're the closest neighbors. Halley and Cliff argued nearly every night, and their fights were bitter. If you don't believe me, ask my husband, Alan. I'm not making up anything."

Joanie's brown eyes were electric with anger. Her hands were clenched inches away from the lethal-looking knife. Suddenly, little Joanie seemed formidable.

"I'm sorry," Josie said. "I didn't mean to imply anything. Thanks for the snack. It was delicious. I'd better go now."

"Yes, you'd better," Joanie said.

Josie left in disgrace. The interview was a waste of time. Worse than a waste, since she'd angered an important ally and inhaled another five thousand calories.

I should give it up, she decided. I'm not going to bother Linda Dattilo today. I'll just commit more blunders.

But Josie was already at Wood Winds. She didn't want to drive back another day to see Linda. What the heck, Josie thought. Mom has already agreed to pick up Amelia. I don't want to try to negotiate another free afternoon. Not after Mom's had to deal with all those deliveries.

So what if I stick my foot in my mouth? I don't live in Wood Woods. Linda won't blame Alyce for my stupid comments. Besides, I can't eat another Chunk-A-Chicken. I'm starting to look like one. My skin is yellow and greasy. My butt is spreading like butter. Tail feathers are next.

Worse, the cinnamon, chicken, and cheesecake were duking it out in her innards. Josie took another swig of Maalox, wiped the chalky stuff off her mouth, and pulled into Linda's driveway.

She'd ask Linda a couple of questions, then get ready for her date with Mike. Halley's best friend should know the names of the other investors. Josie could also ask her about Cliff and Halley's fights. She had to know if Joanie was telling the truth.

Josie rang the doorbell.

"Coming," Linda called. She flung the door open, and gave Josie a startling sight for St. Louis in December. Linda was wearing a pale green bikini. Her red-gold hair was piled on her head. She had a big glass of red wine in one hand.

"Hi," Linda said, raising her glass. "Come join me so I don't have to drink alone."

Linda was slightly sloshed. Halley's funeral must have been a wrenching experience. Linda wasn't a bad drunk, as far as Josie could tell. She was just feeling no pain.

"Wine?" Linda said.

"Sure." Josie figured a liquored Linda would talk. She'd join the party and help her along.

"I'm relaxing in the hot tub," Linda said. "I have a couple of extra suits. Come join me."

"Uh," Josie stalled.

"What's the matter?" Linda said. "Got a hot date tonight?"

"As a matter of fact, I do."

"Well, good for you. Sit with me a little while. You can wash your hair here and wear that black suit you had on at the memorial service for your date. It will look smashing."

Josie started.

"I saw you and Alyce at the church," Linda said. "But I won't tell anyone. I'll even give you my Halley-blue scarf. It will be stunning with that suit."

"I couldn't," Josie said. But she loved that scarf.

"I can't bear to wear it anymore," Linda said. "I was going to give it to Goodwill. I'd rather you have it."

Josie had wanted that scarf. She didn't think about it when she knew it was out of her reach. Now it had been dropped in her lap. Josie couldn't wear a Halley-blue scarf to work, but she could have it on her date with Mike. When he saw what that color did to her hair, she wouldn't be cute. She'd be hot.

"Good. We have a deal," Linda said. "The extra swimsuits are in the guest room closet. Get dressed, turn right, and I'll see you on deck."

Josie chose a modest tank. She'd eaten so much today, her gut would bulge if she wore a bikini. She carried her cell phone with her, in case Jane or Amelia tried to reach her.

Josie opened a sliding door and stepped into the pool area. She stopped, stunned by the view. A piece of the tropics had been built onto the house. The glass room was wonderfully steamy on this cold December day, bright with flowers and palm trees in pots. The warm air smelled of chlorine.

The pool was a deep turquoise. The hot tub was a

warm, bubbling circle off to one side. Linda bobbed in the water, holding her wineglass.

"This is stunning," Josie said. "A pool and a hot tub. What luxury."

"I built this addition with the proceeds from my decorating business," Linda said. "My husband bitches that I don't make enough to maintain them. It costs seven hundred dollars a week to keep the pool and hot tub clean and running. That doesn't include the emergency calls when the damn thing breaks. I don't belong here, futzing with hot tubs. I should be in New York. I've got everything Halley had, except luck."

Wow! Linda was schnoggered, Josie thought. She was definitely ready to spill.

Josie slipped into the hot tub and floated in the warm, bubbling water, hoping she could stay alert. One sip of wine, and she felt pleasantly relaxed and sleepy. Must be all that food at Joanie's.

"What will happen to Halley's company?" Josie said. "Will it keep going?"

"Absolutely. That Halley-blue scarf is a classic," Linda said. "They'll milk it for years. Death never stopped Chanel. Look how many designers have gone on to great success after they died. You can't buy the publicity Halley got."

But I wouldn't want it, Josie thought, and took another sip to avoid saying anything. She was afraid to interrupt this monologue. Linda seemed to be getting drunker. Her eyes were too bright. The conversation was turning slightly creepy.

Josie suppressed a yawn and pinched herself to wake up. The long, stressful day was catching up to her.

"You know, I asked to run the company after Halley died," Linda said. "The investors turned me down. Said they needed someone with New York sensibilities. They acted like I was stomping around here in cow shit. That's why Halley wanted to move to New York in the first place. She was sick of that attitude. I wanted to go with her."

"You'd give all this up to live in New York?" Josie

waved her arm to indicate the incredible pool area.
Whoa. She made a wide swing there. She was getting as
plastered as Linda.

"In a New York minute," Linda said. "Do you think
New Yorkers say that? Probably not. It's just us hicks
in the sticks who talk that way."

"You're too rough on yourself," Josie said. "You're
no hick. You have real talent."

"Who cares, if no one recognizes it? If a decorator
falls in the Midwest, does anyone hear her? I'm going
to spend my life doing cracker-box mansions."

Linda's bitterness began to frighten Josie. She made
a clumsy attempt to change the subject. "Who were Halley's other investors?"

"There were five," Linda said. "Jake was one. The
keyman insurance was his idea, and a damned good one.
One was a lawyer who worked with Jake. Grenville,
Graveby—"

"Granby?"

"That's him," Linda said.

Ohmigod, Josie thought. Granby had another good
reason to destroy Jake and kill Halley. Her murder was
a quick route to his Porsche. Jake's disgrace was the fast
track to his coveted partnership. Did Granby send that
destructive e-mail from Jake's computer? It was such a
simple way to ruin Jake.

"The other two investors were Jake's clients," Linda
said. "Want some more wine?" She climbed out of the
hot tub, lurched over, and topped off Josie's glass, then
sat down heavily on a chaise.

"Uh, can I use your restroom?" Josie said. The wine
was getting to her in other ways, and the bubbling water
didn't help.

"I love that question," Linda said. "What would you
do if I said no—pee in the pool? Of course, you can.
Use the bathroom right off the deck there, so you don't
drip all over the hall floor. I haven't redecorated that
john yet, so don't look at the walls. I'd die if any potential clients went back there, but you're OK. You can't
afford me."

Have I just been insulted? Josie wondered. Well, I wanted her to talk. I got my wish. Linda was still rambling on about the bathroom.

"Those stupid stencils are going. I did them myself—so eighties. I'll replace them with crown molding. The vanity has to be ripped out, too. I decorate other people's houses, but my own is a slum. Towels are on the chaise longue."

Josie wrapped herself in a fat fluffy towel and staggered off to the john. She'd had only a few sips of wine, but she was definitely woozy. Unless she was staggering from all the food she ate. She felt odd. Very odd. Josie wondered if there was something wrong with Joanie's fresh-ground cinnamon.

Even in her woozy state, Josie knew the bathroom wouldn't win any awards for originality. It was powder pink with a boxy beige vanity and a gold-framed mirror. Stenciled near the ceiling was some sort of design. Josie stood on tiptoe for a closer look, then nearly fell backward.

Ohmigod.

It was Halley's famous bird-and-bluebell design, except it was pale pink. It looked so forgettable in that color.

Where did Linda get that design? Did she borrow it from Halley—or did Halley steal it from her?

Suddenly, the puzzle pieces began falling into place. Josie wiped her wet feet on the pink rug and tiptoed through the house to check the theatrical photos in the den again. *Snap!* Another piece fit.

On the way back to the pool, she passed through Linda's kitchen. On the desk there was a pile of magazine subscription cards and catalogs—The Territory Ahead, Harry & David, Omaha Steaks, Neiman Marcus, Tiffany & Co. All the places that had deluged Josie with boxes. *Snap. Snap.* More puzzle pieces fit together.

In the wine rack by the dining room were six bottles of Topolos Alicante Bouschet, the prizewinning California wine. Linda didn't pick up those bottles at the supermarket. She had to order them. And Josie had had a case delivered to her house. *Snap. Snap. Snap.* More pieces. She was getting the whole picture now.

Josie stumbled back out to the pool, dazed by what she'd seen. She had to get out of there. She'd make her excuses and leave. No, run. She wouldn't even bother getting dressed. She'd grab her clothes and drive straight to Alyce's. She could call the cops and Jake's lawyer from there.

"What's wrong?" Linda said. She stood up too quickly and grabbed the chaise arm to steady herself.

"I have to go. I got a call on my cell phone," Josie said. "Mom needs me."

"Your mother called you?" Linda said.

"Just now, when I was in the bathroom," Josie lied.

"I don't think so," Linda said. "Your cell phone is right here on the table. You put it there, remember?"

The phone sat there like a silent accusation.

Without warning, Linda pushed Josie headfirst into the hot tub.

Josie choked, sputtered, and swallowed great gulps of water. She tried not to panic as she flailed around in the warm hot tub. She was bigger than Linda. She could fight her way out. She just had to get her head above the water.

At last, Josie clawed her way to the surface, shook her waterlogged head, and opened her chlorine-raw eyes.

She was staring down the barrel of a pearl-handled pistol.

Chapter 32

Josie could hear the hot tub bubbling like a demented cauldron.

Linda was standing over her, a rabid beach bunny in a pale green bikini. The pearl-handled pistol was small but deadly, like the woman holding it. Looking down that barrel was like staring into eternity.

The fear reached through Josie's fog. Linda didn't seem drunk anymore. She was in control. She had a crazy light in her eyes—the yellow-green that signaled tornado weather. Linda was hell-bent on destruction.

"You figured it out, didn't you, Josie?" Linda said. The soft, alcoholic slur was gone. Her voice was hard and steady.

Keep her talking, Josie thought. Maybe I can distract Linda or pull her into the water. I have to make her drop that weapon.

The adrenaline coursed through Josie's veins like liquid fire, washing away some of the drowsiness. She fought to marshal her scattered thoughts. Don't sit there, she told herself. Talk! But what do you say to a killer?

Josie knew Linda felt unappreciated. She'd try praise.

"Nobody sees how smart you are," Josie said. "You're an actress. The photos were right on the wall, but nobody noticed. You played a boy in *Peter Pan*. It was easy to reprise that successful role and play another young man. You're small and thin. A little dark makeup, a stocking cap, some baggy clothes, and you could pass for a young male shooter. What did you do after—"

Josie hesitated while she searched for the right word. There was no polite way to describe Halley's killing. "After it was over? Run inside the mall and change clothes?"

"You got it in one," Linda said. "I shot the bitch, then ducked into the diaper-changing stall in the women's restroom. I had some baby wipes in my pocket to remove the dark makeup. I took off the gangsta clothes. Underneath, I wore beige pants and a cashmere sweater. Nobody noticed my flats were Dearfoams slippers. They fit right inside my clunky athletic shoes.

"I buried the gangsta clothes and shoes under the smelly diapers in the trash. No one would search that waste can too closely. When I left the stall, I looked like every other woman at the Dorchester. I walked right out of the mall. I was home free.

"You're the only one who bothered to figure it out," Linda said. Admiration tempered the steel in her voice. "The police acted like I was wallpaper. They asked me a few questions about Halley's mood and possible enemies, then dismissed the little woman. I didn't count. The cops knew the killer had to be somebody smart. Only men have brains.

"You're used to being underestimated, too, aren't you?" Linda's pistol wavered for a second. She righted it and pointed it straight at Josie's head.

"The police helped me by arresting some kid running through the other end of the mall. He'd committed that notorious African-American crime, RWB—Running While Black."

Josie wished she had this confession on tape. She wished she wasn't sitting in a hot tub, sick and woozy, with a crazed killer pointing a weapon at her.

Keep Linda talking, she told herself. But it wasn't easy with a gun aimed at her right eye. Josie's mouth was so dry, she could hardly get the next words out.

"Halley stole your design, didn't she?" Josie struggled to stay awake. She wanted to slip into the warm water and close her eyes. What was wrong with her? How could she feel sleepy when she was facing death?

"She's a thief," Linda said. "That pissed me off. She took my design and made it Halley blue. She transformed it with that color of hers. Nobody noticed my design in puke pink. Color is a vital element. I blew it. I admit that.

"I just wanted to go with her to New York. I didn't even ask for a share of her business. I wanted to work for Halley until I got my decorating business going. Her name and contacts could jump-start me in New York.

"You know what she said? I wasn't good enough. She stole my idea and then said I wasn't good enough."

Linda's laugh was corrosive. "I nearly killed her right then. Fortunately, I didn't. They're wrong. Crime does pay."

Snap! The last piece fell into place. "You were the fifth investor," Josie said. "You'll get a share in the key-man-policy money."

If I'm dead and nobody knows you're the killer, Josie thought. She fought harder to remain alert. She wanted to lie down and sleep forever. No! She jolted upright. She saw Amelia, laughing as Josie baptized the giant turtle. Josie had to live. She didn't want to miss one day with her daughter.

"That's right," Linda said. "I invested everything I'd saved to expand my decorating business in her career. A million dollars should be enough to get me out of here."

"What about your little girl?" Josie asked.

The gun shook in Linda's hand, and her finger tightened on the trigger. Oops. Josie had said the wrong thing.

"You mean my little mistake?" Linda said. "She's better off without me. She's Daddy's little girl. If I go to New York, she'll have him all to herself. We never hit it off. Halley and I had that in common, too. Motherhood was a mistake and we both knew it. That's the problem with kids. You can't drop them off at the Humane Society when you get tired of them.

"Oh, don't look so shocked, Josie. Do you know how many women in Wood Winds are bored with playing Mommy? Give them enough wine and you'll find out.

Half the women here would dump the kids like stray kittens if they could get away with it."

Linda's red-gold hair came loose from its clip and tumbled down her back, giving her a wild beauty. Josie could see she was growing more upset. The gun barrel was almost in reach. A little closer, Josie thought. Just a step closer, and I'll be able to grab it. She fought back another wave of tiredness. Calm her down. Keep her talking while you look for an opening. And dammit, stay awake.

"Why did you set up Jake?" Josie said. "Not that I object. He's a jerk." It felt good to say those last three words, even to a double murderer.

"Because he's an arrogant son of a bitch," Linda said. "He was at Halley's house a hundred times and barely remembered my name. Every time we met, he'd say the same thing, 'You're Linda, right?' Then he'd forget and we'd go through that routine again.

"He always remembered Halley's name. She promised to make him rich. Halley knew how to lead men on."

Josie had a sudden flash of inspiration. "Jake did more than forget your name. He cut you out of the New York job, didn't he?"

"See, you are smart," Linda said. "Or maybe you know Jake. I bet he never quite remembers your name, no matter how many times he sees you with Alyce."

"That's right," Josie said.

Jake is facing murder charges because he forgot Linda's name, Josie thought. He made her feel like nothing. And she got her revenge. Amelia was right. The little things we aren't aware of can make a lasting impression on someone else.

"Halley killed me, but Jake put the stake through my heart," Linda said. "The keyman policy required us to have a backup administration in place in New York, in case anything happened to Halley. She was traveling to Italy twice a month, and that wasn't the safest country for a businessperson. There'd been a rash of kidnappings.

"I offered my services as backup. I had all the qualifications. I had a successful decorating business. I knew how to run an office, and I had design experience. Experience? Halley stole my design, although I'd kept my mouth shut."

"Why didn't you sue her?" Josie said.

"Because I still had hopes of riding on her coattails. I thought I could guilt her into taking me to New York. But Halley told the other investors I wasn't talented enough. And Jake, charming Jake, said I was 'only a housewife' with no executive experience or planning skills. So the other investors voted against me, and hired someone in New York.

"That's when I decided to kill Halley and blame Jake for her murder. He'd never guess it was me. I didn't exist for him. Well, he got a taste of my planning skills. I set him up so perfectly he'll never be free. The keyman insurance was my idea, by the way. Jake took credit for it. Maybe he really believed he suggested it. He'll pay dearly for stealing that idea. And me? Well, the million bucks I'll get from the keyman policy is more than I'd get suing Halley.

"Jake had a cold coming on, and he kept sneezing. Halley gave him a tissue. He used it and dropped it on the ground. That was so Jake. The world is his trash can. I picked it up and put it in my purse. It was yucky."

Yucky? A woman who'd murdered two people thought a used tissue was yucky?

"I left it in the hotel room when I tied the scarves on the bedpost. That gave the cops their DNA. I used Halley's key to get in. Jake gave it to her. I slipped it out of her purse. Jake never asked the police if her hotel key was missing. He wasn't a detail man.

"I didn't know about the video in the parking garage, but it helped me. It was like God wanted me to blame Jake."

Josie didn't think God had anything to do with it, but she kept that to herself. The pistol was still pointed at her eye, and Linda was gripping the gun tightly.

"I knew Halley's schedule," Linda said. "When she was in town, she always checked the mall stores on Monday. I picked the Dorchester Mall for the carjacking because it had a crime problem. The purse snatchings and holdups were the talk of Wood Winds.

"Killing Halley was easy. I walked up and shot her. She looked surprised for a second, but she never said a word. She never knew it was me. My disguise was perfect. You know what? It felt good to kill her. I never lost a night's sleep. She deserved it."

Josie shivered in the warm water. Linda wouldn't hesitate to shoot her when this monologue was over.

Keep her talking, Josie thought. Keep yourself alive. And stay awake. She dug her nails into her leg, and the pain brought her back.

"Jake deserved what happened to him," Josie said. She almost believed it. "But why kill Evelyn?"

"I put the suffering artist out of his misery." Linda gave a hard, harsh laugh. "He figured it out. I don't know how, but he knew I was the killer. I'd underestimated him. I never told a soul how I felt about Halley's betrayal. But I put it in a letter and sent it to her. I told her I wasn't going to sue, but I wanted Halley to know that I knew she'd stolen my idea. It was my only mistake. Somehow, Evelyn got it. He knew it gave me a motive for her murder. It wasn't my fault, not really. His own greed killed him. The great lover wanted money to keep quiet. When I refused to pay him, he said someone else would buy that information."

"So he called me," Josie said.

"And tried to get the money from Alyce. I heard you on your cell phone at her house. I knew Alyce would pay anything to save Jake. I had to act fast. I called Evelyn, said I'm meet him at his place that night, and I'd pay twice what Alyce would.

"Evelyn was so trusting. He met me alone in his disgusting little rathole. He thought he could handle a housewife. He'd been drinking, as usual. I put secobarbital in his wine. He passed out in less than ten minutes. I strangled him with a Halley scarf."

Wine. Josie's sluggish thoughts suddenly stirred. "You've drugged my wine."

"That's right," Linda said. "It's starting to work. I've been watching you fight it, but you won't be able to much longer. In another two or three minutes, you'll fall asleep and drown."

That sent an electric jolt through Josie. Her eyes opened wide.

"Don't worry," Linda said. "It won't hurt. I'll have some secobarbital in my wine, too, but not as much as I put in yours. My husband is due home early today. He'll find us. You, unfortunately, will have drowned in the hot tub. I will pass out on the chaise and survive."

"But they'll trace the drug back to you," Josie said.

"Do you think I'm stupid enough to order it at my own address, under my own name? I bought it on the Internet under a fake name."

An angry Linda waved the gun at Josie. "They'll find traces of secobarbital in my wine, too. When they revive me, I won't remember much, except that Jake stopped by to talk to you and I invited him in."

"Jake?" Josie said.

"Yes, Jake. They'll find the secobarbital bottle in his glove compartment. The arrogant twit still doesn't lock his car, even after all that's happened. Some people never learn."

Josie waited for Linda to be distracted, so she could make a grab for the gun. But the demented decorator was too guarded.

"You sent me all those catalogs and packages," Josie said. "You wanted to stop my investigation."

"I wrote down your credit-card information when you were at my house. Women are so careless with their purses. Too bad my plan didn't work. I really liked you, Josie. I wanted you to live."

Linda said that last sentence with such sadness, Josie almost felt sorry for her. Then it penetrated her drugged brain that this woman felt bad about killing her.

"When I couldn't stop you, I started planning to get rid of you. I took you seriously. If you hadn't stopped by today, I would have invited you tomorrow."

Josie searched desperately for another topic. "Granby," she said. "He hated Jake. Is he working with you?"

"That idiot? Of course not. But I did tell him an interesting story I'd heard about a corporate lawyer who was working on a huge takeover. His career was destroyed by an e-mail somebody sent from his computer to the CEO of the takeover target. I could practically hear the lights go on in Granby's greedy little brain. I knew he was desperate to make partner and wanted Jake out of the way.

"But we've talked long enough. Take a nice big drink of your wine and say good night, Josie."

This was it. Linda would force her to swallow the rest of the wine. Then the bubbling water would close over Josie's head. She would never see Amelia again. Never shop for her prom dress. Never watch her go on a date.

Date! She couldn't let her daughter grow up alone and unprotected.

Might as well go for it, Josie decided. She's going to kill me, anyway. She grabbed the hot-tub railing and, with a mighty effort, pulled herself out of the pool. The water felt like heavy wet hands pulling her back into a watery grave. She flopped onto the deck.

"Stop!" Linda screamed. "Get back in or I'll shoot."

"No, you won't." Josie was wet and shivering. She longed for one of the thick towels on the chaise. "Your husband is due home shortly. You'll never be able to clean up all the blood in time. Besides, where are you going to put my body?"

"In the toolshed in the backyard," Linda said.

"Won't work," Josie said. "I'm heavier than I look. There will be drag marks in your sod. Your husband will notice."

"No, he never—"

But Linda didn't get a chance to finish the sentence. Josie lunged for the weapon. "Give me the gun."

"No!" Linda said. "I'll shoot you, and then I'll kill myself. I won't go back to this life. I won't."

"Put the gun down," Josie said.

"You're going to die," Linda screamed.

A tinny tune interrupted her dramatic scene. Linda and Josie both froze.

Josie recognized her cell phone's song: U2, "New Year's Day." That put her a split second ahead of Linda.

Josie kicked her in the bikini wax with all her might. Linda doubled over, but she still clung to the gun. Josie grabbed the wine bottle from the table, and tried to hit Linda on the head. Linda slid sideways on the wet tile, ducked the wine bottle, and brought up the gun. It was pointed at Josie's heart.

"You're going to die, Josie," she gasped. "I don't care anymore. I want—"

Josie swung the wine bottle like a baseball bat, and slammed Linda on the shoulder. Josie heard a crack like a tree branch breaking. The gun dropped from Linda's hand and skidded across the pool tile.

Josie kicked it into the hot tub. She was gasping for breath. She held the wine bottle, poised for another swing.

Linda rocked back and forth on the slippery tile, holding her injured arm. Tears splashed on her bikini top.

"Don't hurt me," Linda said. "Don't hate me. I just wanted out of St. Louis."

Epilogue

"You're alive because you ate five Chunk-A-Chickens," Mike the plumber said. "I don't believe it."

Josie didn't believe she was in this cold hospital room with a hot Mike holding her hand. Too bad an IV was stuck in it with enough tape to wrap every Christmas present in Maplewood.

"Hey, I'm only repeating what the doctors told me," Josie said. "The Chunk-A-Chickens saved my life. Linda drugged my wine, but the chicken grease and Maalox coated my stomach and slowed down the secobarbital. Otherwise, I could have died."

Josie couldn't believe she said that. She could have died, but she didn't. She was floating on painkillers and pure happiness. On the other side of the curtain, her roommate snored gently after gallbladder surgery.

"But you ate five Chunk specials with fries and gravy," Mike said. "That would kill a normal person."

"I know," Josie said. "My horrible boss, Harry, is taking credit for saving my life. He says I'd be dead if he hadn't given me that rotten job."

"He called it a rotten job?" Mike said.

"Well, no," Josie said. "But he made me mystery shop Chunk-A-Chickens because he was mad that my report got his niece fired. Most mystery shoppers refuse to eat that garbage. They pretend to taste it and lie on their reports."

"Your dedication saved your life," Mike said.

"You want to hear the worst part?" Josie said. "Harry

says Chunk-A-Chicken is thrilled by the publicity. They're putting out a press release about the lifesaving properties of their product. They've requested me as their permanent mystery shopper. How could I be so lucky?"

"Actually, you are one lucky lady."

"Don't I know it," Josie said. "It's almost midnight and I'm supposed to be dead."

She was definitely alive right now. In fact, she was tingling all over. She felt like celebrating. No, she felt like ripping off Mike's clothes.

Whoa, girl, she thought. Calm down. This isn't love. It's adrenaline overload. Besides, your mother and daughter are right down the hall, trying to find a soda.

That worked better than a bucket of cold water. Josie knew she was hardly a romantic sight. Her hair was stiff with chlorine, her face was ghost pale, and her gut was distended. Josie prayed nothing awful erupted while Mike was in the room.

"What did they do to you?" Mike said. "And how long are you in here?"

"They put me on this IV, pumped my stomach, and threw some activated charcoal in there to absorb any drugs that were left," Josie said. "They also took about half my blood for liver-function tests."

"Ohmigod," Mike said. He gently petted her taped hand. Josie thought she would drown in the sympathy in his deep blue eyes.

"Wasn't that bad," she said. She almost shrugged, except that would hurt too much. "I'm glad they did it. I'd been mystery-shopping Greta Burgers and Chunk-A-Chickens. I hope this removed the last traces of both. They'll probably have to sandblast my arteries."

"When do you go home?"

"They're watching me tonight. If everything is normal, I go home in the morning."

"Josie, I haven't known you that long, but 'normal' isn't a word that describes you."

"It's relative," Josie said. "My relatives should be back here in about two minutes."

Suddenly, Josie yawned. Long hours in the emergency room, and God knew how many questions by the police, had taken their toll. Josie felt like someone had pulled the plug on her. Mike was sensitive enough to notice.

"You're beat," Mike said. "I'd better go."

"I'm sorry. This isn't exactly the evening we planned," Josie said.

"My grandma used to say, 'If you want to make God laugh, tell him your plans.' Thanks for calling to cancel our date. With all you had going on, I'm surprised you even thought of me."

Josie looked at that rugged face with the *Miami Vice* beard, the broad shoulders and strong hands. "I don't think I can forget you."

She gave Mike a good-bye kiss that made sure he'd remember her.

Josie was asleep when Jane and Amelia returned with three sodas.

The morning sun was like a slap in the eye. Josie's roommate had her TV on low. Josie recognized the announcer's voice. It was her main morning man, John Pertzborn on Fox 2 News.

"Murder charges against Attorney Milton 'Jake' Bohannon were dropped when police found new evidence in the killing of designer Halley Hardwicke," John said. "Linda Dattilo was arrested and charged with the murder of the Wood Winds designer and the West End artist known as Evelyn. Ms. Dattilo is a popular Wood Winds decorator. Police said—"

Josie's phone rang. She knew who it was before she picked it up.

"It's me." Alyce sounded like her old self. "Josie, I'm so sorry you're in the hospital. I can't thank you enough for all you've done. I knew Jake was innocent. I'm glad you believed in him, too. I have to go now, but we'll thank you in depth later. Can you have visitors?"

"I'm going home this morning," Josie said. "I'm fine. Mom will be here. Stay with Jake. He needs you."

Jake was free. That meant Josie was free, too. She didn't have to go out with Granby Hicks. Josie called him and canceled their date. She didn't mention she was in the hospital. The less she talked to Granby, the better.

Granby was furious. She thought he might sue her for a breach of the social contract.

"That's outrageous. You can't cancel," Granby said. "You have a commitment. You made that date days ago. I have reservations."

"I have reservations, too," Josie said. "Serious reservations about going out with a sleaze like you. Goodbye, Granby."

Josie enjoyed hanging up on him.

Thirty minutes later, her mother was glowering at Josie. Her arms clutched a shopping bag full of clean clothes, but Jane held them hostage until she got the answers she wanted.

"I got a call from Mrs. Mueller," Jane said. "Why did you cancel your date with Granby?"

The neighborhood information network never ceased to amaze Josie. Mrs. Mueller had set up that date, and assumed she'd made a perfect match. She probably had Josie's wedding present on layaway.

"He's not a nice man," Josie said.

"Oh, Josie," her mother said. There was a world of disappointment in those two words.

"No, I mean it, Mom. He's a horrible person. After what he did on our last date, I never want to see him again."

"He didn't try to force you to—"

"Yes, he did, Mom." He tried to force me to go out to dinner with him, Josie thought, but Jane, bless her, would assume the worst.

Sure enough, Jane gasped, then clenched her fists. "Where is he? Let me at him. When I finish with him—"

"I've handled it," Josie said. "You don't have to worry. Just promise me no more blind dates from Mrs. Mueller."

"Certainly not. Not when she tried to fix my daughter

up with riffraff! And speaking of riffraff, why on earth did you go to that murderer's house alone, Josie Marcus?"

"Because I didn't know Linda was a murderer," Josie said. "As soon as I figured it out, I tried to get out of there, but it was too late."

"You would have been dead if I hadn't called you at the right moment," Jane said.

Her mother was taking credit for saving Josie's life, too. Josie figured Jane deserved to. Now the scene by Linda's hot tub seemed almost funny. But Josie hadn't been laughing when her cell phone had played the lifesaving tune that made Linda hesitate. The scene had replayed in Josie's head all night long, in an endless loop.

Josie had kicked Linda in the crotch, hit her with the wine bottle, and dumped the gun into the hot tub. Then she'd wrapped the flexible pool hose around the designer's doubled-up form.

For good measure, Josie had pinned her with a heavy wrought-iron chair. By then, the fight seemed to go out of Linda. She clutched her injured arm. She wept for her lost opportunities. That's when Josie realized her cell phone was still ringing.

She'd stood by the steaming hot tub and opened the phone with shaking fingers.

"Josie," her mother had said, "I don't know why you carry that fancy phone if you're not going to answer it."

"Mom, I've got Halley's killer. Call 911."

"Where are you? What's wrong?"

Josie shouted over the bubbling tub and the weeping Linda, "Mom, I caught Halley's killer. Call 911. I'm at the home of Linda Dattilo in Wood Winds. It says 'Dattilo' on the mailbox. I've got the killer tied up."

"Don't go away. Stay on the line," Jane said. "I'll call the police from my other phone. They'll be there in no time to save you and Linda."

"Linda's the killer," Josie said.

"You're not making any sense, Josie. You're in shock. Keep talking to me. The police will be there right away."

Josie couldn't hear what her mother told 911, but in six minutes, Jane had enough law enforcement personnel at Linda's house for a whole season of *Law & Order*. A woozy Josie staggered and stumbled around, trying to explain what had happened. At first, the police thought she was drunk. Finally, they understood she'd been drugged.

Her mother broke all speed records, arriving at the ER with Amelia just as Josie's ambulance pulled up. Good old Jane. She was tough and determined.

"Josie? Why are you staring off into space?" Jane demanded, pulling Josie out of her reverie.

"I was thinking that you were magnificent yesterday, and I can't thank you enough. GBH, Mom."

Josie wrapped her mother in a great big hug, then pulled back in surprise. "Mom, you don't smell like cigarette smoke."

"I quit," Jane said. "It was the only way I could afford the new paint job and porch railings. I was setting fire to my money."

"I'm glad you stopped," Josie said.

Josie would never admit it, but she was also glad that Jane had started. Amelia now thought smoking was gross. Josie wouldn't have to worry about her daughter sharing any more rebellious smokes in the girls' bathroom.

Her daughter was peeking around the room-divider curtain. "Mom, what did you do to your hair?" Amelia said. Jane must have made her wait outside until after the lecture session.

"Like my new style?" Josie said. "It's a special chlorine mousse."

"You're nutso-crazy," her daughter said. "But my friends think you're sweet. None of their moms would catch a killer in a hot tub."

"Thank you." Josie remembered how she'd clung to the idea of surviving so she would see Amelia again. "I couldn't have done it without you."

* * *

A week after Linda had been led away in handcuffs, Josie finally had a chance to sit down and really talk to Alyce.

Alyce had wanted to fix an elaborate dinner, but Josie wanted life to return to normal. She never had dinner with Alyce. She wanted coffee in her friend's kitchen.

It was good to sit at the granite island, surrounded by the warm oak paneling and Alyce's collection of kitchen gadgets.

"So far, the only one who isn't taking credit for saving my life is Linda," Josie said. "I almost feel sorry for her."

"Are you crazy, Josie Marcus?" Alyce said. "She nearly killed you. She tried to destroy my husband. She nearly ruined our lives and left your daughter an orphan. Save your sympathy for someone who deserves it."

"I know. She did terrible things. She killed harmless little Evelyn, and that was unforgivable. She made my life hell. I'm still returning stray magazines.

"But Halley triggered it. Yes, it was wrong to kill her. But Halley almost deserved killing for what she did to Linda. That was cruel and pointless."

"I agree," Alyce said, "though I can't say that to anyone but you. But I wouldn't feel too sorry for Linda. She got what she wanted. It was in the paper today. Her lawyer's already had calls from a documentary producer and a writer for *Vanity Fair*. New York will notice her at last."

"She'll be out of St. Louis, too," Josie said. "If she takes the plea bargain, she'll probably go to the women's prison in Vandalia, Missouri."

Alyce's phone rang. It did that often these days. "Excuse me," Alyce said. "I have to take this call."

She picked up the phone. "Yes, Mrs. Livermore," Alyce said. "The meeting is tomorrow at two. I'll be there. What can I bring? Just myself? I'll see you then." She hung up.

"I can't believe you've rejoined all your clubs and committees," Josie said. "How can you do that after the way those women snubbed you? I'd tell them to go to hell."

"Justin needs his playdates," Alyce said. "Jake has his career. Those people are useful, but I know they're not my real friends. Besides, I'm no longer the boring little wife. I'm the woman married to the former alleged killer. I have my old life back, but I'm much more interesting now."

Alyce looked radiant this morning. She had her floaty walk and blond halo of hair. Josie didn't have to ask if she'd moved back into the master bedroom.

"The lawyer says it looks like Jake's share of the key-man insurance is going to come through," Alyce said. "We'll get one million two hundred and fifty thousand dollars. Linda won't get her share, of course, though they'll hold it in escrow until her court case is settled, then divide it among the other investors, once it's proven they had nothing to do with Halley's murder. Our son will have a million dollars in his college fund."

"That's some trust-fund baby," Josie said. "Are you going to blow the rest?"

"The rest goes into an account just for me," Alyce said. "It was the only way I'd take Jake back."

Josie knew what that account meant. Her friend was no longer dependent on Jake's largesse. Alyce was free to walk away from the marriage anytime she wanted.

"Jake's been completely cleared of any wrongdoing with the takeover debacle. Granby was so eager to nail him that he sent the e-mail from Jake's PC and never bothered to check why Jake wasn't in his office. Jake was in Chicago on business. He couldn't have sent that message from his St. Louis office. He was in a meeting with six other attorneys in the Sears Tower. Worse, Granby was dumb enough to sign onto Jake's machine with his own password."

"So I guess he won't be making partner?" Josie said.

"Granby's lawyering days are over," Alyce said. "The only good news for the firm is that since he's not a partner, their liability is substantially reduced."

Josie heard footsteps on the stairs. Jake came down in a blue chalk-striped suit. Josie looked for signs of stress, but he seemed untouched by the last few weeks.

"Hi, Josie," Jake said.

Alyce beamed, as if he'd said something clever, and kissed him on the cheek.

"Alyce tells me you were a big help with our little problem," he said.

"Right," Josie said. Little problem? She smiled at Jake and thought: I don't have to live with him. I don't have to love him. I don't have to sleep with him. He's Alyce's man and he makes her happy, and so I'm happy for her.

"Thank you for everything," Jake said. "I mean that. If there's ever anything I can do, please let me know." Once again, Josie caught a hint of the charm that so captivated Alyce. Jake's gaze was so intense, he made Josie feel like she was the only woman in the room.

Josie realized Jake was holding her hand when her cell phone rang. She looked at the display number. It was her mother.

Oh, boy.

"Excuse me," Josie said. "I have to take this."

"Josie?" Jane sounded shaky. "There's another mountain of packages being delivered to our house. I swear I didn't order them."

"Packages? From where?" Josie said.

"All sorts of places: Neiman Marcus. Tiffany's. Dell computers. Pottery Barn. Bed, Bath & Beyond. Williams-Sonoma. And something called UGG."

"I didn't order any of it, Mom. Send it all back, please."

"No, don't," Alyce said. "Those are thank-you presents from Jake and me. Why don't you go home and open them?"

"Please, Josie," Jake said. "You'll do us a favor if you'll accept them. We're forever in your debt. There's no way we can repay you."

Josie left the couple holding hands in the kitchen.

Back home, her living room was waist-high with boxes and packages. Josie refused to open them until she picked up Amelia from school.

"Sweet," Amelia said when she surveyed the stacks

of boxes with the pricey labels. "Did we win the lottery or what?"

"We won the friendship lottery," Josie said. "Alyce got us all these things."

"Well, she should," Amelia said. "She nearly got you killed. Anyway, presents are cheaper than a murder trial."

"Amelia!"

It took them an hour to open all the boxes. There were cashmere sweaters for Josie and Amelia, an iPod for Amelia, UGG boots for Josie, and an Elsa Peretti necklace from Tiffany & Co.

"That's for me," Amelia said.

"That's for me," Josie said. "But if you're good, you can borrow it."

The purple bedspread was definitely for Amelia. "My fave color," she said. "Sweet!"

Jane had a new pantsuit and a chic pink suede purse. "That's much too expensive for me," Jane said, blushing with pleasure.

Josie knew she wouldn't be able to pry that purse out of her mother's grip.

When the orgy of box opening ended, there was only one small package left on the end table. It was from Williams-Sonoma.

"The last one is yours, Mom," Amelia said.

Josie opened it, and burst out laughing. Jane and Amelia stared at a metal device that looked like a piece of miniature farm equipment.

"What is it?" Amelia said.

"An herb mill," Josie said.

"Weird," Amelia said. "What herb are you going to put in it?"

"Rosemary," Josie said.

"That's for remembrance," said Jane, who knew her Shakespeare.

"What do you want to remember?" Amelia said.

"Who my friends are," Josie said.

Author's Note

My mother was a mystery shopper in the 1960s. She shopped at supermarkets and fast food places with her best friend, the way Josie and Alyce do. Mom was a traditional homemaker and wanted to be home when the kids got off school. Mystery-shopping let her do this.

There's no way Mom could have made a full-time living from mystery-shopping. There's more to it than "getting paid to shop and eat." It was hard work. Mom sometimes had to drive more than a hundred miles a day on highways clogged with construction and traffic. Her feet hurt from trudging through malls.

Can you really make a living from mystery-shopping like Josie?

Josie is a mystery shopper the way James Bond is a spy. You've probably read newspaper stories about mystery shoppers who make seven thousand dollars a month. That's possible, but unlikely. Most people mystery-shop for extra money, cheap vacations, and free meals.

Sometimes these jobs end up costing you money. Various Web sites have been known to prey on the unwary. Consumer sites warn that most information provided in the handbooks sold on these questionable sites can be found free elsewhere on the Web. Before you sign on with any company, check out David Grisman's site, www.2007topscams.com/mystery-shopping, to learn the pitfalls. He recommends avoiding companies that require you to pay fifty dollars or more to work for them with no money-back guarantee. Remember, the number one rule of working is: "The job pays you."

Grisman reviewed 329 mystery-shopping Web sites and found that 319 were scams. His one sure-fire test is asking: Does the site offer a money-back guarantee? If the answer is no, then beware. You don't want to sign on with them.

Grisman's top three legitimate picks are: Shopping Jobs (www.shoppingjobs.net), Get Paid 2 Shop (www.getpaid2 .com), and Shop Until You Drop (www.shopuntilyoudrop .net). (Just a note: Shop Until You Drop has no connection to my novel *Shop Till You Drop*.)

If you're not sure about a mystery-shopping company, check with your state attorney general's office (www.naag .org), the Better Business Bureau (www.bbb.org), the Federal Trade Commission (www.ftc.gov), or call 877-FTC-HELP.

You can also join Mystery Shopping Providers Association, the professional trade association. MSPA's Web site, www.mysteryshop.org, has a wealth of information for people who want to be mystery shoppers in North America, Europe, and Asia.

"There, they can find information on how to be a shopper with an MSPA company, what jobs are available in their region, and how to access information on the mystery shopper industry," the MSPA site says. If you are looking for a mystery shopper job, make sure your potential company is a member of MSPA and follows their code of ethics

Also, check the MSPA site for the latest mystery-shopping scams. One current swindle has the mystery shopper cashing a large cashier's check to evaluate a bank's service. The unwary mystery shopper then wires the money to an address outside the U.S., and supposedly gets to keep several hundred dollars as a reward.

"The cashier's check bounces several days later and the consumer is held liable for the entire amount of the money they wired to the international address—typically between $2,500 and $3,500," the MSPA says.

Another good source for reliable mystery shopper information is www.Snopes.com/fraud/employment/shopper .asp. Check the "secret shopper scams" section.

Shopping for Accessories

Pucci, Fendi, Chloe, and other designer names can be found at www.net-a-porter.com/Shop/Accessories. Good buys on accessories are available at many online sites, but some may be last year's styles. Try to avoid the color of the season (acid green, for instance) and you'll have an accessory you can use for a long time.

If you must have a designer name, there are bargains available. Chanel, Gucci, Dior, Fendi, and Louis Vuitton are among the major names available at www.designer exposure.com and www.overstock.com, where you can buy discount jewelry, shoes, hats and handbags. Some of the items are overstocks or last year's styles, but $165 for a Unisex Cross Black Perforated watch is a deal. The Diesel hammered silver metal bracelet with the signature coin is $90. Another jewelry site to consider is www.smartbargains.com. At press time, Movado watches were half price.

Can't bring yourself to spend a thousand dollars on a designer scarf?

Target has trendy accessories by Rafe. Bags, belts, sunglasses and shoes run $25 to $50. Target items are smart and stylish, but many customers will tell you they are designed to last for only one season.

Best time for accessory sales: Fourth of July weekend. January is also a good time for sales, especially for winter accessories. Most online sites have sales year-round.

If you're shopping at an actual brick-and-mortar store, many experts recommend shopping on Thursday evenings for clothing. "That's the day stores restock for the weekend, and many retailers start their weekend promotions," Kathryn Finney, author of *How to Be a Budget Fashionista*, told AOL. Finney says Saturday evening, just before closing, is a prime time for bargains at department stores, because the stores mark down items for the Sunday sales. She also recommends printing out the sale preview from the store's Web site, because many store employees will honor the sale price, even if the item isn't technically on-sale yet.

Keepers: A fashion model once gave me this advice: "Never throw out your accessories. Eventually, they all come back in style." She was right, according to an AOL survey of the hottest fashion accessories. Of course, sunglasses are number one for summer, but surprisingly, belly-button rings came in third.

When's the last time anyone you know had her belly button pierced?

There's a whole line of body jewelry on the Web, including a dangling martini glass to decorate your navel. And a tasteful cherry belly ring. My Irish grandmother would spin in her grave if she knew women were now wearing Claddagh belly rings (which cost only $8.99 online).

Inexpensive navel rings can be found at www.body candy.com, along with eyebrow, nipple, toe, and nose rings. They also have vibrating tongue rings.

Shades of the seventies, color-changing mood rings were number seven on the AOL summer search list, right above nose rings. You can buy them at www.moodjewelry.com—along with mood belly rings.

Green accessories: For those interested in saving the Earth, Revival Ink is an eco-friendly site that "eliminates production of new waste by reinventing vintage clothing."

"My mission is to provide fashionable and affordable

styles for the average consumer by reusing existing clothing and fabrics," owner Tara Smith says on her Web site. "I get my clothing from vintage shops, overstock, and organic cotton wholesalers." She also "uses PVC-free textile inks and nontoxic cleaning products."

Revival Ink has scarves for $15 to $25, hoodies for $25 to $55, and tees for $18 to $28.

For more information go to www.revivalink.com

Dress like a star: Greta Garbo's fabulous silver-and-turquoise bracelet. Pamela Anderson's blue earrings from the television show *V.I.P.* Jack Benny's wallet. Angelina Jolie's necklace. These and other celebrity accessories can be bought at various Web sites.

The items mentioned are from www.roslynherman.com and the collector promises a certificate of authenticity.

Celebrity accessories are surprisingly affordable, even for Golden Age movie stars. Jack Benny's wallet is described as "in perfect condition"—and it's $275.

Greta Garbo's silver-and-turquoise Art Deco bracelet is $875, and Garbo's yellow lace headband is $125. Angelina's beads are $225, but the necklace needs restringing. Pamela's blue earrings are $175. You can also buy her six-inch-high Lucite heels for $325. So far, no word on whether Pam's wedding bikini will be up for sale soon.

The New York Times says there's a cottage industry selling off clothes from TV shows and films. Castoffs from *Sex and the City* found their way to It's a Wrap outlet store (www.itsawraphollywood.com) in Burbank, California.

It's a Wrap also sold Tom Hanks's loincloth from *Castaway* for $2,450. (It didn't say if the loincloth had been cleaned or still has the original celebrity sweat.) Denzel Washington's socks from *Courage Under Fire* were $40. Rhinestones that once graced Sharon Stone's ears were on sale for $225 and Jennifer Lopez's lace teddy from *Angel Eyes* was $1000, custom-framed.

Reel Clothes (www.reelclothes.com) is another celebrity wardrobe site, and the *Times* says you'll find many famous fashions. Many of these designer clothes have never been worn—the shows buy two of each in case there's a fashion mishap.

Paris shopping: Heiress Paris Hilton wore a JET hoodie by John Eshaya. Jessica Simpson sported an "Apple" hoodie. Paris was photographed in a red Voom baby-doll dress and a frayed-billed Brokedown cap.

The favorite casual wear of the Hollywood princesses is sold online at Shop-Ashiya (www.shop-ashiya.com). Better yet, you don't have to be a hotel heiress to afford them. The Brokedown skull-and-crossbones cadet hat is $56. Junkfood T-shirts are $20 to $50, and the JET "Love" hoodie is about $80. The site shows the celebrities photographed in the clothes. So far, there are no chic orange jail jumpsuits for sale there.

Grumpy Girl: I'm partial to the Grumpy Girl T-shirt: "I cook . . . Instant Ramen. On Certain Holidays." Grumpy Girl accessories include key chains ($15), trucker visors ($24), and the Grumpy Girl Auto Bird Turd Emergency Kit ($28.95) with the slogan "Because everything is cute until it poops." There's also a line of baby Grumpy Girl clothing.

Big girls should remember that Grumpy Girl tees run small, so if you don't like your shirts too form-fitting, order them a size larger than usual. For information check out www.grumpy-girl.com.

Whose scarves do you wear?

I like New York designer Christian Ruperto, who makes Italian-designed clothing under the name Alta Moda. I first met him in the 1970s when he had a boutique in St. Louis, and I thought his materials were beautiful. Christian's "Tribute to New Orleans" scarf is one of my favorites, and I wear it often.

Christian and his wife, Jeanne, helped me with this book. Here are some things I learned from them:

Many quality silk scarves are made in Como and

Milan, Italy, and Lyon, France. Scarves are also made in China, but are often cheaper, without the depth of color or quality of fabric. The best are handmade. Lighter scarves are one-ply silk, and the heavier ones can go up to four-ply, which is nearly too heavy to be a scarf. The rich colors are usually achieved through a combination of the dyeing process, the design, and the high-grade materials. The process is a closely guarded secret.

Once the materials are chosen, the major production costs are for the screens and number of colors used. For a quality scarf, the first screen can easily cost upwards of $9,000 for one's own print and a sample. Ouch. The cost decreases as the number produced increases. A markup of 100 to 200 percent isn't unheard of for a unique, quality piece retailing for $1,000 to $5,000.

Theft and copying also exist. An expensive, one-of-a-kind collection could be bought, stolen, or knocked-off, then sold as a cheaper version elsewhere. Think of all those New York street vendors and their "Louis Vuitton" pieces.

To contact Christian Ruperto in New York, e-mail alta.moda@hotmail.com.

Don't miss the exciting mysteries in the national bestselling Dead-End Job series from Elaine Viets, which *Publisher's Weekly* has praised for being "humorous and socially conscious . . . rollicking fun." Her most recent hardcover, *Clubbed to Death*, is on sale in May 2008.

Living life on the lam and working wherever she can find a paycheck, Helen Hawthorne has a knack for keeping a low profile. Her latest career cul-de-sac is in the complaint department of a snooty country club, which has lately dropped its standards so low that even Helen's sleazy ex-husband is welcome. . . .

Once people were dying to get into the Superior Club in South Florida. Now they're just dying.

Read on for a sneak peek of *Clubbed to Death.* . . .

"Do you know who I am?" The woman's high-pitched whine sliced through Helen Hawthorne's phone like a power saw cutting metal.

Yes, ma'am, Helen thought. You are another rude rich person.

"I am Olivia Reginald. I am a Superior Club member. I spend thousands at this country club."

Everyone spends money here, Helen thought. That's how they get in. "How may I help you, Mrs. Reginald?" she said.

The power-saw whine went up a notch. "I'm sitting by the pool waiting for you to call. I left a message at eleven o'clock. It took you half an hour to call back."

"I'm sorry, Mrs. Reginald, but we've had a busy morning."

"My husband is *in* the pool but I can't go *in* until I arrange a guest pass for my sister. Laura is staying at our home while we're on vacation. How can I enjoy myself when I have to wait by the phone?"

I'm sitting in a stuffy office on a fabulous January day in Miami, Helen thought. How can I enjoy myself when I have to deal with you?

"I'll fax the paperwork right now," Helen said.

"I am on vacation. I am not sitting by a fax machine. Just give Laura the guest pass. I said it was OK."

"I can't," Helen said. "I need your written approval. It's for your protection. When you give someone a guest pass, she can charge thousands of dollars to your account. It will take two minutes to fax the paperwork to your hotel."

"Well, hurry up. I'm wasting my vacation on the phone."

Helen fought the urge to say something straight out of high school: "My heart bleeds purple peanut butter."

Instead, she summoned heroic willpower and the memory of her new credit-card bill and said, "Yes, ma'am."

"Do you know who I am?" should be the Superior Club's new motto, she thought. In the old days, the members would have never asked that question. Everyone knew the Prince of Wales, the Queen of Romania, and Scott and Zelda Fitzgerald. For the club's gently bred socialites, the question was unthinkable. A lady didn't want to be known outside her circle. The painted mistresses of the robber barons were politely infamous, but always discrete.

The new members were a different breed. They'd invaded the historic Superior Club like a swarm of termites, and they were just as destructive. Helen prayed the balky fax/copy machine was working, or else she'd have to listen to Mrs. Reginald's power-whine again.

Helen never made it to the copy machine. She was stopped by another club member before she got down the hall. This one looked like he'd escaped from the "Early Man" display at the natural history museum, then hijacked a suit. His forehead was so low it seemed to collapse on his thick eyebrows. Make that eye*brow*. The man had only one, and it was fat and furry. Helen was sure his back and chest were covered with a thick pelt.

The surprise was his hands, which he must have swiped from a higher primate. They were long and slender and only slightly hairy around the knuckles.

The creature spoke with an educated accent.

"I'm a doctor," the caveman said. "This is an emergency. I need to speak to the department supervisor."

"I'm sorry, she's out to lunch," Helen said. In more ways than one, she thought. "Solange will be back in about two hours. How may I assist you?"

"You can't." His eyes narrowed to feral slits. Helen wondered if he had a stone ax up his sleeve. "I need someone important and I need him now."

The doctor's simian face was hard, but not from exercise or responsibility. This hardness came from too much cocaine, too much money, or both. It stripped the softness from the personality, leaving only the nasty "gimme" part. Helen had seen many versions of the doctor at the Superior Club, although none quite so hairy.

He was right. She couldn't help him. She was only a clerk in customer care—a polite name for the country club's complaint department. The other staffers didn't even look up when the doctor screamed at Helen. They'd heard these tantrums before.

"How much longer are you going to keep me waiting?" The doctor's soft, smooth fingers drummed the marble countertop. His brownish hair bristled with rage. "Didn't you hear me? I said this was an emergency."

Maybe someone really is dying, Helen thought. He was a doctor, after all. "Let me find Kitty, our manager. May I have your member number, please?"

"What's that got to do with anything?" the doctor said.

"I can assist you faster, sir."

"I'm a doctor," he repeated, as if he expected her to bow down and worship him.

Helen dropped Mrs. Reginald's paperwork on her

desk and sat at her computer. She looked expectantly at the caveman, her hands hovering over the keys. He capitulated. "My Superior Club number is eight-eight-six-two."

Helen typed in the number and saw the confidential profile: *Doctor Rodelle "Roddy" Dell, breast augmentation specialist, married to Irene "Demi" Dell. Status: Paid in full. See comments on behavior.*

A boob doctor. So what was the big hurry: Someone needed an emergency C cup? Of course, there was that young woman at the fitness center who'd picked up too heavy a weight and busted the stitches on her new implants. She had to go to the emergency room. Imagine the embarrassment when you bust your boobs, Helen thought.

"Are you going to stare at the computer all day?" the doctor demanded.

Helen picked up the phone and called Kitty. "Dr. Rodelle Dell is here, and he has an emergency. His member number is eight-eight-six-two."

Helen heard the clack of Kitty's keyboard as she looked up the account. "Oh, no. Roddy the Rod. Is he foaming at the mouth?"

"That would be correct," Helen said. "He says it's an emergency."

"He's too important to have anything else," Kitty said. "Bring him to my office, please. And stay. I need a witness with Dr. Dell."

"This way, Doctor," Helen said. She noticed little hairs were trapped in the gold and steel links of his TAG Heuer watch. He looked like a well-dressed Cro-Magnon.

And what do I look like, in my navy uniform with the gold Superior Club crest on the chest? A nobody. An eleven-fifty-an-hour clerk. The sad part is, this is more money than I've made in years.

Helen knocked on the door to Kitty's comfortably cluttered office. She could hardly see her kewpie-doll boss over the vase of yellow roses, the piles of paper, and framed photos of her children. A teddy bear in pearls and a pink dress slouched next to her computer.

The only empty space was where the photo of her almost ex-husband once stood.

"Please, sit down, Doctor." Kitty indicated a leather wing chair that shrieked "Country club!" Usually Kitty's soft voice and big brown eyes disarmed the angriest club member.

The doctor paced in front of her desk, too agitated to sit. Helen stayed in the office doorway, but he didn't notice her.

"I have an emergency," he said. "I need my bill."

"The monthly statements will be mailed this afternoon," Kitty said. She checked the computer. "Yours will go to your home in Golden Palms."

"That's the emergency, dammit. I can't have my wife see that bill."

"Is there a problem, sir?" Kitty said.

He was too upset to correct her about his proper title. "I treated a friend—a young woman—to a day at the Superior Club. She's one of my office staff. Strictly business. It helps her perform better."

Doing what? Helen wondered.

"She needed to relax," the doctor babbled. "Job stress. We had breakfast in the Superior Room before I went to the office. Then she used the pool, the fitness club, had some lunch, and bought a few things in the gift shop. The total came to three thousand dollars. I let her put the charges on my club account. My wife Demi will completely misunderstand the situation when she sees those charges."

The doctor was sweating, though it wasn't warm in the office. Helen was sure Demi would understand perfectly. That philandering cheapskate. As a club member, the doctor got a 15 percent discount on meals, goods, and services if he used his club card. That could be the most expensive four hundred and fifty dollars the doctor ever saved.

"What would you like me to do?" Kitty's dark hair curled innocently around her smooth forehead. Her lips were soft and pink. Only her determined chin gave a clue to her real strength.

"I'd like you to give me the damned bill right now so Demi doesn't see it," the doctor said.

"I'm sorry," Kitty said. "I can't do that. Your wife is a member of this club. I cannot deny her access to her own account, which she shares with you. Club rules require me to send the statement to your billing address. But I can give you a copy now if you wish."

The doctor's fist crashed down on Kitty's desk. The teddy bear jumped and the children's pictures rattled. "I don't want a copy. I want the bill. I'm entitled. I make all the money."

"But it's also her account as long as you two are married," Kitty said.

"That's just it," the doctor said. "She'll give the bill to her lawyer."

"If I were you, doctor, I'd be home tomorrow when your mail arrives. Then I'd explain those charges to your wife. Have a nice day. Helen, please show the doctor out."

Helen had no idea how Kitty managed to defeat him with her soft words, but the doctor realized he was dismissed. He pushed past Helen and slouched out of the office.

The two women waited until he slammed the mahogany door to customer care. "He is a brilliant boob doctor," Kitty said. "But rumor has it the only way he can cop a good feel is through his specialty. Otherwise, he has to give the ladies lavish gifts."

"But why bring his mistress to the club?" Helen asked. "He knew he was going to get caught."

"That's part of the thrill," Kitty said. "You've only been here a week, sweet pea. You'll see a lot more emergencies like this one. Some idiot brings his bimbo to the club and then tries to cover up his mistake. Do these guys really think their wives won't find out? Demi plays golf and tennis here. One of her friends is bound to spot her husband with another woman."

"If I knew the name of his wife's lawyer, I'd fax the bill to him," Helen said.

"I know Demi," Kitty said. "She's no fool. She won't divorce the doctor during his peak earning years. Besides, he still cares enough to try to cover up. My guess is she'll get another little gift from Harry Winston. When she's finally had enough, Demi will cash in her diamonds for a good divorce lawyer."

Helen saw Kitty staring at the empty spot where her ex-husband's photo used to be. She still loved him. Helen had no idea what caused the split. A single tear slid down Kitty's cheek.

Helen silently shut the door to the office and went back to her desk to unearth Mrs. Reginald's guest pass paperwork. The woman was still languishing by the pool. She'd call back any minute and assault Helen's ears with that power-saw whine.

Jessica, at the next desk, was on the phone with a club member, making placating noises without making promises. It was an art Helen had yet to master.

"Yes," Jessica said in her hypnotic voice. "Yes, I do understand."

It's her acting training, Helen thought. Jessica sounded so sincere.

She had remarkably pale skin for someone who lived year-round in South Florida, and long straight blond hair that was either natural or a first-rate dye job. Helen really envied Jessica's bones. She had razor-sharp cheekbones, a strong chin, and a thin, elegant nose.

Jessica's aristocratic face had earned her small, choice parts in the New York theater, but she made her real money selling champagne and pricey chocolates in TV ads. Four years ago, Jessica and her husband, Allan, moved to Florida. Their luck ran out about the same time as her acting career went on hiatus, and she took a job at the club. Fifty was a tough age for an actress. Jessica liked to say, "My greatest role is pretending to like the members at the Superior Club."

Helen heard her finish another bravura phone performance. "Oh, I'm so glad you're feeling better," Jessica said, and hung up.

Helen wanted to applaud.

"I saw the doctor slam out of here," Jessica said. "What was that all about? Was it really life and death?"

"Yes. His death. The doctor's wife will kill him when she gets this month's statement," Helen said. "He's been fooling around with some bimbo at the club."

"They can't even come up with an original sin," Jessica said.

"You actresses," Helen said. "Always complaining about the script."

Jessica laughed. "I'm not much of an actress these days."

"You're resting," Helen said. "Isn't that the phrase?"

"If I get any more rested, I'll be dead."

"If I don't get Mrs. Reginald her guest pass, I'm dead," Helen said.

The Superior Club was like a stage set, Helen thought. The imposing pink stucco buildings were designed by Elliott Endicott, Addison Mizner's greatest rival, in 1925. Critics called Endicott's semi-Spanish architecture derivative. Helen thought it looked like it came from a Gloria Swanson movie. But that was OK. Gloria was once a club member, too. She must have felt right at home with the lobby's thronelike chairs, massive wrought-iron chandeliers and twisted candelabra.

Behind this imposing front was a warren of battered storage rooms and dark passages that reminded Helen of backstage at the theater. They were used by the staff. But it was the club members who provided the drama. Too bad Jessica was right. The stories were old and trite, and it was easy to guess the endings.

Helen picked her way down the narrow, scruffy back hall of the customer care office to where the fax/copy machine growled and groaned in a former coat closet. The noises reassured her. The beast was working. Mrs. Reginald could receive her forms, sign them, fax them back, and then go soak her head.

Helen's office was part of the stage set. She sat at one of five original desks designed by Elliott Endicott, coffin-sized mahogany affairs carved with parrots and egrets.

Endicott loved parrots and used to have them fly freely around the indoor garden in the lobby, until members complained the ill-mannered birds ruined their clothes and hair.

The drawers stuck on her antique desk and one leg tilted inward. The matching chair, with its original parrot-print fabric, was fabulously uncomfortable. But the view from Helen's window made up for it. She could see the yacht club basin and the seagoing mansions. Today the place looked like a boat show. Yachts the size of cruise ships were docking. Hunky young crew members in tight white uniforms were scrubbing decks and reaching for ropes.

"What's going on?" Helen said. "Where'd all the yachts come from?"

"It's the party tonight," Jessica said, as if that should explain everything. "Oh, I forgot. You're new. Every year, Cordelia van Rebarr, of the Boston van Rebarrs, has a yacht party. She invites some amazing entertainer to perform at a private party for one hundred of her closest—and richest—friends. This year, it's Eric Clapton."

"The real Eric Clapton? Not an impersonator? How can she afford him? The man sells out stadiums."

"The man himself," Jessica said. "Some people have money. Cordy is rich. She hires the major names for her parties the way you'd get a DJ."

"Ohmigod. Imagine listening to Eric Clapton at a private party."

"You won't have to," Jessica said. "Customer care helps out at the party. That's why you're working late tonight. We all work on party night. We'll get to hear Clapton. It makes up for what we have to listen to during the day.

"It's the social event of the season. Cordy's guests arrive by private plane or helicopter. About twenty come by yacht. That's twenty yachts at fifty dollars per foot per day. And none of the guests stay on their boats. They all take rooms at the yacht club for another thousand a day."

Jessica broke off and said, "Look at that one. It's huge, even for this crowd. Must be over a hundred feet long."

The flashy white yacht's dark windows gave it a sinister look, like a drug dealer in a white suit and sunglasses. A very successful dealer, Helen thought. The yacht had a helicopter and a swimming pool.

Then she saw its name.

"The *Brandy Alexander*," Helen said. She didn't even realize she'd said the name out loud.

"Now there's a real-life mystery," Jessica said. "Anyone who says there are no good roles for older women doesn't know this story. That yacht is owned by a merry widow somewhere south of sixty. She's had five—or is it six?— husbands die on her. Her first one, the rich old one, died of a heart attack in his eighties. His death may have been natural. After that, she married one young stud after another. Rumor says they played around on her, and shortly after she found out, they died. Sometimes it was a boating accident, or a problem with their dive tank, or a fatal case of food poisoning. She's never been charged with murder, but she's notorious. I can't remember her name, but she's a club member."

"Her name is Marcella," Helen said. "The Black Widow."

"You know about her?" Jessica said. "She's married again. I wonder how long this one has to live?"

"His name is Rob," Helen said. Her voice seemed to come from far away. "I tried to stop the wedding, but he wouldn't listen."

"Really. How do you know him?"

"He's my ex-husband," Helen said.